Praise for Lowen Clausen's *First Avenue*

"Sights, sounds, smells, and—most of all—real emotion mark this novel as a winner! Clausen is a natural, and I hope *First Avenue* is only the first in a series. I loved this book!"
—*New York Times* bestselling author and former Seattle cop Ann Rule

"When a cop starts to burn out, apparently the last organ to smolder is his heart. In *First Avenue*, Lowen Clausen has written a cop novel that is really about people, and an atmospheric mystery that is actually about the resiliency of the human heart. *First Avenue* is as moody as Seattle in the rain, and just as alluring. It's a skillful, memorable first novel."
—*New York Times* bestselling author Stephen White

"A thoughtful police drama, filled with insight and empathy. More than a shoot-em-up, *First Avenue* offers a glimpse at the human beings who can be found in the shadows of skid row. Clausen is a fine writer with enough talent and personal experience to keep us reading for many more books."
—Bestselling author John Straley

"*First Avenue* by former Seattle policeman Lowen Clausen is a solid debut marked by unfussy prose and straightforward plot lines. . . . The book's chief pleasure, however, lies in its evocation of Seventies-era First Avenue."   —*The Seattle Times*

"Strong narrative style . . . admirably real people. . . . Much of the pleasure of Clausen's book comes from seeing that despite the blue uniform, the lives of beat cops are much the same as anyone else's."   —*Seattle Weekly*

"A quick, compelling, literate read about a Seattle cop whose determination to solve a particularly horrible crime entangles him in unsuspected mysteries and secrets of his own life."
—*Footnotes*

"A satisfying mystery with honest, hardworking characters you hope are based on real people. The authenticity of these characters shines through."   —*Cookeville Herald-Citizen* (TN)

"Lowen Clausen provides a fabulous tale that will leave . . . fans anxiously awaiting his next book."
—*Midwest Book Review*

Also by Lowen Clausen

First Avenue

SECOND WATCH

Lowen Clausen

A SIGNET BOOK

SIGNET
Published by New American Library, a division of
Penguin Putnam Inc., 375 Hudson Street,
New York, New York 10014, U.S.A.
Penguin Books Ltd, 80 Strand,
London WC2R 0RL, England
Penguin Books Australia Ltd, 250 Camberwell Road,
Camberwell, Victoria 3124, Australia
Penguin Books Canada Ltd, 10 Alcorn Avenue,
Toronto, Ontario, Canada M4V 3B2
Penguin Books (N.Z.) Ltd, Cnr Rosedale and Airborne Roads,
Albany, Auckland 1310, New Zealand

Penguin Books Ltd, Registered Offices:
Harmondsworth, Middlesex, England

First published by Signet, an imprint of New American Library,
a division of Penguin Putnam Inc.

First Printing, March 2003
10 9 8 7 6 5 4 3 2 1

*To Ingeborg Kisbye,
a great lady with great stories;
to John,
wherever you are;
and to Steven,
wherever you go*

Chapter 1

From the top of Phinney Ridge, Katherine Murphy saw the Ballard Bridge rising over the Ship Canal that separated Ballard from Queen Anne Hill and Magnolia Bluff. The canal was like a river that separated two states of mind. Seattle's Queen Anne and Magnolia neighborhoods were green and residential while Ballard's industrial waterfront stretched bare and low along the canal as if a flood had swept through it and removed the frills. From the Ballard side, steam rose from a steel mill east of the bridge and dust from a concrete plant to the west. Beneath the bridge a pleasure boat ducked out of the way as a fishing trawler headed out to sea. The fishing season had already begun, and the fishing boats left behind were coming out of dry dock with no time to waste.

On the bench seat of the police car, Katherine sat beside her new partner as she had in the police academy a few years earlier. It was a quirk then of the alphabetical seating that Murphy's M and Stevens's S placed them, the only women in the academy class, in desks side by side surrounded by men. They were still surrounded, but the dark blue cuffs on her long-sleeve gabardine shirt showed the years of daily wear and her black leather gun belt was dulled and bruised. Her deep brown eyes saw more and saw differently than before and seldom rested. From the outside corners of her eyes faint wrinkles fanned out on her smooth skin like tentative pencil tracks on a newly drawn map.

It was Katherine's first day working with Grace Stevens on the footbeat in Ballard, her first hour on the Second Watch. She had moved from the night shift downtown because Grace had asked her, and no one had ever asked her before. She had always been a partner by default, when there was nobody else, when there was no choice.

With a new partner, new surroundings, new uncertainties, Katherine had the same feelings she'd had as the rookie on her first night on the street a few years earlier—except it was high noon, or nearly so, and Grace was not like the training officer who had barely and begrudgingly acknowledged her presence. And Katherine didn't feel sick to her stomach as she had when that first night began and ended, and on many nights thereafter.

Grace pointed out streets and directions to orient Katherine to her new beat. It was usually quiet, Grace said—a drunk fisherman now and then, a merchant's complaint, a panhandler or two. Occasionally something serious would cross their paths, but in Ballard people took care of their own problems.

But Ballard, Katherine thought, of all places for them to work. With its Scandinavian names on business after business and storefront after storefront, it was like another country. She wondered how Grace had ever arrived at this western bulge of the city, why the police department would send her here, and why she would stay even though they did. She could ask herself the same questions. Ballard was so far out of the way of her normal life, the normal roads she took, that she couldn't remember being in the neighborhood more than a few times since she had moved to Seattle as an eighteen-year-old college student.

As Grace entered a long straight street from its southern tip, she turned to Katherine and told her they had come to Ballard Avenue, "the center of the universe." She smiled when she said it.

It was that smile that had interested Katherine from the first days of the academy. There was something about it that set Grace apart from her, from the rest of the recruits. It was a cautious smile that didn't invite or permit anyone to come too close, and yet there was something unmistakably appealing about it, a vulnerability that showed through the caution.

On Ballard Avenue a man crossed in front of the police car, waved to them, and stepped onto the running board of a truck parked in the middle of the street. Farther down, another man crossed with a long pipe balanced on his shoulder, and another passed him pushing a handcart. Katherine had seldom enforced jaywalking ordinances downtown, but here everyone walked from one side of the street to the other as if they had never heard of the law.

Trees rose from the buckling sidewalks with new spring leaves reaching delicately into the lower wires of power lines. Old brick buildings crowded against the street with advertisements painted a hundred years earlier on their walls. For all that Katherine could see, she had slipped back into another time.

"Usually we stop here first," Grace said, "but we'll go a little farther today."

Grace turned and dropped down a gentle decline to Shilshole Avenue. She followed the waterfront west past the Ballard Locks, which divided the fresh water of the Ship Canal from the salt water of Puget Sound. As the street curved north on Seaview Avenue, a marina stretched for a mile behind a rock breakwater and hundreds of sailboats lined up row after row, their empty masts bobbing in the restrained waves. Grace continued into Golden Gardens Park at the far tip of the Ballard sector and swung into a parking stall facing the water.

On Puget Sound a few sailboats chased the wind between Golden Gardens and Bainbridge Island. The Olympic Moun-

tains stood like a faded watercolor far in the distance. On
the beach gentle waves danced onto the sand and then
crept back again. A mother stood with a pair of small shoes
in her hand and watched her child wade into the water.
The little girl screamed with delight when a wave went
higher than she expected and soaked her rolled-up pants
all the way to her waist.

"Brrrr," Katherine said. "That water has to be cold."

"It is," Grace said. "You and I would freeze out there.
Kids don't have any nerves."

The little girl ran back to dry land and stomped her feet
in the sand. Her mother walked over to her and extended
her hand, but the girl headed out to sea again. She jumped
when the next wave came and raced it to shore. Katherine
laughed with the child. The mother looked back at the police car as if she had heard her laughter, but the police car
was too far away.

"There's already talk about us," Grace said.

Katherine turned away from the child and looked at her.
"What kind of talk?"

"You know," Grace said. "Two women working together."

"Men work together."

"That's different. They have no choice."

"Lucky us," Katherine said.

"It doesn't bother you?"

"No more than anything else."

"There are men with a lot more seniority than you and
I who would like to have our beat. There are only two
footbeats left in the north end—one in the U-District and
the one we have in Ballard."

"So why don't they have it?"

"Because we do. This was Wes Mickelsen's beat until
he retired. He was my training officer when I got out of
the academy, but he never took another recruit after me.
I think Rigmor would have given him hell if he dumped
me."

"Who?" Katherine asked.

"Rigmor Jensen. She has a little grocery store on Ballard Avenue. Haven't you heard of her? I thought every cop knew about her."

"Not me," Katherine said.

"You'll meet her as soon as we leave here. I think you'll like her."

"I'm sure I will."

Grace looked straight out the front window toward the endless row of waves that relinquished themselves on the shore. Katherine saw Grace smile at the water, but it wasn't the smile she had seen earlier.

"I remember that about you," Grace said. "You were always sure of yourself. You probably never wonder if you can handle this job."

Katherine was silent until Grace turned away from the water and looked at her.

"I wonder every day," Katherine said, "but I don't know why you would. I remember that academy instructor you threw out the door."

"I didn't throw anybody through a door."

"Off the mat, then. He was supposed to teach us self-defense, but he was nothing more than a bully. He especially liked picking on us, but he picked on you once too often, and you threw him completely off the mat. He wanted to get even, but they sent him to the emergency room instead. I could have cheered right then. I wish I would have."

"That wasn't such a fine moment," Grace said. "It nearly got me fired."

"It was the best moment I had during all those miserable months. You don't know how many times I wished I could have done that."

"It's all in the technique."

"No, it wasn't. You just picked him up and threw him, and he never bothered us again."

"I guess he had it coming," Grace said.

"He sure did. Do you remember how many stitches he got?"

"Seven," Grace said. "I often wished I hadn't done it. You would have used your head instead of getting mad and throwing the guy into a table. I think they respected you more because of that."

"They didn't respect either of us," Katherine said.

Grace looked back at the water, back to the time of the academy classes, and silently nodded her agreement.

The cold water finally chilled the little girl enough so that she allowed her mother to take her hand. The child sat on her mother's lap in dry sand beyond the reach of the waves, and the mother brushed sand from the girl. She pulled warm stockings onto her daughter's feet and slipped shoes over them. Then she pointed to the police car and raised the little girl's arm to wave. The two women waved back to the child and the mother.

"I was surprised when you called me," Katherine said.

"It was Wes's idea."

"Really?"

"I told him about you."

"Me?"

Radio's voice interrupted Katherine's question by asking for their location. Grace picked up the microphone and told him they were in Golden Gardens.

"It's a bit of a run," Radio said, "but all my other cars are tied up. I have a report of a dead body at the Fremont transfer station, 800 block 34th West. Can you handle that for me?"

"Affirmative," Grace said. She put the microphone back into the holder, restarted the car engine, and looked over at her new partner. "This is a fine way to start."

"What's a transfer station?" Katherine asked.

"A garbage dump," Grace said as she backed out of the parking stall.

"It doesn't sound like a call for our footbeat."

"It's not," Grace said, "but we're like an umbrella car,

too. When the district cars are tied up, we'll get their calls."

Grace drove out of the parking lot and onto the main road, driving faster than normal but not using the blue lights until she came to an intersection. Even then she stopped before passing through a red light.

Katherine didn't dread the call as she would have a year or so earlier. It was a dead body that they were going to find, no longer a person. She knew what to do. If there were suspicious circumstances, and certainly there would be at a garbage dump unless it was somebody who keeled over with a heart attack, they would secure the scene and call Homicide. She would have to look at the body, but that seldom bothered her anymore. She had seen enough of them downtown—old men mostly who drank themselves into oblivion.

The North Precinct radio operator went on with other calls—an accident on Aurora, a stolen car in Greenwood, a fight in the University District. Their call became buried beneath the pile that had gathered at shift change.

A line of waiting cars blocked the entrance to the transfer station, and Grace turned into the exit lane. The line continued on the driveway that ran past the weigh station and around a large concrete building where the garbage was dumped. A man standing on the exit scale waved them forward. Katherine rolled down her window, and he bent down to her level.

"It's up there," he said. He pointed to the concrete building.

"What's up there?" Katherine asked.

"A body, I guess," the man said. "Didn't they tell you?"

"They told us," Katherine said.

"Is this the only way out of here?" Grace asked.

The man bent lower so that he could see Grace, too.

"Unless you've got a key for the other gate," he said.

"Did anybody leave since you called?" Grace asked.

"Nope. Roscoe won't let anybody out."

"Who's Roscoe?" Grace asked.

"The shift manager. What do you want me to do with all these cars?" He gestured to the line that flowed out to the street.

"Tell them the dump is closed," Grace said.

Grace drove up to the cavernous building, turned sideways in the driving lane, and blocked the exit with the police car. On one wall of the building lines of castaway appliances stood beside steel bins of glass and recycled metals. On the other side a two-foot-high concrete barrier ran the length of the building. There was a deep pit beyond it. Three garbage trucks stood in a row at the far end of the building, and cars were still backed up to the pit, but nobody was throwing anything in. A short man in white overalls hurried toward them.

"I told everybody to stay just where they are," he said. "I've got a ladder over by the body. Jim saw it when he backed up the bulldozer."

"Are you in charge here?" Katherine asked.

"That's right. Roscoe Burnett." He stuck out his hand. "Damn glad to see you. We get all kinds of stuff dumped here, but I've never had anything like this."

Katherine shook Roscoe's hand, although she didn't shake every hand extended to her.

Grace began walking toward the ladder whose top rungs rose above the concrete curb. Katherine followed her to the edge of the pit and saw the bulldozer twenty feet below. Ten feet in front of it was a large black garbage bag embedded in the mass of garbage, and Katherine could see the form of a knee sticking through the bag. She couldn't see any other part of the body.

"Are you sure it's real?" Katherine asked Roscoe, who had followed her.

"It looks real to me," Roscoe said.

"Did you touch it?"

"No, ma'am. I sure didn't."

"We'd better check it first before we call anybody," Grace said to Katherine. "I've got some rubber gloves in the trunk."

Grace hurried back to the car, and Katherine grabbed the top of the ladder. She pushed on it to see if it was steady. Heights always bothered her.

"I'll hold it for you," Roscoe said. He reached for the ladder and held the rails with both hands.

Katherine swung her leg onto the first step below the curb. The ladder sank farther into the mass of garbage below her. She looked down and then quickly back up. Slowly, a step at a time, she descended into the pit, looking straight ahead at the concrete wall.

"You're almost there," she heard Roscoe say.

She looked up and saw Roscoe at the top. Grace was ready to start down. Katherine stepped carefully off the last rung of the ladder onto a pile of wood and plaster debris. It was firm beneath her feet. She released the ladder and walked carefully around the bulldozer, testing each step before giving it her entire weight.

The height of the ladder didn't seem to bother Grace. She descended quickly to the bottom. Once in the pit, however, she moved just as slowly and carefully as Katherine. She was wearing rubber gloves and handed Katherine another pair.

The knee was real, and the flesh was torn so deeply that it exposed the bone. Katherine brushed away leaves and cut grass that lay on top of the bag until she was sure she had found the head. It felt like there was more than one bag around the body. She tried to gently rip an opening in the bag, but it was hard to get it started. Grace knelt beside her on the other side of the body and clenched the plastic beside Katherine's hands. Together they ripped it away until they could see the face.

"It's a young girl," Katherine said.

Her fingers encased in the rubber glove, Katherine touched the girl's neck to feel for a pulse, even though she knew that life had left this girl long before. Grace stood up and pulled the radio out of her holster.

"I'll call the sergeant," Grace said, "and get another unit here to help us. We need to seal off the whole dump site."

Katherine nodded her agreement. There was nothing they could do down in the pit. All their work was up the ladder that Grace had already begun climbing. Even so Katherine didn't leave. She remained in the pit and looked into the girl's lifeless eyes.

Chapter 2

Katherine stayed at the garbage site all afternoon with Grace, while Homicide searched for evidence around the body. For the Homicide detectives Katherine drew a diagram of the building that showed where each vehicle was parked when she and Grace first arrived. She wrote down the license numbers and the names of the drivers and occupants. With the consent of each driver she and Grace searched the vehicles and released them one at a time until the building was emptied and only the police cars remained.

When the van from the medical examiner's office arrived, the two investigators put the girl into a body bag and carried her out of the pit through a lower door. To Katherine the building seemed eerily quiet and empty after the girl was taken away.

It was after shift change by the time she and Grace left the garbage dump, and the North Precinct was quiet, too. They turned in their reports, shed their uniforms, and dressed in clothes that would allow them to become civilians again, although they could never quite be civilians again.

In light evening traffic Katherine drove downtown to the YMCA, which was a few blocks from police headquarters where she had worked before transferring north. In her car she removed her police revolver from her off-duty hip holster and stuffed the revolver into a gym bag. Then she walked into the building and down the stairs to the swimming pool in the basement. The door to the pool was locked, but she had her own key. She made sure the door locked behind her.

She swam five or six laps before settling into her rhythm. She controlled her breathing by the depth and force of her strokes. Through her goggles, she followed a painted line on the bottom of the pool. She took big gulps of air and exhaled with her face in the water.

One of the few friends she had in the police department told her that she must forget in order to survive. She must force the day from her memory the way she forced air from her lungs. Train, prepare, act, but in the end, she must forget. She pushed her strokes deeper into the water. Two strokes, more air, two strokes.

She had become stronger trying to forget. When she had begun swimming, a few laps would tire her enough that she had to stop and hold on to the edge of the pool until she regained her breath. Now she never stopped until she was done. The familiar ache in her shoulders came and passed, and she adjusted her breathing in the water, not above it.

In the beginning there were five cops from the Third Watch who went to the pool at four each morning after work. Because they were cops, three men and two women, the young Christian men at the YMCA gave them keys without worrying about security or having a lifeguard on duty. It became their own private pool in the hours when no one else could swim. One by one, they stopped. There was a new lover who required time, a second job, a family that could not give up the hours that swimming took from sleep and sleep from the day. Even before leaving the Third Watch to go north, she had been the last one. When she swam during the day on her days off, there would be others in the pool with her, but after eight o'clock the pool was closed. She liked it better when she was alone.

She had changed in the water. Her muscles had hardened

as well as her discipline. Since immersing her face in water, she had not shed one tear in sorrow or anger. What came to her at work she could not control, but she could control the depth of her arms, the speed of her stroke, and the ever-decreasing seconds between one end of the pool and the other.

She followed the straight line back and forth in an endless path that took her nowhere. When others were with her in the pool, their voices ricocheted from the concrete walls, but now there was only the muffled noise of her body in the water—her feet propelling, her arms pulling, her breath rising to the surface in a stream of bubbles. The light was dim, two switches up in a row of a dozen, enough to see where she was going but not where she had been.

When the memory of the girl's face appeared, Katherine pushed it away. When she saw the girl's eyes despite her resolve not to see, she closed her own eyes and swam harder until her lungs burned for air. She had done all that she could. Now she must forget.

Katherine looked up at the wall clock. It was nine o'clock. She had lost track of her lap count somewhere in the pile of garbage. She turned in the water and pushed off for the final length. She rallied strength into her tired shoulders and finished in perfect form. At the end of the pool she let her feet gather under her and pulled the goggles from her eyes. She lifted herself out of the water, her arms so tired that they could barely complete the task.

Chapter 3

It was an argument that woke her—the cook and his wife shouting at each other in Chinese from the back door of their restaurant across the alley. Katherine wondered what their argument was about this time. Had he been out too late? Had she? Did they disagree about the daily special, or was it just a good morning to argue? There was a last shout from the wife as she went back into the restaurant. Katherine knew the husband would remain outside and smolder with his cigarette. She had seen him many times through her bedroom window. He would smoke the cigarette, throw the butt into the alley, and go back inside. She didn't need to look.

Turning from the closed window, she heard the traffic on Broadway a block away. It wasn't loud, but irregular enough to keep her awake once she had been awakened. She closed her eyes and thought about moving to a quiet place where she could sleep, something she had been thinking about for months as her savings grew ever larger in her bank account. If the Chinese argument did not awaken her, something else would. The price and location of her apartment had held her while she was in college, but she was no longer a student. She had not been a student for years. Maybe she should look at houses outside the city as had most of the cops she knew.

Then she remembered that she didn't need to sleep late anymore. She opened her eyes and stared at the ceiling. Seven-thirty at night when her shift now ended was like the middle of the day, compared to three-thirty in the morning. She could get up whenever she liked without paying for it at the end of the shift. If she moved, it would have to be for another reason.

She heard Dale's quick steps on the pine floor in the next apartment. His footsteps never bothered her. She wondered how many miles he walked inside his apartment before she even opened her eyes. Together they shared the second floor of the old brick fourplex. Her apartment was on the north side and his was on the south with the hallway at the top of the staircase linking them.

In the years she had lived in the building, there had been five other neighbors before Dale. The first had been students like her, a man and woman, and she had hated to see them go. She had become more distant with each new arrival and had barely known the last woman with dull eyes who drank too much. None of the neighbors had known she was a cop, except Mrs. Rabin who lived on the first floor. Then Dale came.

She remembered the moving truck and two men carrying a couch down the ramp from the back of the truck. Dale stood at the bottom, guiding the couch carriers over the curb, around Mrs. Rabin's flowers in the planting strip, and up the sidewalk. He surrounded the couch with his quick steps and gesturing arms and exerted more energy directing the progress than those who actually carried the load. He made sure no feet trampled the flowers. Before she even met him, Katherine had liked this man.

He was in his forties, and there were gray streaks in his short hair. His stomach protruded beneath a brightly colored Hawaiian shirt. He talked fast. From her second-floor window, she couldn't understand what he said, but he was saying it fast. He walked fast, too.

There were two trucks—one on the street to the north

and one on the street in front. She wondered if the apartment would hold two truckloads of furniture. His apartment had two bedrooms, but otherwise was no bigger than hers. Nevertheless, the sound of footsteps continued up and down the stairs without slowing. Sometime during the moving day, she heard a crash and went to the window to see what happened. It looked like a wreck. A box had broken open at the bottom of the ramp, and its contents spilled onto the street. Two men chased a metal bowl down the hill. The flower protector shouted instructions, then tilted his head back and burst out in laughter. It made her laugh, too. He saw her in the window and waved. "It's all right," he shouted. "They saved the bowl." Then he laughed again as the two men returned with the bowl, smiling foolishly.

She had given Dale the first gift, but she couldn't remember what it was—something small and simple. At first they had knocked politely on each other's door, and there had been equal exchanges of flowers and food. Then something triggered Dale's unending generosity, and Katherine had given up trying to match him.

She got out of bed and wondered what it would be like to make her own coffee, if she even had any. Dale ground his fresh every morning. It was enough to spoil anybody.

When Katherine tapped on Dale's open door, she heard him yell, "Open," as if she couldn't see for herself. She walked into his apartment in the pink bathrobe and bedroom slippers her mother had given her for Christmas, smelled the fresh ground coffee, and heard Dale in the kitchen. There was a steaming cup ready on the table, and she sat down in front of it in one of his comfortable wicker chairs. He continued to work at the counter, barely noticing her entrance. She took a sip of coffee and looked out the window through the row of plants stacked on the sill.

"I found a new recipe," Dale said. He had been planning for years to open a restaurant, as soon as he found the right location and the right recipes. "It's a crab cake sandwich with melted cheese." He stuck a flat pan into the oven and left the oven door open a crack. "Lovely for a light lunch with a glass of chardonnay. Would you like a little wine?"

"No."

"Too early, isn't it?"

He poured himself coffee and joined her at the table. He turned an open recipe book toward her and pointed to the color picture of the crab cake. She studied the picture and read through the recipe.

"It looks good," she said.

She already had a number of his failed recipe books and was careful to phrase her answers so that he would not put another in front of her door. That was the way he got rid of things. He would place food or a book, a plant, or a piece of furniture that he thought she needed in front of her door so that, when she came home at night, she would have to take it in. By the time she woke the next morning, whatever he had given had a night to become used to her apartment. She wondered how he would work it now that she had transferred to the Second Watch.

"Mrs. Rabin cut fresh tulips," he said. "You take them. I'll get more tomorrow."

"They're lovely right here."

"No, take them. Take the vase, too."

"I already have two of your vases."

"Those are garbage. Take this one. I have another just like it."

"No more vases," Katherine said, "unless you want to give me the Chihuly."

He held his breath until she smiled, and then he laughed as he hurried back to the stove and peered into the oven.

"I'll take the flowers," Katherine said. "No vase."

"They say the Chihuly is worth a fortune now," he said. "My insurance broker told me I need to get special insurance just for the vase."

While he studied his crab cakes, Katherine pulled the flowers to her and smelled them. Mrs. Rabin's flowers already filled her apartment with a lovely fragrance. These would not, but their yellows and reds blended cheerfully together.

Mrs. Rabin lived below Katherine and had been in the building many years before Katherine moved in. Mrs. Rabin's flower garden took up the entire planting strip in front of the apartment. Sometimes the old lady could barely walk, and yet she would spend the whole day among her flowers. It was the best place to talk to her.

The previous fall Dale had come up with the idea to convert his and Mrs. Rabin's parking stalls in the alley to a flower bed, too. Neither of them had a car. He had broken up the hard graveled ground with a pick and shovel and had worked in peat moss and enough manure so that, for a week or two, Katherine thought she was back on the farm of her childhood.

"I think it's ready," he said and pulled the pan out of the oven. He picked up a toasted crab cake with his fingers and placed it on a plate. "Hot." He shook his fingers and laughed as though surprised by the effect of heat. He set the plate in front of her and hurried over to the silverware drawer. As he dropped the knife and fork by her plate, he sat in his chair with a deep sigh and waited nervously for her response.

"Aren't you going to have any?" she asked.

"I don't like crab. I should have asked if you like it. If you don't, just take a little bite and tell me what you think."

He clenched his mouth tight as if that were the only way he would not talk. She was used to this routine. She cut a small piece from the corner of the crab cake and put it in her mouth.

"You have to try more than that," he said. "You won't even be able to taste it."

"I can taste it." She cut a larger second bite. "It's a winner," she declared as she thoughtfully chewed the crab cake.

He rocked back into his chair, looked toward the ceiling,

and produced a brief staccato laugh. She had never heard another like it.

"Here, try it," she said. She cut a small bite and pushed it to the edge of her plate. He picked it up with his fingers, placed it carefully in the front of his mouth, and tasted it with his tongue.

"It's good, I guess, if you like crab. Needs more pepper, maybe. Can you taste the cilantro?"

"Yes, I can taste it." Before Dale, she had never heard of cilantro.

"I'll make you another. I have way too much."

"No, thanks."

"Are you sure? It just takes a second."

"I'm sure. It's nine o'clock in the morning. I'm not even alive yet."

"You'll get used to your new shift in no time. I'm glad you're not working on that other street anymore."

"There was nothing wrong with where I worked."

"Don't try to tell me that," he said. "I know what First Avenue is like. You were ready for a change."

Maybe Dale was right. A new street, a new partner, a new shift. Presto! Everything for the better.

"How did you know when I would get up today?" Katherine asked.

"Guessed," he said. "I knew you wouldn't sleep as late as when you worked nights, but I didn't think you would completely switch to normal hours. It took me months to get on track when I switched from graveyard to swing shift. I'll never do that again."

Dale poured more coffee for Katherine and filled his own cup. He put the silver bowl with crabmeat into the refrigerator but didn't cover it. She often watched him accumulate three or four days of extra bowls in the refrigerator before he dumped them all.

"This is when I want a cigarette," he said, returning to his chair at the table. "Just one cigarette in the morning with coffee."

"Keep thinking about all that black crud in your lungs."

"I think about it, but, God, just one."

"It's supposed to get easier after a while."

"I hope so, but sometimes I wonder if it's worth it."

She wondered, too. Through Dale's plant-framed kitchen window, she saw the tops of downtown skyscrapers, less than a mile away. There were apartment buildings on all sides of them as far down the hill as she could see. They lived side by side in the most densely populated district in the state—thousands of people within a few blocks all wondering if it was worth it. Through the smog and haze thrown off by the freeway, she saw the Olympic range a hundred miles away with the two special mountains she always looked for huddled off by themselves like two children lost in the forest. She turned to Dale, who fidgeted with his fingers on his coffee cup and thought of cigarettes.

"I'll shoot you if you start smoking again."

Chapter 4

Thomas had slept inside the cardboard recycling shed for a week, give or take a few days. Each day he had dared to stay inside longer. The shed was big enough for him to stretch out, and the cardboard made a perfect mattress. He scratched his back and rolled onto his side.

Through the crack of the door, he saw a person peering in. That was never a good sign. He stilled himself within the dark shed and waited for the person to pass. The door pulled gently against the twine that he had tied to the outside hook and held in his fingers. Then it jerked and burned his hand. He saw a man standing in the light.

"You can't stay here," the man said.

The voice was harsh and cold and sent a chill through Thomas even though the shed remained warm. Having heard those words so often, Thomas didn't even think about them anymore. He sat upright on the cardboard, which had been compressed with his weight. The man towered above him. Thomas didn't question the man's authority but began gathering the plastic bags that held his possessions. He saw potato chip crumbs on the cardboard that must have fallen out of his bag while he was asleep, and he began sweeping the crumbs into a pile with his hand.

"Don't bother with that," the man said. "Just pick up your stuff."

"I never leave a mess behind, sir," Thomas said. "I make sure every place is neater when I leave."

Thomas crawled out of the shed and swept the crumbs into the bag from where they had escaped. The man stepped back and gave him room.

"What's your name?" the man asked.

Thomas ignored the man's question.

"I straightened out the cardboard earlier," Thomas said. "Perhaps you didn't notice, but whoever stacks the cardboard doesn't flatten it out very well. If that person were to break down the boxes properly, the shed would hold twice as much. Simple mathematics."

"I'll tell them," the man said.

"I'll just straighten up a little more, and then I'll leave," Thomas said. "You don't have to wait. I'll leave as soon as I finish."

The man did not leave, but his face changed as he continued to look at Thomas. It was not cold after all. Thomas had read that the human species was the only species capable of emotion. Perhaps it was the only species capable of arrogance. He would like to know how a whale might feel, or an elephant, or a dog, for that matter. He would even like to know about the man who was forcing him out of the shed. It had been a fine little place.

"You scared the girl from the art store this morning," the man said. "This is their cardboard recycling shed."

"I apologize," Thomas said. "I certainly don't want to interfere with any effort to save the environment. When you live as I do, you know how close we are to burying ourselves in garbage."

It must have taken a great effort for the man to scowl so coldly. He didn't have the face for it, or the eyes. His smile showed that he had a sense of humor.

"How did you end up here?"

"Do you want the literal answer or something more?"

"Either one," the man said.

"I've not been to Ballard before, but I passed this building and saw that workers were constructing something on the roof. I was curious. It's such a fine old building. I wondered why anyone would want to change it. I walked around to the back and saw this little alley and this shed and the tree right behind it and thought, 'This looks nice and safe. No guard dogs or sharp wire.' I judge places from the back, you see, more than the front. Did you know that that entire garbage can is full of books?"

He pointed to a green garbage Dumpster, which was one of a row lined up along the neighboring building.

"It belongs to the bookstore."

"Why are they throwing their books away? They tore off all the covers."

"That's how it works," the man said. "It's more expensive to ship some of the books back than it is to print new ones, so the bookstore just sends back the covers."

"Lucky for me," Thomas said. "Most of them aren't any good, but look at this." He opened one of his plastic bags and removed two books. "*Simple Laws, Complex Universe,*" he read from the title page. "A wonderful book. This man won the Nobel Prize and explains how the universe works, and they threw it away. And this, *Jude the Obscure.* I never read it before, but everybody knows Hardy. I hope you don't mind that I rescued them."

"I don't mind." The man took the first book from Thomas and thumbed through the pages. " 'The Special Theory of Relativity,' " he read. "Now that's an interesting subject to read back here in the alley."

"It's interesting to read anywhere."

"Did you read it?"

"Not this time, but I'm quite familiar with the theory."

"Do you understand it?"

"Yes. I can't work though all the mathematics, of course, but I understand the basic principles. They're not so difficult."

"I've never understood it," the man said. "Not even the basic parts."

"That's because you have to change the way you think. That's what Einstein did, and he saw something no one had ever seen before."

"If you understand Einstein, why are you sleeping in this shed?"

"Because I want to," Thomas said. "Because I'm a little crazy, I suppose. Not dangerous, not at all dangerous. I can't get up like you and go to work, and even when I have money, I can't pay the rent or the electric bill. I just can't make myself do it. I don't know why. That doesn't make the landlord happy, you know."

"I know."

"So, here I am—in both the literal and metaphorical senses. Is this your building?"

"It belongs to my brother and me, as long as we keep paying the bank."

"What are you doing to it?"

"We're adding another floor."

"Why?"

"So that we can keep paying the bank. As soon as we bought it, our biggest tenant moved out, but we found another company that would move in if we built them more space. So, we're building. What do you think Einstein would say about that?"

"From clutter, he would say, find simplicity. From discord, find harmony. In the middle of difficulty lies opportunity. Those are his rules for work."

The man looked at Thomas without saying anything. They were nearly the same age and nearly the same height. They had the same color of brown hair, although Thomas had a beard that edged toward red. They both wore blue shirts. One shirt was cleaner than the other.

"Look," the man in the clean blue shirt said, "you scared the girl when she brought out the cardboard because she didn't know who you were. You can stay here a while longer if you want. I'll tell them to lean the cardboard against the shed. You can break it down and put it away. A good deal for everybody."

"That's very generous of you."

"No, it's probably not. It's not even my shed."

"My name is Thomas Rosencrantz. No relation to the villain in *Hamlet*." He extended his hand to the man with the big building.

"Jack Morton," the man said, shaking Thomas's hand. "I'm not related to the guy either."

Jack Morton pushed a button on a small black box in his hand, and a garage door opened into the building at the end of the alley. He started walking toward the garage, but then he stopped and turned back to Thomas.

"If Einstein is right," he said, "there must be a lot of opportunity in this old building."

Chapter 5

Five large glossy photographs lay spread across the top of her worn wooden desk, covering files of misery and a half-eaten sandwich. With her right hand, Anne Smith lifted a coffee mug with the Space Needle rising opposite the handle. It was a Christmas gift from her four-year-old great-niece. With her left hand, she picked up a photograph of an older girl, but how much older? Fifteen? Thirteen? The girl's wide unblinking eyes stared from the face of death.

"They found her yesterday at the Fremont dump. A bulldozer ran over her and tore the garbage bags she was in." Detective Fred Markowitz stood beside her chair. He had laid out the photographs and interrupted her lunch. "I forgot," he said. "It's not a dump. It's a 'refuse transfer station.' "

"Of course," Anne said, "and those are refuse transfer bags around her legs."

"Garbage bags," Fred said. "Fifty-five gallons. They're supposed to hold a ton or something like that. There were four of them around the girl. Whoever dumped her first pulled one over her head and then one up from her feet. Then he repeated the process. One over the head. One over the feet. These bags are almost five feet long, so she had a lot of layers around her. If the bulldozer hadn't ripped them open, she might have been pushed into a container and hauled off to Oregon. That's where we ship our garbage now."

"You're kidding. Oregon?" Anne asked.

"That's what they said at the dump."

Fred pointed to the middle picture, which showed torn black bags crushed into a mass of garbage. A slender leg was exposed.

"She was naked, and there was nothing to identify her. No prints on the garbage bags either. We have runaway reports of two girls who fit her general description, but she's not either one of them. They're both from the Central District. It's unusual to have a black victim up north."

"Might have come from the U-District," Anne said.

"Too young for a college student," Fred said.

"Yes, but there are a lot of street kids there."

"True. We're sending out her photograph to other departments. The autopsy showed semen in her vagina."

"Rape?"

"Possibly. There were tears that indicate force."

"She looks so young," Anne said. She picked up a photograph of the girl taken before the autopsy. Her ribs showed clearly through her dark skin, and her breasts had barely begun forming. "So skinny, too."

"Ninety pounds," Fred said. "The medical examiner estimates she's thirteen or fourteen years old. Do you see the marks on her neck? She was strangled."

"You want to know if we've had any cases in Sex Crimes like this?" she asked.

"Like this, except the girls got away."

"Of course," Anne said. "Otherwise the case wouldn't land on your exalted desk, would it?"

Homicide Detective Markowitz smiled with the self-conscious but not self-absorbed grin she liked. He did not take offense to her kidding. Some of the others did. Their humor did not extend to themselves. If she were ten years younger, maybe twenty, she could make him grin in a different way. He would have to change his glasses, however. He was two decades behind with them, too. Black horn-rimmed glasses had gone out with the '60s. Fred seemed little concerned about any style, including the skinny tie he wore.

"Here's something you'll like," Fred said. He laid the initial police report on her desk. "The investigating officers are both women. Partners. What do you think of that?"

Anne picked up the report and read the names at the bottom. Murphy and Stevens. Both had high serial numbers.

"They must be new," Anne said.

"Yes, but they know what they're doing. I worked with Murphy a year or so ago on a case downtown. This was her first day in Ballard. I guess Stevens has worked Ballard since she graduated from the academy, which is sort of strange."

"Why?"

Fred looked over his shoulder and leaned closer to Anne. "She's a black officer," he said softly. "Why would she work in Ballard?"

"Why not?" Anne asked. "It'll give those square heads something to think about."

"I know, but the department is doing all this recruiting to put black officers in the Central District, and then they send her north. Go figure."

"Do you want some coffee?" Anne asked. She wasn't going to figure anything.

"That's why I'm here," Fred said. "For some of Anne's famous coffee."

He pulled a chair into her cubicle as she reached for the percolator, which was nearly as old as Fred's glasses. She looked at the row of coffee mugs on the top shelf of her bookcase—all Christmas and birthday presents from her nieces and nephews—and selected Smokey the Bear. Her niece was sixteen now, but Patsy was only seven when she had given her the mug. The aroma of freshly perked coffee filled the space.

"Is that why you're asking me about this girl," she asked, "to get a free cup of coffee?"

"Yep," he said. "Besides, you're the only one left. Everybody else skedaddled."

Without looking, she knew that was true. There were no voices beyond her gray cubicle walls within the Sex Crimes office. The telephones were silent and would be until well after one o'clock, which was why she stayed. She could think better without all the chatter. She had been thinking about another girl before Fred came in with his pictures.

"It's almost lunchtime," she said. "Maybe you didn't notice."

He smiled as he took the cup from her and looked at the bear's face on the mug.

"I like this one," Fred said. "Who gave you this?"

"Patsy."

"That's right. How's she doing?"

"She's sixteen. What does that tell you? Today there's euphoria, tomorrow there's a crisis. You've got boys, so you don't know what I'm talking about. Boys are either too smart or too dumb to go through all that."

"Smart," Fred said. "Tell Patsy I like her mug."

"I will. Do you want half a sandwich? Chicken salad."

"I don't want to eat your lunch away from you."

"Yes, you do," she said.

She moved two photographs and revealed her sandwich. She gave him the half without missing bites, pulled two Kleenex from the box, and handed them to him.

"You want to be sure you don't stain that lovely tie."

He looked down at his lovely tie.

"It's from Mikey," he said. "He wraps up the same tie and gives it to me for my birthday every year. He picked it out himself."

"When?"

"A few years ago."

"You got to love them, don't you?" she asked. She took a sip of coffee from the Space Needle. At one time there had been a bright red jewel on top of the needle, but it had disappeared into the drain with the first washing.

"The girl took a drug called Ritalin not long before she was killed," Fred said. "Sniffed it like cocaine. Got any suspects out there giving Ritalin to kids?"

"Not that I know about. What happens when you sniff that stuff?"

"It makes you happy, I guess."

Anne picked up a photograph that showed the girl's full body lying on the medical examiner's table.

"She doesn't look happy."

Fred pointed with his sandwich to gashes in the girl's leg.

"Those are from the bulldozer. Nothing to do with her death. The bulldozer didn't even break her legs. It just pushed her farther down into the garbage. Have you ever been to one of those garbage stations?"

"You know me. I don't throw anything away."

"This one in Fremont is a big concrete pit," Fred said. "The garbage trucks come in there from all over the north end, everything north of the Ship Canal up to about 105th, but it's open to the public, too. So, anybody could have dumped her. People back up their cars to the edge of the pit and throw stuff in. There's a big line of cars waiting to get in there most of the day.

"A bulldozer drives back and forth over the garbage, which compacts it, and then it pushes all the garbage into a container down in a lower pit. When the container gets full, it's hauled away and they put another one in.

"The garbage gets all mixed up. She was found in an area of the pit where the garbage trucks dump, but she could have been pushed there from the other end. We checked the garbage around her. It's from all over. She could have been dumped there by dozens of trucks or by anybody.

"If a garbage truck dumped her, it's hard to figure how

the bags weren't ripped apart earlier. Those garbage trucks are not delicate machines. They smash everything together before they dump it out. So she might have been dumped by some guy who just backed up his car and threw her in the pit."

"Pretty risky to do that," Anne said.

"Maybe, but if that bulldozer didn't happen to rip open the bags, she would have been pushed into the container and shipped off to Oregon."

"No witnesses, I guess," Anne said.

"None that know anything. The garbage company sent out a message to all their drivers. Nobody who works at the dump noticed anything. It was a citizen who saw the girl's legs. He'd been cleaning out his garage."

"How long were you down in that pit?" Anne asked.

"All afternoon. We closed the whole dump station. You ought to see what people throw away. I found a whole box of Grateful Dead albums."

"Who?" she asked.

"The Grateful Dead. You've never heard of Dead-heads?"

"Of course, the music group. I think some of the older kids used to listen to them. Do you think the music has something to do with her?"

"I hope not," Fred said. "I took the albums home. I figure some guy from Fremont took too much dope and threw out the wrong box. There are only a couple scratches on the whole lot."

"With some of that music, I can't tell if the record is scratched or not."

"What kind of music do you like?"

"Are you thinking of my Christmas present or my birthday?" she asked.

"When's your birthday?"

"Wouldn't you like to know?"

There was laughter out in the hallway that interrupted their conversation, but it didn't enter the room. It passed

with the footsteps on the tile floor. Anne picked up the
photograph of the girl's face. The picture seemed so perma-
nent that it was hard for her to imagine that the girl had
been alive. Had she ever laughed? What kind of music did
she like? Where had this girl come from that she would
end up in a garbage dump?

Chapter 6

Grace sat on the bench in the locker room, tied her work shoes, and watched Katherine struggle with her locker door. It wouldn't close, and Katherine finally kicked the bottom.

"Maybe it needs a little oil," Grace said.

A faint thin scar above Katherine's left eye folded into a frown and deepened it.

"It needs more than that," Katherine said.

"We're lucky to have this," Grace said. "I had to change downstairs in the bathroom for the first three months. I don't think they knew I was coming."

The two other women in the locker room, both fresh from the academy and working with training officers, paused from dressing and looked to the veterans as if waiting for new instructions.

"Surprise," Katherine said.

The North Precinct was an old two-story wooden building handed down to the police department when the fire department moved into a new brick building down the street. The new fire station wouldn't burn, but the old building looked like it could disappear in a flash. The women's locker room was more makeshift than the rest of the converted police station. It had been squeezed out of a storeroom on the second floor. The carpet and paint were new, but the sink had been there since the beginning, and the lockers, although freshly painted, were as old as the sink.

Grace walked down the old stairs ahead of Katherine and stopped at the car board behind the front desk. No regular car was assigned to their footbeat because the beat existed on only one shift, but she tried to get the same spare every day. Otherwise, there was no way to know what the condition of the car would be. She remembered the day when her old partner, Wes Mickelsen, found their car trashed from the previous user—sunflower seeds on the floor, newspapers on the backseat, paper cups and a pop bottle stuffed under the driver's seat. The gas tank was empty. Wes went through the log sheets until he found who had last used the car. He gathered all the trash into a garbage bag, tied it to the officer's locker, and taped a note to the locker door. Grace never saw the note, but the spare car they used was free from trash for a long time after that. Wes Mickelsen had a way with words. The closer he approached, the softer he spoke, the more convincing he became.

He had convinced her. Since the new policy was to hire women, they might as well get some good ones, he had told her in Rigmor's store, where she worked every Saturday while she was in college, where she had worked every Saturday since she was a girl. She was studying archaeology at the time and had no interest in anything as modern as the police department. Wes gave her the application anyway, added his soft convincing words, and told her she could dig all she wanted once she became a cop. Almost to her surprise she did, and he trained her once she left the academy. She had not imagined, had not wanted to imagine, that he would ever leave. He had been on the beat in Ballard as long as she could remember, and her memory of Ballard went far back into her childhood.

Wes had given her his police whistle in Rigmor's store when she was eight, and she still carried it. In those years her mother worked in the store, more for gratitude and friendship to Rigmor than financial need, but it hadn't always been that way.

After the war her mother—the only daughter, the only child of Norwegian immigrants—had traveled to Norway to visit her grandmother and her father's older brother and send back news to her father and an uncle in America if anything was needed there. The war and German occupation had brought hard times to Norway, and the American family wanted to know what they could do to help. Her mother fulfilled her responsibility, but she sent back more than a financial report. She sent back news about a husband, too.

If he had been a Norwegian, there would have been great satisfaction for the family in Ballard. Secretly, part of the plan in sending her was for her to meet a good Norwegian man. If the husband had been Danish, he would have been welcomed, although with less enthusiasm. Even a Swede could be tolerated over time, but her mother had fallen in love with none of them. She had fallen in love with an American in Paris.

Grace had often heard the story of her mother and cousin taking the ferry to Denmark and then the train to Paris—two young women looking for freedom and adventure. They met Martin in the Louvre. He was a young American soldier sent to France after the war when the Americans were still welcome. He loved France and the language and had spent every free minute learning about both. For the young American woman and her Norwegian cousin, he interpreted the French inscriptions in the museum. He interpreted more than that, because when it came time for the young women to return to Norway, one caught the train and one didn't. Lisa and Martin, her mother and father, married in Paris. Her mother was twenty-two; her father a year younger.

What had they seen in each other, Grace often wondered, that they overlooked the first characteristic everybody else saw in them. Her father, an African-American from Omaha, Nebraska, and her mother, a Norwegian-American from Ballard, joining together in a country where everything was foreign except themselves. Martin wanted to stay in France, but Lisa wanted to come home. She was not ashamed, and she wasn't afraid, and she wasn't going to hide.

On the day Wes had given Grace the whistle, he had handcuffed her older sister, Evangeline, to the refrigerator door. Evangeline had wandered farther from the store than the block on Ballard Avenue where the two girls were supposed to stay when in Rigmor's care, and Wes had escorted her back. Rigmor scolded Evangeline, but such scoldings always passed over her, out the door, and farther away than even Evangeline wandered. Wes handcuffed her to the refrigerator while he went into the backroom to eat. He told her that even if he couldn't hold her, the handcuffs would. Wes Mickelsen had the biggest hands Grace had ever seen, and she couldn't imagine anyone getting out of his grip. Grace had watched her sister try to slip the handcuffs off her wrist, but they were compressed just enough that she couldn't slip free. When Wes finished eating, he gave Evangeline the key to his handcuffs. After she finally freed her hand, he told her to keep the key because she would probably need it someday. It was strange. Her sister always liked Wes, even though there were many days when she didn't like anybody.

Grace stuck the car key in her belt buckle the way Wes had always done and joined Katherine in line for roll call. With Wes beside her, none of the other cops had dared question her assignment. They would now, and like her mother, she wasn't going to hide.

"Mileage?" Katherine asked as they drove away from the precinct after roll call.

Grace looked at the odometer and read out the numbers. She picked up the mike. "2-Boy-8 in service," she said.

"2-Boy-8," the radio operator replied.

"5004 and 4996." She gave Katherine's serial number first, the way Wes had taught her. When she worked with other cops on days Wes took off, some announced the lower number first, and others began with their own number whether it was lower or not. Wes insisted it was like proper grammar. You always put yourself last.

Grace drove down Phinney Ridge from the North Precinct in Wallingford and straight, or as straight as she could, to Ballard Avenue. Today she would not pass through the street as she had done the day before. She had never known Wes Mickelsen to drive the street without stopping at least once. He never said it, but it must bring bad luck.

Grace parked in front of Al's Cabinet Shop and led Katherine up Ballard Avenue to the concrete benches in Marvin's Garden beyond the Bell Tower. Two men were sleeping beneath the cedar trees at the north end of the park. She saw a bottle in a paper sack lying between them, but that wasn't the reason she stopped. She checked her watch and said, "In a minute."

"A minute for what?" Katherine asked, sitting beside her.

Grace nodded to her left as Arne Johansen walked out of Johansen Brothers Meats still dressed in his bloodstained butcher's coat. He crossed the street toward them and waved. Grace raised her hand in response; Katherine sat straighter on the bench.

Arne walked beneath the arch of the round brick Bell Tower that stood in the triangle where Ballard Avenue angled past 22nd. He opened a small steel door on the interior wall of the tower, reached inside the compartment, and pulled a lever. A bell rang above him in the copper dome. It rang each time he pulled. After twelve rings he closed the door, turned toward Grace and Katherine on the concrete bench, and began to sing.

Grace knew the song immediately and even recognized a word now and then in the Italian: *diverse, bruna Floria*. Arne's song gathered strength and stopped three men in long-sleeved work shirts on their way to Vera's Cafe. One of the men crossed his arms and hid his grease-stained hands. The song roused the two sleeping fellows who lay beneath the drooping branches of the cedar trees, and they struggled to rise. A ponderous rank garbage truck rumbled to a rolling stop at the stop sign beside the tower and added a percussional flurry as it continued south on Ballard Avenue. Grace leaned toward Katherine and whispered, "He's singing this for us."

As he reached the conclusion to his aria, Arne closed his eyes, formed his hands into fists, and with all the strength that remained in his aging vocal cords, sent his song high into the air where seagulls circled on wind currents originating in cold Pacific waters.

"Tosca sei tu," he finished.

For a moment there was silence. Then applause erupted from all sides of the tower. Arne smiled and tilted his head to the two men who clapped with boisterous enthusiasm beneath the trees, and he waved to the scattered cheers farther down Ballard Avenue. Finally he bowed deeply and formally to the police officers on the bench.

"Tosca," Grace said as she rose from the bench and walked toward Arne. "It's always my favorite."

"I hope so," he said.

"Arne," she said, "I've brought a foreigner across the bridge. This is Katherine Murphy, my new partner."

"I feel safer already," Arne said, extending his hand to Katherine.

"Do you do this every day?" Katherine asked.

"I'm the official bell ringer," Arne said. He stuttered when he spoke, and it was always a wonder to Grace how he could sing so clearly.

"I mean, do you sing here every day?"

"Only when I have an audience. Otherwise, Grace would haul me away to the funny farm. If I had known you would be here today," he said through his halting speech, "I would have brought my sister Margaret with me. Grace has had to listen to me since she was a little girl, but I could have spared you the pain. Margaret has a lovely voice."

"You have a lovely voice," Katherine said.

"You're very kind. It's gotten a bit rusty after all these years."

"Arne studied opera in New York," Grace said.

"Oh, that was a long time ago. Now I'm a butcher like all my brothers, and Margaret keeps the books, but we can always sing for our supper if we have to."

"What was the song about?" Katherine asked.

"Love, of course. With the Italians it's always about love. This fellow is painting a blue-eyed Madonna on the wall of a church, but he's thinking about his dark-eyed lover. As he paints, he wonders about the mystery of art that mixes such beauties together. 'I only think of you,' he says. '*Tosca sei tu!*' " he sang softly again, clearly and beautifully. Tosca, of you."

Katherine looked up at Grace and then back at Arne.

"Why would he paint a blue-eyed Madonna?" she asked. "Whoever heard of that?"

"It's an opera," Arne Johansen said. "You can do anything in the opera."

They escorted Arne Johansen to the butcher shop, where he left them with a theatrical wave.

"I'll bet you didn't have anything like that on First Avenue," Grace said.

"Nothing like it. What other surprises do you have?"

Grace looked across the street to a sign in once bold but now fading red letters that proclaimed, RIGMOR'S GROCERY. A round table stood outside the door with chairs gathered around it. On both sides of the table were bins of fruits and vegetables. Grace felt like she should have stopped yesterday on her way home after work to make sure Rigmor was okay, but after leaving the garbage dump, she hadn't wanted to talk to anybody. If she had stopped to see Rigmor, the old lady would have known something was wrong. And then she would have wanted Grace to explain, and there were some explanations that Grace didn't want to make even to Rigmor. Besides, Rigmor was fine without her. Over the years different cops came onto the Ballard Avenue beat and felt like Rigmor couldn't get along without them, but eventually the cops left and Rigmor continued.

"Now you'll meet Rigmor," Grace said. She stepped off the sidewalk and started walking across the street.

"How did you pronounce her name?" Katherine asked. She was looking at the sign, too.

"Ree-mor," Grace said with elaborate precision. "It's spelled r-i-g-m-o-r, but the *g* is silent and the *i* is like an *e*. The *r* is different, too, but don't even try that. Rigmor," Grace repeated as she opened the door to the grocery and heard the tiny bell ring above the door.

"*Goddag,* Rigmor," Grace said to the tall woman who stood behind the counter in the back of the store. Rigmor's thick gray hair was held in place with a series of combs that circled her head like a crown. "*Hvordan har du det?*"

"I'm fine, *tak,*" Rigmor said. "Is this Katrin *med dig*?"

Rigmor had never mastered the English *th*. Usually it came out of her mouth as *d,* but for Katherine, she had shortened it to a simple *t.*

"Yes, this is Katherine."

"Ha!" the old woman exclaimed. "So they let you do that. I'm very happy to meet you, dear."

"I'm happy to meet you, too," Katherine said.

"I expected to see you yesterday," Rigmor said to Grace.

"We got a call that took up the whole shift. Did you have any problem closing up?"

"Of course not," Rigmor said. "Are you hungry?"

"You know me," Grace said. "I'm always hungry."

"*Skipperslabskovs* on the stove, or you can make a sand-wich—shrimp or herring or maybe some *leverpostej.* You show Katrin where everything is."

Grace walked behind the counter where there was a large stainless steel pot on the stove. She lifted the lid and sniffed. "Ummm," she said to Katherine. "Sailor's stew. It's the beer that makes it good."

She set the lid down on an unlit burner and stirred the stew with a ladle. Then she picked up a bowl from a shelf above the stove, ladled the stew into it, and tasted it with a spoon she picked out of a gray rubber tub.

"Want to try some?" she asked.

"Just a little," Katherine said.

"Help yourself, then."

Grace nodded toward the pot and walked through a doorway into Rigmor's tiny backroom filled by a wooden table and three chairs. Shelves surrounded a stairway that led up several steps, turned, and went up again to Rigmor's apartment. Katherine came into the room, and Grace pushed out a chair for her. She heard Rigmor talking to a customer on the other side of the wall.

"What language were you talking to Rigmor?" Katherine asked.

"Norwegian. Rigmor is Danish, but I speak Norwegian, and we understand each other just fine."

"Is there any difference? I thought Norway and Denmark were the same."

"Don't tell that to Rigmor," Grace said. "It would be like telling an Irishwoman that Ireland is the same as England."

"Not a good idea, I guess."

"Not a good idea."

"Did you learn Norwegian working out here?"

"No. I learned that at home from my mother. She's Norwegian. I grew up here in Ballard. I used to work in this store after school and every Saturday. That's what Arne meant when he said I've had to listen to him since I was a little girl. Well, he meant more than that, but that's another story. Sometimes I forget to explain who I am."

"You don't have to explain anything to me," Katherine said.

Grace wondered if that were true. She wished it would be—just once. She still remembered her first recognition of how color mattered to people. It was Evangeline who told her. Evangeline, three years older, believed she knew everything. She had told Grace the truth about Santa Claus and the tooth fairy. "They'll call you black," Evangeline had said. It was the day Grace started kindergarten.

"Why?" Grace had asked.

"Because you are, that's why."

"I am not," Grace had answered. She knew her colors— blue and red and black and white and yellow. Yellow was her favorite color. Her sister liked green, but there was green everywhere. She liked yellow. The tulips in the back-yard were yellow, some of them anyway, and so was her dress that twirled with her when she spun like a top. People did not have colors like tulips. People were different. She had never thought about her own color before. "Cramden is black," she had told her sister.

"Cramden is a dog," Evangeline said. "That's not what I'm talking about. Maybe they won't say it out loud, but they'll still say it."

They said it out loud. She had been clumsy as a child, but every so often she would hit the ball too hard, or she would win the Friday afternoon arithmetic contest on the blackboard, and some child would shout the word after her as she ran home. It was an excuse for anger, such strange anger. She was not black like Cramden, and the other kids were not white. Paper was white. Teeth were white. If they were white, they would disappear into the white walls and you would not see them until they stood in front of the blackboard. Why did it matter, she had wondered as a child. She still wondered as a faint tint of red left Katherine's cheeks that were neither as white as chalk nor as dark as the blackboard.

"Where are you from?" Grace asked.

"Eastern Washington. I grew up on a farm."

"Not many black people there, I suppose."

"No."

"Not many here in Ballard either. Sometimes I think I'm the only one, and I'm only half black and not really that. My father is part Indian, too. He teaches French at Ballard High School."

"Do I have to learn Norwegian to walk this beat?" Katherine asked.

"It wouldn't hurt, especially if you want to understand Rigmor. She mixes English and Danish together all the time."

"I would like to understand her."

"I hope you do. There are some things you need to know. We help her close the store every night," Grace said. "Every night except Saturday. It's part of the job for the footbeat. It has been for years. We carry in the vegetable tables from the sidewalk and make sure she's okay. We do some other things, too, but that's the main job. That's how we pay for this food. You'll make Rigmor mad if you try to give her money and, believe me, you don't want to make her mad. She has an official letter signed by the chief that says because of historical precedent and neighborhood traditions the gratuity policy doesn't apply to Rigmor's guests. So don't worry about that."

"Why don't we close on Saturday?" Katherine asked.

"The chief closes on Saturday—at least some of the time. Rigmor lives upstairs, and there is a poker game here every Saturday night with the cops who used to work this beat. It's been going on for as long as anybody can remember. There are a few majors and captains, too, but rank doesn't matter. You get to play if you worked this beat long enough."

"Is this some kind of secret?"

"It's no secret. They play for matchsticks. Rigmor won't let them play for money. 'They come as friends,' she says, 'and they leave as friends.' They close up, too. That's part of the deal. On the other nights, we help her close. Except Sunday. She's not open on Sundays."

"What happens if we get a call at the end of the shift?"

"Radio won't give us a call unless he has to, and then Al closes up if we're not here. He has the cabinet shop across the street."

"This is really good stew," Katherine said.

"Just wait until Friday. She makes seafood chowder with cream and sherry. It's good enough to die for."

"I guess we're not invited to the poker game," Katherine said.

"Not yet," Grace said, "but rules are rules. That's what Rigmor says."

Grace picked up Katherine's empty bowl and carried it back through the door. She put the bowls into the sink beside the stove and turned on the hot water.

"It was delicious, Rigmor," Grace said. *"Tak for det."*

"Velbekommen," Rigmor said.

Grace washed their bowls and handed a dish towel to Katherine.

"How did you like this strange food that we eat?" Rigmor asked.

"It was wonderful," Katherine said.

"Next time, you'll have to try a little more."

"We would eat here all day long if you made lutefisk," Grace said.

"You and your lutefisk," Rigmor said. "You'll die from that stuff."

"Rigmor doesn't think much of our Norwegian specialties," Grace said to Katherine.

"I didn't say that," Rigmor said. "Now don't get me into trouble with the Norwegians."

"That's just between us," Grace said.

"So, then, that's different."

Grace wiped her hands dry and pulled a plastic container out from beneath the butcher block next to the sink.

"You're about out of flour," Grace said.

"Ja, but I'll get some later," Rigmor said.

Grace went into the backroom where Rigmor stored the extra flour.

"Leave that," Rigmor called after her. "You'll get that mess all over your uniform."

Grace carried the flour sack into the kitchen and ripped open the top. She propped it on the edge of the container and tipped the sack slowly. A white plume of dust rose above it, offering a fine contrast to the color of her hands.

When she finished, she folded the sack into quarters and disappeared again into the backroom.

"No *ja*," Rigmor said, placing the English *no* and the Danish *yes* side by side in contradiction to each other. "So much for what I say."

Chapter 7

Late in the shift Katherine settled into the car seat as Grace drove south on 24th Avenue approaching Market Street. They had left a citation with a shoplifter on Crown Hill and were leaving the hill behind, too. Grace curved onto Shilshole Avenue, a flat industrial street that ran along the back side of Ballard Avenue. A mile east the Ballard Bridge rose over the Ship Canal, delaying the late commuters heading home on 15th Avenue. The streetlights began to come on, a few at a time, as their sensors reacted to the change of light.

Grace had introduced Katherine to so many people and streets and businesses all over Ballard that her mind was swimming with details that would take months to master. The districts she had worked downtown were tiny in comparison.

Along the canal the parking lot for the industrial center had emptied while the restaurant lot was becoming full. A large boat was edging into one of the repair docks at Pacific Fisherman, and Katherine turned in her seat to watch it dock. She saw movement that wasn't from the boat.

"Let's turn around," Katherine said.

"Did you see something?" Grace asked.

"I saw some kids back there. Something doesn't look right."

Grace made a U-turn and drove back slowly. A boy and girl were walking along a seldom-used railroad track overgrown with weeds. The bright clothes of the children stood out from the bleak background. It didn't look like a safe place for children to walk.

Grace pulled into a driveway that intersected the railroad tracks a few yards ahead of the children. The boy looked frightened and stopped. The girl could not have been five years old, and the boy was not much older. He tightened the grip he had on the little girl's hand.

"Hi," Katherine said through her open window. "Are you guys lost?"

The little girl broke away from the boy's grasp and hurried up to the car.

"Look, Daniel, it's two lady policemen." She placed great emphasis on the two.

Her small hands grabbed the edge of Katherine's open window, and she jumped up and down to see into the car. Her short fine hair bounced in opposition to her jumps. The boy she called Daniel edged cautiously closer with his head down.

"Where are you going?" Katherine asked.

"Home," the little girl said.

"Where's home?"

"Over there," the girl said. She pointed over the car between jumps.

"It's a little late, isn't it?" Katherine asked. She was charmed by the child's enthusiasm and open smile.

"I don't know. Is that a gun?" the girl asked. She pointed to the shotgun locked into the dashboard clamp.

"It is. What's your name?"

"Mary."

"Do you want to sit in our car?"

"Yes," Mary said and grabbed the handle of the front door.

Katherine had intended for the little girl sit in the back, but that wasn't Mary's intention.

"Okay," Katherine said, "you can sit in the middle."

Katherine picked up the clipboard, which was on the seat between her and Grace, and tossed it on the dash. With a child's agility Mary squirmed past Katherine and reached out to touch the dashboard.

"I won't touch the gun," Mary said. "Look, Daniel. I'm inside the police car."

"Are you her brother?" Katherine asked the boy. He had moved closer to the car but not so close to be within reach.

"Yes. She's supposed to stay with me." He had not smiled once, and his large brown eyes contrasted sharply with his sister's. He was a somber child with a book in his hand.

"We're police officers. Didn't your parents tell you it was okay to talk to us?"

"I—I guess so," Daniel stuttered.

"You can get in, too," Katherine said.

He moved forward another step so that he was just outside the sweep of Katherine's open door, but not any closer. Meanwhile Mary was exploring all the buttons on the dashboard.

"Do you want to turn on the police lights, Mary?" Grace asked.

"Yes, yes, yes," Mary said.

Grace pointed to the toggle switch. "If you push this switch up, the blue lights come on. If you push it down, you get the flashing lights. Which do you want?"

"The blue lights," Mary said.

"Okay. Push the switch up."

Mary reached for the switch and paused when her finger touched it. She looked at Grace for final approval and then flipped the switch. The lights hummed as they twirled in their glass cases on the overhead rack, and their reflections bounced off the metal walls of the building across the street. Mary pushed her head into the front window, but she could not see the lights from there. She slid past Katherine and stuck her head out the open door. Katherine put her feet outside so that they wouldn't be trampled.

Daniel watched the lights, too. As the revolving blue lights reflected in his eyes, he smiled for the first time.

Grace leaned forward so she could see the boy. "Do you want to turn on the siren, Daniel?" she asked.

"I do, I do," Mary said.

"We'll let Daniel do it," Grace said. She turned the blue lights off and patted the seat where Mary had been. "Come over here. I'll show you how."

Katherine got out of the car to remove one barrier for the boy. His sister hung on the door, her feet still inside the car. Daniel looked at the ground and said nothing.

"Come on, Daniel," Mary said. "Don't stand there like that."

"It's all right," Katherine said. "He doesn't have to do it if he doesn't want to."

"I'll do it," Daniel said.

"Okay," Grace said, "but you have to sit over here. You can't reach the switch standing outside."

Daniel climbed into the car, carrying his book past his sister, and sat beside Grace. Grace turned the siren knob so that the siren would come on with the switch. Then she pointed to the toggle on the dash beside the one for the blue lights.

"Now, turn it on for just a second and then turn it back off. We don't want to scare the whole neighborhood."

Katherine sat down in the car. She didn't want to be standing outside when the siren went off. Daniel moved forward so that his feet were firmly on the floor. He flipped the switch on and off so quickly that they barely heard its scream.

"Very good," Grace said. "Now try it again and leave it on just a little longer. I'll tell you when to turn it off."

Daniel flipped the switch again. Mary covered her ears with her hands and managed to jump up and down inside the car. Daniel stared at the switch and at his finger.

"Okay, off," Grace said.

Daniel slowly applied pressure on the top of the switch until it clicked off.

"Wow, that was loud," he said.

"Can I do it?" Mary asked.

"No," Grace said. "You did the lights, and Daniel did the siren. You two make a good team. Maybe we'll have to hire you to run our equipment for us. What do you say to that, Daniel? Looking for a job?"

"You can do that yourself," he said.

"I'll do it," Mary said.

"I'll bet you would," Grace said.

"Where have you guys been?" Katherine asked.

"Down to the lock," Mary said.

"Where?"

"She means the Ballard Locks," Daniel said.

"Do you like to watch the boats, or did you watch the salmon go through the fish ladders?" Grace asked.

"He just likes the trains," Mary said. "That's all he wants to do. I like the ducks. We take bread and I feed the ducks, but he just watches the trains."

"Tell me about the trains," Katherine said.

"They go over the bridge," Mary said.

"I was asking Daniel. I think he can tell me."

"The bridge is for the Burlington tracks," Daniel said. "When a train comes, the bridge drops down over the water. The trains have the right-of-way, and the boats have to wait."

Once, during his brief speech, he looked up at Katherine. Otherwise he fastened his attention on the siren switch, his finger lightly touching it as he spoke. For that moment when Katherine saw his eyes, he had the enthusiasm she would expect in a child. But it was only a moment, and then he looked away.

"When I was a girl," Katherine said, "I liked trains, too."

That brought him back. "Did you?"

"We had tracks that went through our farm. I liked to

watch the trains and listen to the noise they made on the tracks. The trains didn't come very often, but they made me think I could go anyplace I wanted."

"Where was that?" Daniel asked.

"Where did I want to go?"

"No. Where were the tracks?"

"In eastern Washington, close to Davenport. Have you ever heard of that town?"

"No, but it was probably the Burlington. The government gave them the rights to build across Washington."

"It was probably the Burlington, then. You know a lot about trains."

"That's why he has that book," Mary said.

Daniel pressed the book tighter against himself as though it held a secret he didn't want to share.

"It's good to read books," Katherine said. "That's how we learn."

"He stole it," Mary said.

"I didn't either." He gave Mary a sharp look, but the little girl wasn't frightened.

"He was supposed to take it back, but he didn't."

"Is that true, Daniel?" Katherine asked.

Daniel looked at the floor again, and Katherine didn't think he would answer. Every question, even the simplest one, was hard for Daniel to answer. She wondered if he was trying to hide something, or if he was just unnaturally shy. She hadn't meant to frighten him. It was only a book, and he was only a child.

"Well, I checked it out of the library," Daniel said finally, still staring at the floor, "but then I forgot, and now if I take it back, I have to pay a big fine. I don't any have money, so I've just kept it for now. They'll get mad at me if I take it back and don't have any money."

"They'll get mad at you if you don't take it back," Grace said. "Then we'll have to come and arrest you. Here I was thinking you would be my siren guy. You can't run the siren with an arrest record."

Both children looked at Grace with their mouths open as they contemplated the force of the law. Grace returned their look with an expression that they would never interpret.

"Officer Stevens is just joking," Katherine said. "We never arrest anybody for library books, but she is right. You have to take the book back. Maybe the librarian will give you a second chance."

"Let's do it right now," Grace said. "We'll stop at the library and give you a ride home. Prepare for launch, Officer Katherine."

Katherine closed her door and lifted Mary onto the seat beside Daniel. There was room for all of them. Grace made a U-turn and retraced their course on 24th. The library was a few blocks north. Its parking lot was empty.

"It closes at six," Grace said, reading the sign.

"I'll tell you what, Daniel," Katherine said. "You put the book in the night drop, and I'll stop at the library tomorrow and talk to the librarian. I'll make sure she understands. Do you trust me to do that?"

He did not look at her with more than a passing glance. He held the book in both hands and nodded quietly.

"I have to hear the answer, Daniel."

"Yes," he finally said.

"Let me see the book, then. I'll write down the title so that I know what I'm talking about."

He showed her the cover of the book. The book had gotten wet, and the pages had swelled. *The Great Race,* she wrote into her pocket notebook, *by John Jacob Jones.*

"What's your last name?"

"Wilson."

"How old are you, Daniel?"

"Eight," the boy said. "I'll be nine this summer."

"How old are you, Mary?"

"Four," the little girl said. She held up four fingers for clarity.

"And what's your address?" Katherine asked.

Mary shrugged her shoulders and looked at Daniel. "I know how to get there," he said.

"Good. Put the book in the night drop, and we'll give you a ride home."

"We can walk from here," Daniel said. "It's only a few blocks." He made it clear that he didn't want to ride home in a police car.

"Okay," Katherine said. "But I don't want you guys to walk along those tracks after dark. It might not be safe. Will you promise me that, Daniel?"

"Yes."

She opened her door and turned sideways. "Out you go, then."

Daniel climbed out of the car first. He was careful not to bump against Katherine or step on her feet as he got out. Once outside he moved away from the door and waited for Mary in silence. Mary wiggled past Katherine without any of her brother's concern about contact. One hand moved slowly across the dashboard to the shiny badge pinned to Katherine's hat, which was wedged behind the handle of the spotlight. Katherine felt Mary's other hand seeking support as she passed. Katherine held it as Mary jumped down from the car. The child's trusting touch lingered with Katherine. It was an unexpected gift at the end of the day.

When Daniel stopped at the book drop, Mary turned and waved. Katherine waved back. Daniel pushed the book into the book drop, closed the chute, and then checked it a second time. Mary waved again when they reached the sidewalk as if she did not want them to forget her. Then she hurried forward to keep up with Daniel. Grace pulled out of the parking lot and headed south again for Rigmor's Grocery.

Katherine had seen so few children downtown. She turned in her seat for one last look at Daniel and Mary. They stood at the crosswalk on 24th, hand in hand, waiting for the long procession of dangerous traffic to stop.

Chapter 8

Sometimes the fear came from a dream that shook him from sleep—when Daniel tried to run but his legs would not move, or he screamed but his voice was lost. Sometimes the fear did not come until his eyes adjusted to the light, until he recognized the room, until he heard his sister's deep breathing beside him. It was worse when he forgot, when he saw light through the window and thought he was home and could go out to the backyard with Hercules the cat and sit in the sunshine until everyone else was awake.

Then he remembered. He remembered his father shouting, damning him, damning his sister, too, but mostly him because he was older. "Damn those kids," his father yelled. "Nothing for myself because of those damn kids." Those were the last words Daniel heard that night. Daniel knew that *damn* was more than a swear word. The word, the meaning, had haunted him as he waited for another to replace it.

If he could see his father, he would find out what went wrong. If his father came back, he would not ask for toys. He would polish the old truck and the new boat his father wanted. He would line up his father's fishing rods and never ask for one himself. He would untangle the lines on all the fishing reels if his father would come back, if only he would call.

His father had taken the truck and the fishing poles. He

had even taken the toy train, which the two of them would set up together in the basement on special Saturday mornings. His father told him that it had been his toy as a child, that it would be valuable someday when Daniel grew up. Maybe it was valuable now, because his father had taken it, too.

Daniel remembered his mother crying when she talked to the landlord about the rent. She cried when she watched television with his little sister on her lap and when she ate the macaroni and cheese he made. She cried when the telephone stopped working and, finally, when he showed her the newspaper with the help-wanted ads he had circled. He had cried, too, at first, but he stopped.

When his mother got the job at the bar, he took care of his sister and tried to stay awake until his mother came home. He was afraid his mother would damn him and his sister like his father had done. Where did children go when they were damned?

Daniel lay in bed and guessed the time from the sound of cars on Market Street. It had to be late at night. During the day, the cars never stopped coming.

Daniel wondered what happened to Hercules. Rudy said Hercules had found a new home, but Rudy said lots of things that were not true. Rudy said they could be a family, but why couldn't they keep Hercules, then? Hercules was part of the family before his father had damned them.

Rudy was allergic to cats. He had other problems, too, which was why he didn't work anymore. He had worked once, but he could not overcome his problems. He had the apartment, though, and that was where they went. That was why they could not keep Hercules—in addition to the allergic problem.

"Honor thy father and thy mother," Rudy said. He said lots of words that were supposed to help him overcome his problems. They were all waiting for him to overcome. In the meantime, he said those words, but he was nobody's father.

Maybe they could just forget what happened. Maybe they

could erase what happened like Mrs. Murray erased arithmetic problems from the blackboard. Rudy said that without him they would scatter like seeds in the wind. Daniel
was not sure what that meant except it was something like
being damned. If they scattered in the wind, he would never
see Mary again, he would never see his mother.

He pulled the covers away from Mary's face. She didn't
move. She had been asleep when their father left, and she
was too young to understand. He was glad Mary didn't
understand. She didn't have nightmares yet.

He heard their apartment door close and listened for
footsteps. Were the footsteps getting closer or moving farther away? How heavy were they? He closed his eyes and
listened as far as he could. The bedroom door opened, and
he froze beneath the covers. He heard light footsteps come
into the room.

"Mom?" he asked.

"Shhh," she said. "Don't wake Mary."

Daniel sat up in bed, and the covers dropped from his
neck.

"How was work tonight?" he asked.

"The same. You should be asleep."

"I woke up," Daniel said. "Is Rudy here?"

"No."

His mother stood by the bed, and Daniel could see her
from the streetlight that came through the windows. Her
voice sounded tired. Her voice was always tired. Daniel
moved closer to Mary to make room for his mother and
hoped she would sit down. If Mary were awake, his mother
would sit on the bed and Mary would crawl onto her lap.
Sometimes Daniel wished he were as young as Mary and
could crawl onto his mother's lap, too. He remembered
doing that when he was young.

"Did Rudy say where he was going?" his mother asked.

Daniel shook his head even though there was barely
enough light for his mother to see. He didn't like to talk
about Rudy.

"Is it still nighttime in Idaho?" Daniel asked.

"It's the same time in Idaho as it is here," his mother said. "I told you that before."

"I know. I just like to hear about it. We should have stayed there."

"There's nothing there now," his mother said, "not for us."

"Grandma was coming for us, wasn't she?" Daniel asked. "She wanted us to come back."

"Sure."

"We could still go."

"Maybe someday we'll go back," his mother said. "If your father pays us what he's supposed to, we might be able to go. Or maybe Rudy will get a good job. He wants to go to school now. Maybe I can do that, too. I won't stay in that bar forever. Or maybe we'll win the lottery. I bought ten more tickets tonight. Somebody has to win. Maybe it will be us."

"I could make you some hot cocoa," Daniel said.

"You'd better go back to sleep," his mother said. "Rudy doesn't like it when you get up in the night. He must be out walking again."

His mother turned away from the bed.

"Mom," Daniel asked, "do you really think we can go back?"

Chapter 9

Thomas stood outside the recycling shed and organized the plastic bags that held his belongings. His bed had risen a few inches, and he estimated he would stack himself out of the place in another two weeks. He didn't intend to sleep higher than three feet.

Perhaps he could tolerate a few inches above that, and when he calculated an additional factor for compression, it was possible he might stay another week beyond the two weeks of his original calculation. Three weeks plus the week or so he had been there would total a month. He doubted he had stayed a month in one place since the day he had abandoned his apartment in Chicago. On that day he had only intended to walk to the lab, but it felt so good to walk—to be free of time divided into hours and minutes, to be free of the laundry on the bedroom floor, the bills on the kitchen counter, and the telephone that rang when he didn't want to talk—that he kept on walking. He always intended to go back. He wondered how long ago that was.

Maybe he wouldn't stay here either. He had already begun to accumulate possessions—eleven books, a hairbrush, a *Wall Street Journal,* fifteen feet of good rope. He had even considered possessing an office chair with rollers that had been left outside the mechanical garbage machine. It had been a dangerous moment.

The gears on the building garage door whirred loudly as the door began to rise. Before it completed its ascent, Jack Morton pushed through the opening with a wheelbarrow that gained momentum as it descended the ramp. Jack quickened his steps to keep up with it.

"Morning, Thomas. You're up early," Jack Morton said as he passed. He didn't slow down until he reached the end of the alley. There he stopped and removed orange traffic cones from the wheelbarrow. He placed them in a line across the entrance to the street. Thomas ambled after him at his own pace.

"I saw your brother earlier this morning," Thomas said. "He was dressed like you in work clothes. It must be interesting to have a twin."

"It's interesting, all right," Jack said.

"What are you doing?" Thomas asked.

"We're pouring concrete today," Jack said. "Everybody works when we pour concrete. I even get my brother out of the office and put him to work. I have a pumper truck coming any minute."

"Do you need any help?"

"Sure. Do you know anything about concrete?"

"I know that a form of concrete was developed by ancient Egyptians. The Greeks and Romans used it, too."

"No kidding? I thought I was the first guy who tried this stuff!"

Thomas liked the way Jack kidded him.

"What do you need help with?"

"I don't know. This is heavy work, Thomas."

"I don't mind. It might be interesting to gain a little practical experience. There's no telling when it might become useful."

"Do you think Einstein ever worked with cement?"

"I don't think so."

"I bought that book," Jack said, "the one about Einstein's theories."

"I could have found you a copy in the garbage."

"I wanted one with the cover in case I understood what he was talking about."

"Did you understand?" Thomas asked.

"No," Jack said. He had finished arranging the cones that blocked the alley, and he looked down the street. There was no truck in sight. "I've tried to understand this relativity deal since I was a kid. Time slows down with speed. That's what the book says. I can say it, too. I can even believe it, but I don't understand it."

"You mean you don't feel it in your guts," Thomas said.

"That's right. I don't feel it."

"Einstein didn't say that time slows down," Thomas said. "He said that time and motion are relative to the observer."

"Not to this observer." The observer looked down the street again and checked his wristwatch.

"Sure they are," Thomas said. "Let's say you're suspended in space. It's completely dark and you can't see anything. You have no feeling of motion. But then you see your brother floating toward you. He's holding a light that flashes on and off. He waves as he passes by. You wave back. Who is moving? You or your brother?"

Jack stood still, and Thomas imagined what he was thinking. Why would he listen to some fellow who slept in a recycling shed?

"I suppose I'll think that my brother is moving."

"That's right, but that's exactly what your brother feels, too. So, who is moving? That's what Einstein asked. He decided that movement had to be relative to the observer. And if movement is relative, so is time. You can't change one without changing the other. Time and space. They're meaningless without each other. If you understand that principle, I can show you how time changes relative to motion—or how time slows down, if you want to say it that way."

It was up to Jack. Did he want to learn, or would he stand next to the street and wait for the truck? Ideas or concrete? Thomas never tried to predict.

"How can you show me?" Jack asked.

Thomas walked back to the shed and Jack followed, leaving his wheelbarrow at the end of the alley. Thomas removed a pencil from one of his Safeway sacks. He tore off a piece of cardboard from a flattened box in the stack beside the shed and squatted on the driveway beside the cardboard. Jack bent over to watch, propping his hands on his knees.

"This is a light clock," Thomas said. "There are two mirrors, one on top of the other, exactly in line. They're held six inches apart with a piece of metal." He drew two horizontal lines on the cardboard with a dot between them. "A particle of light, a photon, bounces between the mirrors. The photon bounces back and forth a billion times a second. It's an imaginary clock, but it demonstrates the principle. Understood?"

"Understood," Jack said.

"Let's say you have a wristwatch that's synchronized with this light clock. You look at your watch and see that the photon is bouncing a billion times a second. Of course, you have to see this through understanding, not in the literal sense. Also, you have to understand that the speed of light never changes, regardless of your perspective. That's essential."

"The speed of light doesn't change," Jack said.

"Now, imagine that this light clock is on a flatcar connected to a train, and you're standing beside the tracks. If the train is standing still in relation to you, you watch the photon bounce straight up and down between the mirrors. You check your wristwatch and see that the photon is bouncing back and forth a billion times a second. Now look what happens when the train is moving."

Thomas drew new lines below the original lines. This time he drew three sets of mirrors to show a moving clock.

"If you're standing beside the tracks and the train car with the light clock passes in front of you, what happens to the photon? From where you're standing, the mirrors are moving, but the photon is still hitting directly in the center of the mirrors. If it didn't, the photon would bounce out into space and there would be no clock. From your perspective beside the tracks, the photon on the moving light clock has to move at an angle to continue hitting the center of the moving mirror. If the photon moves at an angle instead of bouncing straight up and down, it travels a greater distance. Since light always travels at the same speed regardless of perspective, the photon takes longer to bounce between the mirrors. Greater distance, greater time. You look at your wristwatch, and sure enough, the photon is now bouncing back and forth less than a billion times a second. From your perspective time on the train has slowed down. However, if your brother is on the train sitting beside the photon clock, he checks his wristwatch and sees that the photon is still bouncing straight up and down a billion times a second. The same clock, the same photon, but two different perspectives of space and time."

At the end of the alley, a huge truck pulled up to the traffic cones and blocked the sidewalk and half the street. Its powerful diesel engine caused the asphalt where they stood to vibrate. Jack Morton picked up the cardboard and studied the illustrations of the light clock at rest and in motion.

"Damn," Jack said. "This is it, isn't it?" He held up the cardboard as if it were the tablet from the mountain.

"This is part of it," Thomas said. "Einstein demonstrated his theory mathematically, but he saw it in his imagination first. It's been proven experimentally many times. There was one experiment where they used atomic clocks. They kept one clock on the ground and put the other on an airplane. When they brought the two clocks together and compared them, what do you think they found?"

The truck driver opened his door and climbed down from the cab. Thomas thought he looked annoyed. No one had moved the cones out of his way.

"The clock on the airplane was slower," Jack said.

"That's right. Less time had elapsed on that clock. A few hundred billionths of a second, but measurable and predictable."

"I heard about that," Jack said. "Amazing."

"I think the truck is here," Thomas said.

The truck driver walked down the alley to the recycling shed. Thomas thought maybe Jack should do something, say hello or move the wheelbarrow. Jack showed the truck driver the drawings of the light clock.

"Do you have any idea what this is?" he asked the driver.

"A piece of cardboard," the driver said.

"This is an explanation of Einstein's theory of relativity. Thomas did it." Jack pointed at Thomas. "It makes me want to run down the street shouting 'Eureka.' "

"Is this the place that ordered concrete?" the truck driver asked.

Jack held the cardboard as he guided the truck farther into the alley. He carried it with him to the roof and propped it up against the roof parapet. It distracted him until the concrete began to flow through a giant black hose that hung from the telegraphed steel tubing of the pumper truck.

Thomas was eager to do well, to concentrate on the concrete hose, which was his job to move. He could see that the other workers did not trust him, except Jack's twin brother. There was no difference there.

"We're moving left, Thomas," Jack Morton said.

Thomas pulled the giant rubber hose to the left. It was a fascinating operation. The cement truck emptied its load into the hopper of the pumper truck down in the driveway, which then pumped the concrete through a steel boom that rose eighty feet into the air and then down onto the roof of the building through the rubber hose. The sections of hose were heavy enough when they were empty, but they were unbelievably heavy when filled with concrete. Jack held the end of the hose and aimed the concrete where it was needed. The concrete spurted in rhythm to the pump below. The pump must have tremendous power.

"How high will that truck pump?" Thomas asked.

"High enough," Jack said. "Don't let that hose kink. It'll explode on us."

Thomas knew he shouldn't have asked that question or any question just now. That was the problem he always had. You don't ask what's in the water when the flood is coming at you.

"We're moving back," Jack said. "Pull it back."

When Thomas stepped back with the hose, his feet became entangled in wire mesh and he fell backward. Jack looked at him, but he didn't say a word even though the entire weight of the hose had dropped on him. Thomas jumped back up and picked up his share. He looked down at his feet. They were pouring the concrete onto sheets of evenly rippled steel that reminded him of waves with a constant frequency. A grid of wire mesh overlaid the waves like a four-dimensional view of time and space, and his feet had become entangled in time.

The job became less fascinating to Thomas as his arms and shoulders began to ache. Sometimes when they moved the hose, he stumbled under the weight and wondered if he was holding the hose up or if the hose was holding him.

There was no time to ask. He wondered why they didn't stop to rest.

They stopped only once to remove sections of hose. Thomas uncoupled one of the sections himself and carried it over his shoulder. It felt light and flexible compared to how it felt when it was full of concrete. They pumped concrete until they reached the end of the steel. There was a section of roof farther to the east that had been left alone. Thomas thought about asking why, but then decided he was just glad that they had come to the end.

After the concrete trucks and the pumper truck were gone, the men sat down beside their work. Jack's brother gave the youngest of the crew money to buy sandwiches for everybody. Then he and Jack shook hands, laughed between themselves, and the brother left. The other men talked about how the job had gone, the number of yards poured, how it compared to others. There was a story about concrete that had set up too fast. They guessed how long it would be before they could trowel this mix. "When she goes, she goes," one of the men said. Thomas sat on the roof beside Jack, separated from the others by Jack's body and by experiences he could not share.

Some time after the sandwiches had been eaten, one man stretched and groaned and picked up a small trowel from the edge of the form. He walked along the parapet to where they had begun. One by one, the others rose with trowels in their hands. Jack was the only one who did not move.

"So, what do you think of pouring concrete?" Jack asked Thomas.

"It's interesting. It's hard work, too."

"Where did you learn all that stuff about Einstein?" Jack asked.

"I'm still learning."

"How about the photon clock?"

"In school, I believe."

"What kind of school?"

"I taught physics for a while," Thomas said.

"Where?"

"At the University of Chicago," Thomas said. "Where did your brother go?"

"Disneyland. He's leaving in an hour. He has kids—two girls. It's an exciting day for them."

"What about you?" Thomas asked.

"Not so exciting for me. I get to stay and work."

"I mean kids."

"No kids. I'm not married. How about you?" Jack asked.

"Me?" It was an idea that had never entered his mind. "No."

"Footloose and fancy free, I guess," Jack said.

"I don't know what you mean."

"I don't either. I've been thinking about that light clock."

Jack picked up the remaining trowel and leaned over the concrete form beside him. He smoothed out a section of cement several feet wide. Then he reached into his front pocket, pulled out a Swiss army knife, and opened the small blade.

"Here," he said, extending the knife to Thomas. "Use this and draw that clock for me in the concrete."

Thomas drew the photon clock in the concrete with Jack's knife just as he had done on the cardboard, with three images of the clock side by side and the photon bouncing from the center of one to the next. He retraced a few lines where he had not pressed deeply enough and wiped the knife blade on his shirt.

"So, if I'm standing beside the railroad tracks and that clock goes whizzing by me on the train, how do I know that something else isn't affecting the photon?" Jack asked. "How do I know that the photon isn't distorted by the train?"

"The speed of light doesn't change, regardless of perspective."

"That's the key, isn't it?"

"Yes."

"Next you're going to tell me that the Earth is round," Jack said. "That would be too much for one day."

For a moment Thomas wondered what to say. Of course, it was a joke. Anyone who had wanted to know about special relativity would know about Copernicus. Thomas smiled before Jack did, but he had almost been caught in the joke.

"Have you had enough, or do you want to help me finish cleaning up?" Jack asked.

"I'll help you finish. Do you want to smooth out this concrete?" Thomas asked. He pointed to his photon clock.

"No. Let's leave it. Then I'll know where to go if I forget. Put your initials there on the bottom."

"My initials?"

"Sure, like the artists do with their paintings."

Thomas bent over his drawing again and carefully etched TR into the concrete. Then he saw a few lines in his drawing that were not clear. Had he known his drawing would survive, he would have been more careful. He traced over them again, wiped the excess concrete on his pants, and added another arrow.

Jack checked his watch and looked over at a stack of scrap wood beyond the concrete forms.

"We finished before noon," Jack said, "from my perspective anyway. I promised my tenants that I would have the garage open by one o'clock. I think we'll make it. We'll bundle up this scrap wood and haul it down to the garbage compactor. I'll show you how it works. It's not nearly as complicated as that photon clock of yours."

Chapter 10

Katherine was learning to walk the beat slowly, seemingly without purpose or destination, receptive to all voices, smiles, glances or averted glances. It took a long time to walk a block on Market Street with Grace. As on Ballard Avenue, Grace knew every merchant in the stores that lined both sides of the street. She knew the beggar who stood in front of Ballard Square, and Nero, the seeing-eye dog who was not the emperor of Ballard, she told Katherine as she squatted to scratch the dog behind the ears, but only worked for him. The dog's employer, who was in charge of "Little City Hall," laughed at his new title, extended his hand to Katherine, and welcomed her to Ballard.

From the card shop they collected information about a suspicious man who was selling watches. In the music store they saw photographs of the manager's new baby. In the bakery they stood beside the coffeepot and looked at a nude woman on the wall. PENSIVE, A SELF-PORTRAIT was the title. It was the owner's contribution to the upcoming art walk.

"It's about looking at yourself as honestly as you can but knowing you can never see the whole being," the artist said. She wore a white apron that matched the flour on her cheek.

"You can see enough," Grace said.

The artist remained at her picture, looking for the whole being, as Grace and Katherine walked farther down the street.

"More guts than I've got," Grace said once they were outside the store. "Would you hang up a picture of yourself like that?"

"Never," Katherine said.

At the corner of 22nd and Market Street, they rested a moment in their parked car. They moved it often to keep it close in case they needed to answer a call beyond their walking range. Grace explained that Wes Mickelsen never liked to get more than a block from his car. "He couldn't run any farther than that," she said.

Before moving the car to the next block, Katherine wrote entries on the daily log sheet about the block they had just finished walking. In a regular patrol beat, she would list only calls they were given, or traffic stops, or other unusual circumstances that merited entries, but the footbeat was different. She wrote down the time, *1200 hours–1230 hours,* and a general explanation of their activity: *footbeat, 2200 block NW Market Street.* Then she wrote the description of the man selling watches. She was thinking about the young woman who revealed herself to every customer who bought her bread when Radio dispatched another car, 2-Boy-4, to a call of a "child in a garbage Dumpster" in the 2200 block of NW 56th Street.

"That's just around the corner," Grace said. "What the hell is going on here?"

Grace picked up the mike and told Radio that they were a block away and could handle the call. Radio transferred the call to them. Katherine dropped the clipboard onto the seat as Grace turned on the blue lights, pressed down the accelerator, and made a U-turn on Market Street. As Grace turned north on 22nd Katherine tried to get her seat belt buckled, but gave it up when she saw the man waving at them from the sidewalk. Grace pulled to the curb beside him and turned off the blue lights. Katherine hurried around the police car but stopped beside Grace when she saw the man's grim face. Another man, somewhat older, stood off to the side.

"I tried to pull him out," the first man said, "but I could see it wouldn't do any good. He's still in there." He pointed to a hulking machine behind him.

"All right," Grace said. "Is that man with you?"

She pointed to the man with an unkempt beard who stood away from them.

"Yes. He's with me."

"Stay here, then. Both of you," she said.

The garbage compactor partially blocked the entrance of the alley and was at least five feet tall. A wheelbarrow lay overturned beside it. Katherine steeled herself in preparation for the sight she expected to see in the gaping mouth of the machine.

"God," she muttered when she saw the boy's face suspended in the garbage. Her stomach lurched, and she swallowed hard. At first she thought it was only the head. Then she saw the boy's body stuffed farther back into the garbage that was packed solidly around him. She pulled torn strips of black plastic away from his ghostly white face. His eyes stared at her in horror. Reluctantly she pressed the artery on the side of his neck. Nothing.

"It's the same damn thing," Grace said. She took a deep breath, looked above the garbage machine, and exhaled.

From the street they heard the screaming siren of an aid car shut down just as it began to rise again. The aid car jerked to a stop beside their police car. Two firemen bailed out of the red and white van, one of them carrying a large medical case that tilted his body to the side. Other sirens were approaching in the distance. The boy's face did not change.

The firemen shut down like the siren on the aid car when they saw the boy. One of them reached out and touched the spot on the boy's neck that Katherine had already touched. He shook his head.

"He's been dead awhile," he said. "Do you want us to pull him out?"

"No," Grace said. "Leave him where he is."

"Do you have other units coming?" Katherine asked him.

"Medic One and an engine company," the fireman said.

"Call them off," she said. "We need to protect this area for Homicide."

It was too late to call off the engine company. They had built up steam and roared to a stop in the middle of the street. The noise from the siren and engine were loud enough to hurt everyone's ears except the boy's. Two men riding on the back of the truck in full fire gear jumped off. Katherine went out to stop them, but the others were intent on passing her to join the others at the garbage compactor.

"Hey! Stay back." Katherine grabbed one of the men by the sleeve. He was surprised by the interruption.

"There is nothing you can do. Stay back."

There were soon five firemen from the truck surrounding her while the fire department radio blared from a speaker. The lieutenant in his white hat worked his way to the front of his men.

"Your guys have already checked the boy," Katherine said. "He's dead. I don't want anybody else going over there."

People began gathering to watch the show. They came out of the bank, which was on the other side of the fence, and from the pharmacy across the street. Some of them inched forward for a better view. There was barely room for all of them on the sidewalk.

"Anything you want us to do besides get our butts out of here?" the lieutenant asked.

"Got any yellow tape?" Katherine asked.

"Rolls of it. Tell us where you want it."

"Tie off on the fence and stretch it over to our car. Find someplace to tie off on that brick building." She pointed to a single-story brick building that ran along the entire west side of the alley. "And push those people back a little, will you?" she said, nodding in the direction of the sidewalk.

The firemen responded energetically. Two of them moved the curious citizens farther back on the sidewalk while the others set up a barrier of plastic tape, crisscrossing to the police car from points high and low on the fence and from two different places on the building.

Grace led the two men who had found the boy away from the firemen. She stopped opposite the garbage compactor beside a wire fence where ivy wove itself among the wood slats that obstructed the view into the bank parking lot.

Katherine returned to the open mouth of the compactor and looked at the boy again. It was hard to tell his age. It was hard to look beyond his staring eyes. When she joined Grace at the fence, the man who had flagged them down was telling Grace what happened.

"We were pouring concrete this morning on top of the building," he said, "and I was showing Thomas where to dump wood scraps from the forms. We didn't notice anything when we threw the boards into the compactor. I pushed the button on the compactor to shove everything back. When I opened the lid again, I saw his head—at least, part of it. A nail from one of the boards went into his neck. I yanked the board away, and then I tried to pull him out, but his feet are wedged way back in there. I could see it wouldn't do any good anyway. I don't know if the boy crawled in and we crushed him, or what might have happened."

Wood and cardboard were scattered on the ground around the compactor, evidence of his effort to get to the boy.

"He was dead before you started the machine," the other

man said. He was also covered with gray splatters, but his clothes were more deeply soiled. He had not spoken until then. Unlike the first man who had turned away from the compactor, this man was still looking. "If you look where the nail went in, you'll see that the boy didn't bleed at all. He was already dead when that happened."

Katherine and Grace followed the man's instructions, and Katherine moved a step closer to the garbage compactor. The second man was right. There was no blood. A puncture wound would bleed very little, but the nail had left a jagged opening. There was no blood at all from this wound.

"I read mystery books," the man said. He smiled in an oddly gracious manner.

"What is your name, sir?" Katherine asked. She removed her notebook from her shirt pocket.

"Thomas Rosencrantz," he said. "With a *z*."

"Where do you live, Mr. Rosencrantz?"

"At the moment, right over there." He pointed down the alley.

"In that building?" Katherine asked. She pointed to the large building behind the garage door.

"No, that one," he said and pointed again.

"Thomas has been staying in the cardboard recycling shed," the other man said.

"I'll need to see identification from both of you," Katherine said.

As both men reached for their wallets, the aid car pulled away from the curb. The engine of the fire truck gathered strength and moved off slowly down the street with its silenced siren and exterior speakers. The spectators began drifting away, too. The man who had first met them handed Katherine his driver's license. His name was Jack Morton.

"I have several checks, but no identification as such," Thomas Rosencrantz said. He showed her his open wallet, which was stuffed with money.

"Jesus, Thomas," Jack Morton said as he stared at the wallet.

Thomas handed Katherine a frayed check, then fingered through layers of bills in his wallet and gave her a check that was not worn or frayed. It was made out to Thomas C. Rosencrantz for $4,609.22.

"The first one is a dividend check, and the second is for the sale of Ford stock. I'm buying General Electric right now. I recommend it."

Katherine gave the check to Grace. The address on the check was in care of a brokerage firm in Chicago.

"You live in that shed?" Grace asked.

"As long as Mr. Morton allows it. That is, until the cardboard gets too high."

Mr. Morton continued to look at the fat wallet that Thomas held. Thomas smiled as he scanned their faces.

"Have you ever been arrested, Mr. Rosencrantz?" Katherine asked.

"No. Oh, I see. You have to consider all known possibilities. Yes, that would make sense. I should have thought of that. I'm over there; the body is here. Certainly, you have to consider that."

"We have to consider everything," Katherine said.

"But you can't, of course," Thomas Rosencrantz said. "The uncertainty principle. What you observe is affected by your observation, and the other way around. Einstein disliked the whole idea. Nevertheless, there it is."

"How much money do you have in your wallet?" Katherine asked.

"Do you mean cash?" Thomas asked.

"Yes, cash."

"Twelve hundred dollars, I believe. I don't usually carry this much, but I'm holding cash right now. When the time is right, I'll buy more General Electric. It's going to go up soon. They're adding to their company as fast as Mr. Morton is adding to his building."

"We're not too interested in the stock market right now, Mr. Rosencrantz," Katherine said.

"Of course not. I thought I would explain why I had the money so that it wouldn't seem strange."

"We appreciate that," Katherine said.

"I heard noises last night," Thomas said. "I heard somebody by the shed moving cardboard. As you can see, there is cardboard in front of the body. After the noises around the shed, I heard the garbage compactor start up."

Katherine looked into the machine again and tried to focus on the material around the boy's face, but it was hard not to see the boy. As Thomas Rosencrantz said, there was cardboard crushed around the body.

"When I went to sleep last night, there were seven flattened cardboard boxes beside the shed. I flattened two of them myself. I don't think there are seven boxes in the stack anymore."

"That stack?" Katherine asked and pointed toward a pile of cardboard at least forty feet away beside the shed.

"Yes. Mr. Morton doesn't want cardboard lying around the alley, and I intended to put them inside the shed this morning, but I went to work with Mr. Morton instead."

Katherine walked over to the stack. She turned back frequently toward Grace and the two men. The second man with his money and strange ideas seemed harmless, but she wouldn't bet on that. She wouldn't bet on anything. She counted the flattened boxes, using her pen to separate them.

"Four boxes left," she told Grace when she returned to their group. "What time did you hear the noises, Mr. Rosencrantz?"

"I'm not certain, but it was late. I don't have a watch, but it was late enough that I didn't hear any traffic from the street."

"Did you see anybody?" Katherine asked.

"I didn't open the door. It doesn't pay to become too

curious in the middle of the night. The person may have been alone, however. I didn't hear any talking."

"How can you be sure there were seven boxes?" Katherine asked.

"I count things," Thomas Rosencrantz said.

Chapter 11

Grace was standing outside the car with Jack Morton when the sergeant arrived from the station. Rosencrantz sat in the backseat of the patrol car, and Katherine was inside the car with him writing the incident report. Several of Jack Morton's tenants had driven up while they waited, intending to park in the garage, and he had directed them to another lot. During the intervals he remained somber and quiet.

The sergeant parked his car behind their patrol car. There wasn't enough room, and it blocked part of the entrance to the busy bank parking lot next door. He turned on his amber flashing lights. They flashed less conspicuously than the bright red lights of the fire engine, but they still confused a driver who intended to park in the bank lot. The bank customer stopped his car in the middle of the street and looked for a way around. The sergeant flung his door open and crawled briskly through the yellow tape to their patrol car.

"What do you have?" he asked. His voice was as brisk as his walk, and his new uniform fit his small frame with careful tailoring. He didn't wait for an answer before he turned his eyes from Grace and surveyed the scene.

"We have a dead boy in the garbage compactor," Grace said. "Mr. Morton, who owns the building and the garbage compactor, found him."

Jack Morton nodded to the sergeant as she announced his name, but the sergeant, who was from the sector north of Ballard, said nothing to him. He looked at the building owner in his concrete-splattered work clothes, nodded curtly, and walked over to the front of the compactor. Grace told Jack Morton to remain at the car and followed the sergeant. By then there were more cars stopped in the street waiting to enter the bank lot.

"Why don't I move your car ahead so that it won't block traffic?" Grace asked.

"There's plenty of room," the sergeant said without looking. When he did turn, he waved his hand impatiently to the driver who could not see his gesture. Slowly and carefully, the elderly driver inched his car around the sergeant's car into the bank lot.

Katherine got out of the police car and came up to join them. The sergeant was intently studying the inside of the garbage compactor.

Grace pointed out the wound in the boy's neck and the cardboard crushed around his body. She told him about the noise Thomas Rosencrantz said he heard and about his count of the cardboard in the stack beside the shed.

"So, maybe the kid crawled into the machine and got crushed," the sergeant said, "or maybe the witness killed him. He sounds strange enough. You advise him yet?"

"No," Grace said. "He's still just a witness."

"Okay, but be sure you give him his rights if he starts blabbing a different story."

It was good advice, Grace supposed, but she already knew it.

"He didn't crawl into the machine," Katherine said.

"How do you know that?" the sergeant asked.

"He has garbage bags around him," Katherine said. "The one over his face is torn away, but if you look from the side you can see how it's wrapped behind him."

The sergeant moved to the side of the compactor and leaned into the space below the lid. Grace looked at the boy's face again. Each time she saw something new. The boy had the first wisps of whiskers above his lip. He had probably never shaved.

"Any idea who the victim is?" the sergeant asked. He stood upright and hit his head on the lid of the compactor. The sergeant frowned at Grace as if it was her fault he had bumped his head. He smoothed back his neatly trimmed hair and looked at the palm of his hand.

"We don't know who he is," Grace said, "but it's the second body we've found like this. Monday we got a call of a dead body at the Fremont dump. It was a black girl, but she was stripped and wrapped in the same kind of garbage bags. They're too similar not to be connected. We haven't called Homicide yet. Detectives Markowitz and Richards investigated last time. I imagine they'll want to come here, too. We thought we should use a land line so we don't get a bunch of reporters out here."

"I'll do that," he said. "Do you have any other cars assisting?"

"No," Grace said. "We have the area secure."

"What about an area search? What about crowd control?"

Grace looked back to the street and saw that a few people were beginning to gather close to the sergeant's car with its blinking lights.

"We sealed off the alley," Katherine said. "There's nothing for anybody to do until Homicide arrives."

Turning away from them, the sergeant raised his portable radio to his mouth. He commanded the operator to send two more patrol cars to the scene and held the radio there as if he might need to issue another command. No other command came forth. He walked away and inspected the alley south of the garbage compactor. He walked all the way up to the building at the end. Katherine looked at Grace questioningly, but neither followed the sergeant.

"Where did he come from?" Katherine asked.

"Nora sector," Grace said. "He was just promoted last month from some administrative unit."

"He reminds me of the barnyard," Katherine said. "We

used to have a bantam rooster like him on the farm. I don't know why we kept it. All he did was strut around and get in fights with the other chickens. He was too small to eat."

"Are we supposed to follow him?" Grace asked.

"I'm not," Katherine said. "I'm going back to the car to do the paperwork."

"I'll stand here and look official," Grace said. "Let me know if you need help with crowd control."

The sergeant may have realized he was walking alone because he left soon after, having found nothing more to command. Boy-1 found nothing in the area to add to the investigation and also left, as did Boy-3, who had found no crowds to control.

It was a long wait for Homicide. Grace remained outside the car with Jack Morton and wrote her officer's statement standing up. A few citizens walked by on the sidewalk, but it wasn't heavily used. No more of Jack Morton's tenants drove up to park. The word about the boy must have gotten out to them.

Finally a plain dull green Dodge Dart parked in front of their patrol car beyond the barricade of yellow tape. Two detectives got out of the Dart. Grace asked Jack Morton to stay beside the car and joined Katherine at the tape.

"I hope this doesn't get to be a regular thing," Detective Markowitz said.

"I do, too," Katherine said. "This is enough for me."

"Our sergeant and maybe the lieutenant will be out here soon," Markowitz said, "but we'll get started. Who found the body this time?"

"Mr. Morton," Grace said. "He owns this property."

"Is that the fellow beside your car?" Markowitz asked.

"Yes."

"And the guy in the car?"

"His name is Thomas Rosencrantz. He was with Mr. Morton when they found the body."

Markowitz nodded. "Well, let's have a look," he said.

Markowitz pushed his heavy glasses back onto his nose

after bending down to get through the tape. It was only a few steps to the garbage compactor, but Grace was growing weary of the trip. The shock of seeing the boy's face diminished each time she saw it, but it didn't disappear completely. And the questions about the boy—Who are you? Why are you here?—became more pressing.

Richards and Markowitz pulled latex gloves out of their suit coat pockets and put them on. Markowitz chased away a fly that had landed on the boy's cheek. The color of the boy's face was nearly the same as his latex glove.

Katherine explained how the boy had been found, and she pointed to the shed where Thomas lived with the cardboard stacked beside it. Markowitz listened to her without interruption and followed her hand as she changed its direction to the garbage bags that surrounded the boy. She explained how the steel ram compressed the garbage against the back wall.

"We'll take some pictures and get the boy out," Markowitz said. "He's been in there long enough."

Markowitz went back to his car and put a blue jumpsuit over his white shirt and dress pants. Detective Richards took pictures of the compactor and the alley from different angles using two different cameras. The first was a Polaroid, which gave them an instant record, while the other had .35 mm film that would be developed later. He laid the Polaroid pictures on the lid of a green garbage can that was next to the compactor, and the images began appearing.

Markowitz bent into the mouth of the compactor and pulled out a bag from the bottom of the machine. The bag dripped grease onto his shoes.

"Oh, would you look at that," he said. "I just polished them last week."

Reaching to the bottom again, he pulled out a slice of pizza and a piece of wire and placed them on top of large plastic bags that he stretched over the concrete driveway. He bent back into the open mouth of the garbage machine and pulled out scraps of lettuce, more pizza, and other food along with cardboard posters of rock and roll stars. He organized the refuse in the order he found it.

"Look at this," he said, emerging from the opening. He held up a beaded chain from which dangled a small golden cross. "Somebody lost their rosary."

He laid the cross on a bag by itself, and the other three police officers gathered around looking for a revelation.

"Might have been dumped with the other junk," Richards said.

"Might have," Markowitz replied, "but it doesn't look like it fits. Do you think the owner could identify this garbage? It might help establish a timeframe if we knew when this stuff was dumped."

"I'll ask him," Grace said. "He seems kind of shook up, though. I don't know if he wants to look at this again."

"Who does?" Markowitz asked. "He can stand off to the side. He doesn't need to look at the boy."

Grace went to the car where Jack Morton remained standing and asked him if he would help them identify the garbage. He came readily enough, even if he didn't want to look.

"They're probably from the Backstage," he said when Markowitz pointed to the posters that lay on the garbage bags. "It's a nightclub in the basement. They use the compactor, too."

"I've been there," Markowitz said. "Were they open last night?"

"I think so."

"And this food?" Markowitz asked.

"Probably from Dimitrio's restaurant. They have their own garbage cans, but sometimes a new dishwasher dumps it in the wrong place."

"How late is the restaurant open?"

"Ten or eleven, but they're here in the morning, too. That cardboard," Jack Morton added as he walked slowly toward the mouth of the compactor, "around the boy. I think that's from the art store. Those girls would never throw it in here. They recycle everything. Thomas said he heard somebody last night picking up cardboard."

"You don't need to look in there again, Mr. Morton."

"I've already seen him."

Markowitz reached into the mouth of the compactor with one hand and tugged on the cardboard that had been crushed beside the boy's head. It barely moved. It was part of a large section wedged tightly into the compressed mass. Markowitz leaned farther in and grabbed the cardboard with both hands. He jerked it down and away from the boy. As the cardboard came loose, the boy's head flopped sideways into the newly freed space. It came to rest at an inhuman angle. Markowitz dropped the cardboard onto the ground.

"Ah, Jesus," he said, staring at the boy. "His neck is broken. We need to get the top open so that we can crawl inside. I want to get that boy out of there."

He walked away from the mouth of the compactor and examined the top lid. He pushed on it, but it wouldn't budge.

"Do you know how to get this thing open, Mr. Morton?"

The building owner looked at him but didn't seem to understand the question.

"Come back here, Mr. Morton. It won't do any good to keep looking at that boy. We need some help getting this lid up."

He understood and walked toward the back of the compactor. Grace followed to see if she could help.

"There are two levers," he said, reaching for the one closest to him.

"You just give me the instructions," Markowitz said. "I don't want you touching anything here."

"Sorry, I already touched it."

"That's all right. We aren't going to worry about that. I see how it works."

"It's hinged on the front," Jack Morton said. "Once you push it up halfway, you have to let it go. It's too heavy to stop. It's going to flop down over the mouth."

Markowitz released the two levers that clinched the lid tight to the frame. Detective Richards lifted one corner with his rubber-gloved hand. The lid was solid steel.

"You need something to push it high enough to flop it over," Jack Morton said. "I have some two-by-fours in the garage."

"Would you mind getting them for us?" Markowitz asked. "A ladder, too, if you have one."

Jack Morton looked relieved to do something useful. Grace had seen how difficult it was for him to wait, to do nothing about the boy except think about him. It had been difficult for her, too. She would dream about that face, but probably not with the same dreams as Jack Morton.

"I'll give you a hand," Grace said.

"Thanks," he said. "I'd appreciate that."

He had a garage door opener stuffed in his back pocket. He pulled it out and pushed the button to raise the garage door. As he entered the garage, he looked back at the garbage compactor. He was too far away now to see the boy. Grace stopped beside him at the entrance to the dim garage and saw moisture glisten in his eyes as he looked outside into the brighter light.

"I should have locked that compactor," he said.

"I don't think it would have made any difference to the boy," she said.

He looked at her and nodded.

"I wonder where he came from," he said.

"We all wonder," Grace said.

Chapter 12

The telephone woke her, and Katherine stumbled into the living room to answer it. She saw that it was daylight, but she didn't see much more. As she reached for the telephone she stubbed her little toe on the corner of the bookcase, and she swore before she picked up the receiver.

"Hello," she said sharply into the mouthpiece.

She sat down on the couch, lifted her foot off the floor, and held it in her hand. The toe hurt more as she woke up.

"Officer Murphy?"

It was a woman's voice.

"Yes," Kathcrine said as she rubbed her toe and tried to see how much damage she had done.

"This is Detective Smith, Seattle Police Department. Is everything okay there?"

"Yes. I just stubbed my toe whcn I picked up the phone."

There was a deep hearty laugh in the receiver. Katherine put her foot down tenderly on the floor. She didn't see any blood.

"That does hurt, doesn't it? Don't you just hate it when you do that? I hope I didn't wake you up. I saw on your report that you work the Second Watch, so I thought you would be up by now."

"I'm awake. What time is it?"

"Seven o'clock."

"What did you say your name was?"

"Detective Anne Smith, Sex Crimes, serial number 2205. I'm calling about the two kids you found in the garbage. I've read your reports. It was good work. You should see some of the junk I get."

Katherine pulled her foot up. The toenail had broken in half and hung by a sliver. She pulled it away and grimaced.

"We think the girl was sexually assaulted. That's why I'm involved. Detective Markowitz called me about the second case last night. Fred has an autopsy scheduled this morning, but it's clear that there are already lots of similarities to the girl at the garbage dump."

"That's what we thought," Katherine said.

"I'm wondering if you've ever seen these kids before. I assume you haven't, because you didn't say anything about that in your statement, but I thought I would ask anyway. Or maybe you've seen somebody who could have been one of them but you're not sure."

Katherine placed her foot back on the floor. She ran her fingers through her hair and quietly took a deep breath.

"I don't think I have," Katherine said, "but I've only worked in Ballard a few days."

"So I understand. Detective Markowitz told me about that case on First Avenue. What a piece of work that was."

"I didn't have much to do with it," Katherine said.

"That's not what Fred said. Is there any chance you have seen either of these kids downtown?"

"I don't think so, but their faces were pretty distorted." Katherine closed her eyes, and the two faces reappeared in a grotesque combination so that she couldn't be certain that she was seeing each one separately. "Did you find out who they are?"

"No. That's the worst part—not knowing their names. When the suspect stripped their clothes from them it was like he was trying to take away their identities, too. We don't have any runaway reports that match. I'm looking at the photographs Markowitz took. This boy is absolutely white. I mean his whole body is white, like he's never been out in the sun. Here we are, spring has arrived, and it's still winter for that boy. He's wearing makeup, too. Eye shadow and lipstick. Maybe he was turning tricks and ran into the wrong guy. Maybe the girl was, too. That's why I was wondering if you had seen them downtown."

Katherine tried to imagine the boy and girl on First Avenue. Would she be one who stared at her in contempt and defiance, or would she hide when the police car drove by? Would he swagger and sneer, or would he tremble with fear of the cops, with fear of the streets, with fear of himself?

"Do you want me to come down this morning and look at the pictures?" she asked Detective Smith. "Maybe I'll remember something if I just see the pictures."

"No, that's not necessary, but I would like you to show me around the alley where the boy was found—you and Officer Stevens? I'll show you the pictures then. How about one o'clock?"

"Sure."

"I understand Officer Stevens is a woman, too."

"That's right," Katherine said. "We went to the academy together."

"I think that's great," Detective Smith said. "I never thought I would see the day when three women cops would be looking at a crime scene. God knows, we love these men, but it's been a long time coming. I'll be the one with red hair. I guess you two won't be hard to spot."

"We never are," Katherine said.

She stood at Dale's door and listened for him. It was early, and there were no footsteps that told her he was up. Without disturbing him, she went back to her apartment, opened the window in her living room, and listened for a voice she might recognize—Mrs. Rabin talking to a neighbor about her flowers or even the argument in Chinese from around the corner. She leaned out the window and looked at the flowers. They stood quietly waiting for the old woman, their heads raised in anticipation.

Leaving the window open Katherine returned to the telephone that had awakened her. She dialed a number from memory and listened to the rings. She could see the other telephone on the kitchen wall and could hear its distinct ring drawing to it anyone who was close by. Katherine could picture her mother rising from the kitchen table, where she lingered after breakfast with coffee and her latest book. She imagined her father hurrying in from the back porch in his coveralls, or her brother who had stopped for a cup of coffee, turning toward the telephone from where he stood at the sink, from where he had been looking out the window toward the machine shed where the old combine was being repaired for one last year. Her sister might be home for a visit, and she might be walking down the stairs just at that moment, planning her day or thinking about the night before, a night so different from Katherine's.

If her father answered, Katherine would ask him how tall the wheat was. If she heard his voice, she would be able to picture the wind currents rolling through the fields and see the precise color at that moment of the thousand colors that marked the wheat from beginning to end. If her mother answered, she would ask if Mrs. Gray had new kittens, if the squirrels had gotten into the bird feeder again. She had questions for everyone. She let the telephone ring a long time, so that one of them would have come if she had heard it, if it had been within his reach.

Katherine could imagine every valley, every field, every corner of every building on the farm. She could see her brother on the tractor, her mother in the kitchen, her father beneath the raised hood of the combine, her sister raking hay on summer weekends. But she saw herself only as a child there—never as the grown-up Katherine. She had thought the new image of herself would come from natural evolution—child to teenager, teenager to college student, college student to adult—and she had waited a long time for this self-image to show up somewhere else, to grow and cast its shadow in some other place.

Katherine looked out the window to the west. A jet airplane passed silently through her view so slowly that she wondered how it remained in the air. A horn blared and rose above the ever-present murmur of the freeway at the bottom of the hill. A heavy motor rumbled in the alley, and the engine whined shrilly as the hydraulic forks of a garbage truck lifted the refuse container and muffled the careless indifferent banging of the garbage Dumpster.

Katherine sat quietly before the window and watched the sunlight find the eastern slopes of the two mountains in the Olympic range that stood off by themselves. They must have names, these two mountains. Even mountains had names.

Chapter 13

Markowitz had given her simple straight instructions, which Anne had lying on the seat beside her, but she had gotten into the wrong lane and couldn't make the turn on Market Street. She turned left at the next block, and a car honked even though she was sure that there was half a block to spare. She turned back to Market Street where she expected the streets to increase in number one at a time in an orderly fashion. They didn't. The streets went from 15th to 17th to 20th on one side and had different names on the other. The taverns must have already been in Ballard when the old boys started naming streets.

22nd Avenue NW came after 20th. She almost expected that, but the light was red before she could see where to stop. By that time she was over the line and a Metro bus bore down on her as if she weren't there. It stopped with its squealing bus brakes as she began her turn onto 22nd. Then two old guys, one following the other, darted across the street in front of her against the wait sign and made her stop again. The one who followed looked at her with guilty eyes while the first one with gray hair and a round face laughed without remorse and waved him forward. She thought the Norwegians were supposed to have square heads.

It was no wonder they killed people out here.

It was raining, too, but not hard enough to keep the wipers going smoothly. They screeched unhappily across the windshield. At the stop sign on the next corner a steady stream of people crossed the street between the bank and the drugstore. No one hurried. They bowed their heads to the rain and paid no attention to the cars waiting for them to pass.

She saw the blue and white police car waiting half a block down. Maybe it was a whole block. Who could tell the way they numbered their streets? Across from the police car Anne found a place to park where she could pull straight in without having to squirm into a parallel parking stall. After picking up the manila envelope beneath Markowitz's instructions, she got out of the car and looked for a crosswalk. To hell with it, she decided. She darted across the street with the envelope above her head as a rain cap to keep her hair and glasses from getting wet.

The driver of the police car reached over the backseat and pulled up the lock. Anne slid into the car with a heavy sigh and pulled the door closed behind her.

"Where the hell did this rain come from?" she asked. "It was perfectly nice when I left home this morning. Anne Smith," she said, extending her hand over the seat for either of them to take.

"Grace Stevens," the passenger said as she shook her hand.

"And you must be Katherine," Anne said as the driver turned farther in the seat to accept her hand. "These people are terrible drivers out here. I thought they'd kill me before I got here."

"That's why we walk most of the time," Grace said.

"Don't blame you. So, this is the place where you found that boy."

"Right there." Grace pointed to a hulking steel machine that stood in the alley next to their car.

No one walked by them on the buckling sidewalk that passed the garbage compactor. Anne looked up and down

the street. There were only parking lots and a few stores—
no trees, no fancy storefronts, nothing pleasing to com-
mend it.

"Lousy place to end up," Anne said.

After opening the envelope, she took out a group of
pictures. She moved to the center of the backseat, leaned
over the backrest of the front seat, and held the photographs in both hands.

"See what I mean about this boy never seeing the sun.
Go ahead, you can take it," she said to Katherine. "The
discoloration in his legs and feet is because of the way he
was stuck in that compactor. The blood settled there."

Katherine took the picture and held it so that her partner
could see it.

"By the way, the autopsy this morning showed that the
boy had been sexually assaulted and then strangled to
death. There were bruises on his throat, but you might not
have seen them yesterday. The boy had traces of the drug
Ritalin in his system. It's a stimulant. The girl you found
was killed the same way, and she also had taken Ritalin.
Here, you can see his neck better on this one," Anne said.

She pointed to a spot on a new picture that she held
across the seat. "See the marks there? Those are finger
marks. The person who choked him was facing him. The
boy's larynx was crushed, although that's not what killed
him. He was strangled to death. Not easy to do, really,
especially from the front the way this boy was strangled."

Anne went through the next three pictures quickly.
"These are just different angles," she said, "except this
one." It was a close-up of the boy's hand, the sixth and
last picture. "Do you see the number on his palm—the blue
ink? It's smudged, but you can still see it. It's a phone
number. Somebody stripped the boy of everything that
might tell us who he was, except for this number. He
missed that. It's the phone number for the King Arthur
Motel off Aurora. You guys probably know all about it. I
understand there's not much chivalry there anymore."

Anne settled back in her seat and took a second batch of pictures out of the envelope.

"I've never heard of it," Katherine said.

"Union sector," Grace said. "Just east of Aurora. A lot of people wish it would burn down."

"Not until we find out about this boy," Anne said. "That motel is the best information we have so far. The boy couldn't have had the number on his hand too long. It would have washed off or worn off pretty fast. Richards went out to the motel this morning and got the registration forms from the last two weeks, not that anybody told the truth on any of them. He told the manager he was investigating a credit card ring. We decided not to show anybody there a picture of the boy yet or say anything about the phone number. They don't have a reputation for cooperating with the police. Here is an autopsy picture of the girl you found."

Anne passed the picture to the front of the car. It revealed a girl from the chest up. Her dark skin contrasted with the white table where she lay. Grace took it and studied it before she handed it to Katherine.

"We don't know where she came from, but the garbage truck that picks up this route dumps at Fremont. Like the boy she was stripped, and also like the boy she had been sexually assaulted and strangled. If you look closely, you'll see finger marks on her neck, too."

Anne pointed to the finger marks that were less apparent on the girl, but the outcome was just as distinct.

"When I say sexually assaulted, I mean there was semen in both victims. It was in the vagina of the girl and the anus of the boy. From the semen we were able to determine the blood type of the suspect, and it's the same in both victims. That only tells us that the rapist could be the same guy for both. It doesn't tell that he is for sure, but I'd bet a month's pay that it's the same guy even though one victim is a girl and the other is a boy. Another interesting fact," Anne said, "the boy had gonorrhea, but the girl didn't. The boy had the infection before this last sexual act. It might mean he was sexually active.

"We don't know if the victims were willing or not, but if the murderer is over eighteen, the victims' willingness doesn't matter. It's still rape, and they're still dead. I'm just wondering if any of these pictures remind you of somebody. Sometimes it's not so easy to look at the faces when they're right in front of you."

Katherine held two pictures side by side and shook her head slowly.

"I've never seen them before either," Grace said. "I would have noticed the girl out here in Ballard."

"Yes, I guess you would."

As soon as she said that, Anne wondered if she had stuck her foot in her mouth. She considered herself an expert at that. Well, they didn't pay her to be sensitive. They paid her to find out what happened to the kids.

"I'm supposed to provide information and research to Homicide from the Sex Crimes unit, but I'll tell you something. I wouldn't mind finding this sick bastard myself. Now," she said as she dug in her purse for her plastic rain hat, "would you ladies mind giving me the tour?"

Anne was first out of the car and walked over to the garbage machine, which was just a few feet from the police car. She couldn't figure out how it worked. Grace came up beside her and Katherine came around the car. The two officers were as different as they could be, Anne thought. They would be an interesting sight walking down the street together. Neither wore a hat, however, to protect her hair from the rain. Neither had hair long enough to matter.

"The garbage goes in on the other side," Grace said.

"Ah, I see," Anne said. "I don't know much about these things."

She followed Grace to the other side of the machine. There was still fingerprint powder on it, but the rain was washing it away. A chain passed through several handles on the machine.

"The building owner must have locked it up after we left," Grace said. "There wasn't a padlock here before."

"A little late for that," Anne said.

"That's what he thinks, too," Grace said.

It was an interesting comment. She waited for Grace to say something more, but the young woman said nothing else.

"So, how does it work?" Anne asked.

"This handle on the bottom releases the lid," Grace said. She pointed to a thin metal handle. "When you pull it, the lid pops up. Then you dump in the garbage, close the lid, and push that green button." She pointed to a box about two feet tall that stood off to the side. Two rubber hoses connected it to the compactor. "That starts the hydraulic ram. The ram is hinged on the bottom, and the top is pushed forward up to here." Grace pointed to the edge of the curved section behind the lid. "The owner said the ram is strong enough to crush wood, but it doesn't go all the way to the back so nothing would be crushed unless there's a lot of stuff already there."

"There must have been a lot of stuff when the boy was dumped," Anne said.

"Yes, there was," Grace said. "It looked like the ram shoved the boy back into the other garbage and broke his neck."

"It broke his collarbone, too," Anne said, "but the autopsy showed he was dead before he ever got here."

"That's what Thomas thought," Katherine replied.

"Who?" Anne asked.

"Thomas Rosencrantz," Katherine said. "He was with the owner when they found the body."

"Oh, yes, Mr. Rosencrantz. The man who lives in the cardboard recycling shed. He sounds like an interesting character. Any sign of him today?"

"No," Katherine said, "but we didn't look inside the shed."

Anne looked farther down the alley.

"Is that Mr. Rosencrantz's home?" She pointed toward a small shed close to a ramp that led up to the garage door.

"It was," Katherine said. "We don't know if he's still there."

"Let's see, shall we?" Anne said.

She walked down the rough rutted asphalt of the alley toward the recycling shed and noticed how neat everything was, as if the entire alley had been swept clean. The two officers followed her.

"Was the alley this clean when you were here before?" she asked Grace.

"No. It's been cleaned up."

Anne Smith tapped on the door of the shed and then opened it a few inches to see inside. No one was there, but three plastic bags were arranged in a neat row on top of the layers of cardboard.

"His stuff?" Anne asked.

"Yes," Katherine said.

"Anybody know what the Supreme Court says about searching recycling sheds?" she asked.

"Detective Markowitz looked yesterday," Katherine said. "Rosencrantz has more books than anything else."

"Any children's books?" Anne asked.

"I don't know. I only saw that there were books." Katherine looked at her partner with a serious expression. They were serious young women.

"I didn't look at the books either," Grace said.

"Did Mr. Rosencrantz object to Fred looking?"

"No."

"Maybe he won't mind if I take a look, then," Anne said.

She pulled one bag closer to the door and arranged its contents on top of the cardboard stack. There were two cans of low-salt chicken noodle soup, a can of black beans, and a bag of potato chips.

"Must be his supper," she said. "There are a spoon and can opener in there, too."

She put everything back in the sack and set it back in its

place. She looked into the second sack, which contained soiled clothing. Without gloves, she wasn't eager to stick her hand into it.

"Did Fred look in here?" she asked.

"Yes," Katherine said. "He took everything out."

"All right. We'll leave Mr. Rosencrantz's underwear alone. These must be the books," she said as she pulled the third sack toward her.

She laid the books out on the cardboard, bending forward through the doorway to examine them. There were eleven books. All but one had the paper covers torn away. She fingered through the front pages to find the titles.

"Interesting selection," she said. She picked up a thin book and read the title to the officers. "*The Immense Journey,* 'dedicated to the memory of Clyde Edwin Eiseley, who lies in the grass of the prairie frontier but is not forgotten by his son.' We should all have sons like that," she said.

She flipped through the pages and read chapter titles out loud. "The Flow of the River, How Flowers Changed the World, The Secret of Life. Wouldn't we like to know?"

She picked up the one book with a hardbound cover, *Leaves of Grass* by Walt Whitman. It was worn and the cover was dirty. She opened the book where a scrap of paper marked the page and read silently, but she had to share it with the two officers. "Listen to this poem," she said.

"*When I heard the learn'd astronomer,*
When the proofs, the figures, were ranged in columns
*   before me,*
When I was shown the charts and diagrams,
to add, divide, and measure them,
When I sitting heard the astronomer where he lectured
with much applause in the lecture-room,
How soon unaccountable I became tired and sick,
Till rising and gliding out I wander'd off by myself,

In the mystical moist night-air, and from time to time,
Look'd up in perfect silence at the stars.

"Maybe Mr. Rosencrantz has the right idea. Keep everything you need in a few bags and to hell with the rest of it. Maybe he's normal, and the rest of us are crazy. What do you think, Katherine?"

Without hesitation Katherine said, "I think whoever killed this boy knows something about garbage compactors."

Anne closed the book of Whitman's poems and slipped it back into the plastic bag. She stacked the other books on top of it.

"Why do you say that?" she asked.

"That machine isn't easy to get into. You would have to know where the lever is and how to release it. You would have to know about the start button, too. It was dark. There was light from the streetlights, but the button is set back in that box. It would have been hard to find. Thomas said he heard the compactor start up after somebody picked up the cardboard."

"He could be making up the story," Anne said.

"Yes, he could," Katherine said.

"But you believe him."

"My gut feeling is that he didn't push the button."

"And the building owner? He knows how to work the machine. What do we know about him?"

"We know that he called us," Katherine said, "and that he opened up the compactor with a witness beside him."

"Maybe to set up the other guy," Anne said.

"Maybe," Katherine said, "but it wouldn't make any sense for him to dump the body here. He would have taken it somewhere else. We ran his name through records. He's never even had a traffic ticket."

"What does your gut tell you, Grace?"

"I agree with Katherine. He wasn't covering up anything. He'd been working with concrete in the morning and talking about some scientific theory that Rosencrantz had explained, and then they find this body. I don't think either one of them had anything to do with it."

"Relativity, as I understand it."

"What?" Grace asked.

"The theory was about relativity. Fred explained it to me. Something to do with time that Einstein thought of. Did you see the drawing on the cardboard?"

"We heard about it," Grace said.

"Mr. Rosencrantz apparently understands this theory and a whole lot more. If he understands theories from Einstein, I imagine he can figure out how to start the garbage machine."

"Not necessarily," Katherine said.

"True," Anne said. "I've seen really smart people who can't tie their shoes. But what about the money? He has a wallet stuffed with money, and he's living in a recycling shed? I could think of better places to lead the simple life, if that's what his intentions are. Fred is looking into his story about coming from Chicago. I was hoping we might find Mr. Rosencrantz this afternoon. I'd like to meet him. Maybe you two would let me know if you happen to see him again."

"What if he doesn't want to talk to you?" Katherine asked.

"I'm hoping you'll pass on how delightful I am," she said.

Anne closed the door to the shed and walked back toward the street. Katherine and Grace walked on either side of her. The young officers' estimation of the rain proved correct, and Anne removed her plastic head covering.

"There weren't any prints on the garbage bags," Anne said. "Our suspect must have been wearing gloves. The garbage that was found in front of the boy was all from the nightclub, except the cardboard. We all know about that. The pizza and lasagna and other stuff that Fred pulled out were made at Dimitrio's restaurant and then taken downstairs to the nightclub. The kitchen fellow from the nightclub said he dropped two garbage bags into the garbage machine at about three in the morning but didn't press the compactor button. He said he didn't notice anything inside the machine either, but it was dark. We understand he had a few drinks before making his garbage run.

"Fred is hung up on that rosary he found, but then he's Catholic. He's pushing the lab to get some partial prints off the cross. He even wants them to work on the beads. What do you guys think? Anything to it?"

"It looked expensive," Katherine said. "So maybe it wasn't thrown away intentionally."

"What do you think, Grace?"

"I don't know what people would do with their rosaries," Grace said.

"They pray," Anne said. "And if it belongs to our suspect, we'd better find him before he misses too many of his prayers."

Chapter 14

Late in the afternoon Katherine and Grace walked into an argument in the Valhalla Tavern that had begun the previous summer in Alaska. Two fishermen were about to use their pool cues to settle a dispute about nets. Katherine led one man outside and listened to his complaint. She knew nothing about crossing gill nets, but she told him he would miss his boat if he didn't settle down. He heeded her warning and directions and marched down the sidewalk in a curving line that would cross every net on Market Street. Grace called a cab for the second man and gave his car keys to the bartender.

While they waited for the cab to arrive, Radio asked if they were free to handle a service call at the hospital, which was across the street from the tavern. It was not urgent, he said. They could handle the hospital call whenever they cleared the tavern.

By the time they crossed Market Street and approached the emergency entrance, something had changed the level of urgency. A hospital employee stood in the ambulance drive and signaled anxiously to them.

"This way," she said.

The employee didn't run, but she walked as fast as she could down a hall and around the corner and pointed toward a treatment room where a group of people in hospi-

tal clothing was gathered at the door. The group parted to
let them through, and Katherine saw a man with unkempt
dirty hair on the far side of the treatment room with one
hand strapped to a stretcher and the other flailing wildly
with a pair of scissors. He seemed to be fighting demons
that only he could see. He repeatedly jerked his strapped
hand to get away from the stretcher, and the stretcher
lunged toward him and frightened him each time he jerked.
A security officer and a doctor were inside the room, but
neither was moving closer to the patient.

"We have a problem," the doctor said. He was a young
man, tall and thin and scared. "This man was dropped off
for treatment, but he is not coherent, and his friends left.
We don't have authorization to treat him, and we don't
have control."

That was clear. His patient was sky-high.

"Let's get his arm," Katherine said to Grace.

"Watch out, he's crazy," the security guard said.

That was clear, too.

"No mace," Katherine said as they slowly approached
him. There was no way to predict what mace would do if
he were high on drugs. It might make him more violent,
and they would be stuck inside the closed room with nox-
ious fumes that might affect them more than him.

The patient was big. Katherine wished he were smaller,
much smaller.

The man was aware of the new danger as Katherine and
Grace got closer. Grace tried to calm him, to talk to him, to get
him to drop the scissors, but he recognized nothing from her
soothing voice. His eyes moved erratically back and forth as he
tried to watch each of them circle opposite sides of the stretcher.

The doctor followed close behind Grace, who continued
to talk to the man even though her words made no difference. The patient backed away from them until he bumped
into the counter. Then he whirled around as though he had
been shocked. Grace lunged for his free arm and Katherine
went with her, but the man was too strong for them to
hold. He broke free and raised the scissors above his head.

Katherine grabbed him from behind around the neck with her right arm, jerked him toward her so that he lost his balance, and squeezed as tightly around his neck as she could. Grace grabbed the man's arm again, this time with the doctor's help. With her left hand Katherine pushed on the wrist of her right hand in order to tighten the vise she clamped on his neck. She tried to keep her feet on the floor and to use her hip as a lever to tilt him back. He thrashed about even more, and Katherine was lifted off the floor and slammed against cupboards mounted on the wall. She was afraid he would break free, and she held with every bit of strength she had until his violence ebbed. The vise she made with her bicep and forearm squeezed the arteries in his neck and shut off blood to his brain—what was left of it. His body shuddered and then collapsed.

"I've got the scissors," Grace said. "Let's get him on the stretcher."

Katherine released her hold so that blood would again flow to the man's brain. By then there were many hands on him, and they dragged him onto the stretcher. The nurse tied his free hand to the railings with restraining straps and started tying down his legs. The doctor felt for the man's pulse. He nodded to Katherine as though to tell her that all was well. She knew it wouldn't last long. The man was already reviving.

"I can't do anything until I know what he's taken," the doctor said.

"His friends said he took angel dust," the nurse said, pulling hard on her knots.

"PCP," Grace translated.

"I can't rely on that information. I need to take a blood sample, and somebody has to authorize treatment. That's why we called you officers in the first place. His friends disappeared when we started asking questions."

"You need us to authorize treatment?" Katherine asked. It was hard to believe.

"I'm afraid so," the doctor said.

The man was beginning to fight within his confinement

and was able to move much more than seemed possible with all the straps around him and all the hands that pushed him down. The stretcher began to rock back and forth.

"Treat him," Katherine said, "but let's get going."

The nurse was ready. She swabbed the man's arm through an opening in the straps. The doctor held the needle next to the man's arm, but the man was now moving so violently that he could not stick the needle in. He turned to Katherine.

"Officer, are you able to apply that tranquilizing technique of yours again?"

Katherine moved to the man's head, bent down, and carefully wrapped her arm around his neck. He struggled to get away from her, but there was no place to go. She applied pressure gradually and held it until the man stopped struggling. It didn't take nearly as long as the first time.

The doctor took the blood sample and pulled the needle out of his arm. Katherine released the pressure around his neck. Everyone else got into position to hold the man down when he regained consciousness.

Katherine wondered why it would take so long to test blood. They strapped more bands on the man's arms and legs, but still he thrashed around until the doctor finally had the blood results he needed. He administered a sedative that eventually quieted the patient.

They remained standing around the stretcher in silence—Katherine and Grace, the doctor and the nurse, the security guard and three others who had come to help—expecting the man to rise in desperation once more. He did not rise.

Katherine felt the muscles twitching in her right arm and shoulder, and she felt pain in her left shoulder blade. She suspected she had pulled a muscle. The nurse, who had closed the door to the treatment room so that no one else could observe the unconventional treatment of their patient, was the only one who seemed able to leave the man and get on with her work. She came up behind Katherine and tugged on her shirt collar.

"You're bleeding, Officer." She tried to pull the collar away from Katherine's neck.

"Let's have a look," the doctor said, and he joined the nurse behind Katherine.

"Unfasten your top button," the nurse said.

Katherine pulled her clip-on necktie away from her collar and unfastened the top button of her shirt.

"One more," the doctor said as he pulled her collar away from her neck. "We might need to do something about that cut."

Katherine wore a T-shirt and a bulletproof vest under her uniform, and she wondered what they could possibly see. Grace walked behind her to see what he was talking about. Katherine wondered if everyone intended to line up and look. She felt a rush of heat rise up her neck.

"You have to excuse us," the nurse said. "We have no dignity here. Come on, I'll take you to another room."

"I'm sure it's nothing. Just give me a Band-Aid. Our shift is almost over."

"You're already bleeding through your shirt," the nurse said, "and your shirt is torn. We'll take care of this right now."

The nurse turned and headed out the door, making it clear that there would be no additional discussion. She reminded Katherine of her mother, who was also a nurse. Her mother tolerated no dissension either when she was treating a wound or an injury. Katherine and her brother and sister did what they were told, confident and glad that they were receiving competent care but also fearful of provoking a scolding if the injury was from unusual foolishness. Katherine felt like that child as she followed the nurse down the hall to an empty room.

"Take off your shirt and that other thing you have there. What is that, by the way? Some kind of brace?"

"It's a bulletproof vest," Katherine said.

"My goodness. I guess I should have known that. You can just put it on the chair."

Katherine finished unbuttoning her shirt and took it off.

The fabric was torn and there was a bloodstain around the tear. She unfastened the straps of the bulletproof vest beneath each arm and lifted the vest over her head. Blood had soaked into the fabric of the vest—more than was on her shirt. The nurse lifted Katherine's T-shirt above her shoulders.

"Oh, yes," she said. "I don't think a Band-Aid will quite do the trick."

She opened a drawer and withdrew a hospital gown. "Take off your T-shirt and bra and slip this on. You might be more comfortable if you remove your gun, too. I know the doctor will be." She chuckled softly.

The nurse, who was close to her mother's age as well as her disposition, removed items from a cabinet mounted on the wall. An assortment of packaged products began to accumulate on the countertop. Katherine couldn't believe all of it was necessary for one cut.

Katherine unsnapped the leather straps that anchored her gun belt to the belt that held up her pants. She snapped the straps into a loop and dropped the loop over her gun. She unhooked the gun belt and pulled it away from her. She felt much lighter without it strapped around her waist.

"You can just put it there on the counter, if you want," the nurse said, less certain about what to do with it than the clothing.

Katherine was not sure what she wanted to do with it either, but she followed the nurse's suggestion. She put on the gown, which was open at the back, and sat on the examination table. She crossed her arms beneath her breasts while the nurse swabbed the cut with antiseptic. The antiseptic added a sharp burning to the deeper ache.

The doctor came into the room and washed his hands at the sink.

"How does it look?" he asked.

The nurse pulled the swab away from the cut. "See for yourself," she said.

The doctor walked behind Katherine, and she felt his fingers probing her back.

"It's a jagged cut," he told Katherine. "It needs a few stitches. We can fix it up in a jiffy."

"Okay," Katherine said.

The doctor walked around the examination table and sat on a short stool with wheels. He rolled close to her and looked up at her face. "How did it happen?" he asked.

"I think I got pushed into the corner of the cabinet."

"I'll bet you did," the doctor said. "That was quite a ride you had. We weren't expecting him to go off like that. I was most impressed by the way you went into that room— you and your partner. When he went crazy and grabbed the scissors, the rest of us bailed out of there in a hurry. You had more guts than we did."

"We're trained to do that."

"I'm trained, too," he said. "I want you to know I was right behind you." He smiled up at her, and she could see that he did not mind making fun of himself. "That was a nifty hold you put on that guy. It shuts off the blood in the carotid arteries, doesn't it?"

"If you get it right."

"You got it right. What do you call it?"

"A choke hold."

"Really? I think I'll use another term for the record. How about an arterial restrictive maneuver? That sounds better. Have you ever done it before under medical supervision?"

"This was the first time," she said.

He was not like her mother dispensing medicine.

"This is on the house," the doctor said. "Emma, don't even write it up," he said to the nurse, who was now organizing utensils onto a steel tray.

"Fine with me," Emma said.

"It's the least we can do to show our appreciation," the doctor said.

He crossed his legs and laced his fingers over his knee.

He had long fingers. His relaxed position gave her the same feeling. The pain had nearly disappeared. She wondered if he took this much time with everybody.

"You should leave the stitches in for a week or so. Anybody can take them out, of course, but I think you should come back here so that I can make sure everything is okay. It will save you a few bucks, too. I have a crazy schedule, but for the next three weeks I work every Friday—twenty-four hours straight. You can't miss me on Fridays."

"You have worse hours than I do," Katherine said.

"I'm finishing up my residency, so I work when I'm told to work. After that I'll get a better deal, but I'll still have a hundred years of school to pay for."

"You won't make any money if you give away your services like this," Katherine said.

"None of us will make any money if the doctor spends all day talking," Emma said.

The doctor looked up at Emma and smiled. Then he winked at Katherine and stuck out his hand. "Joe Bradshaw," he said.

He used no title to separate himself from her. She liked that, just as she liked his smile. She unfolded her right arm from her chest and took his hand.

"Katherine Murphy."

"Remember," he said, "every Friday."

When Grace parked the patrol car beside Rigmor's store after leaving the hospital with Katherine, Rigmor was sitting outside smoking a cigar. The shadow of her store reached across Ballard Avenue and crept up the west-facing wall of Al's Cabinet Shop. Grace pulled two chairs away from the outside table and gestured for Katherine to take the one closest to Rigmor. Slumping into the other, Grace extended her legs so that the heels of her shoes rested on the sidewalk. She put the portable radio on top of the table and turned the volume down.

"No *ja*, it's almost over," Rigmor said, blowing a puff of smoke into the air. Wisps of hair fluttered across her forehead. She still wore her long apron, but she had untied the strings around her waist.

Katherine sat straight in the chair with her police jacket covering her torn shirt. She had not said a word about pain, but her face was pale, and Grace could see that it hurt her to move. It looked like the pain was getting worse.

"How are you feeling?" Grace asked Katherine. "You don't look so good."

"I'm fine," Katherine said abruptly.

"Hvad?" Rigmor asked. She sat forward and looked at Katherine's face. "Are you sick, dear?"

"I'm fine," Katherine said. Her voice was less sharp than when she had said the same words to Grace.

"Well, I'm not," Grace said. "I feel like a truck ran over me, and I didn't even get hurt."

"That's because you controlled his arm the way you were supposed to."

"It took three of us to hold it down. You should have seen her, Rigmor. She held on to this man who went crazy in the hospital and choked him until he was unconscious. He was twice her size. Don't mess with her. She fights like a bulldog."

"I guess I won't," Rigmor said. "Where are you hurt, dear?"

"I have a few stitches in my back," Katherine said. "It was an accident. The man was so high on drugs that he didn't know what he was doing."

"So then he should leave those drugs alone."

"Yes, he should."

"These people make this mess of themselves, and then you have to clean it up and get hurt, too. It's not right. *Hvad?"*

"No. It's not right," Katherine said.

"Would you like some coffee? *Skat,* make some coffee for Katrin."

"No coffee, thanks. I'm fine, really. Let's just leave it alone."

"Leave it?" Rigmor asked. *"Ja,* we can leave it. Of

course, we can. You should have a shot of whiskey anyway, not coffee. I don't suppose you can do that?"

Grace smiled as she watched the color return to Katherine's face. She knew how successful her partner would be in getting Rigmor to change the subject. As Katherine squirmed under Rigmor's sharp eyes, Grace began to feel better, too. The truck that she had talked about earlier no longer seemed so large.

Across the street Al Johnson closed the door of his cabinet shop and wiped his bald head with his hand as he crossed the street toward them. He checked his hand for sawdust.

"Good evening, everybody," he said as he stepped onto the sidewalk on Rigmor's side of the street.

"You're working late tonight," Rigmor said.

"I was finishing up an order."

"You help Grace with the tables," Rigmor said to him. "These drug people hurt Katrin. She shouldn't lift anything."

"I'm fine, Rigmor. We're not going to talk about it anymore. It won't hurt me to lift something."

"So we won't say anything more about it, but you sit here. These two have done it lots of times."

Rigmor got up from her chair with a groan, and her apron hung loosely from her neck. Stiffly she walked into her store. Grace got up from her chair and put her hand on Katherine's shoulder.

"Stay here," she said, "unless you want to hear Rigmor scolding you the whole time."

"I'll stay," Katherine said.

"At least it's the end of our week. I'm ready for a couple days off. I've written more reports and statements in the last few days than I would in a month with Wes. Maybe nobody told you. This is supposed to be a nice quiet beat."

"You told me."

Grace walked over to one of the tables and lifted the end off the sidewalk. Al grabbed the other end as Rigmor had instructed. Grace backed through the door and down the center aisle where the table would stay until Al took it out with the first customer in the morning. Rigmor was mumbling to herself as she opened the sliding door of the refrigerated display case.

"Can you imagine hurting that girl?" she asked. "*Hvad?* Somebody hurts you, and they have me to answer." She shook her finger at Grace. "They piss me up, these people. They take those drugs and expect you to take care of them. No *ja*, but I have some sandwiches for Katrin to take home. I made a hundred *stykker smørrebrød* for Sam Pedersen's birthday tomorrow. He won't miss a few. Do you think she will like herring? No, maybe not," she said before Grace could answer. "*Laks,* and some roast beef with *agurke salat. Ja,* she will like that."

Rigmor was still talking, still deciding what Katherine would like, when Grace went out for the second table.

Chapter 15

Grace was third in line at Ballard Hardware. The morning had not gone well, but it seldom went well when she was working on her house. A two-hour plumbing project was now in its fourth hour with no end in sight and no water, except the annoying drip that continued to slip past the main shutoff. She had intended only to replace the corroded shower pipe, but she was now in the basement, having removed one corroded section after another looking for the end of corrosion. The end, she realized, wouldn't come until she replaced them all.

She heard the bell up the street and unconsciously counted the rings. The man in front of her was eating a sandwich, which made her think about stopping at Rigmor's. She looked back over the display of drill bits pointing to the ceiling and out the plate-glass windows with duct tape patching their cracks and could almost taste Rigmor's Friday chowder. Of course, she might get hung up in the store and not get her water turned back on. As she weighed the options she saw Jack Morton come through the door. He joined the line behind her.

"Not working today?" he asked.

"I'm working," she said. She showed him the list of supplies she had scribbled on a sheet of typing paper.

"Are you a plumber?"

"I am today," she said. "I have an old house, so I'm learning how to do everything. I imagine you know all about that."

"I do."

"What are you getting?" she asked.

"Replacements." He raised a two-foot-long drill bit with a corkscrew shaft an inch thick. It had been through rough work.

"Carbide tip," she said. "It must be for your concrete."

"It is, except my guys seem to think it will go through steel, too. We broke two tips this morning."

"So now you spend your lunch break getting more."

"That's right. I'm not going to pay somebody construction wages to walk down here and stand in line to get a bit for the rotohammer. Neither will those guys." He nodded toward the two men in front of them. "This line will get pretty long in another five minutes. We beat the rush."

"Aren't we lucky?"

He smiled and she watched his face change. He had been thinking of broken drill bits when he walked in the door, and he had probably been reminded of the dead boy when he saw her. Neither of those thoughts created his smile. She liked a smile that didn't hide anything or press in too closely, one that was simple, like the line ahead of them, which decreased by one person and shifted them forward.

"I could use a good plumber," he said.

"You wouldn't want me. I spend half a day soldering a few Ts and elbows. Then I don't have something, and I'm back down here."

"Me, too," he said.

The customer ahead of them walked rapidly down the aisle toward the door with the last available employee. Grace advanced to the counter and moved to the side so that there was room for Jack Morton. The counter had three feet that was more or less clear. It was the place all the orders were written, boxed, and signed. There was a hardware store closer to her home, but she knew Ballard

Hardware had everything she could possibly need, including advice.

The owner's son, Doug, stood up at his desk behind the pulley display. The desk was a new development, having been in the store only three or four years, and some customers who lined up down the aisle still talked about it as though it threatened the core of the business.

"Hi, Grace," Doug said as he came to the counter. "What are you working on today?"

"Plumbing," she said, "but I'll let Mr. Morton go first. He needs to get back to his crew."

Doug looked at Jack Morton and raised his eyebrows. "Mr. Morton?" he questioned. "What have you been telling this lady, Jack?"

"I've been telling her how hard it is to find good help these days. But go ahead and help her first. I know you didn't get out of that comfortable chair for me."

The pink cheeks of the owner's son glowed brightly.

"I'll help both of you at the same time. What do you have, Grace?"

She gave him the list, and he glanced through it.

"Jack?"

Jack raised the rotohammer drill bit. "One-inch Milwaukee, spline shaft. I need three more."

"I might be able to handle that. Follow me."

They followed Doug through a swinging wooden door, beaten and worn, into an adjoining room where they walked single file through a maze of shelves. The son found the drill bits without getting lost. He pulled a box toward him, tilted it down from the shelf, removed three bits, and shoved the box back in place. He picked up another box of drill bits lying at his feet on the wood floor and shoved it onto the shelf beside the other box. There were three more boxes on the floor, but he stepped over those as he led them around the aisle.

"I need some concrete anchors, too," Jack Morton said. "Do you know where they are?"

"I think I do."

Jack broke off from them and headed down an aisle. Doug watched him. "A little farther," he said. "Left side."

Jack raised his hand to signal he had found the anchors, and Doug continued on to the plumbing bins. Grace knew this area well. Bins overflowing with copper fittings took up the entire wall. He found a small box of fittings and emptied its few contents into one of the bins. A copper elbow fell onto the floor. He picked up it and several others among the mixed array there and threw them into the appropriate bins. He filled the box with the items on her list and wrote the quantities and stock numbers on the side.

"What kind of solder?" he asked.

"I don't know. Not too heavy."

Doug pulled a coil off the shelf and showed it to her.

"That'll work."

"Do you have enough flux?"

"Yes."

"What about this pipe?" he asked, gesturing to the list. "You don't want flexible pipe, do you?"

"No. Rigid."

"I'll call down to the pipe shop and let them know you're coming. Anything else?"

"That's it."

"Any news about that boy?" he asked.

She had no news for the hardware store.

"It's a bad deal, that's for sure. Dumped there like garbage behind Jack's building. I guess you figure he was a runaway."

"We don't know who he is."

"It makes you wonder when something like that happens right here in Ballard. I mean, who would do something like that?"

"I don't know."

"We're keeping our eyes open, that's for sure. I told my son to stick close to home, not talk to strangers, all those things you hate to tell your kids."

"How old is your son?" Grace asked.

"Six. How do you tell a six-year-old about all the bad people there are?"

"I don't know. I'm just a plumber today."

"So you are. Let's see if we can find Jack. I think he got lost."

Jack was not lost in the maze, but he had moved to another aisle where he was squatting beside a box of heavy black bolts.

"Hey, Doug, I didn't know you carried anchor bolts. I would have bought them here instead of from Western Supply."

"You should have. I could have saved you twenty percent. That's why I sit in that comfortable chair and answer the phone. You call me, and I'll have them waiting for you when you come. Then you don't have to stand in line."

Jack Morton stood up and grinned. He looked at his hands, which were black from the bolts, and wiped them off on the front of his pants.

"I like that line," he said.

Doug led them back through the door and to the front of the line that had grown longer, just as Jack promised, and dropped Grace's box of fittings at the end of the counter. She looked down the line and wondered what Jack Morton meant. What was there to like about a line?

"I should have one in there," Jack told the owner's son who was sorting through a stack of invoices on a shelf behind the counter.

"Here we are," Doug said. "How about you, Grace? Do you have an invoice running?"

"I don't think so," she said.

Doug removed a nameplate from the third of four wooden boxes, slipped the plate into a stamp machine, and pressed her name onto a new invoice. He wrote down the quantities and stock numbers of her order, flipped the invoice around, and dropped his pen on top. She scribbled her signature on the bottom of the invoice. He tore away the yellow copy and dropped it into her box. Her order was done, and she picked up her box of plumbing supplies.

Doug squeezed the stock numbers for the concrete anchors and carbide bits onto the bottom of Jack's crowded invoice and dropped his supplies into a heavy paper bag.

"Thanks, you guys," Doug said. "I'll call the pipe shop," he said to Grace as she and Jack Morton stepped away from the counter. Another customer moved forward and put his list in front of Doug. The owner's son wasn't going back to his desk just yet.

Grace started for the door. She thought it was strange that she didn't recognize anyone in the line. She heard Jack's name from one of the men, and he answered back, but he was behind her when she opened the wood and glass door that led outside. She held the door for him.

"How long have you been building stuff?" he asked as they stood on the sidewalk.

"Since I was little. My father made me a workbench one Christmas and put it in his workshop down in the basement."

"He must have liked your company."

"I think he decided that he wasn't going to get a boy."

"Did he?"

"No."

Jack stood north of her in the direction of his building. Her plumbing pipe was in the shop a block south.

"I called the detectives a couple times about the boy," he said. "They won't tell me anything. They won't even tell me his name."

She knew there were many reasons to protect information or the lack of it. They might even think Jack Morton was a suspect, but the detectives didn't meet their witnesses in line at the hardware store.

"They don't know his name," Grace said.

"I see."

He paused, and she thought he was going to ask another question.

"Thank you," he said.

Jack Morton turned away and started up the sidewalk. He shifted the sack of drill bits so that his hand supported the bottom. After a few steps he turned back to Grace.

"Good luck with your plumbing," he said.

"Good luck with your concrete," Grace said.

Chapter 16

Breaking away from the line of cars that backed up for blocks on Market Street during the Sunday migration to Shilshole Bay, Katherine approached Ballard Avenue from the south and parked in the angled stalls beside the Bell Tower. In contrast to the arterial streets that surrounded it, Ballard Avenue was a quiet oasis. If not for the few cars that meandered by as Katherine walked down the tree-sheltered sidewalk, the street would seem deserted.

Grace had taken the day off in addition to their normal days and had warned Katherine that Sunday would be a quiet day. To Katherine this wasn't quiet. Quiet was noon on the farm when a screen door slamming was the loudest noise for miles, when the summer dust floated endlessly in front of the windows of the haymow while beads of sweat gathered beneath her hair, rippled down the side of her face, and left tracks through the dirt on her skin as she looked in silent determination for baby kittens hidden by their mother beneath bales of ancient hay.

Besides, she had not switched to the Second Watch for excitement. She had switched to leave the drunks on skid road, the prostitutes on Pike Street, and the stench of run-down hotels. She had changed shifts in order to find people who did not feel anonymous, uncounted, and uncontrolled. And she wanted to get out of that police car—cruising the streets downtown, listening to the endless yammer of her partners, being seen but seeing little. She wanted to accomplish something that could not be found in the tally of arrests, traffic tickets, and days worked gathered each month by the sergeant. She wanted to go home and stop asking herself what she was doing and why she was doing it.

She looked through the window of Rigmor's store. The produce tables were aligned differently in the center aisle. Grace placed them in a practical position so that she could walk through the break in the aisle, but perhaps the poker players had forgotten. Perhaps they didn't want to be practical.

In the backroom of Rigmor's store Katherine had seen a large photograph of Ballard Avenue from the 1920s. In the picture an electric trolley line ran both ways on a busy mercantile street. The trolley was gone, and most of the merchants had relocated to Market Street or beyond to the shopping centers off the freeway. A customer could no longer buy a bow for her hair, but Katherine counted three different shops that would fabricate sheet metal into any shape she wished.

At the front window of an artist's studio, metal sculptures stood in line, waiting for buyers. Katherine wondered if one of the sheet metal workers had grown tired of flat mechanical shapes and had turned to art. Do you turn to art, or does it turn to you? She heard voices behind a tall wooden fence that stretched across a vacant lot between the art studio and the next building to the south. Through a small opening in the upright weathered boards she saw a man and woman sitting in chairs on a green plain of grass. Flowers outlined the perimeter of the lot, and a clothesline reached between two poles. Squares of colorful fabric hung from the wire. Katherine imagined the two people were artists discussing their latest works in their secret garden.

What would it be like to create something, to brush paint across canvas or words across paper that someone would remember? When she was a student at the university, she had bought a sketch pad and charcoal and had sat by herself on the campus lawn and gone through the motions of drawing trees and brick buildings, long stairways with students like her drawing students like her. No life rose from her creation. A child could have done better. She threw away the pad and the charcoal.

Once she had known a poet—not that he called himself that. Words were different for him. He could see the same child as she and the same smile, hear the same voice, and make them all different. He could arrange words together in combinations that made her think beyond them. She loved the way he used his words. She might have loved him, too, if he had brought her inside his words, if he had taken her in his kayak across peaceful water instead of troubled seas. If the timing had been better, if she had been a year or two older and he had been a year or two younger, if he had not loved before with consequences he had never imagined, he might have loved her. Was love a creative urge? Surely it had to be creative or else she would have found it by now. Sometimes she burned to find it, like the cut healing on her back as the stitches rubbed against the coarse shell of her bulletproof vest.

Katherine turned around and headed back the way she had come. A half block ahead, a small boy emerged onto the sidewalk from a narrow void between two buildings. He stopped when he saw her as though he had done something wrong—the same expression he had had when she had seen him at the railroad tracks.

"How are you, Daniel?" she asked.

"Fine."

He was dressed in a long-sleeved shirt buttoned up to his chin. His brown hair was carefully combed and wetted down, but he needed a haircut.

"Where are you going?"

"I was just going to see if Al is home."

"Do you know Al?"

"He has trains in his apartment. They go through the walls."

"Really?"

"It's a model train, of course."

"Of course. I've seen the train in his shop window."

"That one doesn't go anywhere. You ought to see the trains he has upstairs."

Daniel didn't look well. There was something in his face, a pallor that made him look as if he had been sick.

"Are you feeling okay?" she asked.

"I'm okay."

He looked away from her. He wasn't able to look at her more than a moment at a time. He looked above her, below her, beyond her, but not into her eyes. When she placed her hand on his forehead to feel if he had a temperature, his body froze but his skin turned red.

"I guess you're okay," she said, not wanting to bring him more torment. "Where's your sister today?"

"She's with my mom. Do you want to see the trains?" He remained determined to get to his destination.

"Sure."

Daniel started across the street, then reached back and took her hand unconsciously as he would for his little sister. She could not help smiling to herself. Daniel quickly realized what he had done. His hand would have slipped away, but she was not ready to let it go. She could have held it all afternoon—down the street, past the garden to the railroad tracks that led to the locks and the drawbridge where each could dream of someplace else. Daniel didn't say anything about her hand as they crossed the street, but when he stopped in front of the cabinet shop, he glanced down as if he wondered whether she still held it. She released his hand before he could pull away.

"Thanks for the escort," Katherine said. "That was very much like a gentleman."

Daniel smiled, and she saw a flash of the child spirit inside the small sober body. Without taking her hand, he led her up wooden stairs on the outside wall of the cabinet shop. Rounded smooth at the edges, the stairs were impressed with a hundred years of footsteps. Daniel tapped softly on the door.

Al opened it and was surprised to see them. He was surprised to see her anyway.

"She'd like to see the trains," Daniel said.

"I met Daniel down on the street," Katherine said.

"Come on in."

He opened the door wide and looked outside after Katherine and Daniel had entered the room.

"Where's Grace?" he asked.

"She took the day off. So I'm on my own."

Daniel headed over to a round oak table in the dining room. Half the table was clear, but the other half was piled with train equipment. There were two control boxes on a cabinet next to the table, and levers and wires pointed in all directions.

"Do you want to start her up?" Al asked.

"Sure."

"Turn on the switch and let it warm up a minute." He turned to Katherine. "It's a hobby of mine," he said. "I've been interested in trains since I was a boy."

Daniel examined the tracks while he waited for the machine to warm up. Al had made tunnels through the walls of each of the rooms just as Daniel had described.

"This is amazing," Katherine said.

"The Burlington was off the tracks," Daniel said as he came out of one room she thought must be the bedroom.

"Old Snoops has been climbing around again. She's the cat," he said to Katherine. "Did you fix it?" he asked Daniel.

"Yes."

"All right, then, get her started."

He stood beside Daniel as the boy slowly turned a knob to start up the train. The engine emerged through the wall on tracks that were supported by a shelf running the length of the room. The train cars passed miniature buildings and a painted mountain with evergreen trees above the front door. The door was part of the mountain.

"Okay, now start up the Santa Fe," Al said.

Daniel turned the knob on a second black box. A train began to move beneath the windows. It passed cactus plants, palm trees, and adobe buildings that stood in sand. Everything in the room was part of the train fantasy except a wooden cross above the kitchen door.

"My nephews used to come over, but I guess they're too old now. Daniel seems to enjoy it," he said.

"What child wouldn't?" Katherine asked. "I'm fascinated myself."

"It kind of grows on you," Al said. His voice had to rise above the roaring sound of train wheels on tracks and a piercing whistle that was receding into the distance.

Al hurried over to the control bench. "We'd better turn down the volume a little," he said. "I recorded these sounds from the Burlington tracks in the Cascades."

To compensate for the lower volume Daniel turned up the trains' speed. He had been adjusting one dial or another ever since the trains began moving. Al flopped a worn engineer's cap on Daniel's head so that the brim dropped over the boy's eyes. Daniel tilted the cap back but left it on.

Katherine announced she was leaving. Daniel acknowledged her farewell with a nod of his head, but the Burlington was approaching the mountain again and required all his attention. She ducked as she went beneath the train even though the door had not shrunk in size. Al followed her out to the stairway, and another loud whistle followed them. Al laughed with the shyness of a boy, and she was sure that he would not turn down the volume a second time.

Back on the street, Katherine headed toward her car. She heard Radio send Boy-3 to find a lost child at the zoo. There was an alarm in the University District, an accident on 145th Street, gunshots in Ravenna Park. Soon she would be able to screen out the calls that did not affect her, but she had not yet trained herself to her new number. All the troubles of the city on a Sunday afternoon sputtered into her consciousness.

Chapter 17

On Monday morning Thomas was thinking. He sat on a pile of cardboard beside the shed and looked at his feet. His big toe came through where he had worn a hole in the top of his right tennis shoe. What would it be like, he wondered, to have one idea that no one else had ever thought, to be like Einstein sitting at his desk in the Swiss patent office in 1907 when he had what he called his happiest thought? Acceleration. If you were standing on the floor of a spaceship accelerating at a moderate speed, it would be the same as standing with your feet on the earth. While gravity was mysterious and ethereal, acceleration was understandable. If you could understand acceleration, you could understand gravity. Thomas wondered what would have happened if Einstein's boss had walked into the patent office ten seconds before his happy thought and had told him to get his feet off the desk and get to work.

Thomas looked up at the sun. Einstein showed that not even gravity travels faster than the speed of light. If the sun explodes, the Earth will continue its orbit until it finds out about the explosion—93 million miles away, light traveling at 186,000 miles per second, eight minutes of ignorance. It was possible that the sun had exploded seven minutes and some odd seconds ago, and he wouldn't know because the Earth's orbit had not changed. Before he completed this thought, he might be dead and not even know it.

Gravity—such a basic concept—but how many people had watched the apple fall before Newton first thought of it? Would he, Thomas Rosencrantz, keeper of the recycling shed, ever wonder why the apple dropped instead of floating away? Had he, Thomas Rosencrantz, who was sitting in the warm sunshine in spring, ever had an original thought?

Thomas wiggled his big toe through the top of his shoe. His sock had a hole in the exact same place as the hole in his shoe. He had a toe looking for freedom.

A car turned into the alley, and a lady with hair the color of a bright sunset lowered the car window and stopped the car beside him.

"Are you Mr. Rosencrantz?" she asked.

"I am," he replied.

"My name is Anne Smith," she said. "I'm a detective with the Seattle Police Department."

She showed him a silver badge. He liked the way it curved across the top. Then her hand came through the window opening and presented a paper bag.

"I hope you like almond croissants," she said.

He stood up and accepted the sack.

"Thank you." He had not yet thought to be surprised.

It felt like more than one, but it would be rude to check. Next, she handed him a paper cup with a plastic lid and a small elliptical hole on the side of the lid that slanted up from the rim of the cup.

"Starbucks," he read. "They make good coffee."

"It's a tall latte, regular not decaf."

"Why bother with decaf?"

"I was surprised to see Starbucks here in Ballard. I found a parking place right in front of their store."

"I hear they're going public and opening a lot of stores," Thomas said. "I'm thinking about buying some stock when they do."

"Maybe we all should. Would you mind if I asked you some questions?"

"I don't mind at all."

"Did you ever see the boy before that day you found him

in the garbage machine?" Detective Smith asked. "Here's a picture of him. He might look a little different in the picture."

Thomas put the coffee cup and the sack on top of the cardboard and took the picture she handed through the window. She was right. The boy looked different, but it was the same face.

"No," Thomas said. "I never saw him until that day."

"Never in the alley? Never somewhere else in the neighborhood?"

"I don't think so."

"How long were you here before you found the boy—in this shack, I mean? About how many days?"

Days were so hard to remember. He seldom thought of time in days.

"I'm not sure," Thomas said.

"Was it a long time or a short time?" the detective asked. She smiled, and her face was friendly.

"What is a long time to you?" he asked.

"Goodness," the lady said. "I wish I knew."

"I don't think about time that way," he said.

"All right. Here's a picture of someone else," the detective said as she gave Thomas a second picture. "Have you ever seen this person before?"

Thomas looked at the second picture. Now he had a picture in each hand. The second picture was a girl lying on a table.

"She's dead, too," he said.

"That's right."

"They must be connected, these two deaths."

"We're all connected, Mr. Rosencrantz. Have you seen her before?"

"I might have seen her somewhere," he said. "She might have passed in front of me, and I didn't notice. So many people walk by, you know. I look but I don't always see everybody."

"Did you ever talk to a girl like her?"

"How would I know what she's like?"

"To her, then, Mr. Rosencrantz. Did you ever talk to this girl?"

"No," Thomas said. "I never talked to this girl."

"Thank you," the police detective said. "I won't take any more of your time."

She took the two pictures back from Thomas and put them on the car seat beside her. It was not a very nice car. Thomas saw her check the rearview mirror that would let her see backward down the alley.

"Did you ever have a thought that nobody else ever had?" Thomas asked.

The detective removed her hand from the gearshift that was beside the steering wheel. She rested her other arm on the car door.

"How would I know?" she asked.

"You would know," he said. "Newton saw the apple fall, and he had an idea. Gravity. Everything attracts everything else. He developed mathematical equations that could accurately predict planetary orbits, rockets taking off from the Earth, and the trajectory of a baseball that Joe DiMaggio caught in center field. We still use the equations, but he was wrong. Einstein thought of an idea that changed everything."

"I thought Newton was right," the detective said. "Didn't we learn that in high school?"

"Probably, but that's the seventeenth century. It takes us that long to learn something even if it's wrong. Einstein showed that gravity doesn't have anything to do with mutual attraction, at least not the way Newton saw it."

"That's too bad," the detective said. "I like the mutual attraction idea."

Thomas smiled at her. That was good, he thought.

"Do you ever wonder if there are laws like Newton's or Einstein's that control the way we are and not just objects floating in space?"

"I thought you said Newton was wrong."

"He is, unless Einstein is wrong." Thomas did not always think of them as being in the past. "Is there a mathematical theory that could explain why the garbage truck came early today before the first car drove into the garage, or why the box from the office on the third floor had shredded newspaper for packing instead of Styrofoam, or why Jack asked me to help him pour concrete instead of telling me to leave? Do you ever wonder that?"

"What are you thinking, Mr. Rosencrantz?"

"I'm thinking about how this coffee got here." He looked down to the cardboard, and the coffee was still there. The paper bag was there, too. "What would have happened if the parking space in front of Starbucks had not been open or if I hadn't been here in the alley?"

Another car entered the alley, and the detective looked in the mirror again.

"I believe I'm in the way," she said. "It's been a pleasure."

The second car backed out of the entrance, and the police detective backed her car slowly and crookedly past the garbage machine and out into the street. Thomas picked up the coffee cup and sack and sat down on the pile of cardboard where he had been before the detective entered the alley. He carefully placed the cup on the uneven asphalt at his feet and looked into the sack. Two croissants. He looked up at the sun.

"Another ten minutes would be appreciated," he said.

Chapter 18

The picture stopped Daniel in his tracks. A steam loco-
motive had crashed through the second floor of the
building and hung down to the street. Bricks and stones
were scattered on the sidewalk like his toy building blocks
after Hercules ran through them. It was an old picture. It
reminded him of pictures he had seen of his grandfather in
the war. Nobody wore hats like that anymore. The cars
looked strange, too, unlike any he had ever seen.

Mary tugged on one hand, and the grocery bag tugged
on the other. He knew she was hungry, but he had to figure
out this train. How could the engine crash through a building above the street and smash its nose into the sidewalk?
People in the picture stood looking at the train like he did;
only he was farther away.

Mary pulled away from him and drew a line on the glass
past the train. The train picture was on sale—today only.
He knew that today was Tuesday because he had been in
school only two days even if it seemed like a whole week,
but why would they only sell the picture on Tuesday? What
would they do with it tomorrow?

He liked to study the pictures more than the books at
school. The pictures were always interesting, and the art
store showed new pictures in the window every week. Mary
liked to go inside and sit at the children's table where

she would play with the stuffed animals or put the puzzles together even after he told her that the table was for kids whose parents were buying pictures. He knew his mom couldn't afford the picture even if it was on sale. Mary always promised not to go in, but sometimes she forgot if he studied the pictures too long. Then he would have to wait on the sidewalk until she finally came out.

"Let's tell Al about the picture," Daniel said. "You can play with Snoops."

Mary forgot that she was hungry and ran down to the corner ahead of him. He tried to catch up with her, but he had to hold on to his grocery sack. He wanted to yell at her to stop, but there were people everywhere on the sidewalk. Mary stopped at the corner and waited for him.

"Don't do that," he said when he caught up with her, but he knew she would do it again.

He held her hand tightly and waited for the light. Market Street was the busiest street they ever crossed. He didn't trust the cars there. Sometimes the cars or the bus ran through the red light without even slowing. He could imagine how much it would hurt if a car hit him or Mary.

It was quieter across the street. He liked to leave the noise behind. When they came to the park on the corner, Mary pulled him through the tower with the bell on top. She screamed so that her voice came back to her from the bell, and she jumped down the steps with her voice chasing her.

He liked to hear her laugh. When they played tag she would laugh so loud that she could not feel his touch. In their bed she would laugh beneath the covers as she hid from the ghosts who were waiting if he pulled the covers away.

A man came through the trees at the end of the park and watched Mary beneath the bell. The man smiled at her, but Daniel knew that some smiles could not be trusted.

As he led Mary away from the bell he did not mention the man who smiled, and he did not look back. Sometimes it was better not to look.

Mary found a new reason to skip ahead. The lady police officers were carrying tables inside the grocery store. Daniel walked fast so that he would not lose Mary's hand, but he didn't dare skip along with her. His sack was beginning to tear.

Mary pulled away from him again and peeked in the door after the lady police officers. He didn't think they would mind if she watched. Everybody liked Mary. The police officers had guns like on television, but on television the police never carried vegetable tables.

"Hello, Mary," one of the police officers said. There was still one table outside. "How are you?"

"Fine," Mary said. "What are you doing?"

"We're helping Rigmor close up. What are you doing?"

"Daniel bought some food at the store, and now we're going to see Snoops."

Daniel moved behind a tree, but it was too small. He looked up to the leaves and reached out to a branch with one hand and held the sack in the other. He pulled on the branch and felt the rough bark, wondering if it would make a dent in his hand if he pulled hard enough. Right then his sack broke and dumped everything on the sidewalk. A can of soup rolled toward the street, and he lunged after it.

The lady police officer came toward him as he tried to put the can back into the sack. There was a rip in it bigger than the can. He rolled the top of the sack down over the hole.

"What did you buy at the store?" the police officer asked. She squatted down on the sidewalk and picked up the box of macaroni that had spilled out with the soup. "Macaroni and cheese," she said, answering her own question. "Are you the cook tonight?"

"Yes." He wondered how he would get the macaroni from her.

She handed it to him, and he opened his sack with the hole big enough to let everything out.

"Do you remember my name?" she asked.

Of course he remembered. She had her name spelled out on her shirt. He would have remembered without it being spelled. He nodded that he remembered and looked down at his shoes and pulled on a lace. He wasn't sure why.

"I forgot to tell you yesterday when I saw you, but I talked to the librarian about your book," Officer Murphy said. "You can go back and get more books now."

"I can?"

"Yes."

He hadn't intended to say anything about the book. He was sure she wouldn't remember anything about it. Nobody remembered things like that. Except Al.

"What else are you cooking tonight?" she asked.

He looked at the soup can. He wondered why she couldn't see it. The whole side of the sack had ripped open. He read the label for her anyway. "Tomato soup."

"That sounds good. I used to cook when I was your age. Do you stand on a chair to see over the stove?"

"No, I can see."

"I used to stand on a chair," she said. "You're taller than I was."

He liked her voice. She didn't seem to mind that everything had dropped out of the sack. She was smiling, too. He didn't expect that. He was lucky that nothing had broken.

"What did you cook?" he asked.

"Hamburgers, I think, and canned vegetables. Potatoes, too. We had to have potatoes. I cooked when my mother was working."

"I do, too," Daniel said. He thought she had pretty teeth.

"Good for you. Is your mother working tonight?"

"Yes." He didn't want to talk about his mother. Rudy said it was nobody's business about them. Daniel tried to push the sack together, but it was hopeless. He had never had a sack that ripped so easily. "She has to work," he said.

"Everybody has to work," Officer Murphy said. "I'm working, too. Officer Stevens and I come here every night to help Rigmor close up her store. That's part of our job."

Her voice was soft, the way his mother used to talk.

"Do you have kids?" he asked. He thought she must if she could talk like that.

Officer Murphy was not smiling the same way as before. He wondered if he had said something wrong.

"No," she said softly, "but I wish I did. Then somebody could make macaroni and cheese for me when I got home."

"It's not hard," he said. "Even I could do it."

Chapter 19

Katherine twirled the dial on her combination lock. It clicked softly and she pulled it open. She lifted her shirt from the locker and inserted the loop of the wire clothes hanger through the air vents at the top of her open door. It covered her locker and the one to the left. She smelled the solvent used in cleaning as she inserted the silver pin of her badge through the cloth pathway on her shirt. A locker door slammed on the other side, and she felt the force transferred through the steel frame to her.

"You might want to hold off on that."

Katherine turned away from her locker and looked at Grace, who stood in the doorway.

"The sergeant wants to see us in the captain's office," Grace said. "He has a plainclothes detail for us."

"The captain's office? What kind of detail?" Katherine asked.

"I don't know. Detective Smith is down there."

Anne Smith was not alone. Fred Markowitz stood against the wall on the opposite side of the captain's desk beside a man whose hair was slicked back into another time. Markowitz raised his hand in greeting. Lieutenant Olson, who was in charge of the Second Watch at the North Precinct, stood behind the captain. He smiled as they came in. Katherine had not seen him yet without the smile. The captain sat stolidly in a swivel chair behind his desk. Their sergeant followed them into the room and closed the door.

"We've assembled the inquisition," Anne said. She sat in one of the three chairs in front of the captain's desk. Her lipstick was an even brighter red than before. "Sit down, Officers. I'm not sure you know Lieutenant Vick from the Vice Squad."

Lieutenant Vick nodded his head. Not a hair moved out of place.

"Detective Smith and Detective Markowitz have asked for your help," the captain said. "I don't have a problem in assigning you to them temporarily, if you don't."

Katherine supposed she was part of the "you," but he had never spoken to her before. Beyond that she wasn't sure if he was asking them or telling them. She looked to her right to see if Grace knew.

"What would you want us to do?" Grace asked Anne.

"Lieutenant Vick's men have been staking out the King Arthur Motel all week," Anne said. "A couple of them even spent the night there, but they didn't come up with anything, except they seemed to reduce the occupancy a little. It was like they were wearing signs on their heads that said 'cops.' I suggested to Fred that we use you two. Nobody will suspect that you're police officers."

"I worked Vice before," Grace said, looking at Lieutenant Vick. "I wasn't any good at it."

"I wasn't either," Katherine said.

"I can't imagine that," Anne said. "When I was new like you two, we never even tried to catch the men—only the women. Isn't that the way you remember it, Jerry, all those years ago?"

She looked at the captain and gave him a bright red smile.

"It might be," the captain said without conviction.

"Of course, women weren't really cops then," Anne continued, without acknowledging the captain's reply. "This detail will be different from that interesting line of work

Lieutenant Vick had you doing before. We need you to become ladies of the night, all right, but you won't be out trolling for tricks on Pike Street.

"The motel phone number on the boy's hand is the best lead we've got, but we don't know what it means. There aren't any boys out there working the streets as they do downtown. So why did this kid have that phone number written on his hand? Did he meet a trick there? Did he know somebody? Was he teaming up? We don't know.

"We want you two to set up shop in one of the motel rooms in the King Arthur for a few days," Anne said. "We'll keep the Vice guys in the area for surveillance and backup. They'll also be your customers. We'll have you out on the streets some of the time, but we don't want you to blow your cover by arresting some gentleman who just wants to have a good time. We want you to be seen and to keep your eyes open. We're hoping you'll get through a few doors that these old guys wouldn't be able to get through."

Anne nodded her head toward the old guys, who had remained unusually quiet.

"Why don't you find a couple cops who could dress up like boys?" Grace asked. "Isn't that what you're looking for anyway?"

"That wouldn't work," the captain said.

"Why? I know a few who would be perfect," Grace said. "Put them into tight black pants and who knows what would happen."

Lieutenant Olson laughed and nodded his head. "I know them, too," he said. "And it's a good idea. It would get them out of my hair for a few days."

"That's not who Detective Markowitz asked for," the captain said. He was not laughing. "I made it clear that I won't order you to do this job. It's up to you. I'm not so excited about it myself. Our manpower is already too low."

The captain's description of his workforce irritated Katherine more than usual. Everything about him irritated her, including his deference to Detective Markowitz and the way he tried to ignore Anne, even though she was the one who presented the plan.

"I'll do it," Katherine said, "as long as Detective Smith is in charge."

"That's not my call," the captain said.

"There's no problem with that," Markowitz said. "This was Anne's idea in the first place. I asked her for help. Besides, she's smarter than the rest of us."

"Meaner, too," Lieutenant Olson said.

"I still don't understand what you want me to do," Grace said, looking past Katherine at Anne. "You want us to look like whores, then what?"

Anne leaned forward so that her head passed over the top of the captain's desk. She looked directly at Grace, but Katherine felt that she was also within Anne's view. The others were excluded.

"Not just a whore," Anne said softly, her voice more serious than before. "We want you to look like a young whore. Remember, we have that girl, too. I'll bet a month's pay it's the same murderer who killed them both. He doesn't seem to discriminate. We don't know who we're looking for, but we know somebody out there has a fondness for youth. There's got to be a connection with that motel. We want you there. We want you to find out as much as you can without taking risks. The captain is right about the boys in your squad. If somebody gives them a little squeeze in the wrong place, they'll defend their manhood and ruin everything. You know how to work your way through that. You both do. You wouldn't be here if you didn't."

And neither would she, she seemed to say—but not with words.

"All right," Grace said, "but I won't sleep in that place."

"I don't blame you," Anne said. "I wouldn't sleep there

either. We'll make sure you get home. If you don't make any progress in four or five days, we'll call it off."

"We sure will," the captain said, but his voice was far in the background.

Chapter 20

"What have you done to your hair?" Rigmor asked.

"It's a new look," Grace said. "Don't you like it?"

"It's fine. It's good to have a new look sometimes. I thought you were working today?"

"I am working. I've become a prostitute. That's why I have the new hair."

Grace walked behind the counter that Rigmor had covered with buttered slices of rye bread. The back work counter was covered with slices of bread, too. Rigmor had begun spreading liver pâté and pointed the flat knife toward Grace's face.

"What is that on your face?"

"Lipstick."

"No, the other stuff."

"Rouge, or base, something like that," Grace said. "It's supposed to be a match for my complexion, to make me look younger."

"I don't like it," Rigmor said.

"You should see my dress and shoes. I'll be a hot number tonight."

"You have to do that again, that prostitution business?" Rigmor asked.

"Something like it."

"You didn't change like this before. You went like a schoolteacher last time."

"I put on a dress, Rigmor, and they told me I looked like a schoolteacher. This is supposed to be different. We're trying to catch somebody who kills kids."

"That boy up there?" She inclined her head toward the street where they had found the boy. She spoke softly even though the store was empty.

"Yes."

"But if they're looking for boys, why do they send you?"

"You see, they should put you in charge. I asked the same question."

"So what did they say to that?"

"There was a girl, too, at another place."

"That's terrible. Do they think these children were prostitutes?"

"They might have been."

"Such a shame, to waste life when you're so young."

"The public isn't supposed to know."

"Of course not," Rigmor said. "The public won't know anything about it, but it's still a shame."

Rigmor took in a quick breath that carried with it a mournful inflection. Grace's mother made the same sound when distressed.

"Who ordered the sandwiches?" Grace asked.

"Lars Krogh. For Liberation Day. His daughter is here from Denmark, and he wants to have the party before she leaves."

"So nobody was liberated today?"

"No, it's a few days yet, but that doesn't matter."

"What's the liberation about?" Grace asked.

"It's the day Denmark was freed from the Nazis. And that was a day, I'll tell you. I still remember like yesterday. When we heard on the radio that the Germans had surrendered, everybody ran out into the streets and hugged each other and laughed and cried. We tore down all the black cloth that covered our windows. It was a day none of us who were there will ever forget. You Norwegians should have more celebrations. Learn to enjoy life a little."

"We have celebrations."

"Like your Christmas? That's not a celebration. It's more like punishment when you have to eat that lutefisk. And then the Seventeenth of May? That's supposed to be the big deal, but what do you do? You have a parade, and some of you walk in the parade and some of you watch. What kind of party is that? *Hvad?* If you had some clowns, maybe it would be worth watching. Or if you carried the flag at the head of the parade instead of those old men, then I would watch."

"That job goes to somebody important."

"Who?"

"I don't know. The king, maybe."

"You see what I mean. They could have you carry the flag, and then we would come. But, no, they have some old man carry it. And it won't be the king, I'll tell you that. He's not going to carry the flag all the way down Market Street. No, I was here the year he came, and he didn't carry any flag."

Grace could not dispute that. She, too, remembered the year the king came. She was eleven years old. Her mother had made Norwegian dresses for her sister and her—long traditional red and black dresses that took a month to make. Something happened a few days before the parade. Her sister wouldn't wear her dress. Evangeline wouldn't say what it was, but she wouldn't wear the dress. She wouldn't go to the parade either. Her father was going to make her, no matter what had happened, but her mother said to leave her alone. Grace felt like a traitor going to the parade when her sister would not, but she knew she would feel like a traitor, too, if she didn't go. Besides, she liked the way the dress twirled when she spun around.

She stood on the corner of 22nd and Market Street in front of her mother and father, wearing her long red and black dress and waving a small Norwegian flag as the king came down the street. Rigmor was right. He was not carrying a flag. The men beside him carried the flags, but he left the flag bearers and came across the street to her and shook her hand. He was shaking a lot of hands. In English he told her how pretty she looked and was about to walk over to the next girl at the curb when she told him in Norwegian that he looked pretty good, too. *"De ser temelig godt, også."* It was a silly thing to say to a king, but at least it was in Norwegian. He asked her how old she was, and she told him. Then the entire parade stopped while she talked to the king in Norwegian. The marching bands marched in place, the folk dancing groups danced in stationary circles, the Norwegian princess from Poulsbo waved to the same people over and over, and the fire trucks shifted into neutral. She didn't know all the details until later when she read the story in the newspaper beside the picture of her talking to the King of Norway.

Her sister wouldn't talk to her for days after that. Grace thought Evangeline sometimes made more problems for herself than was necessary. When Evangeline finally did speak to her, it was to ask questions.

"Don't you think there is something strange about that picture?"

"No."

"Do you see anybody like you?"

"Yes, the girl next to me."

"She's not like you."

"We're wearing the same dress."

The other girl had long blond hair, obvious even in the black and white photograph. Grace knew what her sister meant, but she was not going to talk about it. The king was talking to her, not to the girl with the blond hair.

"You don't want to do this job, do you—this prostitution business?" Rigmor asked, interrupting Grace's reverie.

"No. I don't like to pretend that I'm somebody else."

"Did I ever tell you about Jesper Paulsen?"

"I don't think so."

"We worked together in the Resistance."

"Is he the tall man you kissed?"

"He's the one. Then I have told you."

"Not enough. You said you never told your husband about him."

"I never told my husband about any of it. He never knew I worked with the Resistance. Can you believe that? I can't believe it myself sometimes."

"How old were you when he kissed you?"

"Old enough to know better, that's for sure."

"How old?"

"Thirty-two, thirty-three. Heinrik was a child. But it wasn't that kind of kiss."

"What kind was it, then?"

"Oh, you have it all mixed up. It was after the Germans occupied Denmark, and I was working with the Resistance to smuggle the Jewish people to Sweden. Jesper had a fishing boat that we used. You see, the fishermen went out every night to fish, and the Germans couldn't tell them not to fish because they ate the fish, too. So it was a good way to get these people to Sweden.

"I brought a family to Jesper's boat, a mother, father, and two children—two little girls. I was just about to sneak home when Jesper grabbed me and kissed me. Luckily I didn't hit him, because I could have. He whispered to me that German soldiers were coming toward us. We weren't supposed to be out at night past the curfew time. They could shoot you on sight.

"It was some kiss, I'll tell you. He grabbed me like a drunken sailor who had been to sea a month. The Germans recognized Jesper. He was so tall that everybody knew him. He laughed when the soldiers stopped beside us. 'You won't tell my wife on me, will you?' he said to them. The Germans laughed with him. You see, I wasn't the only lady in the area, if you know what I mean. So sometimes we have to be somebody different for a while.

"I wasn't afraid. I can't believe it now, but I wasn't. On

the way home I didn't even think about the German soldiers. But, let me tell you, I did think about that kiss."

Rigmor looked out to Ballard Avenue where the shadow from the top of her building drew a line on Al's Cabinet Shop and the auto repair shop across the street. A man walked by her big glass windows and waved to her. Rigmor raised her hand. *"Goddag,"* she mumbled. The man continued walking through the shadow of Rigmor's building.

Grace quietly opened the knife drawer and removed a flat-bladed butter knife like the one Rigmor held. Dipping the knife into the liver, she removed enough to cover a sandwich and crowned the pâté the way Rigmor had taught her, covering every centimeter of the bread.

"He shouldn't have been so tall," Rigmor said. "He was too easy to recognize. The Germans caught him a few months later. They sent him to a concentration camp. We never heard what happened to him after that."

Rigmor turned to Grace and looked straight into her eyes. Rigmor and her mother were the only women Grace knew who stood as tall as she. When Grace was a little girl, Rigmor had always seemed bigger than everyone else. She was still that way. Jesper Paulsen must have been a tall man to be tall in her eyes.

"When I was a girl," Rigmor said, "my father told me I was too dumb to do anything by myself. Can you imagine a father saying that? Why would anybody say that to a child? Your father would never say that. And my husband said the same thing, just about. Then came this war. They were bad times, but they were some of the best, too. Smuggling the Jewish people to Sweden was the simplest thing I ever did. I never doubted if I was right or wrong. I never thought about what would happen to them later, or what would happen to me. It's wonderful to find something that is so simple and right. My husband wasn't brave enough to help these people, but I was, and they thought I was plenty smart."

"Smart enough to run this store, too," Grace said.

"Ja, and it's pretty smart to get you to make my sandwiches while I stand here and talk. Don't you think?"

"It's the price we pay for your stories."

"The stories had better be pretty good."

"They're pretty good," Grace said.

"So, then, I should see the dress."

Grace stood perfectly still for a moment as she considered Rigmor's instruction. It was an instruction, she decided. She never knew what might happen in Rigmor's store. They might be making *frikadeller,* and Rigmor would send her to Market Street for ice cream. She had not done that for a while. Now she was more likely to send her upstairs for beer or to make martinis if it was after four so that they could sit outside and sip their drinks while the sun played hide-and-seek with the shadows on the street. Rigmor was particularly delighted to hear that it was against the law to drink alcohol on the public sidewalk. The one time Grace brought down the drinks in regular glasses, Rigmor made her go back for martini glasses.

"You won't like the dress, Rigmor."

"How do you know what I like? Half the time, I don't even know."

It was after four o'clock as Grace headed out to her car for the dress.

"And the shoes," Rigmor called after her.

She brought the dress in and held it up in front of her as though she were before a mirror in a clothing store deciding whether to try the dress on or put it back on the rack. She would have put this one back.

"You didn't buy that dress, did you?" Rigmor asked.

"No, the police department paid for it. And for this hairdo."

"They have money for such things?"

"They have money for everything," Grace said. "You just have to know how to pull the strings."

"And you pulled them?"

"I didn't. A woman detective pulled them. She's in charge of this operation."

"Well, let's see how she did. Go upstairs and put it on. Then come down and show me. Make us a martini while you're at it."

Grace should have known that Rigmor would have to see her in the dress, that holding it up would not be enough. As she climbed the stairs with the dress draped over her right arm and the shoes in her left hand, Grace heard the old lady chuckling to herself. Grace smiled, too, as she entered Rigmor's apartment and smelled the familiar odor of her imported Danish cigars. Manna from heaven, Rigmor called them. Grace draped the dress over the back of the sofa and dropped her shoes onto the floor.

It was familiar territory and had hardly changed since she was a girl. There were a few more pictures crowded onto the wall, and the row of blue and white Christmas plates mounted below the ceiling had turned the final corner and was approaching its origin. Even after Grace's sister had stopped speaking Norwegian and stopped going to any Norwegian events, she would still come to the apartment. Rigmor didn't care what language she spoke. Rigmor's younger son, Peder, had stopped speaking Danish, too.

Grace went into the kitchen and took down the bottle of Beefeater gin from the cupboard above the sink. There were three bottles of Beefeater, as well as whiskey, scotch, and cognac, all top quality. Rigmor did not like cheap liquor, and the poker players kept it well stocked. They also made sure there were boxes of her Manna Cigars in the china case.

Grace removed the martini shaker and glasses from the cupboard beside the alcohol. Without needing to measure she poured gin for two drinks. In the refrigerator she found the scarred lemon that Rigmor would eventually use for something more than martini twists, but not yet. From the freezer compartment she got ice and the bottle of Aalborg Akvavit, which was the clear Danish liquor Rigmor preferred to mix with the gin. She cut twists from the abused lemon and wiped the rims of the glasses with the inside of the rind before dropping one sliver into each glass. Then she splashed akvavit over the ice cubes in the shaker, shook, waited, and poured to the rim of the glasses. She dumped the ice into the sink, rinsed the shaker, and put everything in its place.

She left the martini glasses on the kitchen counter and went back into the living room where her dress still lay over the back of the sofa. She hoped it might have left by this time. She took off her jeans and T-shirt with paint spots on the front and slipped the sleeveless knit dress over her head. It hugged all parts of her body equally and stopped well above her knees. Anne Smith had wanted to buy one with tiny shoulder straps that would not even cover bra straps, but Grace had refused to try it on. Now she wondered how she had been persuaded to get this one. She sat on the couch, stuck her feet into the high-heeled shoes, and stood up. It was difficult to even stand in them.

She clumped into the kitchen for the martini glasses and clumped back to the stairs. She had not walked in high heels since she was a girl, and she had been better at it then. She stopped at the top of the stairs, a martini glass in each hand, and seriously considered how to get down. She was not worried about spilling the martinis, since she disliked the taste of them anyway, but she could easily imagine herself falling and breaking both legs. Slowly, a step at a time like a person with both feet already in plaster, she worked her way down.

"I'm not sitting outside with this thing on," she said to Rigmor as she came through the door. She was watching the liquid surface of the martinis. She had already spilled some and had drunk some on the way down and was trying to retain the rest before it was a total loss. She intended to stay next to the door in case a customer came in. She could only imagine what her father would say if he walked into the store just then. "We're going to drink them right here." And that was final, she added to herself.

"*Ja vel,*" Rigmor said as she turned toward Grace.

"Oh, great," Grace said when she looked up from the martini glasses.

Jack Morton stood at the counter and just looked. He said not a word.

"Do you know Mr. Morton?" Rigmor asked. "He comes for my curried herring."

"How are you, Mr. Morton?"

"Jack," Mr. Morton corrected. "I guess you're not working today, on plumbing that is."

"This is too complicated to explain," Grace said. She would have waved her hand across her dress, but she still held the martini glasses and they would tolerate no waving.

"You don't have to explain anything to me. I just came for herring."

"*Ja,* and now you have it," Rigmor said. "I can tell your mouth is already watering."

Jack Morton smiled.

"I'm trying to decide if I need anything else," he said.

"No, you have everything you need," Rigmor replied. "You think you're making her blush, but that's just the stuff she has on her face."

"I'm blushing, Rigmor. Here, take this glass before I drop it." She held out the martini glass that was in her left hand.

Rigmor took it from her and raised it in a toast. "*Skål,* dear," she said. "Happy birthday."

"Happy birthday to you," Grace said. It was Rigmor's toast no matter what day it was.

They drank from their glasses and brought them down to their hearts.

"*Ja,* pretty good," Rigmor said as she placed her glass on the counter next to the plastic carton of curried herring. "Next time we'll make a drink for you, too," she told Jack Morton. She put the herring into a paper sack.

"I'd like that," he said.

Jack paid for the herring and lifted the sack off the counter. "Thank you, Rigmor." He nodded at Grace. "Until next time," he said.

Grace nodded back but said nothing. She thought the quiet would surely explode before he got out the door, but nothing happened until the little bell above the door rang its foolish note. Then Rigmor bent over in laughter. No one could resist that laugh. It was not melodic or soothing in any way. It went high and low in unexpected turns, but it had been too hard earned to resist. The gin and akvavit rippled in Grace's martini glass as her whole body shook in her tight pink dress.

Rigmor straightened and reached for her glass. She raised it, clinked it against Grace's, and took a large drink between the high and low notes of her laugh.

"Poor man," she said. "He never knew what hit him."

"It wasn't me," Grace said. "This doesn't look like me."

"No, *Skat,* you look like you. And I'll tell you something else. If you carried the flag wearing that dress, a lot more people would come to your parade."

Chapter 21

Walking back and forth the length of the block, Daniel waited for the police car to come. He carried a paper sack folded twice at the top, and he was careful not to let the sack tear like last time. He was sure it was the same time that Officer Murphy had come before.

A man walked toward him on the sidewalk, and Daniel turned away from the street and looked in the window of the car repair shop. There was a truck there the same color as his father's truck. He wondered what was wrong with this one. There was always something wrong with his father's truck.

When Daniel looked across the street again, he saw Al and the tall lady pick up one of the tables and carry it inside. It was the police lady, but not the one he hoped to see. Maybe Officer Murphy was inside the store. He wanted to talk to her, but even if she came out to the sidewalk, he might not be able to do it. She might look the other way. She might not remember him. How could he even start?

He walked down the sidewalk until he was directly across the street from the grocery store. The sun shone in his eyes and blinded him. He shielded his eyes with his free hand and tried to see inside.

When Al came out, Daniel hurried across the street before Al could disappear again. Al saw him and waved.

"Hi, Daniel, what are you up to?"

"Nothing," Daniel said.

Now the tall lady came out, too. She looked different than when she was in her uniform.

"Do you want to give me a hand here?" Al asked.

"Sure." He was willing to do anything with Al.

Daniel went to the opposite end of the table and started to lift. The table was too heavy, and he needed both hands completely free. He placed his sack into the box of apples in front of him and lifted again.

"Maybe I can help," the tall lady said.

Anybody could see that she could carry the table better than he could, and Daniel started to back away.

"No, you lift, too," she said. "Then it will be easier for both of us."

Daniel stepped back to the table and lifted. With the tall lady he backed through the door and down the aisle until they came to the other table. There he was blocked and could not get out until she did. For a second he thought about crawling under the table and getting away, but he stayed where he was. What a dumb idea, he thought. He would stand very still and wait for her legs to move.

"Thank you for the help," the tall lady said.

Daniel looked up and saw that she was smiling. He wanted to keep looking, but he couldn't. It seemed that every time he looked too long something bad happened.

"You should put the tables on wheels," he said, looking down at the floor.

"You mean Rigmor should," the police lady without the uniform said. "This is her store, and she decides how things go here."

Daniel decided that it was not a good idea to make suggestions.

"Besides, if the tables had wheels, there wouldn't be anything for us to do."

"You could still sweep outside," he said. He looked up

briefly before he remembered that he was not going to give any more ideas.

"That's right. We could." She was smiling so maybe it wasn't so bad. "Maybe you would like to sweep."

"Sure," he said. He didn't mind helping. He picked up his sack from the apple box.

"What do you have there?" she asked.

Daniel looked at the sack and wondered how he could explain what was in it. He was ready to sweep, but the tall lady stood in his way, and he could not move until she did.

"It must be a secret," the tall lady said.

"It's not a secret. I made them for the other police lady. She said she wished somebody would make her something."

"What did you make?"

"Cookies," Daniel said. "You can have them. I can make lots more."

He held out the sack. It would be good to get rid of it. It was in his way every time he tried to move. The tall lady took the sack and looked inside.

"Chocolate chip cookies," she said. "They look delicious. Did you make them yourself?"

"Yes. Well I got the tube from the store. All you have to do is cut up the dough and bake it."

"I'll make sure Officer Murphy gets them," she said.

"Where is she?" he asked. "Did she have to go somewhere else?"

"She and I have a different job for a few days, but she'll be back."

"Are you a police officer now?" She didn't look like one.

"Sort of," she said. "If somebody did something bad, then I would have to be a police officer, but that's not why I'm here. I'm here to talk to Rigmor and help her close. Come on, let's get the broom."

Daniel didn't mind that everyone else sat in the chairs while he swept the sidewalk. Even though there was an extra chair, he didn't want to sit down. Rigmor said that he was doing a good job. He liked the way she talked. Her voice was different from everyone else's. She reminded him of his grandmother, what he remembered of her. When Rigmor laughed, it was the way he wanted his grandmother to laugh. As long as he kept working, he knew he could stay close enough to listen. When he finished the sidewalk in front of Rigmor's store, he decided he might as well sweep in front of the secondhand store next door while he was at it.

Chapter 22

Katherine felt conspicuous driving her own car into the police garage. It was eight o'clock at night, shift change, and Lenny was on G-deck with his clipboard, directing traffic. She had her badge ready to show but dropped the badge case onto the front seat as he waved her forward and bent down to look into her window.

"Hey, kid, what are you doing back here?" he asked.

"Special deal," she told him. "They told me to park down on A-deck."

"Vice, huh?"

Lenny abruptly straightened and whistled through his fingers. "Hey! I said forty-two, not thirty-two," he shouted to a car backing into a stall in front of her. Then he used his fingers to repeat four and two in case the driver did not understand. The driver understood and headed farther down the row.

Lenny turned to her again. His smile was back, and he laughed as though someone had told him a good joke. "You know how these guys are," he said. "Think they rule the world." Then he motioned her to continue. "Easy as it goes, kiddo."

Once past the bustle on G-deck she drove rapidly down through the garage in a spiraling orbit to A-deck, where most of the cars were solid-colored Dodge Darts. A few of the private cars were for officials far above the rank and privilege of street cops. She parked in the stall that Anne Smith had directed her to on the telephone. Grace's car was a few stalls away.

Katherine headed for the back stairway so that she would not run into cops who would recognize her and want to know what she was doing. It had taken a long time to smile just right, to show impersonal friendliness that would be interpreted properly. Even then it didn't always work. No longer was she the novelty that she had been as one of the few women on Third Watch, but she was not sure how her revised smile would work with the hairdo and makeup Anne had arranged for her that afternoon. Pigtails. She hadn't had pigtails since she was a girl.

Even before her present pigtails, she was checked every time she bought a drink. There could be a dozen cops with her, and she would still get checked. There had never been a dozen, she corrected herself, except for the celebration after the last day of the academy when to everyone's surprise she was still there. Too small, too young, too much like a woman, not enough—she had heard every reason why she wouldn't make it. But she had.

That was the easy part. The police recruiter told her that she would be able to work her way off the streets into Juvenile or Sex Crimes where her size wouldn't be such a disadvantage, but she was still on the streets and wasn't sure where she wanted to go. She knew it wasn't Sex Crimes, and she knew it wasn't the King Arthur Motel.

Katherine walked into the Sex Crimes office on the fifth floor. Anne was sitting at her desk emptying a large knit bag. Grace was watching her and did not look happy. Sergeant Parker, whom she recognized from her last Vice detail, sat on the edge of a desk in the cubicle across from Anne, Lieutenant Vick sat in a swivel chair between the desks.

"Sit down, Officer Murphy," Anne said. "We're just going through your bag."

"My bag?" Katherine asked.

"Unless you brought one."

"I brought a purse," Katherine said. She showed Anne the black purse she had bought when she joined the department.

"Lovely," Anne said. "It makes you look like Cadet Murphy. Did you ever see a prostitute with a little bag? You have a lot of stuff that goes in here." She pointed to the items on her desk. "You've got rubbers, gum, Kleenex, pint of vodka, paper, pen, not to mention you might want to carry a gun with you because you can't exactly strap it around your waist."

"Where did you get a bag like that?" Katherine asked.

"It's mine and so are these rubbers. I want them all back, too. No extra stuff on the side."

Lieutenant Vick and Sergeant Parker chuckled from their perches. Grace looked at them, but she didn't laugh. Katherine thought about the time Grace threw the self-defense instructor off the mat.

"Relax, ladies," Anne said. She had seen Grace's expression, too. "We outnumber these guys for once. Besides, these rubbers are the large size. Wouldn't fit anybody here."

The two men chuckled again, but their humor was a little shorter than before. Grace picked up one of the condom packages and read the label. The room, which was empty except for the five police officers around Anne's desk, became very quiet.

"Katherine, have you met Sergeant Parker?" Anne asked.

"Yes. It's been awhile."

Sergeant Parker scooted off the desk to shake Katherine's hand. "It's nice to see you again," he said. "There are no favorites here. Anne treats us all with the same respect."

"And you love it," Anne said. "Now here's what we've got planned for tonight, but remember you two will make the final decisions on all of this. Your butts are on the line out there, and we don't want you to take any chances. To start with, we just want to get you into that motel and be seen. We don't know who will be looking, or if anybody will. Dear Mrs. Miller, who lives across the street, has given us a whole page of license plate numbers. She's been recording them for the last month at the suggestion of the district car, but no one has shown any interest in them until now. A few cars reappear quite regularly, and we're checking them out.

"After you establish yourselves, we're hoping somebody will come to you. If not, you might have to take the first step. Better if they do it. At the very least, we'll get to know a lot more about this place.

"We have a Thunderbird with Nevada plates for you. Narcotics confiscated it as part of a drug bust last month, and they haven't used it yet. We'll have you register at the King Arthur for three days. Tell the clerk you don't want cleaning service. A dump like that, they might not have it anyway. Don't use the phone. It might go through the office, and we don't trust anybody who works at that place.

"If you can, get a room on the second floor. Lieutenant Vick has decided he will grace us with his direct attention and will be watching the motel from Mrs. Miller's house across the street. You'll be easier to see if you're on the second floor. We plan to have you set up shop on Aurora. Sergeant Parker will be your first pickup. Tell them what you're thinking, Sergeant."

Sergeant Parker cleared his throat. While the lieutenant wore a sport coat and tie, Parker had on a nylon windbreaker and jeans. He was the older of the two men. On Katherine's previous Vice detail, Parker had been on the street with his squad.

"We want you to stay on the east side of Aurora," Parker said. "There's a stairway at the underpass across the street from the motel."

"I know where it is," Grace said.

"Good. You'll be Car 209. The lieutenant is 200; and I'm

201. These are bogus car numbers for this detail. We're going to be on frequency 6, and we'll tell Radio to ignore our call numbers unless we specifically ask for him. We want you to call me when you're ready to leave your room and tell me that you'll be out of the car a few minutes. Make sure nobody hears that radio outside the room and that you use F6. Lieutenant Vick will watch you and tell me when you reach the steps. We'll use different codes each time in case somebody is listening on a police scanner. I'll wait ten minutes after you get to Aurora, and then I'll head across the bridge. I'll be in a blue Ford station wagon.

"We want you to walk north so that you're close to the next street. That's 39th. If there are girls already there, go to the next block. I don't want to show up too early in case somebody is watching, so if a trick beats me to you, you have to get rid of him. The trick will probably slow down and look and then turn onto the side street. Aurora is too busy. Nobody will stop there. You'll know when you see that look. Do you know the routine, what to say?"

"We know the routine," Katherine said. "We're not fifteen years old, even though we're supposed to look like it, I guess."

"I'm not talking about a prom date," Sergeant Parker said, his voice edged with a note of irritation.

Katherine had her own sources of irritation, and they went back to the last time she was assigned to Vice. She reminded herself that this was supposed to be different. Anne looked worried, as if her idea were not so great after all. Katherine shifted her chair toward Parker, crossed one leg over the other, and smiled as sweetly as she could. She leaned toward the sergeant.

"What are you talking about, big strong man like you? Hey, baby," she cooed, "looking for a good time? Oooh, you're so cute I don't even want to charge, but got to pay the rent. Got any money tonight, sugar?"

The transformation was immediate. Parker was entranced with her message, even though he had to know that none of it was true. He had to know that her smile was fake, but he watched her until it disappeared from her face. Anne chuckled softly.

"Okay," Sergeant Parker said, "you know the routine, but this time it will be a little different. Tell the trick you only work together and it costs. Tell him it's a hundred bucks. If he's got a hundred bucks, tell him that's only for the warm-up, and it'll cost him two hundred for a good time. Or tell him he looks like a cop, and you're not interested. Something like that, but get rid of him.

"When I show up, I'll slow down and turn onto 39th or whichever street is north of you. I'll roll down my passenger window and talk to you for a few minutes. Then one of you will get into the front seat and one in the back. I'll drive to the motel, and we'll go into your room. I'll stay there for half an hour or so, and then I'll leave. Like Anne said, we're just trying to have you seen, to set up a pattern.

"We have four pickups arranged tonight, including myself. Here's the list." He gave Katherine a sheet of paper, which she read and passed on to Grace.

"It has all the information about the cars and who the officers will be. They'll show their badges right away. I know you don't like this detail, so you won't have to sweet talk them unless somebody is close by. A smile might be good though, just like you did in your little act before." He smiled to show what he meant.

"The last time I did this," Katherine said, "you had a few guys who didn't know when to stop acting. I hope that doesn't happen again."

"It won't," Lieutenant Vick said. "Sergeant Parker and I will make sure of that."

"You can tell them, Lieutenant," Anne said in a most pleasant voice, "that these ladies might be smiling, but they have guns now."

Chapter 23

Katherine stood with Grace on the second-floor walkway of the King Arthur Motel. She heard the traffic on Aurora and the whine of wheels on the steel grating of the Aurora Bridge. In the parking lot below there were six cars, including their Thunderbird. The Thunderbird was the latest arrival. No car had arrived since they checked in at nine o'clock.

Television laughter escaped from an open window at the end of the walkway, and blue light from the television screen flashed against the drapes. There was light in one other room on the second floor. Their own room was the last on the north end of the building. Like the others it had a large window on the side of the walkway, but it had a smaller window facing the houses that were squeezed between the commercial buildings on Aurora Avenue and Stone Way.

Across the street a solitary woman walked a dark stretch of sidewalk. Trees shaded her from the streetlight. She stopped, looked toward them, and resumed her singular vigil.

Katherine started down the concrete steps. Grace held the railing and came down behind her in her high-heeled shoes and tight dress. Katherine decided she had gotten the better deal. She wore low-heeled shoes and a loose-fitting white blouse tucked into white pants. Anne had made sure that she was white everywhere, including the two ribbons in her hair.

After they crossed the street Katherine looked back at the motel. It resembled a decrepit make-believe castle, with trash-strewn streets surrounding all sides instead of stagnant moats. She climbed the stairway to Aurora and saw no one on the sidewalk on either side of the busy highway. A concrete barrier in the center prevented any cars from turning, and the cars drove by at fifty miles an hour after crossing the bridge. Leaving Katherine behind, Grace took off at a rapid pace toward 39th Street, where they were supposed to meet Parker.

"Slow down," Katherine said. "You look like you're trying to catch the bus."

Grace stopped and turned around, surprised that Katherine had stopped her. Katherine walked slowly toward her to catch up. Her heels touched the sidewalk and her weight rolled slowly up onto her toes before she stepped forward, as if she had forever to get to the corner. She turned her head slightly toward the street, but not enough to be obviously looking.

"Where did you learn how to do that?" Grace asked.

"I've been watching the ladies on Pike Street," Katherine said. "See, you're not going anywhere. You're just walking and waiting. You've got the strut down pretty well, though."

"I don't have anything down," Grace said. "It's these shoes. You either move your hips or you break your knees. I'm going to get cramps in my legs wearing these things."

They passed a two-story office building that had a stairway on both ends of the second floor landing and an empty parking lot in front. Beyond it was a one-story building with a big sign next to the sidewalk showing a real estate agent smiling with white shining teeth. There were no trees to create shadows on this block—no trees and no people—and her shadow scattered in all directions as she passed from the arc of one street lamp to the next.

A car slowed down as it passed them. The driver did not

turn his head, but she could tell he was looking. They were still only halfway down the block, and he would have to wait for them if he turned the corner. He didn't turn. Katherine moved closer to the street on the paved-over space between the sidewalk and the curb and let her purse dangle close to the ground.

A blue Ford station wagon slowed as it passed. Katherine bent down to look at the driver. The car turned at the corner and stopped, and she walked toward it with more speed. Katherine looked over her shoulder several times before arriving at the corner.

Sergeant Parker reached across the car and rolled down the window on the passenger's side. Katherine stopped a few feet away from the car. Parker leaned toward the open window.

"Any problems?" he asked.

"One car slowed down," Katherine said, "but it didn't stop." She moved a step closer to the window.

"We'll play this game right from the start," Parker said. "We don't know who might be watching. I'll take out my wallet and look for money. Then you get in. Smile though. Don't forget that smile."

The sergeant leaned forward and removed his wallet from his back pocket. He showed them a dollar bill.

"It takes two bills," Katherine said. She looked back at Grace, smiled and transferred the smile to Sergeant Parker. He fished out another bill from his wallet. The second was a five-dollar bill.

"That's better," Katherine said. She reached through the window and took the money from his hand.

Katherine straightened, looked around one more time, and got into the front seat. Grace crawled into the back, and Katherine handed her the five-dollar bill.

"You're going to give me my money back, aren't you?" he asked.

Katherine turned and looked into the backseat. "What do you think, Grace?"

"Nope."

"Smile, Sergeant," Katherine said. "Somebody might be watching."

The sergeant smiled as he put his station wagon in gear and drove downhill. He turned at the next corner and headed for the motel. The woman beneath the trees was still pacing, and Katherine saw her face as they went by. She could not have been eighteen years old.

The sergeant parked beside their Thunderbird. Katherine noticed one new car in the lot parked close to the manager's office. From habit she noted the license plate number, Washington ORK 896, and the make of car, a dark green Oldsmobile.

Grace led the way up the stairs with Sergeant Parker next. They didn't talk among themselves. A man laughed in a room below them, and Katherine looked down toward the laughter.

A single lamp between the double beds lit their room, and the air conditioner fan masked any noise. Sergeant Parker put his ear against the wall that separated their room from the next one.

"Anybody next door?" he asked softly.

Katherine shook her head as she sat on one of the double beds. Grace sat beside her and removed her shoes. Sergeant Parker moved a chair over to the bed and sat down in front of them. He checked his watch.

"How did it go checking in?" he asked. "Did the clerk seem suspicious of you?"

"You mean Elvis?" Grace asked. "I don't know. I couldn't get past the smirk and sideburns. What do you think, Katherine?"

"I'm pretty sure he didn't make us, if that's what you mean," Katherine said. "In fact, I'd say cops were the last thing he had on his mind."

"Friendly, huh?" Parker asked.

"Yes, friendly," Katherine said. "I don't think he's the one going after boys."

"Did you see anybody else while you were checking in?" Parker asked.

"No," Katherine said.

"All right. Keep your eyes open. I figure I'll stay about half an hour and then leave." His voice remained just above a whisper. "We'll change the time a little with each guy. You can send a few of them out in ten minutes, especially the ones you don't like. Make them your quickies. We'll vary the time on everything, how long you're here with the tricks, how long it takes for you to get picked up, how long you wait in here after they leave. Tonight we'll come back to this room two more times. The last time, we'll pick you up and call it a night.

"Lieutenant Vick is in the house across the street. He's watching the motel. We've got a car with two officers hidden in a driveway across the street from you on Aurora. They'll have you in view all the time you're up there, and they can get to you in a hurry if you need them. They'll take down the license numbers of any cars that stop or look interested. I know you don't want to stay here, but you should think about that again. This routine will be okay for a day or two. It'll look like you found a trick who is taking you some other place, but it's not going to look right very long."

He pushed on the mattress and looked around the room as though he were the one who was going to stay. "This isn't so bad. I've been in worse places. We can get you extra time off to make up for it if you change your minds. Of course, who knows how long we'll work this operation? It's taking a lot of people. We have to come up with something pretty fast or bag the whole thing. The old lady across the street is already driving Lieutenant Vick nuts. When I leave here, I'm going over there to replace him."

"Aren't you the lucky guy," Katherine said.

"I don't mind. I'd rather be doing this than setting up a two-bit gambling raid in Chinatown or rousting whores on Pike Street. I know you don't like this, but I wish I could be in your place."

"You might look real cute in this dress," Grace said.

Sergeant Parker smiled. There was even an extra dash of color in his cheeks.

"That's a real nice shirt, though," Katherine said. "We wouldn't want you to change."

Sergeant Parker looked at the brightly colored Hawaiian shirt he was wearing beneath his windbreaker. "My wife gave it to me for my birthday. She's determined we're going to Hawaii for our anniversary in December, and she's been giving me little reminders whenever she can. I thought it would make me look like a tourist out on the town."

"Oh, it does," Grace said. "You look like you're ready for a good time."

"I think you should go," Katherine said.

Sergeant Parker checked his watch. When he looked back to Katherine, she saw that he was confused. She hadn't meant to confuse him.

"I've only been here ten minutes," he said.

"To Hawaii," Katherine said. "I think you should go to Hawaii, you and your wife."

"Oh, I see," he said, but then he shook his head as if he didn't. "I'm going to tell you straight out that this is new to me. I've worked with women officers a half dozen times as prostitute decoys, but that's it. From what you said, Officer Murphy, we didn't do a professional job when you worked with us before, and I've been thinking about that. When the women officers come in, they're uncomfortable and we're uncomfortable, and sometimes both sides make little jokes that they probably shouldn't make. I hope it's not more than that, but I suppose it could be.

"I think we can do some good work here, but we all have a ways to go. Do you know what my wife wanted to know when I told her about this? 'Are they pretty?' That's what she asked me. She works in an office and supervises more people than I do, and I don't ask her if the men in her office are good-looking. What am I supposed to say? 'No, they're ugly as hell. That's why we think they'll make good prostitutes.'

"Now, I've told these guys tonight, every one of them,

that I expect them to act professionally. We've got somebody going around raping and strangling kids and dumping
them in the garbage. I don't want any jokes. I don't want
this operation messed up. Anyway, that's how I see it. You
think I'm off base on any of this, you tell me, but tell me
first. Fair enough?"

It was fair. And honest. What Katherine wouldn't give
for more of that. When Sergeant Parker got up to leave,
thirty minutes after arriving, he told them to wait fifteen
or twenty minutes and then head out to the street again.
He suggested that they mess up the beds and make it look
like the room was used in case somebody sneaked in while
they were out.

Katherine got up first, pulled the covers off the other
bed, and inspected the sheets. She turned the pillows over
and inspected them, too.

"Find anything crawling there?" Grace asked.

"No."

"These shoes are giving me blisters," Grace said. "What
if I had to chase somebody? I don't care what anyone says.
I'm not wearing them tomorrow."

Chapter 24

Daniel wanted to leave, but Mary wanted to play with the new doll Rudy had bought her. She hung a blanket over a chair in their bedroom and made a house beneath it.

"You can bring the doll with you," he said.

"Rudy said we had to stay here."

"He's sleeping. He won't wake up if we're quiet."

Daniel could never guess what Rudy wanted. Sometimes Rudy told them they couldn't leave. Sometimes he made them leave and go to the park across the street and wait until he came for them. There was nothing to do at that park, but they couldn't go to the locks or someplace interesting because Rudy would get mad if they did. Sometimes Rudy left them without saying where he was going. Daniel didn't mind when Rudy left them alone.

Daniel wished they could go with their mother to work. He thought they could help in the kitchen or sweep out the bar, but his mother said it was against the law for kids to go there. A bar wasn't safe for kids, she said. Sometimes he thought, his mother wanted to get away from him and Mary because they just caused problems. Problems and problems. Daniel didn't want to be a problem. Sometimes he didn't want to be anything.

"I'll make you a better house if you help me find some wood," Daniel said.

Mary stuck her head out of the house she had made with the blanket.

"Will it have a door?" she asked.

He thought about that. He remembered the door in their old house that went out to the yard. He liked to go out there and climb the apple tree that grew apples no one could eat. His father said they should plant a tree that was good for something, but he never did. The tree was just the right size for climbing—not so big that you got hurt if you fell, but big enough for you to get off the ground and hide in the branches.

"I can make a door," he said, "and we'll get a tree for the backyard."

She came out from under the blanket.

"You can't put a tree in here."

Daniel closed the door to their bedroom and sat down on the bed. He didn't feel good, but he still wanted to leave.

"We can get a little tree," he said. "They grow everywhere."

"A real one?" She was excited by that idea. She explained to her doll what they were going to do and wrapped the doll in a small blanket to protect her from the cold. It was snowing outside, she told the doll. The wind was blowing a hundred miles an hour. They had to find the tree before it froze, or they wouldn't have anything to eat all winter.

Daniel waited for her to finish her story.

"We have to be quiet," he said. "If the bears hear our footsteps, they'll come after us and eat us."

Mary's doll had begun to cry. "Shhh," she told it. "We'll be okay." Then she hugged the doll close to her and stuck out her hand for Daniel.

He led her down the stairs, one at a time, with each creaking noise sounding like an explosion in the storm. It was only a game, he told himself. Rudy was asleep upstairs. He would sleep through anything after he took his medicine.

Mary forgot about the snowstorm when they got outside.

She released his hand, ran over to the tree planted in the sidewalk, and bent down to look for small trees in the dirt around it. She told her doll to look for trees.

"Is this a tree?" she asked. "Is this?"

"Those are just weeds," he said.

He looked down the street that went past the Bell Tower. He didn't see the police car, but Officer Murphy might have parked farther down where he couldn't see. He wasn't sure what he would do if he did see the car. Maybe Officer Murphy would see him and know what to do even if he didn't say anything. How could she do that? Nobody could see.

"Let's go this way," he said. "Sometimes there's wood beside the grocery store."

Mary jumped up from the tree and ran toward the corner. Daniel followed behind her. He hoped he wouldn't have to run after her. She stopped by herself, but he wished she wouldn't run right up to the edge. While they waited for the light, she jumped up and down as if there was something exciting waiting for her across the street. He didn't feel good enough to jump. He hurt inside. He wondered if Officer Murphy had gotten the cookies.

DON'T WALK stayed red for a long time. They had to cross the narrow street in front of their apartment before they could turn and cross Market Street. People were standing in line to go into the restaurant on the corner. He knew they were watching him. He took Mary's hand, held it tighter, and waited for the WALK signal.

Mary wanted to run as soon as she saw the green light, but he wouldn't let her go. A car came late and rushed by them so fast that he could feel the wind behind it. The driver looked straight down the road and didn't see them. Mary put her hand over her mouth as if she had said something she shouldn't have said, but she hadn't said anything. He didn't say anything either, but they both understood what could have happened. Mary waited until he took the first step before starting across the street.

When they came to the place where the two streets met

beside the Bell Tower, Daniel could see all the way down the Ballard street. The police car wasn't there. The tall lady said that Officer Murphy would come back soon, but she still wasn't there. She wasn't there last night, and she wasn't there again tonight. He wondered if Officer Murphy would ever come again. Lots of times people said things that weren't true, but he remembered her smile. When she bent down to help him with his torn sack, he had forgotten to be afraid—just for a moment. He was sure she would come back.

A stranger was outside the grocery store. Daniel didn't want to walk past anybody he didn't know, but he had to choose which way to go. Mary didn't pull him in any direction. The car had scared her, and she waited for him to decide. She held her doll close to keep it warm. He could walk down the Ballard street, or he could turn around and go back. He didn't want to go back, and he didn't want to walk down the street past the stranger at the store. If he went in the other direction where his mother worked in the bar, he wouldn't be able to go inside. If he walked straight ahead down to the railroad tracks, it would get dark before they could come back. It was too late to see the trains. It was too late to see Officer Murphy. It was too late to go anywhere. He led Mary into the tower beneath the big bell and walked around and around the circle.

Chapter 25

By midnight on the second night of their plainclothes
assignment, Katherine was convinced that their cha-
rade on Aurora was a waste of time. They had not seen
anything that could not be as easily seen from the stakeout
across the street. Bob or Bill or Boyd, some name like that,
waited for his time to pass in the chair positioned at the
table across from Katherine. Grace had propped herself up
with pillows on one of the beds and was reading a magazine.
She listened to the police radio through an earphone. A rock
and roll song played on the cheap plastic radio on the
nightstand between the beds. They left the television off.

The Vice officers had been well instructed. They did not
joke. They did not laugh. They did not smile. They barely
talked. Vice had run out of available men to pose as customers and planned to repeat everybody with different cars.
Parker would be next in a green Plymouth.

Katherine and Grace had agreed to stay in the motel
room through the night, one night only, although it seemed
unlikely that it would make any difference. They had not
even seen a prostitute out on the streets, except for themselves. Certainly there were no boys around. The streets
had been eerily quiet, without police cars even. Lieutenant
Vick had asked the district patrol cars to avoid the area.

The Vice Squad detective left, and Katherine heard his

footsteps on the concrete steps. She got up and locked the door behind him.

"There's a kegger in Golden Gardens," Grace said, adjusting the volume to her earphone. "Want to go?"

"It would be more exciting than sitting around here."

"You sure got those boys to shut up."

"I know. Maybe that wasn't such a good idea."

"It's fine. Parker will be glad to hear his men are such gentlemen."

Grace pulled the radio plug out of her ear and turned off the radio.

"How many more customers do we have?" she asked.

"Parker, and then one more," Katherine said. "Are you going to sleep in that bed?"

"I don't know. If I do, I'm not getting under the covers."

"How long do you want to do this?" Katherine asked.

"It's not as bad as I thought it would be. How about you?"

"I guess we'll see how it goes tonight."

Grace looked at her watch and stuffed the police radio into the bottom of her purse. She walked over to the mirror above the dresser and applied fresh maroon lipstick. She smacked her lips, faced Katherine, and thrust her hips to the side. She wore new tight-legged jeans with low-heeled shoes.

"How much would you pay for this?" she asked.

"You're asking the wrong person," Katherine said.

"Let's ask Parker, then, and get this over with."

Katherine followed Grace down the stairs and past their Thunderbird. There were three cars and an old pickup truck in the parking lot, the same as earlier in the night. All four vehicles had Washington plates. They were silent as they crossed the parking lot toward the street that would take them up to Aurora.

She could tell by the way Grace changed her pace that they saw the man at the same moment. Katherine pulled her purse to the side and stuck her right hand into the knit bag where she found the grip of her .38 revolver. The man was smoking a cigarette beneath overgrown bushes at the edge of the parking lot. From where he stood it was too dark to see his face.

"Going for another walk?" he asked as they approached.

Katherine recognized his voice and withdrew her hand from the bag. She stopped ten feet away from him. He was the Elvis impersonator who had checked them in at the motel.

"What's it to you?" Katherine asked. She wanted her voice to sound disdainful, and it was easily accomplished.

"Nothing. Just asking. I've been watching you, that's all."

"So watch somebody else," Grace said.

"Hey, take it easy," he said. "I don't mean no offense."

"What do you mean, then?" Katherine asked. She tried to take a little of the edge off her voice.

He stepped away from the bushes, and his face became illuminated by the streetlight.

"Just passing the time, talking a little, you know." He pulled air through the cigarette, and the glow increased. He ran his fingers through his greasy hair and raised the cigarette in front of him. It gave him an inspiration. "Would you ladies like a cigarette?"

"We don't smoke," Katherine said.

"I noticed your license plate. You must be from Nevada."

"It doesn't matter where we're from," Katherine said.

"Sure, that's right. Everything okay with your room?" he asked.

"We've seen worse," Katherine said.

"If you're interested, I could arrange something. Say, knock off the rent for a day or two, if you know what I mean."

"We already paid for the room."

"Through tomorrow," he said. "I thought maybe you'd want to stay a little longer."

"Why would we want to do that?" Grace asked.

"It looks like you have lots of company."

"And maybe you want to trade a little company for a room. Is that the deal?"

"Could be."

He seemed to be gaining confidence. After taking the last drag on his cigarette, he tossed it onto the blacktop and walked toward them with smoke pouring out of his nostrils. Katherine's right hand moved slowly back toward her bag, and Grace moved another step away from Katherine.

"We don't plan to stay in this dump long enough to make up for any little something you could arrange," Grace said.

He stopped a few feet away and looked back and forth over the separation between the two women.

"I could set you up with some people. Make it worth your time."

"You want to pimp for us?" Katherine asked. "What are you going to do, protect us, give us everything we need, take all our money? Do we look like fools who need a pimp?"

"I know people who would appreciate you. Most of the girls here have been on the street too long. You girls have some class. These people would like that."

"What people?" Grace asked.

"Business people."

"Who was it last time was going to set us up?" Katherine asked Grace. "What was that guy's name? Billie Ray or Ray Billie. He checked us out and never showed up again. What's your name? Don't tell me you're another Ray Billie."

"These people are different," the man said, without telling her his name. "They'll pay up front."

"How much?" Katherine asked.

"Depends. How old are you, if you don't mind me asking?" He looked at Katherine whether she minded or not.

No, she didn't mind. Just keep talking, she thought to herself. She heard Anne Smith's instructions to the hairdresser. "Make her young. Do something that makes her look like a girl." Katherine reached for one of the short pigtails on the back of her head and twisted it with her fingers.

"How old do I need to be?" she asked.

She looked at Grace to see how she had done.

"That was good," Grace said.

The motel clerk nodded in agreement and shook out another cigarette from his package. He lit the cigarette with a match, sucked the smoke into his lungs Hollywood style, and threw the match into the shrubbery.

"I could tell you ladies were different when you checked in," he said. "Most girls here work alone. I wonder what you do when you get the guy up there."

"You got some fantasy?" Katherine asked. "Two at a time. Salt and pepper. Is that what you want?"

When he grinned in reply, Katherine saw that he was missing a tooth. She could smell his body.

"Anybody wants us together," Grace said, "it's two hundred an hour. More for any kinky stuff. You want a cut, it's above that."

"No problem."

"Why did you ask how old she was?" Grace asked. "You worried about jailbait?"

"I'm not worried. They ain't either."

"We don't plan to stay here long," Grace said. "We're on our way to Vancouver. If they want to talk, they better talk soon. And we don't want anybody to come knocking on our door either. You call us before you come. Make sure we're not busy. You understand what I mean?"

Katherine doubted he understood anything that Grace said. He didn't seem able to look above her chin.

"Sure," he said. "How about that trade?"

"You got something to trade, we'll talk, but take a bath first. Come on, Shelly, let's go."

Grace turned her back on the motel clerk and headed for Aurora. Her hips moved even without the big shoes, and she held her head high. After she took a few steps, she turned back to the clerk. He had not moved an inch.

"And call," Grace said. "Don't forget to call."

Neither of them looked back to the motel until they crossed to the other side of the street. At that point they were close to the house from where the Vice Squad was watching them.

"What are you thinking?" Grace asked.

"I think you're getting the hang of this," Katherine said. "Maybe we'll stay another night after all."

"Do we push it, or do we just sit and wait?"

"I think we wait, but let's ask Parker. Finally we've got something to talk about."

They walked up the steps to the strip of Aurora between the underpass and the footbridge where they set up shop. A young girl in a tight dress watched them from across the concrete divider that ran down the center of the highway. She was the first prostitute they had seen that night. She scowled at them and walked toward the bridge. She was too heavy for the dress.

"I don't think she's happy to see us," Katherine said.

"How old do you think she is?"

"Sixteen, seventeen. I wonder if Elvis tried to make her a deal, too."

A car slowed on the girl's side of Aurora, and the driver leaned down to look at her but then sped up and headed south across the bridge. The girl looked after the car and continued walking in its draft.

"That was a no, I guess," Katherine said.

"It's like standing against the wall during a school dance," Grace replied.

"Don't tell me you want these cars to stop."

"No, but a slowdown now and then would be nice."

A car slowed just as Grace wished, and it was not Sergeant Parker. It was a small Chevrolet with a single man inside. The car turned the corner on 39th and stopped.

"Now look what you've done," Katherine said. "Let's walk the other way."

They turned away from the car as though they had not seen it and walked toward the bridge against oncoming traffic. They had not walked more than a few steps before a big sleek Buick stopped on the on-ramp at 38th Street. The car did not move after the traffic cleared. A third car on Aurora began slowing from the inside lane. Its right turn signal came on.

"Can you believe this?" Katherine asked.

"I do now," Grace said. "Look up there." She nodded toward the sky. "Now all the crazies will come out."

Katherine looked heavenward and saw what Grace meant. Emerging from an eastbound bank of clouds was the full moon reflecting light toward the bridge and toward Aurora.

With its turn signal flashing, the approaching car slowed to a few miles an hour. The driver leaned toward them, and Katherine saw Sergeant Parker's face through the window. She bent down to engage his eyes.

Parker turned onto 39th Street and stopped. The Chevrolet that had been there was gone. Katherine walked quickly in the direction of Parker's car. She looked back over her shoulder and saw the Buick creeping up on them. They were thirty feet from Parker, but the other car was so close that Katherine heard the automatic door lock release. The passenger window lowered remotely. She saw that the man was wearing a shiny suit. Five feet to his car, twenty to Parker's. His hand gestured to the door, spread and opened so that she saw a gold ring on his finger. He bent toward the passenger window, and she saw the confident expression on his face. He knew he was offering a higher bid.

Katherine fluttered her fingers toward Parker in a friendly wave. He was wearing a baseball cap with a sports logo. He didn't look like he could afford a hot dog at the game much less a tumble with two high-priced players. Five feet from Parker's car, she bent down to the level of his window and smiled at him. Grace bent down with her. The Buick accelerated with a powerful roar.

"Jesus Christ," Katherine said, trying to hold her winning smile, "what took you so long?"

"I came by once," he said, "but you weren't here."

"Long story," she said. "Don't you look like the big spender."

She got into the back, and Grace sat down in the front seat. Parker checked his mirror to make sure that they had drawn no one else around the corner and eased into the driving lane.

"What held you up?" Parker asked as they turned the corner and headed toward the motel.

"Elvis," Grace said.

Parker turned and looked at her.

"The clerk or motel manager, whatever he is, was waiting out by the parking lot. He wanted to exchange some favors for free rent."

"What did you tell him?"

"Grace told him to take a bath," Katherine said from the backseat.

"Oh, there's more to it than that," Grace said.

They entered the parking lot of the motel. As they walked up the stairs Katherine had the unwelcome feeling of being watched, even though they wanted to be watched. They had always expected it, but the motel clerk's interest made it certain. From the railing on the second floor, she looked toward the office but saw nothing that proved her suspicion.

Light glowed at the edges of the heavy curtains in their room just as it did from another room at the end of the walkway where the L-shaped motel turned right. Grace unlocked the door and entered the room. Parker followed her inside, and Katherine came last and closed the door. She pushed the lock button on the doorknob and turned up the volume on the rock and roll radio station.

"Tell me about this guy," Parker said.

"He said he had people he could set us up with," Grace said. "He wanted to know how old Katherine was."

"What did you tell him?"

"I asked him how old I needed to be," Katherine said. "He wasn't worried about it. He was hoping I was young."

"Bingo. Anne was right. She said she could make you look like a girl. How old are you, anyway?"

"How old do I need to be?"

They had one last trick planned for the night. They were to look for Lieutenant Vick driving a red MG convertible. Parker said it was Lieutenant Vick's pride and joy, and he had offered it reluctantly as their meager source of cars ran dry. It didn't have a backseat, and Katherine and Grace would have to cram into the one in front. "Whatever you do," Parker said as he was leaving, "don't scratch the damn thing."

It was almost two in the morning, and the bars were closing. Katherine watched the spectacle from the sidewalk as cars sped down the highway. The quiet of the early night was like a worn-out joke. A horn blared twice from a pickup truck, and the passenger stuck his head out the window and howled. The truck swerved from lane to lane but didn't slow down.

"I'm staying away from the curb," Katherine said. "Half these people are drunk."

"We should have skipped this last one," Grace said.

"That's what I'm thinking."

The moon had slipped farther to the west. A huge distant ethereal ring now circled it. Her father would declare there was moisture in the air and that rain was coming. It might be pollution, she thought.

Walking toward 39th Street, they stayed as far from the curb on Aurora as they could, acting more like careful adults than tantalizing streetwalkers. When they were close to 39th Street, too close to the corner to turn the other way, a large black car slowed on Aurora, turned the corner onto 39th, and stopped. Katherine heard Grace swear.

The man in the passenger's seat looked straight ahead. His arm rested on the window opening, and his fingers tapped the curve of the door like he was playing a musical instrument. The muscles of his tanned forearm rippled with the rhythm of the taps. He expected them to approach without effort from him.

"Careful," Grace murmured without moving her lips.

"Hey," Katherine said softly as though she didn't want to startle him.

He slowly turned his head. "Hey," he said back to her. He had eyes that looked cruel even when he smiled. It wasn't really a smile. It was a bare recognition of their existence.

Katherine bent down to get a look at the driver. She didn't intend to move any closer to the car door. Ten feet was close enough.

"You ladies looking for a ride?" he asked.

She tried to estimate his age. At first she thought the passenger was a least thirty-five, but now she wasn't sure. He might have been younger. The driver was certainly older.

"How do we know you're not cops?" Katherine asked.

He snorted his contempt. "The same way we know you're not."

The driver handed the passenger money, which he folded together and stuck in the crack between the door and car frame. Showing was a hundred-dollar bill, but there was another bill inside.

"We don't go with two guys," Katherine said.

"Why not? Two of you, two of us. My partner is a big old teddy bear. He wants the black one. I'll take you."

Katherine smiled for a reason this man would not understand. It would be a risk to their cover to arrest them, but there was something about this man that made her think the arrest would be worth it. She turned to Grace to see if Grace shared her suspicion. Grace had already moved her hand to the top of her purse. Katherine turned back to the man and moved a step closer. She put both of her hands behind her back and positioned her knit bag between them. She bent forward at the waist so that her pigtails dropped over her cheeks. She stuck her right hand into her bag as she smiled encouragement and found the grip of her revolver, right where she knew it would be.

"I'll get in the backseat with you," Katherine said to the man. She wanted him out of the car. "Ginger likes to be in front."

He hesitated a moment, but the driver nodded. Katherine turned her head slightly to make sure Grace was ready. She hoped their backup across the street was ready, and she looked for the driveway where she knew the backup car was parked.

She saw the red MG instead.

Its turn signal was flashing, and it was slowing as it approached their intersection. She saw Lieutenant Vick behind the windshield; the convertible top was down. The lieutenant pulled into the curb lane and slowed more. Another car, coming fast from the bridge, moved to the inside lane. Katherine could see the accident before it happened. With 39th Street blocked by the black car, Lieutenant Vick began moving back into the street, intending to go by. He didn't see the car coming up on him. The other driver's reaction was slow, and he didn't brake until his car clipped the left rear fender of Lieutenant Vick's MG. The sports car spun neatly around, its wheels screaming shrilly as they skidded sideways on the blacktop, and barely missed the rear end of the car stopped on 39th. The car that hit the MG pulled sharply to the curb and bounced over the sidewalk a few feet from Katherine and Grace who jumped away from it. The car grazed the bumper of the parked black car, hit the curb on the north side of 39th Street, and bounced to a stop. The MG finished its ninety-degree spin against the concrete barricade that divided Aurora.

The big car squealed away with such speed that the force of acceleration slammed the passenger's head into the headrest. Grace ran south on the sidewalk, waving her hands wildly in the air to stop oncoming traffic. Katherine ran north to see if she could help the lieutenant. After one car swerved past him dangerously close, he put his sports car into gear and crossed over to the curb with the rear fender scraping against the wheel. He parked in front of the car that hit him.

The other driver got out of his car and weaved back and forth beside his door. "What happened?" he asked. Katherine pulled him over to the sidewalk. Grace was doing all she could to slow down traffic, but the oncoming drivers were more distracted than warned.

"What happened?" the man asked again. He was obviously drunk. She led him over to a wire fence that he could use for support. She saw plainclothes cops running toward them on the sidewalk on the other side of the street. Katherine intercepted Lieutenant Vick before he got to the other driver.

"Are you okay?" she asked.

"I'm okay," he said. "Did you see what happened?"

"Yes."

"That damn black car was in the road, and I had to go around."

"I know. This other guy was moving into your lane when you did that."

"Damn," Lieutenant Vick said. The expression he bore said that he knew it was his fault. "Is he hurt?"

"He's drunk," she said.

"No kidding," Lieutenant Vick said. His face brightened. "And he's not hurt?"

"No."

"I'll get a patrol car here to handle the paper," Lieutenant Vick said. "You and your partner get back to the motel before we blow your cover."

"Some of your guys are across the street."

Lieutenant Vick saw the two officers who were waiting for a clearing in the traffic before daring the crossing. Lieutenant Vick waved them away. Grace was already heading back.

"You can list us as witnesses if you have to," Katherine said.

"I think we'll keep this as simple as we can," he said.

"Good idea," she said.

Katherine crossed back over 39th Street and met Grace on the corner. She saw blue lights flashing on the far side of the bridge. She took Grace by the arm and led her down the hill toward the King Arthur Motel. The accident had blocked out the image of the two men in the black car until she noticed the folded paper bills lying in the gutter just past the spot where the car had been. She picked up the money and unfolded the bills as they walked away from the accident. There was a hundred-dollar bill on the outside and a single greenback within.

Chapter 26

Dear Mom and Dad, Katherine wrote.

Grace had fallen asleep on top of her bed with her shoes on. In another hour it would be Katherine's turn to sleep, but she was reverting to her old night schedule, and unless she began to feel tired, she would let Grace sleep longer. She listened to police radio through the earpiece. The accident on Aurora had been cleared away as well as the debris from other revelers that had scattered over the North Precinct after the bars closed. Shift change was approaching, and there were stretches of silence broken only by the distant sound of Aurora traffic.

I can't wait to see the new baby colt. Is it a boy or girl? Have you named it yet?

Her mother had written about her father's plan for the colt. Her brother, John, and his wife were expecting a baby in the fall, and by the time their baby was old enough to ride, her father reasoned that the colt would be mature and safe like Silver was for them. Katherine suspected that the plan came later to justify the colt since the colt had been conceived first, but her father always had his own interpretation of events.

Since Silver is the grandmother, I have to believe her offspring will make a great horse for kids. But I wonder who will train it? Did John ever tell you how he would coax

Susie and me to ride with him? Then he would guide Silver under the clothesline and wipe us off. We never saw it coming. Or he would take us out into the pasture and ride up and down the gullies until we slid off her back. We should have pulled him with us, but he held on to the mane, and we would let go and tumble into the sandburs. We were so dumb that we believed him every time he told us he would behave. Your son is not trustworthy. Don't let him train the colt.

The streetlights provided a glow through the window curtains sufficient for her to see what she was writing. She sat at the table beneath the window where the curtains had not been opened since their first moments in the room. Dirty finger marks on the wall above the table and the knit purse from Anne Smith blurred from her sight as she thought about a different place.

How tall is the wheat? Have you had enough rain? Are the pastures green yet? I'll bet the wild roses will soon be blooming along the fence at the old farm. I can see them now. Susie and I used to collect the pink buds when we played house in the granary. We wouldn't let John play if we were mad at him.

You should see Mrs. Rabin's flowers. She already has English daisies, primroses, peonies, and more that I can't remember. Dale brought up an armload of peonies yesterday, and I have a bunch of them in a vase on my kitchen table. I wish they would last longer. They're like the roses we put in the peanut butter jars out in the granary. They don't like being cut. Dandelions lasted much longer.

Her mother disliked the telephone. They had been on a party line too many years for her to feel comfortable having a conversation there. She had the feeling people were listening. Katherine suspected that there was more to it than that. Her mother wrote long letters instead, sometimes two a week, and Katherine heard her mother's voice better through letters than the telephone.

I think I may have fallen in love. (over)

It was a clever bit of luck to have it as the last line on the page. She smiled as she imagined her mother's outburst, turning the letter over and slapping it down on the Formica top of the kitchen table.

His name is Daniel, and he's eight years old. He has a little sister named Mary, and he looks after her. He would never ride Silver under the clothesline if Mary were riding with him. He holds her hand like a little gentleman when they cross the street.

They live in an apartment in the area where I work, and we seem to run into each other quite often. His mother tends bar in one of the local taverns. There doesn't seem to be a father. Earlier this week I saw that he was carrying home groceries, and he told me he was going to make dinner for him and Mary. I told him that I wished somebody would make dinner for me, and he said he could do it. (Make sure John reads this letter.)

Grace and I have been working a special assignment (nothing exciting), so I haven't been in Ballard for a few days. Grace was at Rigmor's store at closing the other day, and Daniel brought in a bag of chocolate chip cookies he had made for me. He's only eight years old, and he has already learned the way to a woman's heart. Now I have to think what to do in return. Any ideas?

She wondered if he would like the zoo. There was a miniature train that ran around the grounds, and she was sure Daniel would like that. Maybe it would be wiser to just buy him a book. He could take a book with him wherever he went.

There's a full moon tonight with a big halo around it.

Before she could ask her father if that meant anything about rain, she heard a car engine that was too close to ignore. It rumbled in a stationary position and then stopped. She pried open the curtain where the two ends met in the center, but she couldn't see below the railing. She pushed her chair back, picked up the portable radio with the earpiece still stuck in her ear, and retreated to the corner of the window. Headlights went dark from a long black car that parked next to the office. An interior light came on in the car, and two men got out. She could see only their silhouettes, but it was enough. The driver hoisted a bag over his shoulder.

"Grace," she whispered urgently. "Grace."

Grace sat up abruptly in the bed. She looked around in confusion for Katherine's voice.

"Over here."

Grace bolted from the bed and joined Katherine at the window. Katherine pulled the curtain another inch from the wall.

"That black car just pulled into the lot," she said. "It's the same two men who tried to pick us up on Aurora. They went into the office."

"What time is it?" Grace asked.

"A little after three."

"Anybody else with them?"

"No."

"What are they doing here?" Grace asked.

"I don't know," Katherine said. "I'll call Parker." She brought the radio up to her mouth and keyed the mike. "Car 209 to Car 201," she said as evenly as she could.

"Go ahead, 209," Parker said.

"We have activity in the area," Katherine said.

"Affirmative," Parker replied. "We have it in view."

"Parker saw it, too," she told Grace. She reached inside her bag and found her Smith & Wesson revolver. Carefully withdrawing it, she pointed the barrel at the floor, popped open the cylinder, and felt the six cartridge ends of the .38-caliber shells with her finger. She pulled back the curtain an inch until she could see the office door again.

Katherine felt Grace's hand on her shoulder as they looked through the slotted view of the parking lot. A light went out in the office. The outside window of the office was now completely dark.

Katherine pulled back slightly from their window. "Did you see that?" she whispered.

"Yes," Grace whispered in her ear.

"I don't have a good feeling about this," Katherine said.
"Neither do I. Look."

Three figures emerged from the darkened office and stood in the shadow of the overhanging deck. They walked beneath the deck, past the parked black car, and disappeared from sight.

"They're heading this way," Katherine said.

Parker was on the radio alerting her to the movement. She brought the radio close to her lips and keyed the microphone. "209 receives," she said softly.

"Parker is watching them," she told Grace. "Do you suppose these are the businessmen Elvis was talking about?"

"How would they have known we were on Aurora?"

"Maybe he called them."

"He's not calling us," Grace said.

"What do you want to do if they come to our room?" Katherine asked.

"Nothing," Grace said. "Let's wait for them to do something."

"They might come in anyway. We'd better split up. I'll stay here by the window," Katherine said.

"I'll get behind the bed," Grace said. "If they come through the door, I'll shine my flashlight on them. Look for their hands."

Katherine felt two pats on her shoulder as Grace hurried away. Grace picked up her flashlight and gun off the nightstand and crouched down behind the far bed. While Katherine backed into the corner, away from the window, she saw Grace point her unlit flashlight toward the door.

"201 to 209," she heard through her earpiece. "Three men are going up the stairs to your location. Do you receive, 209?" Parker asked. His voice was tight with urgency.

Katherine clicked the mike twice in silent acknowledgement as she saw shadows pass the window. She pointed her gun toward the door, raised her left hand with the radio still in its grasp, and used the radio to support her gun.

There were no voices and there was no knock, but she

heard a scratching noise at the doorknob. Of course, she thought, Elvis has a key. Parker was on the radio again, telling her he was moving in. She had fastened the chain lock, but that lock was anchored to the molding with a few short screws. It was worthless.

The chain secured a burglary charge, however, even though she was sure they were not breaking in to steal anything. It was burglary no matter how they came in, but if they broke through the chain, it was absolutely clear—a felony, grounds to shoot if necessary.

The door opened slowly until the chain halted the swing. She heard whispering outside and then saw a hand reach through the door and feel the chain. The hand disappeared, and the door crashed open.

Grace turned on her flashlight, and Katherine screamed, "Police officers! Freeze!"

"Freeze! Police!" Grace echoed.

The men bunched up at the doorway. Elvis held the doorknob, and the other two were behind him. Katherine stepped forward, shouting her cold instructions, and pointed her gun at the second man's head. He had nothing in his hands. The third man bolted from the door and took off running. She couldn't worry about him.

"Hands above your head!" she shouted. Her attention was focused on the second man. In the black car he had been the passenger who had made all the offers. He was not offering anything now. The doorway behind him was unobstructed. He could run like his partner, but first he would have to release his eyes from the gun barrel that was three feet from his head. He raised his hands.

"Keep your hands up," Katherine said. She was no longer shouting. "Turn around. Put your hands on the wall."

Elvis already had his hands above his head and was turning to the wall. The second man was slower to respond, but he finally turned, leaned forward, and put his hands high on the wall.

Grace came up beside her with her gun and flashlight pointed toward Elvis. Katherine heard Parker shouting after the man who had run. Katherine flipped on the light switch beside the door. She pulled the earphone from her ear and pulled the cord out of the radio.

"Car 209," she said. "Come in, Radio."

"Go ahead, 209," Radio said. His voice filled the room.

"We have two burglary suspects in custody at the King Arthur Motel just north of the Aurora Bridge. One suspect has fled. Send us backup. We are plainclothes. Car 201 is in the area with us."

The chief dispatcher came on the air and broadcast the call. "All units responding to the King Arthur Motel switch to F6. Keep the air clear. Repeat. All units responding to the King Arthur Motel switch to F6. Car 209, you have units on the way. Advise of your situation."

"Car 209," Katherine said, "we have two suspects under control in room 15 of the King Arthur Motel. Car 201 is pursuing the third suspect on foot. Car 201 is also plainclothes. Repeat. Car 201 is plainclothes."

As the chief dispatcher put out the information she had given him, she heard Parker again in the parking lot giving the third suspect the drill. Katherine moved closer to the doorway but kept her gun pointed on the second man.

"Car 201 to Radio." Parker was breathing heavily into his radio.

"Go ahead, 201."

"We have one suspect in custody. What is the status of Car 209?"

"Car 209 advises that they have two suspects under control in room 15," the chief dispatcher said. "Are all suspects in custody?"

"Murphy, are you okay up there?" Parker asked her directly on the radio.

"We're fine," she said. "Car 209 to Radio."

"Go ahead, 209."

"All suspects are in custody," she said. "Slow down the backup units."

Katherine heard the first patrol car roar into the parking lot.

"Let's get them cuffed," Katherine said. "This one first."

She was not worried about the motel manager. Grace had quickly frisked him, and he had shrunk into the wall and was struggling to hold himself upright. But the second man, who was a foot taller than she and twice as big, was paying too much attention to them. He was like a snake coiled and ready to strike. She established herself firmly behind him with her right foot between his legs, her gun pointed at his back, and her left hand just above his waist.

"I'm going to pat you down," she told him. "Spread your feet farther apart."

He started to turn his head.

"Don't turn around," she said. "Spread your feet out." She tapped his left heel with her shoe.

His hands inched down the wall as he slowly and reluctantly spread his legs.

Her gun in her right hand, she reached under his arm with her left and felt the unmistakable impression of a handgun beneath his jacket. His body tensed even more, but the tension was interrupted when she pressed her gun into his spine. "Don't move," she said through gritted teeth.

"He has a gun," she told Grace. "Cover me."

Grace put her left hand on the neck of the motel manager and pointed her gun toward the other man's head. She nodded at Katherine.

Katherine reached beneath his jacket and felt the square butt of an automatic. It was in a holster slung across his shoulders and anchored with another strap through his belt. She flipped the holster snap, grasped the gun butt firmly, and pulled it slowly and deliberately from the holster. From all the people she had frisked, this was the first time she had found a gun in a holster. She had found one stuffed in a man's pants, another hidden in a bag, and a few under car seats, but she had never found one carried professionally before.

Katherine pointed the man's automatic at the floor and handed it to Grace. Katherine frisked him thoroughly from top to bottom. He had no other weapons. She reached behind her and pulled her handcuffs out of the knit bag on top of the table. After stuffing the handcuffs into the waistband of her pants so that one cuff pressed against her skin and one cuff dangled outside, she reached under his coat and grabbed his belt from the back.

"Listen to me carefully," she said. "You're going to get on the floor exactly the way I tell you."

He started to look at her again. Another car screeched into the parking lot. He saw Grace's gun pointed at his head.

"Look at the wall," Grace said.

Katherine reasserted the contact between her gun barrel and his back, and her finger pressed tighter on the trigger where it had been throughout the search. He turned back to the wall. His body trembled as his coil began to unwind.

"Back up," she told him. He shuffled his feet backward, putting more of his weight on his arms. "More," she said. "Back up more." His feet shuffled back a few more inches. "Get on your knees. Keep your hands on the wall." He sank to his knees, his hands pushing futilely on the wall as they went down. "Back up more," she said. "More." He scraped his knees backward on the worn carpet. Two guns followed him. When he was stretched as far as he could without falling, she told him to lie flat on the floor. He lowered himself slowly to his stomach with his head tight against the wall. She put a knee into his back and told him to stretch his hands out to his sides.

She heard footsteps on the stairs and looked up to see Parker's face in the door. She waved for him to come in. Two patrol cops came behind him. For the first time since watching the men leave the motel office, the numbers and weight were on her side. From her waistband, she reached for her handcuffs and stuck her revolver where they had been. Then she grabbed the suspect's left hand, pulled it behind his back, and slapped one of the cuffs around his wrist. It could only ratchet a few clicks before it was tight. Parker knelt beside her and grabbed the man's right hand.

"He had a gun," Katherine said. "In a shoulder holster." She tapped her left side to show where the gun had been. "How about your guy?"

"No weapon. He had a movie camera."

Katherine stared at Parker for a moment as if she were trying to see the words he had said. Parker nodded that she had heard correctly and jerked the suspect's right hand back to meet the left. Katherine circled his right hand with the second cuff. The veins in the man's neck distended as though lying still required great exertion.

"You got nothing on me," he said.

Katherine squeezed the last cuff a few notches tighter and bent forward so that her face was close to his.

"I forgot to tell you," she said softly. "You're under arrest."

He spit to show his disdain, but the spit came nowhere close to her.

The two patrol officers who had followed Parker into the room handcuffed the motel manager while he stood against the wall. One of them removed the room key from the man's hand.

"I'll take that," Grace said.

She put the key in her pocket.

"It's my job to have that key," the manager said. "I didn't know you were cops."

The man on the floor flopped his head to the other side, scraping it against the wall as he moved, and faced the manager.

"Shut up," he said.

"Look, man, how was I supposed to know they were cops? You saw them, too."

"Keep your mouth shut," he hissed.

The manager recoiled in the grasp of the two patrol officers and shut his mouth.

"Get him out of here," Parker said to the patrol officers. "Put him in your car."

The patrol officers pulled the manager toward the door. The lead officer stepped over the legs of the other suspect lying prone on the floor and jerked the manager along with him. It was much closer than the manager wanted to get. The prone man twisted his head to the other side.

"Keep your mouth shut," he shouted again to the manager as the patrol officers guided him through the door.

"Hey, that's enough," Parker said. "You're the one ought to keep your mouth shut."

The man sneered with a closed mouth, showing he intended to do exactly that.

Grace still had the automatic in her hand, and she moved away from them. She disarmed the gun and dropped the shells onto the bed where she had been sleeping. Two more patrol officers appeared on each side of the doorway.

"Sergeant Parker, Vice Squad," Parker announced to them. His knees creaked as he stood up.

The two patrol officers came into the room. Katherine didn't know them, but she hadn't known the other two either. Although their blue uniforms were familiar and welcome, she must have looked strange to them—a young woman, a girl maybe, with her knee in the back of the handcuffed man. The younger of the two cops knelt down beside her and looked at her with questions he was not going to ask.

"Katherine Murphy," she said and extended her hand.

He took her hand and smiled. "Hank Riley. You working with Grace?"

"Two weeks and she gets me into this mess."

Hank Riley looked down at the handcuffed man who lay with his forehead frozen to the wall.

"Looks like this guy is in the mess, not you."

"Watch yourself with him," she said. "He was carrying a gun. We got him on a felony—burglary for now, but there might be more. Read him his rights when you get him in the car. Don't let him talk to his buddies down there." She nodded toward the parking lot.

"No problem. He won't be talking to anybody."

Katherine and Hank Riley stood together, lifted the suspect's arms, and pulled him to his feet. Riley quickly frisked the man again and headed him toward the door. Just as they were about to go through, the man stopped and looked back at Katherine. Riley shoved him roughly through the door and Riley's partner got a hand on him, too, but he delivered a message that she would not forget: It did not matter at all that she was a cop.

"You guys okay?" Parker asked. He was looking to Katherine for the answer.

She was still staring at the door.

"We're okay," she said.

"What the hell happened? Bernie Miles was with me across the street. As soon as we saw them at your door, we started coming. We didn't see what happened after that."

"They didn't knock," Katherine said. "The manager opened the door with a key, but we had the chain lock fastened. They broke it open anyway. The man with the gun and the one you got with the camera tried to pick us up earlier tonight on Aurora, just before Lieutenant Vick had the wreck. They were in the car stopped at the corner on 39th. The drunk hit the back bumper of their car when he came up on the curb. I recognized the car when they pulled in."

Katherine went over to the table and dumped out the contents of her bag. She found the folded hundred-dollar bill the man had offered, showed it to Parker, and then opened it to reveal the one-dollar bill inside.

"He stuck this in the car door above his window. We could see the hundred-dollar bill, and we could see that there was another bill behind it, but we couldn't see what it was. One buck. A hundred and one bucks. When Vick hit their car they took off, and the money dropped onto the road. I found it when we were leaving. If we got into their car, they didn't intend to pay anything."

She threw the money on the bed beside the bullets.

"Elvis must have called them," Grace said. "They were

the people he was talking about. You said the guy you caught had a movie camera?"

"Yeah. It was in his bag."

"Bastards," Grace said.

"We caught him running for his car," Parker said. "He's older than the suspect you arrested and didn't give us any trouble. This guy here is bad news. Damn lucky he didn't have that gun out."

"He didn't think he needed it," Katherine said.

Katherine walked over to the table and picked up the letter she had been writing. After folding it carefully in half and half again, she stuffed it into her back pocket, but she knew she would never send it.

"Let's do what we need to do and get out of here," Katherine said. "I'm sick of this place."

Chapter 27

Anne Smith unlocked the office door and turned on the lights. She walked over to her cubicle, pulled the cord from the back of her silver percolator standing on top of the file cabinet, and headed for the women's bathroom down the hall to fill the percolator with water.

"Oh, dear," she said as she looked in the mirror and saw her face in the unkind glow of the fluorescent lights.

She usually never left her apartment without touching up a little, but she had been afraid that Katherine and Grace would get to the station ahead of her. After setting the percolator on the sink counter, she shuffled through her purse for lipstick and powder. There were three tubes of lipstick. She selected the deepest color and, leaning toward the mirror, quickly circled her mouth. After dusting powder on her cheeks, she decided she needed more help than powder could give. With the lipstick she drew a mark across each cheek and rubbed the red streak into her skin with her fingers.

"What do you expect," she asked the mirror. "It's four-thirty in the morning."

She dumped the previous day's coffee grounds into the wastebasket and rinsed off the percolator parts. After filling the percolator with fresh water, she walked back to the office and propped open the office door. She scooped seven tablespoons of coffee into the percolator, added one more in consideration of the time, and plugged it in. She cleared off her desk as much as she could without risking chaos, stole a chair from her neighbor's cubicle, and sat down behind her desk to wait for them.

They came in together, young faces that didn't need makeup even early in the morning. Katherine had combed out her carefully braided pigtails, but her hair still held the wave. Anne picked two mugs off the top shelf. C.C. had given her the wolf howling at the moon, and Steven had found the donkey at the Grand Canyon. Most of her mugs had animals on them. She wondered why. There was scarcely an animal she could tolerate. For herself she selected her favorite mug with the Space Needle.

"Cream or sugar?" she asked.

"No, thanks," Grace said.

"I told Parker not to call you," Katherine said. "There's no reason for you to get up and come down here."

"I told him to call if anything happened. I would say that something happened tonight, wouldn't you?"

"Maybe," Katherine said. "But these guys might not have anything to do with the girl and boy we found."

"They broke into your room," Anne said. "God knows what they intended to do. That's enough for me."

"Me, too," Grace said, "but Katherine is right. You didn't need to come down here."

"Okay, let's stop worrying about my beauty sleep and get you ladies home. You've had a long night."

Anne opened a drawer on the side of her desk and ripped off several officer statement forms from a pad of statements. She rolled one sheet of paper into an electric typewriter on a stand beside her desk.

"One of you can use my typewriter, and I'll set up another one over here."

As she inserted the second statement form into the carriage of a neighboring typewriter, she thought about the men she hadn't seen. She already had an image of them seated in her mind.

"I wish I could have seen their faces when they saw your guns. I would have walked the streets for that. Are you two hungry? Would you like a doughnut or something? There's nothing open yet, but we have doughnuts in the vending machine in the hallway."

"No, thanks," Grace said.

Katherine shook her head on her way over to the next desk, where she sat down at the typewriter.

"They taste like cardboard anyway," Anne said.

Within a few moments Katherine had the electric keys tapping the page in a fluent staccato. Grace sat down in Anne's chair and looked at the blank page for a moment before raising her hands. Then she typed in her name and serial number, the date and the current time.

"What time are you using when we talked to Elvis?" Grace asked.

"Twelve-fifteen," Katherine said without stopping the typewriter keys.

Grace wrote the time down on scratch paper. "And when the black car stopped on Aurora?"

"Two o'clock," Katherine said. She stopped typing and looked at Grace. "Three-oh-five when I saw the car drive into the parking lot and three-fifteen when they broke into the room."

Anne looked at the window beyond Katherine's desk. Daylight would be coming soon. Detectives would fill the empty desks, and they would talk about baseball, repeat rumors, and tell jokes. She would be the only woman in the room. But not now. For another few hours they had the office to themselves. There were no jokes, and nobody talked about that pathetic baseball team.

If Parker had made the arrest himself, he would never have called her. These young women had changed that. They chose her, not Parker or Fred or the captain, and she was going to come, by God, whether she was needed or not. But Katherine was right about the arrest. It was a long way from the motel room to the garbage compactor and to the dump in Fremont. They might never get there. Then again, they just might.

Anne watched Grace type her first sentence, spraying
letters across the top line beneath her name. I saw, I heard,
I did—one simple sentence after another. Katherine made
it look easy, as if she was getting rid of something as fast as
she could. Grace pressed the keys as if she felt each word.

The telephone rang on Anne's desk, and she picked it
up and punched the lighted button.

"Smith," she said and nodded to Grace, who had stopped
typing when the telephone rang. Anne listened to Parker
explain what he was planning. She was particularly pleased
to hear him ask if she had other suggestions.

"No. That sounds good to me," she said.

"That was Parker," she told the young officers under her
charge after she hung up the telephone.

Katherine stopped typing and listened, too.

"Parker is getting a search warrant for the motel office.
It's a good thing we were careful about the radio. When
Parker checked the motel office for more suspects, he heard
a police scanner in the backroom. I can't image that clerk
had it just to keep him company. I think he's going to hear
all the police talk he wants in the next few days.

"They're keeping the suspects downstairs in the patrol
holding rooms. The pervert with the camera is demanding
to talk to his lawyer, and the patrol officers are diligently
waiting for somebody to show up and escort him to the
telephone. In the meantime all our suspects are sitting on
their little benches demanding their rights. It must be a
pitiful sight. Parker will book them when they finish up at
the motel. You guys will write up your statements and get
the hell out of here."

Grace took a slow deliberate sip of the fresh coffee and
inhaled the steam that rose from the wolf. Katherine left
her cup untouched and returned her attention to the typewriter. After several minutes she pulled out the first sheet
of paper and inserted another. Anne walked over to Katherine's desk and picked up the finished page. She set the
Space Needle on top of a file cabinet.

Reading the report, Anne could-feel the danger in the motel room. It wasn't what she had planned. Somebody could have been killed, and it might have been the young officer who typed with such certainty. Anne wondered what she felt, if she had been afraid or even angry. The report said nothing about that. None of them ever did.

When Katherine pulled her second sheet out of the typewriter, she handed it to Anne. Only a quarter of the page was filled. Katherine got out of her chair and walked over to Grace's desk. Anne finished reading the report standing up.

"This was good work," she said. "Too dangerous, though. I didn't intend to put you guys in such a bad spot."

"It just happened," Katherine said. "Sometimes it's dangerous walking across the street."

"Go home," Anne said. "Get some sleep."

"I'm past sleeping. How are you doing, Grace?"

"I have a ways to go," Grace said. "Go ahead and shove off."

"You told me Ballard Avenue was a quiet place to work."

"We weren't on Ballard Avenue."

"And you won't be for a day or two," Anne said. "You're still assigned to me, and I'll make sure you get a couple of days off. Nobody else around here works for free."

"Sounds good to me," Katherine said.

Katherine made a copy of her report and gave the original to Anne. After Katherine left, Grace did not lift her fingers from the keyboard. The young officer was closer to the end than she thought.

Chapter 28

Katherine awakened early in the afternoon, still feeling tired deep inside, the sort of tired that sleep interrupted but did not reach. She lay in bed and tried to think what day it was.

It was Friday, she remembered. She had gone swimming after leaving Anne's office, even with the stitches still in her back. She might have been pushing it to go swimming so soon, but without exercise she would become soft in no time. Besides, the doctor had told her she could have the stitches removed on Friday, so she should be able to do whatever exercise she wanted by then.

She hadn't slept well even after swimming. Her schedule was off. Just as she had gotten used to sleeping at night, she had to change again to work the plainsclothes detail. It would take time to readjust.

She knew that it wasn't only the schedule that interfered with her sleep. Anne Smith said she wished she could have seen the men's faces with the guns pointed at them. Maybe Anne would have seen what she wanted, but Katherine didn't think so, at least not with the man who had a gun of his own but didn't think he would need it. Katherine had seen his face. She wondered what others had seen, boys and girls, prostitutes and runaways who could not protect themselves.

Without her gun she could fight such a man, but she could swim for the next ten years, and she still wouldn't be strong enough to defeat him. Maybe a fight would only make a better movie. Was that what he wanted? Did the second man have the camera ready when he came through the door?

She listened for footsteps next door and heard heavy rain instead. She rose from her bed, walked into the living room, and lifted the window. Below her, the full ripe heads of Mrs. Rabin's peonies bobbed up and down in the rain. Mrs. Rabin's daisies looked up at the downpour in open-eyed disbelief. The city moon had been right after all.

Some of this rain would surely make it over the mountains, Katherine thought, but too often when she had been sure there was enough rain to water the whole Earth and certainly their farm a few hundred miles to the east, she had been disappointed to hear that the western slopes had taken it all in greedy disproportion. So was her father. Especially during dry years, she felt somehow responsible for the excess on her side of the mountains.

Rain days on the farm were always good days, unless the rain came just before the wheat harvest. Her father liked company on rain days, and she often rode with him in the pickup as he anticipated what effect the rain would have on the lush green stems in the wheat fields or the sparse grass in the pastures where the ground was too rough for wheat or hay. He would tell stories then, and she never grew tired of them; he parceled them out as stingily as the rain that so seldom blessed their farm.

Nobody worked in the rain—spring or summer. They must have feared they would melt. Sometimes they would go into town and have a hamburger and milk shake at the Uptown Grill, even if it was the middle of the week. On those days there would always be boys at the pinball machines. Her brother might join them with coins he had saved for rainy days. She never played. Girls never played pinball. She would watch them from her wooden booth, lean down to tie her new shoes that she wore to town, straighten her socks, think about the color of lipstick she might someday apply to her dry but willing lips, and wonder if boys would ever look away from their games.

Katherine saw a black winter coat on the sidewalk below her window. Mrs. Rabin was heading out to her flowers. The old lady's hoe tapped the sidewalk like a pilgrim's staff. More and more, Mrs. Rabin used her hoe as a walking cane as well as a tool to do her work. Mrs. Rabin dropped a handful of wooden stakes into a pile on the sidewalk and stepped into her flowers.

Mrs. Rabin pounded a stake into the flower bed using her hoe as a club. From her apartment above, Katherine watched the old lady pull a string out of her coat pocket and tie fallen peony blossoms onto the stake. Mrs. Rabin happily cut armfuls of flowers and distributed them to anyone in need, but she could not bear to see any of them destroyed by the rain. Katherine looked back to her table where she had a clear glass vase stuffed with Mrs. Rabin's newly cut peonies. Several drooped, even though no rain beat on them, and their heads hung forlornly like neglected children.

Katherine walked to her bedroom in the back of her apartment and dressed in a sweatshirt and a pair of old jeans. When she bent down to tie her shoes, she wondered what happened to all those boys who played pinball on rainy afternoons. Did they go on to new toys, or did they finally look up and find something more interesting? She slipped on her raincoat, walked down the apartment steps and out into the melting rain.

Mrs. Rabin was pounding another stake forcefully into the ground with her hoe, holding the hoe close to the blade with one hand and guiding the stake with the other. The handle of the hoe rose and fell like the baton of a drum major leading the band down the street. Her aim was remarkably sure.

Mrs. Rabin's back was bent to her work, but it was bent

even when she was not working. Her head trembled as she looked up past the brim of her old straw hat. One eye was clouded, and she did not see well out of the other, but she had an uncanny ability to sense Katherine's presence and never seemed surprised to see her.

"Hard rain like this knocks down these big flowers," the old lady said.

Katherine knelt beside the stake and gathered a group of stems in her hand.

"You'll get muddy in this dirt," Mrs. Rabin said.

"I grew up in the dirt," Katherine said. "I'll hold these together while you tie them."

Mrs. Rabin pulled another string out of her coat pocket and encircled the flowers while the handle of the hoe rested in the crook of her arm. The old lady's hands were covered with mud, and rain dripped off the brim of her hat into the middle of the gathered flowers. She tied the ends of the string, and Katherine released the stems, which then expanded within the permitted circle. Katherine moved to the next bunch of peonies, being careful not to trample any flowers.

"You didn't come home until early this morning," Mrs. Rabin said. She had a habit of smiling after every sentence.

"Did I wake you up?"

"No. Old ladies never sleep; we just fade away. You're too young to remember that." Mrs. Rabin often had short sayings that Katherine was too young to remember.

Katherine reached for a stake and stuck the point into the ground. When she realized what she had done, she felt stuck herself but bravely told Mrs. Rabin, "Go ahead and pound it in."

"I might hit your hand."

"You didn't hit yours."

"That's different. Both hands shake the same so I have a good chance of hitting the stick. Here, you do it." She handed the hoe to Katherine.

Katherine took the hoe and hit the stake the same way

Mrs. Rabin had done, but the blade bounced off without sending the stake any deeper. Concentrating on the second blow, she hit the stake with the portion of the blade closest to the handle. She hit it three more times before sending it deep enough into the ground to hold the flowers. Mrs. Rabin tied off another bunch of the peonies.

"I hope you weren't at work all that time," Mrs. Rabin said. She smiled, and her unclouded eye was alive with humor.

"I worked late, and then I went swimming after work."

"By yourself? You shouldn't swim by yourself. You could drown."

"The pool is only four feet deep."

"I've heard of people drowning in bathtubs."

"I've heard of people drowning when they tie up flowers in the rain," Katherine said.

The old lady laughed with a high musical note. "Only the crazy ones," she said.

The apartment door opened and Dale darted outside carrying an umbrella. He walked so fast that Katherine doubted he would be able to stop in time."

"What are you two doing out here?" he asked.

"Trying not to drown," Katherine said.

Mrs. Rabin thought that was funny. She handed a piece of string to Katherine, and Katherine encircled a new group of peonies. Dale moved closer to Katherine so that the umbrella would keep the rain off her head. In doing so he could not quite fit under it himself. He was wearing scuffed wooden shoes without socks.

"You'll both catch a cold out here," he said. "I've made some tea. Come inside before you get soaked."

Katherine looked at the stakes remaining on the sidewalk and pointed to them. "Four more to go," she said. She pulled a few weeds around the base of the flowers.

Dale gathered up the stakes and followed Katherine to the next bunch of peonies.

"I thought I would have to call the police last night and

see if you were okay," he said as he handed her a stake. "You didn't come home until after six o'clock."

Katherine looked at him for a second as she thought about responding. There was nothing she could say. Instead she hit the stake with the blade of the hoe. Again it glanced off without making an impression. Dale handed the umbrella to Mrs. Rabin and knelt down to the flowers. He held the stake with both hands and nodded for her to hit it again.

"I might hit your hands."

It was either a warning or a threat.

"I hope you don't," he said.

Chapter 29

Katherine stopped behind a line of cars as the horn blared and cross arms descended across the traffic lanes on the Ballard Bridge. The massive steel platform of the drawbridge rose with the sound of bells. Two sailboats met each other beneath the bridge, and the tops of their empty masts passed before her. From the west, still a distance away, a huge blue ship approached while the two sections of the bridge remained standing at attention.

In the growing double column of vehicles behind the bridge, she shut off her car engine and walked across the empty traffic lanes to the railing on the west side. The rain kept all the others in their cars. It didn't bother her. She raised the hood of her raincoat over her head and took in a deep breath of the rain-fresh air.

Below her on the closest pier of Fisherman's Terminal, a fisherman repaired his nets, as indifferent to the rain as she. Fishing boats of different shapes and sizes, worn and weathered, rocked in their berths along the docks that reached into the bay like the fingers of a sleeping giant. Each boat had a name. *Foolish Dream* rubbed its side against *Sweet Mary*. *Patty Anne* turned away from *Majestic Star,* which was dirty and neglected and the least majestic boat among them.

Out in the canal a man and woman in a kayak paddled

through the gentle rain beneath the bridge and headed west toward the locks. The synchrony of their strokes was beautiful to watch. The man in the front stopped paddling and leaned back toward the woman. They might have been talking, or he might have leaned toward her just to get closer.

How long would it take before she saw a kayak and didn't remember? The kayak was only part of it, but it was intertwined with the quiet mornings while she waited for him to arrive, the occasional touch of his calloused hands. It was intertwined with Olivia, the baby they found together in the rundown hotel on First Avenue. He told her to forget, to push the child away, but she had felt like it was her own child, not a stranger. He couldn't push her away either. Had he forgotten by now? Had he forgotten her, too? Kat, he called her, the only one who ever had.

She wouldn't go through that again. When she saw the girl and boy discarded in the garbage, she began pulling herself away—just as he said she must—seeing them without hearing their cries or feeling their pain. She must forget about the man and his kayak, too. She must.

The fisherman on the pier rolled out another net. In the beginning the roll was as tall as he was and he had to push hard to make it move. When the net was in a long straight line he began pulling it apart. He pulled, retraced his steps twenty feet, and pulled again. He followed the same procedure on the opposite side until the net lay open on the pier. When he found a tear in the net, his hands moved quickly to repair the damage. She wondered which boat was his, certain that it was not the *Majestic Star*.

A week had passed since she had choked the man in the hospital and had received the scar on her back. She recognized landmarks across the bridge that would have been anonymous to her then—the seldom-used railroad track, the tranquil green of Ballard Avenue as it hid behind the warehouses that followed Shilshole Avenue, and the stark straight bulk of the hospital building.

As the big ship passed through the open bridge, its engines growled and smoke spewed from the smokestack. The raised sections of the bridge began to drop. Before returning to her car Katherine picked up the course of the kayak. The paddles were entering the water again in perfect harmony, and the kayak glided smoothly away from the great blue ship.

She parked on a street close to the emergency room of Ballard Hospital, where Joe Bradshaw worked every Friday. He had been specific about that day. He wanted to remove the stitches himself. Did it mean more than that? Had she interpreted the signals correctly? And if she had, is that all it took? Someone says, 'Hello, I'm interested?' Didn't it take more? If the security guard had told her when he worked, would she have paid any attention? She could barely remember anything about the guard. What did she remember about Joe Bradshaw? Did he have brown eyes or blue? Was he fat or skinny? Was he tall or short? He was taller than six feet, and he had long fingers and bony wrists. Enough, she thought. In a week, he had probably forgotten all about her.

Most men saw her with her gun and blue shirt and couldn't see anything else. Joe Bradshaw saw her blue shirt and saw her choke another man unconscious, and he wanted to see her again. Who knew what they wanted? This was better, if it were anything, but the blue shirt was still in the way. It's me, she wanted to say—not the shirt, not the badge, not the gun—just me. Beneath her raincoat she wore a simple white blouse that buttoned up the front and no makeup and no jewelry. She had left her gun hidden in her apartment. He would see her as clearly as she could make herself be seen, and nobody else.

The emergency room door opened automatically as if it had been expecting her. She walked down a tiled hallway a short distance to the reception counter, where the receptionist was busy with papers. Six or seven people were in the waiting room. Katherine could not tell who was waiting to see the doctor and who was waiting for family or friend.

She recognized nobody, and nobody paid any attention to her. They would have paid attention if she had been wearing her uniform.

"Can I help you?" the receptionist asked after a few moments.

"Is Dr. Bradshaw working tonight?"

"Yes. Dr. Morgan and Dr. Bradshaw."

"I would like to see Dr. Bradshaw about some stitches in my back. He told me to come tonight and have them taken out."

The receptionist handed a clipboard to her across the counter.

"Fill this out," she said, along with something else that Katherine did not hear. A tall doctor with curly brown hair walked out of a treatment room and stopped in the middle of the hallway. There is his smile, she thought. She remembered that, too. His hospital jacket was too short for his arms.

"So, here you are," he said. "I'll take care of this, Lois," he said to the receptionist who had given Katherine the clipboard. "Officer Murphy saved our bacon last week when she subdued a patient high on drugs. She earned a few sutures in the process."

Lois didn't seem impressed.

"Which rooms do we have open?" he asked.

Lois hesitated before looking down on her chart. "122 and 126," she said.

"Come on," he said to Katherine and headed down the hall. Katherine followed him, carrying the clipboard.

"I don't mind waiting," Katherine said. She had to hurry to keep up with him.

"I know. I was beginning to wonder if you would come at all."

He pushed open the door for room 122 and held it for her. She walked in ahead of him. The door closed when he released it, and he took the clipboard from her hand.

"Not necessary," he said.

"We have insurance that covers this," she said.

"I certainly hope so." He opened three cupboards before finding an examination gown for her. "Any problem with that cut?" he asked as he handed her the gown.

"It itches."

"Good, but no swelling or infection?"

"No."

"Good. You can slip the gown on. I'll be right back."

He did not leave immediately. He stopped at the door and smiled, then nodded his head once as though he agreed with what she said before he dashed away. She had not said anything.

Katherine unbuttoned her blouse and hung it on a rack beside the door. She slipped her arms through the loose-fitting gown and tied the top string around her neck. The gown remained open in the back. She sat down on a stool beside the examination table and waited.

She felt isolated, hearing footsteps from the hallway but nothing else. She had always hated medical rooms. They were places for shots when she was a child and embarrassing examinations when she was older, but the stitches were nothing. She'd had stitches before when her brother ran over her in the pickup truck.

Footsteps stopped outside the door, and she looked up to see him come in. He had the same smile as when he left.

"Let's see how I did on this," he said as he stood beside her and shifted the gown away from her cut. "Looks good. In a couple weeks, you'll barely be able to see it."

"I can't see it now," she said.

He went to the cupboard and placed a few utensils on a stainless steel tray. He put the tray onto the examination bench and used it for a table. She felt little tugs on her skin. He dropped fragments of thread onto the tray.

"That's it," he said. "Good as new."

He pulled a chair close to the stool, crossed his legs, and then clasped his hands over his knee so that he crossed himself in all directions. His knee rose higher as he leaned back into his chair.

"I was beginning to wonder if you would come," he said again.

"Here I am," she said.

He uncrossed his legs and leaned slightly in her direction.

"There's a nice little Irish pub a few blocks from here. I was thinking, 'Murphy, good Irish name. I wonder if Murphy would tell me to go to hell if I asked her out for a beer?' They have an Irish band on Friday and Saturday nights."

"Are you asking me?"

"I am. Are you going to tell me to go to hell?"

"Is it the one on Ballard Avenue?" Katherine asked.

"That's the one."

"I'm off tomorrow," she said.

"So am I. Is eight o'clock good for you?"

"It's good for me," Katherine said. "I'll meet you at the bar."

He rose from the chair and extended his hand the way he had done the first time they met. He must like shaking hands. His hand made her smile, and his wrist wasn't nearly as bony as she remembered.

Chapter 30

Dale sat at the table reading the French cookbook he had bought the day before. His head hurt more than it should with just a glass of wine and a cognac or two. It was probably the cigarettes that made him light-headed. He dumped the cigarette butts into the garbage from the soup bowl he had used for an ashtray. He had thrown out all his ashtrays a month ago. There weren't enough cigarette butts in the bowl to cause his headache, he decided. Then he remembered he had emptied it once the night before when he had thrown the remaining pack into the garbage. And then, he remembered now, he had decided to have one more cognac and had dug through the garbage to find the pack of cigarettes. Now they were gone. That was the last pack, and he would hang himself from the window if he bought another.

He saw the cognac bottle in the garbage. He forgot he had finished it off, too. Both were gone. He sealed up the bag and carried it down the stairway and around the apartment to the Dumpster in the alley. His bedroom slippers flopped on the steps as he hurried back up the stairs. He was out of breath when he reached his apartment. "Damn cigarettes," he muttered. That was it. No more.

It wasn't a good sign to drink alone in the kitchen. He hadn't done that for a long time—except that night after his birthday and that time when he had watched Bogart on the late movie. How could he forget how lousy he would feel?

Despite his clogged sinuses he could still smell the stale residue of the cigarettes. He opened all the windows in the living room. He supposed it would make him look guiltier to Katherine, trying to get rid of the smell, but he didn't really like it himself. It had smelled better the night before. Coffee, cognac, cigarettes—all delightful and not one good thing about them. Why couldn't he crave something that was good for him, sit-ups maybe, or at least something that he didn't have to hide? He had already gained five pounds since he quit smoking. Wouldn't it be nice to be young again like Katherine and never worry?

He turned on the coffeepot and sat on a kitchen chair with a heavy sigh. Maybe she wouldn't come this morning. He hadn't heard her come home, or was that the night before? Who could keep up with her schedule? She usually worked six days straight and then had two off and then an extra day off now and then, and then she switched to nights for a while. It was too confusing. The police department should be able to devise a better system than that. They were lucky they could get anybody to work there. Since when, he wondered, had he started worrying about the police department?

He remembered the panic he had felt when Mrs. Rabin told him that the young woman in the apartment next to his was a police officer. It was bad enough with the men cops—their cruel jokes that he heard at the hospital, the disrespect, the casual dismissal as if he were not even alive. All he wanted was to be left alone. All he wanted was to hear no more faggot jokes, and then he moved next door to a cop. No wonder the apartment was so cheap.

He had immediately started packing. Two weeks in the apartment, and he was packing again. He had never even seen the girl in her uniform. He would have left, he was ashamed to remember, if he had not found the jar of choke-

cherry jam at his door. He had never heard of choke-
cherries. In the careful handwriting he would come to
recognize, she welcomed him to the building and explained
that her mother had made the jam. It still made him
ashamed to think about it.

In response he made Katherine a batch of light vanilla
cookies with a drop of semisweet chocolate in the center
of each one. The plate shook in his hand as he knocked
on her door. Although he said he couldn't stay, he stayed
for more than an hour. She made coffee so weak that he
could barely taste it and showed him a picture of her
mother who made the jam. She showed him pictures of the
rest of her family, too. There was not one picture of a cop,
not one sign of that occupation anywhere in her apartment.

There wasn't much of anything in her apartment. The
girl had almost no furniture. She was the one who could
pack up and be gone in an hour, while he had unpacked
boxes still stacked on top of one another in the living room.
There had been the new boxes, too, added in his panic.

He didn't pack more after receiving the jam, but he
didn't finish unpacking for weeks, as though he were waiting for something to happen. Nothing happened—nothing
at all. She went to work at the police department and came
home. He went to work at the hospital and came home.
She was so quiet that he had to strain to hear her moving
about in her apartment. He spread her mother's choke-
cherry jam on toast every morning until it was gone, and
he didn't choke once.

Katherine had been surprised, maybe even sad, when he
finally told her months later how close he had come to
moving. Where they lived, she told him, it was safer and
easier for him to tell the truth about himself than it was
for her. That might be, he realized, but the truth that she
was talking about had never been easy for him. The young
men and women who walked down Broadway now had
signs on their shirts announcing all sorts of things about
themselves, but he could not. Neither could she. She never
wore her uniform home. She brought it into the apartment

from the cleaners or took it to work in a black plastic bag, and no one ever saw it.

He became the protector of her secret and invited Mrs. Rabin to his apartment one afternoon to enlist her support. After all, she was the one who told him about Katherine, and it had been her flowers that had attracted him to the apartment in the first place. Over apple tarts and French vanilla ice cream, he suggested that it would better if the two of them were the only ones in the neighborhood who knew where Katherine worked. There were people who might try to harm her if they knew. Yes, he said in response to her surprise, the neighborhood, the city, the world, had become a dangerous place where such a fine young woman had to hide something like that. They needed to keep the secret to themselves. It was nearly a full-time job.

He heard her up and moving around. Now he would pay the piper. It was the last time he would smoke those damn cigarettes. "Damn it," he muttered. He heard her at the door. "It's open," he yelled before she even knocked.

He got up and looked in the refrigerator that was packed so full he couldn't find anything to eat. Nothing. He still had dishes in the sink from the grand dinner he had eaten alone the night before. The asparagus was in the sink along with the dishes. He had dumped it when what's-his-name called and expressed his regrets. Wasn't that how he said it, or was that in the Bogart movie?

"How about some asparagus?" he asked as Kathcrine shuffled into the kitchen in her bedroom slippers.

"No, thanks."

"Nice slippers," he said.

"Yours, too."

"Coffee is ready. You didn't bring your gun, did you?" She stopped in the middle of the kitchen.

"There were just a few left from an old pack."

"I thought the smoke was from Rafael."

"There was no Rafael. Rafael was a figment of my imagination. We'll have no more talk about that."

"What happened?"

"He couldn't come, that's what happened. Canceled at the last minute. Said he was called back to work, if you believe that."

"That's too bad."

She sat down at the table, and he pulled his chair out to join her.

"Do you believe him?" he asked.

"Why shouldn't I?"

"He works in a steak house. Anybody could have filled in for him. No, there was something in his voice. He didn't have to come. I just wanted his opinion on a few things. I made those crab appetizers and had them in the oven when he called. Do you want one? I could heat one up for you."

"No, thanks. I'm sure they were delicious."

"Who knows? Maybe he doesn't like salmon. That's what I planned for the main course. I could have made Steak Diane, but I would think he'd have enough steak in that place where he works. They have piles and piles of raw beef there like a warehouse or something. Your dad would probably like it."

"Do they use linen napkins?"

"Of course."

"He wouldn't like it, then."

He went over to the counter and filled two large mugs with coffee. He was beginning to feel better. She hadn't shot him. Once he cleaned up the kitchen, he could erase the night from his mind. He put her coffee in front of her.

"I'll put the salmon in your refrigerator this afternoon. You can have Salmon a La Rainier for dinner some night."

"Please don't bother, whatever that is."

"Bother? It's no bother. I have to get rid of it somehow."

"Why don't you give it to Mrs. Rabin?"

"I will, but I'll put a nice piece in your refrigerator. It will definitely not be on my menu." He laughed as he considered the new resolution that was added to the others. He was beginning to feel better. No more cigarettes, no more cognac in the kitchen, no Salmon a La Rainier on the menu. Settled.

"What's wrong with linen napkins?" he asked. "For your father?"

"Too fancy. It's like going to a place where they don't put toothpicks on the table."

"Toothpicks?"

"Or at least have them at the cash register."

"I see. In one of those little glass cases where you turn the knob to get one to roll out."

"You can leave them in the box, too."

"Of course."

"Or put them in a whiskey shot glass with pheasants on it."

"Delightful," he said. "Could you have other birds?"

"Only if you can kill them."

"Sometimes I think it would be more fun to have a restaurant like that," he said. "You could put it in an old house with tables in all the rooms."

"They would have to be kitchen tables," she said.

"And chairs that don't match. We could use newspapers for placemats, and you can wear your hat while eating."

"No," Katherine said. "That would be uncivilized. No caps while eating."

"No caps? What would we do with the caps? I know. We could make a rack out of barbwire. I remember you talking about barbwire."

He was beginning to see it in his mind. Wouldn't it be funny if he actually did something like that? What's-his-name would have nothing to do with such a restaurant.

"Did you work last night?" he asked.

"I had last night off. I went swimming."

"Ahhh," he said.

"What do you mean, ahhh? I went swimming."

"You've been swimming a lot lately. You used to go with that group after work, and there was one guy who was such a dedicated swimmer."

"Nobody is dedicated anymore. I went alone. You should do that instead of sitting around here smoking cigarettes."

"All right, all right. Your shoulder must be feeling better. Is it okay to go in the pool with your stitches?"

"Yes, its okay. Besides, I had the stitches taken out last night."

He saw something in her face. Whenever she tried not to smile, there was a certain glow that gave her away. She tried to show such a straight face, but she might as well smile and be done with it.

"Last night? Why would you have them taken out at night?"

"It was the same doctor who put in the stitches. He works in the emergency room on Friday nights."

"And you went back to him?"

"Yes. He wanted to take them out, to make sure there was no problem."

"Any doctor could have done that. I could have taken the stitches out."

"You're a respiratory therapist—one that sneaks a cigarette in the backroom."

He came close to being diverted, but he caught himself before he responded. He was on the trail now.

"Friday nights," Dale said. "I would guess he's in his residency. How old is this young doctor?"

This was too good—the way her face lit up, the smile she wouldn't let out.

"Young." She gave up holding it back.

"Of course he is, and so considerate. I can tell there's more. I won't say a word to anybody."

"He just thanked me for helping with that crazy guy on dope last week."

"And . . ."

"He invited me out for a beer sometime."

"Oh, I like this man," Dale said. "You never told me about the doctor."

"I told you about him."

"You told me he encouraged you to choke that poor sick man nearly to death, but not that he was some handsome young guy."

"I didn't say he was handsome."

"Is he?"

"I don't know."

"Oh, this is good. I hope you didn't agree to go out right away. It might look like you're too eager, but, then again, if you put him off too long, he might think you're prudish or something."

"Prudish? We're only going out for a beer."

"Oh, sure. Of course this guy has seen you in action so he's not going to mess with you. On the other hand, he might be kinky, too. You have to consider that. What kind of guy gets excited watching you choke somebody?"

"I don't know why I tell you anything."

She knew. Oh, this was good. Now he had to behave himself or she wouldn't tell him any more. But this was just too good.

Chapter 31

Daniel cut through the back of the park where the branches of the cedar trees drooped in the rain and wept circles on the ground. Across the street water dripped from the metal rim of the basketball hoop in the storage lot and smoke rose through the rain from the kitchen fires of the Cajun restaurant. He hoped he would see the police car. It had been a long time since he had given the sack to the tall lady. Maybe Officer Murphy didn't like the cookies, or maybe she never got them.

Daniel reached the corner when the butcher began ringing the bell. The noise startled him even though he had heard it before. He wondered why the butcher rang the bell when nobody else did.

Rudy hated it. From the window of their apartment Rudy would shout bad things when he heard the bell. Daniel was afraid then. So was his mother. He didn't understand why his mother would stay when she was afraid. He wished Rudy would leave like he said he would whenever he got mad. If Rudy left, nothing about the bell would scare anybody.

The police car wasn't there. Daniel knew that Officer Murphy wouldn't be inside the grocery store, but he looked anyway. The other police lady had been there even without the car. On his tiptoes, he looked through the window beside the apple box and then moved carefully toward the door. He didn't know what else to do, but he didn't know what he would say to her either. Then the song began.

The bad weather had made everybody else go away, and the butcher was looking at Daniel as he sang. Daniel didn't know what he should do. He stood still in the rain and waited. The song would have to end soon. He tried to stand still even when he felt the hand on his shoulder. Carefully he looked up without moving his head any more than he had to and saw Rigmor behind him.

"Why are you standing outside in the rain?" she asked.

He didn't mean to stand in the rain. He looked at his shoes to see if they were wet. He had ruined shoes once by getting them wet, and his father had gotten angry about buying new shoes when all he did was ruin them.

When the butcher stopped singing beneath the bell, Daniel heard people clapping from all over the street. He wondered where everybody came from. He hadn't seen them before.

"Beautiful," Rigmor said in her way of talking.

She must have understood the song. Everybody, all the people clapping, must have understood. He had not understood a single word.

He lifted one shoe and then the other to make sure they were okay and moved his feet an inch or two away from Rigmor's warm hand.

"No *ja*," he heard her say, and he was not sure if she meant yes or no. It didn't sound like no. Her words were different, but they didn't scare him. They sounded round and soft.

"Of course, you are too big for that," she said.

Then her hand was gone, and his shoulder felt better or maybe it was his stomach, but he wished he would not have moved because he probably had to keep moving once he started. He thought about explaining the shoes so that she would understand why he moved his feet, but he would have to tell her about his father if he told her about the shoes.

"Do you want me to sweep your sidewalk?" he asked.

He looked up at her to make sure she heard him and saw her face, which was as soft and round as her words. Her hair was stacked in a circle on top of her head, and he tried to remember if his grandmother had looked like that. He thought she was round, too. He hoped she was. He thought round was a good way for grandmothers to be.

"No," she said, "but there is plenty to do that's not in the rain. I have to make *kringler* for the card party tonight. Do you want to help with that?"

"Sure," he said.

"Do you know what *kringler* are?"

"No."

"Cookies. I know you like to make cookies, but these are good Danish cookies. Maybe you would like to make some for your mother and your little sister. Where is your sister today?"

"She's asleep."

"Still asleep so late in the day? What kind of business is that? *Hvad?*"

He didn't know what to say and wondered if her questions meant he could not make cookies with her. He had thought it was all right to leave Mary. She was sleeping with their mother. She did that sometimes after Rudy left, and his mother would get angry if he went in the bedroom to wake them up.

Rigmor opened the door into her store and held it open. *"Kom så,"* Rigmor said. Her words sounded like words he knew, but he couldn't be sure. Maybe she was telling him to go away until Mary woke up. He wondered if Mary had heard the bell or if she was still asleep. He looked back where the two streets separated and saw the singing man coming toward them. The clapping was over, and all the other people had disappeared again. He looked back at the door. Rigmor was still there.

"Come," Rigmor said softly.

He understood that word.

He walked down the middle aisle behind her toward the

white refrigerator case that was taller than he was, and he heard her humming a song as she walked. It was not like the song outside. The song outside would have been too loud for the store. Rigmor stopped and moved a can to the front of the shelf. Daniel could see other cans that should also be moved if she wanted them straight. Maybe he would do that when they finished making cookies.

He followed her behind the white refrigerator with doors on the back and heard a motor running close to the floor. He could feel the motor shake through his shoes. Rigmor sighed as she bent down to a shelf behind the counter and moved things around.

"So, here is the mixing bowl," she said and put the bowl on top of the counter.

It was a big bowl, bright and shiny.

"We'll make a double batch today. You're strong enough to mix that. *Hvad?*"

He was strong enough, he told her. *"Hvad,"* he whispered to himself. *"Hvad,"* he repeated, bringing his teeth onto his bottom lip as Rigmor had done.

He heard the little bell ring at the door, and Rigmor looked that way. Daniel could not see over the refrigerator case. Instead he peeked over the rim of the bowl on the back counter to see how much would fit inside. A lot, he decided.

"Hi, Arne," Rigmor said.

"Ten pounds of ground pork and beef," the man said as he placed two bags on top of the counter beside the cash register.

"That's good," Rigmor said. She pulled a yellow piece of paper off one bag, opened her cash register, and put money on the counter. Arne put the money into the pocket of his coat that was wet from the rain.

"Have some stew," Rigmor said.

"I will, thank you," he said. "Who's your helper?"

Daniel could see the man now. He was the man who sang beneath the bell. The singer was talking about him.

He wondered where he should look, and what he should do. He looked at Rigmor and stood very still.

"This is Daniel. Say hello to Mr. Johansen."

"Hello," Daniel said. He hoped he would not have to say anything more.

"He's shy," Rigmor said, "but that's all right," she said, looking back to Daniel. "Plenty of people to talk, not so many to work. We're making *kringler* today, aren't we?"

The bell rang again, and that meant there was another customer. Daniel wondered how they could start making cookies if customers kept coming in the door. Mr. Johansen walked past him to the stove and ladled the stew into a bowl. It smelled good. Daniel liked the way the store smelled. It wasn't like their apartment or the bar where his mother worked. He had been in there one time, but he didn't like it at all. Mary had held her nostrils together, but he didn't do that at least.

The other man wanted cheese from the big white case. Rigmor opened the back and cut it on a shelf below the sliding door. He saw Daniel but didn't say anything, and Rigmor didn't make him say hello.

"I'll have a shrimp sandwich, too," he said.

Rigmor opened the sliding door next to the cash register and removed a small paper plate wrapped in plastic.

"Those sandwiches always look so good I can't pass them up."

"That's why they're there," she said.

The bell rang again and Daniel was sure now that they would never start. Rigmor told the man how much he owed and rang up the cash register. Daniel shifted from one foot to the other.

"You can wash your hands in the sink," she told him before anyone else came to the counter. "Wash them real good. We don't want dirt in the cookies."

Daniel scrubbed his hands harder than he had ever scrubbed before. One time the teacher made him wash his hands because they had gotten dirty at recess. He thought he had done a good job then, but this time he washed twice as hard. Rigmor was laughing at something as she put a metal cup beside the bowl.

"Now, then," she said. "There is flour in that bucket there. We want four cups of flour in the bowl. Can you do that?"

"Yes."

"Pull the bucket over here. It has wheels there under."

Daniel pulled the big bucket with wheels there under over to the counter. It wasn't really a bucket, but that was what Rigmor called it. He took off the lid and looked inside. It was almost big enough for him to crawl into. Of course, he wouldn't do that. He filled the cup. "One," he said as he dumped the flour into the bowl.

Daniel was careful not to let any flour drop to the floor. He didn't look anywhere else until he had counted to four. Then he looked at Rigmor, who was still standing beside the cash register.

"That's good," she said. "I may hire you after all. Now we put in a little salt and a little butter and start mixing."

She dumped salt into her hand from a round paper box and turned her hand over the bowl. She scooped a large spoonful of butter from a plastic tub on the counter and dropped it on top of the salt and flour. "Maybe a little more," she said. She added a little more.

"Now you mix that until the butter disappears."

She showed him how to roll the ends of a strange-looking tool inside the bowl so that the butter mixed into the flour. He had never seen a tool like this. He had never used flour before either. His cookies had come from the round paper carton, and he had only to slice the roll of dough and put the slices in the oven.

It was hard to make the butter disappear. Once he almost tipped the bowl over, but he saved it just in time. Rigmor talked to customers, but he kept working the tool in the bowl even after he couldn't see the butter anymore. He was sure she would tell him when to stop.

"So, now we need the cream," Rigmor said. "It's over there." She pointed to the refrigerator against the wall. It had sliding glass doors, too, but they were on the front instead of the back. "Bring us a pint."

Daniel walked over to the refrigerator with the big glass doors. He looked through the glass, but he saw no cream. He was not sure what a pint would look like.

"Over to the left," Rigmor told him.

Left, he thought. Left. He always got that mixed up. He guessed which way to move.

"Wrong way," Rigmor said. "Look at me."

He looked at her. Part of her was behind the refrigerator case.

"Raise your hand like you do in school," she said.

He raised his hand like they did in school, although he never raised his hand there.

"Is that the hand you always raise?" she asked.

He said it was, even though he had never raised it.

"Look at it, then," she said. "That's your right hand. Say hello to your right hand."

He looked at his hand but didn't say anything. He thought she was kidding about talking to his hand.

"Say hello," she said again. "Hello, right hand."

"Hello," he said to his hand.

"What did it say?" she asked.

He laughed at the idea of his hand talking. "It didn't say anything."

"*Hvad?* Nothing? Then why would you talk to it? They'll take you to the funny farm if you start talking to your hand. But now you remember. The right hand is the hand you talk to, but only when nobody is listening. Now you can turn around and find the cream. It's on the top shelf on the left side."

He looked up to the top of the refrigerator on the left side. He still couldn't see the cream.

"No, but you might not be tall enough yet. No wonder you can't see it. Anyway, you learned right from left. If you learn right from wrong, it will be a good day."

Daniel moved farther to the left as Rigmor walked over to the refrigerator. Left was the hand he didn't talk to, but now it was right when he turned around to watch her. Right changed directions as fast as he did.

Rigmor carried a carton of cream over to the bowl and set it down. He followed straight behind her. She opened the cream carton and poured most of it into the bowl. She held out a big fork for him, and he took it in his right hand.

"Now you stir," she said, "until the flour and cream come together. That's all there is to it. Flour, cream, butter, a little salt. Sprinkle sugar on top afterward. It has everything that will make us fat. *Hvad?*"

Daniel stirred slowly. He held the fork in the fist of his right hand and the rim of the bowl in his left. The dough was hard to mix. He didn't think there was enough cream to mix into the flour. He kept stirring anyway, and the dough began to get softer. Other customers came into Rigmor's store to buy food, and the singing man left the backroom. Rigmor looked into the bowl now and then, muttering something that sounded like he was to keep stirring, and he did.

Finally Rigmor pushed a hole into the dough with her finger. "Pretty good," she said. She added more cream. "That gets mixed in, and then we roll it out. You're doing good so far. Maybe you'll be a baker yet."

Daniel looked into the bowl and wondered how long it would take to mix the rest of the cream. His right hand had begun to talk after all. It was getting tired. He shook it to make it quiet. He could not make circles anymore with the fork, so he pulled and pushed the fork back and forth through the dough until he couldn't see the cream.

Rigmor stuck her finger into the dough again, and this time pinched a little from the bowl. She put the dough onto her tongue and nodded her head.

"That's good," she said.

He liked hearing those words.

She sprinkled flour onto the countertop and dumped the bowl upside down so that the dough flopped onto the counter. Flour puffed up into the air, but she didn't seem to care. She scooped up a little of the flour and dropped it on top of the pile of dough.

"I like the way it feels. Don't you? Push on it," she said, and she pushed on the dough with her hand to show him.

He did the same as Rigmor and laid his fingerprints over hers.

"Now we flatten it out with the rolling pin," she said. "Can you do that?"

She handed him the rolling pin that looked like a long green stone and was as heavy as a bucket of rocks. He had no trouble smashing the dough flat.

"Forth and back," she said. "Make it flatter." She sprinkled flour in front of the rolling pin.

He pushed the rolling pin forth and back until the dough was as thin as he thought it could be. He looked at her to see if he had done that part right. "Good," she said. She took the rolling pin from him and made a few quick rolls herself.

"Now we measure the dough." She stretched out her thumb and long finger, measured a section onto the dough, and cut across it with a small knife. She pulled the cut piece of dough off to the side.

"You measure, too," she said. "Your cookies get bigger as you get bigger."

He stretched his fingers as far as they would go and measured his own section. Rigmor sliced through the dough where his long finger had made a dent. She put a knife like hers on top of his dough.

"Now we cut it up into small slices," she said. "Then we do the fun part."

She cut her dough into thin strips no wider than her finger. He followed her example. Soon he had a whole row of cut-up dough that looked like flat white worms stretched out on the board, but they were not crawling anywhere. They were just lying on the counter and waiting. Most of them were straight.

Rigmor picked up each end of her first strip of dough and made loops back to the middle of the strip so that it looked like a big B when she finished. He made a B with his dough, too, and pushed on the spot where the ends met the middle so that it would stay together. His B was not as big as hers.

"That was good," she said. "You don't have to push too hard."

He had flattened the dough quite a bit where he pushed on it, and he noticed that the top loop was bigger than the bottom. Her loops were the same size, but she didn't say anything about that. Instead she reached down to the shelf below the counter for two baking pans. She poured oil onto both pans and smeared it around with her hand. She used her hands for everything. On the pan beside his dough, he traced his finger through the oil. It felt nice and slippery.

She lifted his B and placed it at the corner of his pan.

"Make a row and then start a new line," she said. She put her B onto the second pan.

Sometimes his Bs were even, and sometimes they looked like the letters his sister made. He tried to straighten one where the top of the B was way too small.

"No, but it doesn't matter how they look," she said. "They'll all taste good anyway."

He wondered what they would taste like. They didn't have any chocolate. He made more Bs than Rigmor. She had to stop every so often and help a customer. He didn't have to stop. He made all his dough into Bs and then started on hers. He tried to make rows as straight on the pan as she had made them, but they got a little crooked. They would taste good anyway, he thought.

When the pans were full of Bs and there was no more dough, Rigmor brushed some of the whites of eggs on the Bs and then sprinkled sugar on top. He picked up the sugar from the bowl in his fingers like Rigmor and sprinkled it over his cookies. Sometimes they got a little extra, but he was sure it didn't matter. They would all taste good.

Rigmor put the pans into the oven. He felt the heat come out of the stove. He wondered how long they would take, and what he should do while they waited.

"Have you ever seen such a cookie?" Rigmor asked.

No, he was sure he had not.

"They are to kill for," Rigmor said. "They melt in your mouth like nothing you have had. My oldest son would eat a whole pan if I didn't watch him. He wasn't so good to make them, but he ate them like everything. Peder, my youngest son, was better to help—right here when he was no bigger than you. We have made lots of *kringler* here in this kitchen.

"These cookies I make are for policemen who come tonight to play cards. At the end of the night, they eat them like my oldest son, except with a little coffee and cognac. But then, that's another story."

"Will the police lady play cards tonight?" he asked.

"You mean Katrin, don't you? No. It's not like that, you see. These men who come tonight used to work here like Grace and Katrin, but now they just come to talk and play cards."

"When is she coming back?" he asked.

"I don't know. Pretty soon, I think. If you like, we can put some of the cookies in a can and save them for her."

"Will they still be good?"

"Oh, yes," Rigmor said. "These *kringler* are good for a long time."

Chapter 32

"I've been thinking about the boy we found," Thomas said.

He continued sweeping between the garbage compactor and the red-brick building to the west and pushed the debris toward the pile he had made in the middle of the alley entrance. Jack Morton stood beside the open mouth of the machine. Jack lifted the flat shovel out of the wheelbarrow and positioned it next to the pile. Thomas swept the dirt and debris onto the shovel, and Jack emptied it into the machine.

"Do you know anything about quantum mechanics?"

"I thought you were thinking about the boy," Jack said.

"I am. That's why I asked you about quantum mechanics."

Jack set the blade of the shovel onto the asphalt and tightened his grip on the handle. "I don't understand at all."

"Nobody understands it," Thomas said. "I asked if you knew anything about it."

"Okay, I'm ready," Jack said. He leaned on the shovel for support.

"It's like this. If you shoot one photon after another at a photoelectric plate, most of the photons hit the plate in a predictable pattern. But a few go somewhere else, and nobody knows why. One might go right through the plate without stopping, or one might go around the plate and out into the universe. The best you can measure is a probability of a certain outcome. Einstein couldn't believe it. In his view, physical laws are constant; they are not a matter of probability. He said, 'God doesn't play with dice.' "

"I'm with Einstein," Jack said.

"He was probably wrong," Thomas said. "It certainly looks like he was wrong."

The garage door opened and a small car spurted down the ramp like one of the photons Einstein refused to acknowledge. It stopped abruptly, inches from the wheelbarrow. Jack Morton raised his middle finger, and the man driving the sports car returned the gesture. Then both men laughed. Thomas thought their behavior was as strange as the photons.

The man got out of the car and joined them in front of the garbage machine. Thomas had seen the man in his office, which was beside the elevator on the second floor. The man had waved to him as Thomas pushed a wheelbarrow down the hallway, but Thomas could never wave back. Both hands had to be on the wheelbarrow handles, or either Newton's or Einstein's gravity would dump the mess right on the floor.

"George, this is Thomas," Jack said. "We were talking about quantum mechanics."

"What kind of mechanics?" George asked.

"Quantum mechanics," Jack said. "What's your opinion? Does God play with dice?"

"He plays with whatever he wants," George said. "But what's this about dice?"

"This mechanic theory is like saying that one of those expensive watches you fix will suddenly jump ahead an hour without explanation."

"I'd like to see that," George said. "One of my watches jump ahead an hour? When I finish repairing a Patek Phillipe, it will be accurate up to one minute a month."

"George is a watchmaker," Jack said. "Old as sin, too. He's been here longer than all the rest of us combined."

"I've seen your sign," Thomas said. "Someday I'd like to see how one of those watches works."

"Stop by, I'll show you," George said. "And you can show me the clock you showed this guy." George nodded toward Jack. "He thinks he's a genius now because he can draw a Ping-Pong ball bouncing up and down."

"Did he show you that?" Thomas asked.

"He shows everybody."

"It's a photon."

"What?" George asked.

"It's a photon clock, not a Ping-Pong ball. It's theoretical. It doesn't really exist."

George removed a package from his shirt pocket and shook it until a cigarette rose an inch above the opening. He placed the cigarette in his mouth with long slender fingers. His hand extended the cigarette package to Thomas.

"Ah, thank you," Thomas said. He contemplated which one to take.

George shook the package again, and one cigarette emerged as the chosen one. Thomas removed it from the package, and George put the package back into his shirt pocket and lit the ends of their cigarettes with a lighter. Thomas tasted the burning tobacco on his tongue and blew smoke into the air. He watched the molecules rise and disperse.

"Why do you live in that shed?" George asked.

Thomas looked at the shed as if he had not seen it before. He thought he saw it in a new light. Another stack of cardboard had gathered that afternoon since the rain stopped. He intended to rip apart the taped ends and stack them efficiently inside. He would do it before the next rain. If they became wet, they would mold inside the shed. Air could not circulate in his densely packed layers.

"Why," he said, sounding the word so that it was not a question. "Why is the most unusual form of the interrogatory, don't you think? It might be the central question of our existence or a foolish human idea. Who, what, when, where, how? Simple questions. But why, that's different. Sometimes we ask, 'How can this happen?' but we mean why. How is simple. Einstein showed how to measure time and distance with a beautiful logic no one had seen before, but he was no better with why than the rest of us. How far back do we have to go to answer the simplest why? If you tell me that, I will tell you why I live in the shed."

"Do you play chess?" George asked.

"Now and then," Thomas said. "I read Reinfeld's book when I was a boy. He had a wonderful approach to the game."

"Have you ever read Lasker?" George asked.

"I've never heard of him."

"Maybe I would have a chance, then."

Beyond the shed the garage door rose again and another car came into view. It was the red car belonging to the pretty lady who stopped and talked to him sometimes when she was driving in or out of the garage. Jack saw the car, too, and moved the wheelbarrow out of the way. The alley was not wide enough for two cars to pass. George walked back to his car and got behind the steering wheel. As he drove past them, he tossed his package of cigarettes over the top of his car. Because of the car's momentum, the cigarettes landed on the asphalt beyond Thomas.

As the lady passed in her red car she waved to him, even though he was only a few feet away.

"Hi, Thomas," she said.

He waved back. He had forgotten her name. The garage door made a loud noise as it closed. Maybe the door was too heavy. The machine would not last long if it had to work so hard. If the watchmaker's watches had gears that were too small, his clocks would never work without giving up time.

Thomas picked up the package of cigarettes and offered it to Jack.

"I don't smoke," Jack said.

"I don't either," Thomas said. He looked at his new possession and wondered if he should throw it into the garbage. He would keep it, he decided. If somebody wanted a cigarette, he would have a cigarette to give. He wondered if the pretty lady would like a cigarette when she passed. It couldn't hurt to keep the package for a short time.

Jack placed the broom and shovel in the wheelbarrow. He closed the lid of the garbage machine and pressed the button that started the hydraulic motor. While the hydraulic ram pushed back all the debris they had loaded into the machine, Jack wrapped the chain around the handle and fastened the padlock. He was in a shadow that extended beyond the driveway. The shadow would have reached the bank parking lot beyond the fence if the wood slats had not interrupted it. Thomas wondered if a shadow could be interrupted. How would you know if you could not see it?

Jack lifted the handles of the wheelbarrow and backed into the alley.

"Everybody is going home," he said. "I'm calling it a day, too."

"Why wasn't the rest of your crew working today?" Thomas asked.

"It's Saturday. Only fools work on Saturdays."

Thomas didn't believe Jack was a fool. He liked talking to Jack whenever he came by the shed. Saturday—that explained why the others weren't there.

"Are you working tomorrow? I could help if the others don't come."

"Sure. How's your geometry? I'm going to start laying out walls in the morning."

"Euclidean or Pythagorean?" Thomas asked.

"Whoever says that the square of the hypotenuse is the sum of the squares of the sides."

"Pythagoras," Thomas said, "but that's only for a right triangle."

"He's my man tomorrow. We won't have to worry about

quantum mechanics, will we? I'm hoping simple geometry will get us through."

"Geometry should be sufficient," Thomas said.

"In case you're interested," Jack said, "I talked to a friend of mine who owns an apartment building up the street. He has a basement apartment that he would rent out cheap. It would be a better place to live than that recycling shed."

Thomas looked back to the shed. He knew he couldn't stay there much longer, but he didn't want to think of another place just yet. It had been warm and dry all afternoon, and he had almost finished reading Hardy. Besides, the depth of the cardboard was just getting comfortable.

"I'll think about that," Thomas said.

"Okay, you keep thinking," Jack said. He pushed the wheelbarrow forward toward the garage.

"Why would somebody pick your garbage machine to dump the body when it could have been a million other places?"

Jack stopped walking, but he didn't lower the wheelbarrow braces back to the ground.

"Bad luck, I guess."

"Maybe, like the one photon out of billions that goes right through the photoelectric plate. There's a more likely answer, isn't there? If you think backward from where the boy was found with the idea that he was put in the place with the highest probability, where does that take you?"

Jack Morton lowered the wheelbarrow. "Where does it take you?" he asked.

"It doesn't take me very far from here," Thomas said. "I would guess that somebody knew about this machine and knew how to make it work. Chances are good that he is not far away. I think he carried the body here on foot. If he had a car, he would have taken it out of the area."

"Maybe that's what somebody did," Jack said, "and this is where he dumped it."

"Possibly, but then you're back to calculating the probability that this machine was picked out of all the others, that this place was picked instead of somewhere remote. It's more probable that the man lives close by, that he has no car, and that he knows how to make this machine work."

"Somebody like you," Jack said.

It was strange how well he matched his own description, Thomas thought.

"You showed me how to work the machine," Thomas said.

"I did," Jack said. "What would Einstein say about your theory?"

"He wouldn't use physical theories to predict human behavior."

"Is he wrong about that, too?"

"No, he's probably right. It is strange, though. Einstein won the Nobel Prize for his work in light quanta, not for relativity, and then his ideas were used in quantum mechanics, which he spent the rest of his life trying to disprove, at least the random nature of it. He wanted to unify relativity and quantum mechanics, but he never succeeded. Nobody has. You have these two extraordinary theories that contradict each other, that don't work together. And yet they must. It's very strange."

Jack agreed. At least he seemed to agree as he lifted the wheelbarrow handles and headed for the garage, shaking his head. He stopped at the bottom of the ramp and pushed the garage door opener that he had in his back pocket. The door growled and vibrated as it opened. Someday somebody would have to fix that door.

Chapter 33

"I miss the golden color of the harvest," Katherine said, "and that cold blue air in the winter."

She sat with Joe Bradshaw beneath a charcoal portrait of James Joyce, whose head was cocked toward them in a position to eavesdrop. Music played from stereo speakers, soft lilting music of green hills, heroes, and death. Lost love, too—the heartbroken girl sinking beneath the waves.

She was trying to tell Joe something about herself, how she had traveled from the farm she still called home to the city for which she had no simple description. She had to begin there. If he couldn't see the forms and colors that shaped her childhood, if he couldn't see the beauty in the changing fields of wheat, he would not likely see any in her.

Joe moved closer when her thoughts traveled to wheat country, while the man in the picture continued to stare over them with his bad eyes, as if caught in an unblinking moment of concentration with his hat raised high on his forehead—thinking beyond the words he heard, thinking what they meant, thinking too much for happiness.

"I worked on my grandparents' farm in Iowa," Joe told her.

Iowa, she thought. Such a short word that took so long to say. It seemed as far away as Ireland from where the music originated that prompted her to tap the floor with her foot. She decided she would see that place someday, get on the road when the wheat died in summer and head off for Iowa and maybe just keep on going to Ireland while she was at it. Mostly she had been thinking about traveling to Pacific islands, but she could go the other way, too. She wondered if it ever got warm in Ireland.

The Irish band began playing at nine, and she leaned close to him to hear his voice through the music that ricocheted off the high brick walls. They sat on a bench that stretched from the front door to the back where the band played. All along the bench were narrow tables like the one behind the sofa in her grandmother's parlor. Pints of black beer dominated the tables. She had thought one beer was the same as another, but this black beer did not taste like any other. The more she drank, the better she liked it.

"Did you have horses?" he asked.

"Yes."

"And cows?"

"Lots of cows."

"I'll bet you used the horses to round up the cattle."

"We used the pickup truck for that," she said.

"You had horses and you used a pickup truck?"

"My dad would scoop ground corn into the back of the truck, and the cattle would follow him from one pasture to another."

"That wouldn't be any fun," he said.

"It wasn't any fun. I remember one pasture off by itself that was always trouble. We had to move the cattle down the county road to get there. My job was to stand on the road beyond the gate where they were supposed to go in and not let any cattle get by me.

"Cows have brains the size of peapods, and steers have brains that are even smaller. Every time we moved cattle to that pasture, we had trouble with the steers. A few of them always wanted to keep on going down the road. I was still in high school the last time I helped. That day the whole bunch tried to get by me. I yelled and flapped my arms like I always did, but those steers went right on by. Then some of the cows decided to follow those stupid steers instead of following the pickup through the gate. My brother and sister were back on the road pushing the herd from behind. They didn't see what was going on. They just kept pushing.

"Dad saw the problem and jumped over the fence to help me, but he was too late. My father is not capable of giving a single clear instruction. He shouted to go this way or that way and I did. The herd took off past me anyway, and there was nothing I could do. Dad ran to get ahead of them. I ran, too, but that just spooked them more. He yelled, 'What the hell are you doing, scaring them like that?'

"That was enough for me. I climbed over the fence and headed home. It was a three-mile walk, but it could have been twenty for all I cared. Dad never said a word to me about leaving, and I never helped on that road again."

She laughed with the man who imagined the steers going by, although she had almost become angry again by telling the story.

"You should have had a horse," he said. "A horse would have stopped them. At least you would have had a ride home."

"What's the deal with you and horses?"

"If I could get a job riding a horse, I'd quit everything else," he said. "My grandparents had horses on their farm—two mares, Ship and Shape. I loved those horses."

"What kind of horses had names like that?"

"Quarter horses. My grandfather named them. He always wanted to be a sailor."

"And you want to be a cowboy. That's hard to imagine, you know."

"Why?" he asked.

They had been together an hour, and the black beer was almost gone from their glasses. She didn't want to tell him how her imagination failed her, that she had seen him in his white coat and had trouble taking it away. He was more capable of seeing her away from blue.

"I'm beginning to see it," she said. "Do you like to dance?"

"Do you?"

"Yes."

"Let's give it a try, then."

She had grown up dancing polkas and waltzes at the VFW hall on Saturday nights, and she thought that if she could follow her cousin Eunice's lead she could follow anybody. She might have been wrong. Joe tried to compensate with energy for what he lacked in skill. She suspected that they didn't dance much in Iowa.

A short man with gray hair tied into a ponytail came up to them at the beginning of a new song. They were debating whether they should try one more or sit down.

"Here now," said the man with the ponytail. "Let me show this young lady a turn about the floor. This is a waltz, not the shimmy jimmy. Young fellow, you sit down over there with my wife and watch."

She was ready for a turn with this man. She had watched him and his wife glide over the floor as though their feet did not touch the wood. Each knew every nuance of every move the other made, and they floated like butterflies in the wheat fields. Joe accepted his dismissal with good cheer and relief and joined the man's wife at a table off the dance floor.

The man began to dance, slowly and deliberately, signaling to her each move with a light touch on her shoulder or on her hand, which he held without pressure. He was no taller than she, and his ample belly separated them so that they barely retained contact. It was enough, and she became surer of him and he of her, and his directions became subtler. Occasionally she made a false step, but he would bring her back effortlessly. They rarely spoke, and he did not invite her with words for the next dance and the next, but she accepted anyway. She began to smile. She had smiled since the beginning, but she began to smile now because there was no way to stop.

They stayed on the floor until the band stopped for intermission. She wondered how long they had danced. It seemed like a short time, but it could have been longer. Joe gathered two extra chairs and smiled without reproach for neglecting him. He ordered four beers for the table, announcing he was capable of that.

"Watching you dance," he told her, "made me want to take dance classes. What other talents do you have?"

"I can drive a tractor," she said, "but every farm girl can do that."

"Oh, my," he said, shaking his head as though it were too much to believe.

When the band began playing again, Joe asked if she would give him one more chance. She would. He must have picked up a step or two watching from the side. At the very least, his steps were slower. The man with the ponytail danced with his wife, and Katherine was glad for that. She didn't wish to be rescued again.

It was hot inside Dubliners. Sweat formed on Joe's forehead, and every now and then a drop flowed down the substantial slope of his nose until he wiped it off with the back of his sleeve. She had removed her sweater during the break, and her silk blouse clung to her body. She felt Joe's hands as if they were on her bare skin. Her hand rested easily over the indentation of his spine.

As they danced together their abandoned beer warmed to the room. Smoke rose in a cloud at the front of the pub where the serious drinkers sat surrounding the bar and was carried past the picture of Mr. Joyce and out the open door.

When the band leader announced the last song of the night, the floor filled with dancers, and all moved closer together. Katherine and Joe occupied a small piece of territory at the center of the floor.

"You're beautiful when you dance," he said.

When last had she heard that word? Had she ever heard it before?

"You're beautiful, too," she said.

She reached up to his beautiful face, pulled it down, and kissed him on the lips.

The fine waltzers surrounded them on the perimeter of the dance floor and circled them with graceful steps. Leaning into his body, she pressed her cheek against his chest and heard his heart beating beneath her ear. She didn't want the night to end. She wished she and Joe could stay right where they were. She wished everyone would stay right where they were.

Chapter 34

For the first time since transferring to the Second Watch—maybe the first time since she had started working at the police department—Katherine walked down the stairs from the locker room into the assembly room with the confidence she envied in others. Perhaps it was because she had survived the test in the motel room and had moved on. She knew she and Grace had done good work that few would have been able to do, certainly not the men who had resisted them so long. There might be a simpler answer, and there might be no answer at all.

She was early for roll call, so early that there was not another person in the assembly room. She heard muffled footsteps from the wood floor above in the men's locker room. For once they were easy to ignore.

From its hook on the bulletin board, she removed the clipboard that held a thick stack of information bulletins and sat down at a table to read what she had missed over the last week. Flipping back to the first day of their off-duty assignment, she read a new procedure for taking time off at Christmas. Wonderful, she thought. It's the beginning of May, and somebody has time to think about Christmas. The second item reported that there had been a problem with the last shipment of mace. All officers with type WTO-214 were to exchange their mace immediately. She pulled

her mace canister out of its holder, checked the number,
and slipped it back. Not her, she decided.

Police manual item I., 5., vii., a., concerning dangerous
animals, was now amended to read . . . She didn't read it
and flipped the whole stack back to its original position on
the long U-shaped rings. Instead of dangerous animals, she
thought about dancing.

A chair scraped on the floor beside her, and Katherine
looked up as Grace settled in beside her.

"Did we miss anything?" Grace asked as she pointed to
the thick stack of bulletins in front of Katherine.

"Nothing," Katherine said.

"Did you do anything worthwhile on your days off?"

"I listened to the rain," Katherine said.

"Me, too. I'm about sick of it."

"I like it," Katherine said.

"Uh huh. You're not turning strange on me, are you?"

"Maybe. What did you do?"

"I worked on my bathroom," Grace said. "Pretty soon
I'll be able to pee in style."

A third person entered the room, and her sharp heels
tapped loudly on the hard tile floor. Katherine and Grace
looked up together.

"I'm starving," Anne Smith said. "How about you
guys?"

Rigmor was at her place behind the counter when Grace
entered the store with Katherine. Immediately Grace
smelled the *frikadeller* and the sharp pungent odor of vinegar in the red cabbage. It made her mouth water.

"*Davs, Skat,*" Rigmor said. "So, you are finally back here
today. Are you all done with that other business?"

"As far as I know," Grace said.

"And how are you, dear?" Rigmor asked Katherine.

"Fine, thank you."

Katherine's face brightened with Rigmor's attention, as
every face did.

"I have a present for you," Rigmor said.

She walked over to the refrigerator with sliding doors, removed a red coffee can, and gave it to Katherine, who held it in both hands like an aunt holding a baby with a wet diaper.

"*Ja,* but you have to take off the lid," Rigmor said.

Katherine pulled off the lid and looked inside. She carefully removed a torn piece of paper. " 'For Officer Murphy,' " she read out loud, " 'from your friend, Daniel.' "

"We made *kringler* Saturday. He made those for you. Two times now he has made you cookies. That says something, I think. See how carefully he stacked them around the can. I can tell you it's not easy to do that without breaking them. I thought he would never get done."

"Thank you," Katherine said. "They look delicious."

"You have to try one so that you can tell him how good they are."

Katherine put the plastic lid on the counter and tucked the note into her shirt pocket. She took a bite of one of the fragile cookies. The unbitten portion crumbled in her hand. She caught most of the pieces before they fell to the floor, but some escaped. She gave out a sound of surprise and bent down to pick up the pieces.

"No, but don't worry about that," Rigmor said.

Katherine swept the crumbs together with her hand.

"Leave that," Rigmor said more forcefully. "It's just a few crumbs. These men bring in dirt more than that on their boots. Leave it," she said more gently.

Katherine obeyed her and left the crumbs gathered in a small pile on the floor.

"You should have seen him stirring up the dough," Rigmor said. "I thought his arm would fall off, but he kept going. Of course, every shape is not perfect, but he did the best he could. I hope he comes after school. He's hanging around all the time looking for you. Anyway, have you ever tasted something so good? *Hvad?*"

"No," Katherine said, "I don't think I've tasted anything better."

Katherine held out the can to Grace. Grace had the recipe herself. The one Christmas she made them, her father had eaten them like they were a delicacy from heaven. Actually they had been tough and doughy. Rigmor's *kringler* were like bites of clouds.

"I could eat the whole can," Grace said.

"No. That you may not," Rigmor said, "but I made *frikadeller* today. *Nok til* an army."

"We invited a detective to eat with us so that we can talk about some of the things that we're working on," Grace said. "It's the woman detective I told you about, Rigmor."

"Is that right? Well, that's good, isn't it?"

"I suppose it is," Grace said.

While they waited for Anne Smith, Grace went into the backroom to check if Rigmor had gotten deliveries while she was gone. For her it was a constant worry that Rigmor would hurt herself someday by lifting a box that was too heavy. Katherine followed her and got the broom and dustpan from the corner beside the door.

Three cardboard boxes were stacked on top of each other against the wall opposite the table. Grace ripped open the lid of the top box. Inside were small jars of *lumpfisk* caviar. She picked up the box and carried it past Rigmor who sat on the stool beside the cash register.

"Einar must have delivered," Grace said as she put the box on the floor beside the shelf that held the caviar and imported herring. Katherine was sweeping a broader area than her pile of crumbs.

"He did," Rigmor said. "His son just graduated from law school. Did you know that?"

"I knew he was in school. What's he going to do?"

"He takes some test at the bar, and then he gets rich. I remember him as a little snot-nose kid who came with his dad. Do you remember that?"

"I remember," Grace said. "He used to tease me."

"Ah, but that's not so bad. Boys tease all the time. That's how you know they like you."

"He didn't tease like that," Grace said.

"Is that right? Well, now you can put him in jail—big shot or no big shot." Rigmor turned her attention to Katherine, who did not have the same history in her store as Grace. "Katrin," she said, "we sweep at the end of the day. What will people say if they come in the door and see a police officer sweeping the floor?"

Before Katherine could answer, the small bell rang and the door opened just as Rigmor anticipated. Katherine stopped sweeping and held the broom at her side. Grace straightened up from the caviar. The customer stopped at the caviar shelf even though there was room to pass.

"What do you do with these?" Jack Morton asked, picking up one of the jars of black fish eggs off the shelf.

"Eat them," Grace said, "with slices of hard-boiled egg and tomato."

"I'll bet they're good. I saw your police car out front as I was walking by."

"On your way to Ballard Hardware again?" Grace asked.

"Yes." Jack smiled for a moment before his face returned to the expression she had seen as he stood in his garage and looked out to the garbage compactor. "Maybe I shouldn't bother telling you this, because you've probably thought about it already. Thomas was talking about some theory of physics that relies on probability, and then he told me that the probability of somebody picking my garbage compactor out of all the compactors in the city is too small to calculate. He believes there is a reason why the person chose mine. He thinks the person who killed the boy lives close by and doesn't have a car. If the killer had a car, he would have taken the body away. I imagine you've already thought about this, but I didn't think it would hurt to tell you."

"It doesn't hurt," Grace said. She tried to remember if she had considered the same theory. She didn't think so, not completely. "Thanks for telling me."

"Sure."

"It looks like you're making progress on your building," Grace said.

"Slowly but surely. How's your bathroom project going?"

"I'll be done by Christmas."

Bells began ringing together, but they weren't Christmas bells. Anne Smith came into the store, and the little bell above the door rang at the same time Arne rang the big one up the street. Arne may have started first.

"Mr. Morton," Anne said in greeting as she stopped in the aisle where Grace and Jack Morton stood. "We meet again."

"Good afternoon," he replied.

"Officer Stevens told me this was the best lunch in Ballard. You must agree. I can tell you that it's harder than hell to find anything out here. You can't make a left turn on Market Street, and you can't turn on Ballard Avenue either. I had to go all the way around your building to get here."

"We like to make it confusing."

"Well, it sure is. I hope I didn't keep you guys waiting," she said to Grace.

"Don't worry about that," Grace said. "We logged ourselves out on a follow-up. Mr. Morton and I were just comparing construction notes."

"That must be interesting," Anne said and walked away. She raised her hand to wave at Katherine and introduced herself to Rigmor while she was still walking down the aisle. Her voice was loud enough to be heard anywhere in the store.

Grace stacked the last four jars of *lumpfisk* caviar and picked the cardboard box up off the floor. Four men came in together and greeted her as they headed for the counter.

"What do you recommend today?" Jack asked.

"Rigmor has *frikadeller* sandwiches on Mondays—sliced meatball sandwiches—or she has sausage and red cabbage. Of course, she always has shrimp sandwiches. They're more expensive, but they're delicious."

"Shrimp for lunch," he said. "That's pretty high living."

"If you're privileged enough to get into the backroom,

she has warm *frikadeller* and red cabbage. Now, that's high living."

"I've got to get back to work, so I suppose I'll have to settle for a shrimp sandwich," Jack said with a smile. He paid Rigmor for the sandwich and left the store as Grace joined Anne Smith and Katherine in the backroom.

The three women sat around Rigmor's small table with meatballs and steaming red cabbage on each of their plates. Grace wondered if the other two would like the food. Not everyone did.

"The guy at the motel had a few porn flicks but nothing illegal," Anne said. "We didn't find anything yet on that creep you arrested either—Albert Gillette—but the other guy, the one who took off running from your motel room, that's another story.

"His name is Keller, Jonathon Keller. He owns a string of porn shops up and down Highway 99 all the way from Everett to Tacoma. He calls them 99 Video. On his signs the first 9 is backward and faces the second 9. Cute, huh? This guy is just full of ingenious ideas. Homicide and Vice worked together and served warrants on three of the porn shops inside the city before word got out. By the time they got to the fourth place, his attorney was down at the station demanding to see his client. We searched his house, too—a big fancy place out in Laurelhurst—but we didn't find anything. There must be lots of money in his business. He made bail as soon as we charged him.

"We found a few interesting videos locked up in a closet in his store down by the First South Bridge. We think Keller has an under-the-counter business there for special customers—probably for big bucks. Maybe they're Boeing executives. Boeing is down in that area, aren't they? Anyway, these videos have numbers written on them, like thirty-one or forty-four. We think the number identifies a customer. The film quality isn't good, but let's just say that the films are unusual.

"There was one that looked like a scene they had in

mind for you. We're sure that it was the same motel, and Vice is checking out all the rooms this morning to see if they can match it. The girl in the video had a tough time of it. The men wore hoods, so identifying them will be interesting. We're sure one is the motel manager, but we don't know who the other guy is. It's not Keller or Gillette. By the way, Keller had two hoods stuffed in his camera bag."

Grace had stopped eating sometime earlier, but now she put her fork down. In contrast, Anne raised hers above her plate and gestured with emphasis.

"These meatballs are delicious," she said. "I wonder how she makes them so light?"

"Pork fat," Grace said.

Anne looked at the last half of the last meatball on her plate.

"Oh, well," she said. "The diet starts tomorrow."

Katherine stopped eating, too. Grace wasn't sure if it was the pork fat or Anne's story that caused the interruption. Katherine looked down at her plate and spread out the remaining strands of red cabbage.

"Was the boy in any of the movies?" she asked.

"Not the boy you found. There was another one, though—for customer number four. Number four must be a real special guy. The kid was so spaced out that I'm not sure he knew what was going on. The boy looked like he was twelve or thirteen years old. I know we're on the right track, but we just haven't put everybody together yet.

"Well, that's enough of that," she said and put her fork down on her plate. "We're getting pictures made that we can use to identify the victims and suspects. We'll sanitize them so that we can show them around. I'll bring them out to you and see if you recognize anybody."

"Is there any way to find out who these customers are?" Katherine asked. "Number four, maybe?"

"We don't know yet. The flunky at the porn shop says he doesn't know anything about these special videos. He didn't have a key on him for the closet where they were locked up. How does that song go? 'Those who know don't say. Those who say don't know.' I think that's it."

Anne looked to Katherine and Grace as if they might know. Grace had never heard of such a song.

"Anyway, Keller isn't saying anything. Neither is Gillette. I talked to Gillette Friday afternoon. He says he's just the driver for Mr. Keller. Where Mr. Keller says to go, he goes. According to him Mr. Keller has never engaged in anything but saintly activities. He claims he lives with Keller."

"Gillette wasn't driving when they stopped us on Aurora," Grace said. "Keller was driving."

"Interesting," Anne said. "The guy has no record. We ran him through NCIC, and there's nothing on him anywhere. A guy like that can't be clean. I don't know how you two feel, but he gives me the creeps. We sent his prints to the FBI, but that can take forever. I'm pretty sure that Keller used to be someone else.

"He asked Fred and me why you two didn't come to question him. He said he'd been looking forward to that. The way he said it, the way he looked, made me want to shoot him right there. It probably doesn't mean anything, but be a little careful for a while. Keller posted bail for him. I don't trust that bastard at all. If he became somebody different once, he can do it again. He doesn't seem worried about anything. A man in his position should be worried."

Grace gathered their plates and scraped off the remains into the garbage. Usually there was nothing left. She hoped Rigmor wouldn't think that there was something wrong with the *frikadeller*. Out in the store Hans Pedersen from Pacific Crab was talking to Rigmor in Norwegian about the *lefse* that she stocked in the cooler. Hans thought Rigmor should make her own. He could show her how to do it. Rigmor was having none of that. She told him she bought *lefse* from the Stanwood bakery because they made it better than anybody else. Grace knew what she really meant. She bought *lefse* because she wouldn't waste her own time making it. The same conversation had gone on for years.

Grace tried to remember if Gillette had said anything to her in the motel room. Katherine had searched him and handcuffed him. She could barely remember his face. It was fading from her memory as fast as the Stanwood *lefse* in Rigmor's cooler. Hans Pedersen was buying the whole stack.

Chapter 35

After school Daniel got off the bus before it reached Market Street and walked away from the apartment. If his mother asked why he was late, he could tell her that he missed the bus, or he could tell her that the bus was full and he walked. He could tell her that he didn't want to come to the apartment anymore and hope that she would ask why.

She wouldn't ask. She would tell him that they were lucky to have a place.

He always asked his mother if she would be there when he came home from school. She said she would, but sometimes she and Mary left and there was no way to know who was there before the door opened. Sometimes it was only Rudy. Rudy was always there when he got home. His stomach hurt thinking about it.

It had rained all day. It had rained for so long that he couldn't remember when it wasn't raining. He had watched it fall outside the window of the schoolroom. It dripped from the new leaves of the big tree in the playground. He wondered if the leaves could drink any of the water that fell on them, or if they had to wait for the roots to bring it up. How long could the rain fall before the skies were empty?

He walked away from the bus and from the apartment,

and he felt the rain soak through his hair and run down the side of his face. There was nothing he could do about it.

On Sunday Rudy had made a new rule for Mary and him. They couldn't go across Market Street anymore. Rudy said it was too dangerous. He said he had watched Mary and him go across the street and had seen cars almost hit them. Daniel didn't believe Rudy, but his mother did. His mother believed everything Rudy said.

Everybody he wanted to see was on the other side of Market Street, except his mother and Mary. Al was there and Rigmor and Officer Murphy who smiled at him when his sack fell apart. He had liked the way she looked at him. Usually he didn't want anybody to look at him, but he didn't mind her. Would she ever come back? People always seemed to leave just when he started to know them.

If he walked far enough from the apartment, nobody would know if he crossed or not. If he went as far as the locks where the train crossed the water, no one would see him. That was the secret. If nobody knew, it didn't happen. Al told him that there was salt water on the other side of the locks. Al said that the ocean began in the water beneath the train bridge. Daniel thought the ocean had big waves and big beaches where you could walk forever. He could not imagine that he had already seen it, but Al said the ocean was right below the bridge. Even if he had to cross Market Street to get there, Daniel wanted to find out for sure.

He walked behind the lumberyard where wood was stacked as tall as a building. At the fence he stopped and looked through the holes in the wire. Al would never leave his wood outside in the rain. He stacked his wood inside his shop where it would stay dry until he cut it, and then the smell would be so good that Daniel didn't want to leave. Al used all the wood, even the small pieces, except those he gave to Daniel. With the wood Al gave him, Daniel made trains and cars and ships—anything that he imagined would take him away.

Daniel looked up at the sky and caught drops of rain with his tongue. It had no taste. He wiped the rain from his face and started running. He ran until he smelled the French fries that smelled so good it made his stomach hurt. He wished he had eaten all the food at school, but the green beans and meat had gotten mixed together, and he didn't like anything mixed. He wanted everything separate. He wanted to eat the beans first and after that the meat. He had planned to eat when he got home. He hadn't known that he would get off the bus and walk the other way.

His grandmother had mixed things, he remembered, but that was different. When she told him the food was good, he believed her. He would eat anything she made. He believed her, too, when she told his mother that there was nothing better in Seattle than what they had in Idaho. They had moved so that his father could get a better job, but the job didn't help them. His father left anyway, and it would have been better if they had all stayed in Idaho. He had sent his grandmother the picture from school and told her that he didn't like Seattle. His grandmother had written back that she was coming to get them before she couldn't recognize him anymore. Now she was farther away than the ocean.

A tire blew up when she was driving down a hill. That was what his mother said. He imagined that his grandmother was on the way to get them when the tire gave out. It made him feel better to think that she was coming. After that his mother said they could be like a family with Rudy if everybody tried, but that wasn't true. None of it was true.

He stayed on the street away from Market Street even though he had to walk halfway up the hill to the street that went down to the restaurant that had the totem pole out front where the French fries smelled good. He stood on the corner where he thought Market Street went to Ballard and looked back toward the apartment building. He couldn't see it. He was sure nobody could see him either.

Rudy could be standing in the window where he always stood, and he wouldn't be able to see him.

When he saw no cars in either direction, he ran straight across to the other sidewalk. Looking back where he had been, he saw a number on the green street sign. It said NW 53rd Street. It wasn't Market Street like he thought. For a moment he stood on the sidewalk and wondered where Market Street had gone. He had not crossed it after all. Was it better that he had found a way to get across without lying? He would have crossed it anyway.

He walked through the gate of the black iron fence and followed the path through the garden where the trees stood a hundred feet tall. He was alone on the path. The rain hardly reached him through the trees. When he came out of the garden he saw people standing at the railing of the locks with umbrellas over their heads. They spoke in a language he didn't understand, and he moved away from them. He walked on the sidewalk along the railing as far as he could toward the train bridge that pointed up to the sky.

From where he stood, a wire fence ran along the edge of the concrete wall of the first lock. The water was twenty feet below him. There was no way to reach the water on this side of the locks. On the other side, there were steps that went down into the water—a hill with grass and then steps.

He had never stepped on the narrow walkways that led across the locks. How could he be sure that the steel doors would hold back the water? How would he know if the dam beyond them would hold? Water gushed through an opening and flooded the lake where Al said the ocean began.

Daniel watched the people with the strange language and umbrellas walk across the footbridge of the first lock. The bridge was so narrow that they walked one after the other. They stopped on the other side, too far away for him to hear their voices. They continued on to the second bridge.

Daniel followed them. He looked to the left and saw the

water from Ballard dropping behind the door. There were four boats inside the lock. The boats had ropes that kept them in place as they dropped. If one of the ropes got tangled up on the steel posts at the top of the wall, the boat would hang in the air as the water left the lock.

He entered the footbridge of the second lock, which was smaller than the first. He didn't look down at the water. Instead he watched the rush of water ahead of him as it shot over the dam. Fish flew out of the water like birds, except they didn't keep flying. They splashed into the dark water below the dam and disappeared. The water looked strong enough to wash away the steel jaws that held it back. It looked like it would flood over the top of the sidewalk and take everything with it.

He had to go. Holding on to the steel railing, he walked slowly forward on the sidewalk that vibrated with the released water. Spray shot up from the steel jaws of the dam and mixed with the rain.

He reached the far side and looked back from where he had come. The boats in the first lock had dropped out of sight. More water and more fish poured through the dam. Two people stood above the rushing water and looked down where it landed. He wondered why they weren't afraid. What if the water washed away the bridge and swept them away?

Daniel ran down the sidewalk beneath the hill toward the railroad bridge. He stopped on the last concrete step above the water that moved up and down as if a giant were walking through the canal. He knelt on the step. When the water rose up to him, he stuck his hand into it and held it there until the water dropped away. He put the tip of his finger on his tongue and tasted it. Al had told him the truth. It was salt from the ocean.

Chapter 36

They had finished checking the hard-drinking bars on the upper end of Ballard Avenue where the cigarette smoke hung from the ceiling like late-afternoon fog and were returning to the shelter of Rigmor's Grocery. Katherine breathed deeply of the washed air as rain dripped from the plastic brim of her hat.

Grace stopped first. She was closest to the gutter. Katherine turned after her and saw Al hurrying across the street toward them with his upraised hand. She had never seen him without his smile.

"We've got a problem," Al said. "Daniel is upstairs in my apartment. He doesn't want to go home."

"Why?" Grace asked.

"I don't know. He came into my shop about a half hour ago shivering like a cold kitten. I've got him upstairs getting warm. He walked down to the locks after school because he was afraid his mother might not be home. Something is not right."

"What did he say?" Katherine asked.

"He said he found the ocean."

"He found what?" Katherine asked.

"The ocean," Al said. "He's afraid to go home. He said he's not supposed to come across Market Street anymore. There's something bad going on."

The machines inside Al's shop were silent. A large piece of plywood stood upright in a frame with a saw stopped halfway through its cut. Beneath it a pyramid of fresh sawdust lay on the floor. Al led them through a door at the back of the shop and up an enclosed stairway that opened into his kitchen.

Daniel was sitting on a chair at the kitchen table drinking a cup of hot chocolate. His feet did not touch the floor. He wore a man's denim shirt, which was long enough to cover his legs. The sleeves were rolled up above his wrists. His wet clothes were draped over a chair on the opposite side of the table. Like a fortune teller reading tea leaves, he concentrated his attention on the cocoa.

Katherine and Grace sat down in chairs on either side of him. Katherine smiled even though he was not looking at her.

"How are you, Daniel?" she asked.

"Fine." He looked up briefly.

"I've been hoping to find you so that I could thank you for making me all those cookies."

"Did you like them?" he asked. The cookies brought his head up from the tea leaves.

"They were the best cookies I ever ate. I had to take them home. I was afraid Officer Stevens would eat all of them."

"I could make more," he told Grace.

"I'll bet you could," she said.

"Al told us you don't want to go home. Can you tell us why?" Katherine asked.

Daniel shook his head and looked down again to his cup. He had both hands around it.

"You have to trust us, Daniel. We can't do anything if you don't tell us what's wrong."

Daniel looked up to Al, who had remained standing. Al nodded his head.

"He said he would take Mary away," Daniel said.

"Who said that?" Katherine asked.

"Rudy."

"Who is Rudy?"

"My mother's boyfriend. We live with him."

"Why would he say that?"

"He said if I told anybody about him, about what he does, he would take Mary, and we would never see her again."

"Did Rudy hurt you?" she asked softly.

He moved his head so slightly that she barely saw his answer. He was looking beyond her, but she thought he could see her, if only in the remote corner of his vision.

"Can you tell me about it?"

She wanted to look to Grace for help, but she did not dare look away from his face. If she did, she might lose him completely.

"Don't be afraid," Grace said as if she intuited Katherine's thoughts. "We'll make sure that Mary is safe."

Daniel looked back into the cup but didn't answer.

"Maybe it would be better if I went downstairs," Al said.

Daniel looked up in fear. Of all the people in the room, he didn't want Al to go.

"Al will stay," Katherine said. She picked up Daniel's clothes from the chair and moved them to the table. "Sit down right here," she said to Al.

Al sat down in the chair, reached his callused hand across the table, and patted Daniel's arm. "Don't you worry, bud. Plenty of help here now."

With Al at the table, Daniel kept his head up. When he looked down they were all lost. Katherine removed her notebook from her shirt pocket and flipped it to an empty page. She put the notebook before Daniel with her pen beside it.

"Can you write your name for me there?" she asked. "Right on top." She pointed to the top of the page.

Daniel picked up the pen and scooted forward on his chair. Katherine pushed the cocoa cup out of his way and moved the pad a little closer to him. He printed DANIEL in large block letters where she had pointed.

"Very good," Katherine said. "Now can you draw a picture of yourself right below your name?"

He looked at her as if she was asking strange questions, and she was. She was going to ask questions that no one should ever have to ask.

Daniel drew a circle for the head, but the lines did not come together exactly. He drew arms below the head and then added a body between them. He drew straight legs and big feet, studied the picture a minute, and looked at Katherine. He seemed to be done.

"Good."

"I forgot the hat," Daniel said.

He carefully drew a cap. It appeared that the cap was on sideways in relation to the rest of the body, but it was difficult to tell because the face was entirely blank. The hat was the most detailed element of his picture.

"It's an engineer's hat," Daniel said. "Those are the stripes."

He pointed to the carefully drawn lines that filled the hat.

"Very good. Now, on this picture, can you show me where Rudy hurt you?"

Daniel swallowed and any pleasure from the engineer's hat followed the saliva down his throat.

"He hurt me everywhere. One time he threw me over the couch, and I hit the wall."

"Was there any place that hurt most?"

Daniel looked at the picture for such a long time that Katherine was sure he was not going to say anything, but then he lightly touched the intersection of the boy's stick-figure legs.

"Did he hurt Mary, too?"

"I don't think so. She never told me."

"Did you tell your mother about that man hurting you?" She had already begun thinking of Rudy as the sort of person who did not deserve a name.

"No. It seems like he's always there, and she believes whatever he says. He said he would take Mary if I told anybody."

"I understand," she said. "What's Rudy's last name?"

"Hagan."

"Do you know how to spell that?"

Daniel shook his head.

"Do you know his middle name?"

"He never told me."

"Do you know how old he is?"

Daniel stopped to think. Katherine could see that any memory of Rudy Hagan caused him pain.

"My mom is twenty-six. Rudy is older than her."

Katherine tried to keep her voice even and soothing, her expression neutral, as she asked Daniel questions about the way Rudy Hagan had hurt him. Grace and Al remained silent, but Al's face turned increasingly pale as Daniel told a brutal story in a child's voice. The veins in Grace's neck bulged as though she were lifting a heavy weight, but her only movement was a slight nod of the head and a forced smile on those rare times Daniel looked at her. Katherine took notes as inconspicuously as she could, even though she was not likely to forget anything she heard.

Daniel seldom looked up from his hands that he kept on his lap, but he seemed to gain strength as he told his story, as if it were a relief to get it out. Katherine hoped that was a good sign. He would need all the strength he could find.

"Daniel, what that man did was very bad," Katherine said. "You're brave to tell us about it. Nobody should hurt children like he hurt you."

"What will happen now?" he asked.

"We're going to find Mary and your mother first. Then we're going to arrest Rudy so that he won't hurt you or other children anymore. We have to take you and Mary to the doctor and make sure you're okay."

"Can Al go?"

She looked at Al and saw that he was willing to go anywhere.

"Sure he can."

Grace inched her chair closer to the boy, and he noticed her movement. He shifted slightly in the opposite direction.

"Daniel, did other kids come to your apartment?" Grace asked. "Maybe friends of yours?"

"I don't have any friends."

"Somebody else, maybe. Did Rudy ever bring people to the apartment—older boys or older girls?"

"I never saw anybody, but sometimes he left us after we went to bed when my mom was at work. I'd hear him come back."

"Did you hear him talking to anybody?"

"I don't know."

"Did you hear any noises that sounded strange?"

"I don't know. I didn't want to look. I didn't want to hear him."

"I understand," Grace said and patted the small boy on his hands.

Daniel dropped his hands to his sides so that they were out of reach. He looked back at Katherine.

"What will you do with my mother?" he asked.

"What do you mean?" Katherine asked.

"Rudy said she wasn't fit. He said you would take us away."

"Rudy is a liar," Katherine said. Her anger was beginning to rise, and she struggled to push it back down. "Try not to believe anything he said. Somebody like him should be put away forever."

Tears silently gathered in Daniel's eyes. He had not cried a single tear, and even these tears did not fall.

"Why is he here, then?" Daniel asked.

"I don't know," Katherine said.

Chapter 37

"What's taking them so long?" Katherine asked. She paced back and forth on the sidewalk in front of the door to Al's Cabinet Shop. In the couple weeks they had been together, Grace had not seen her partner so agitated—not even after the men broke into their motel room.

"They're coming," Grace said.

Katherine stopped pacing and looked across the street to Rigmor's Grocery.

"He wanted to tell us," Katherine said. She turned back to look at Grace. "He kept coming to find us and we weren't there. Can you imagine what he's gone through?"

Grace stood in the doorway of Al's shop, waiting for their sergeant and a backup unit. Katherine had already parked their car in front of the shop so they would be ready to leave as soon as their backup arrived. Grace looked past Katherine's question and saw two men walk out of Ballard Hardware together and head up the street toward Rigmor's Grocery. One carried a red metal box and the other a paper bag. Three Bowie Electric vans stood double-parked in a line that extended beyond the intersection where Ballard Avenue branched off to 22nd, and the electricians scurried in the rain to restock their vans for the next day's work. She watched a rare occurrence, an old chest of drawers being carried out of McCain's Secondhand where all the seconds went inside and seldom reappeared.

"You might as well wait in here," Grace said. "They won't come any faster with you standing in the rain."

"I didn't even think about the boy in the garbage compactor," Katherine said. "It's practically next door to their apartment."

"Either you come in or we'll both have to stand out there," Grace said.

Katherine took a deep breath and came back inside the cabinet shop.

"When Jack Morton came into Rigmor's today, he told me about a theory that Thomas has about the murderer. Something about probability."

"Thomas Rosencrantz?" Katherine asked.

Grace saw the doubt in Katherine's expression. She had doubts herself.

"I know what you're thinking," Grace said. "I remember now. Jack said that Thomas believes that the probability of somebody getting rid of the body in that particular compactor out of all the compactors in the city is so small that it can hardly be calculated. There is most likely a reason the boy was dumped there. The suspect probably lives close by and doesn't have a car. That was his theory."

"Damn," Katherine said. Her expression showed that her mind was opening to new probabilities. "I should have asked Daniel if Hagan has a car."

"Let's ask Hagan," Grace said. "I see our backup now."

Two cops got out of the patrol car that parked in the last empty spot at the curb. Jessen was a huge man with a soft lisp. His partner, Clark, was smaller, except for the chip that rode on his shoulder and seemed to grow every time he came close to Grace. She tried to ignore it.

"What have you got?" Clark asked abruptly, as if he didn't want to be bothered.

Clark stood on the sidewalk in the rain even though Katherine had moved out of the doorway so that he could enter the cabinet shop. Grace knew Clark wouldn't come in. He had ridiculed the cabinetmaker once in front of

Rigmor, and it had made Rigmor so angry that she'd banned him from the store. The insult to his status was an old wound that festered anew every time he came to the street. Grace kept her voice flat and controlled as she explained why they wanted backup to cover the escape routes from the apartment. She didn't intend to tell Clark more than he needed to know.

"Is the kid here?" Clark asked.

"He's upstairs," Grace said. "He came here looking for help."

"From him?" Clark asked and tossed his head upward.

"They're friends." Grace felt her vocal cords tightening even though she told herself to let it go.

"I'll bet they are," Clark said. He chewed a piece of gum with open-mouthed disdain. "The guy is probably screwing the kid himself."

Grace felt the heat rising up to her face, but before she could let it vent, Katherine surged into the doorway with her finger in Clark's face.

"What's the matter with you? You have trouble hearing? The suspect is up the street, not here."

"Watch your mouth, lady," Clark said. "You don't know anything about this."

"I know all I need to know. Get out of the way." Her finger took a sharp turn as she dismissed Clark and looked back at Grace. "Let's go, Grace. We've waited too long already. We'll get another backup unit if we need one."

"We'll back you up," Jessen said behind Clark. His voice was soft, without any disdain. Grace could never understand how he tolerated working with Clark. "Don't worry about that." He smiled at Grace as though he had not heard anything Clark and Katherine had said. "What's this fellow look like, Grace?"

With Katherine seething in front of her and Clark moving away from the door, Grace described Hagan to Jessen and told him about Hagan's threat to kidnap the little girl. Before she finished, the sergeant passed slowly on the street looking for a parking spot. He gave up and double-parked behind the service trucks.

The sergeant passed Clark and Jessen and entered the shop, and Grace started her explanation over and added the information that Hagan's apartment was less than a block from where they had found the dead boy in the garbage compactor. Jessen came closer to the door and leaned against the frame. Clark looked away as if none of the conversation interested him.

"How old was the boy you found in the garbage?" the sergeant asked.

"Fourteen or fifteen," Grace said. "He hasn't been identified."

"And this boy is eight?" the sergeant asked.

"Yes," Grace said.

"From what I understand, the dead boy was probably a prostitute and got mixed up with the wrong guy. Did you ask your victim if he saw anybody who looked like this other kid?"

"We did," Grace said. "He hasn't seen anybody, but he said the suspect sometimes left them at night and then came back."

"Well, we'll keep it in mind," the sergeant said. "Do you think you got the straight story from the boy? He could be making it up."

"He didn't make it up," Grace said. Out of the corner of her eye she could see Katherine gathering steam again. Grace wondered if Katherine intended to get in the sergeant's face as she had done with Clark. Clark she didn't mind, but it wouldn't be such a good idea with the sergeant. "The little girl could be in danger," she said. "We can't afford to wait any longer."

"All right," the sergeant said. "The boy's statement gives us probable cause. Let's go see if we can find this guy."

Katherine struggled to get her anger under control. If Grace had not warned her, she would have driven straight up 22nd to the apartment. She had forgotten Daniel's description of Hagan always standing at the window and looking down at the street. There was something about Hagan at the window that frightened Daniel. But what was the matter with that guy Clark? He was worse than the worst idiot she'd had to deal with downtown.

Grace pointed her into a narrow alley that ran west behind the apartment. Thank God, Grace was thinking. Katherine stopped ten feet from the sidewalk on 22nd with a bank on one side and a movie theater on the other. The sergeant stopped behind her with Jessen and Clark behind him.

"I don't want those guys to go up with us to the apartment," Katherine said.

"They won't," Grace said. "We'll have them cover the building from the street."

A woman pushing a baby stroller with a little boy tagging behind walked in front of them on the sidewalk. The little boy stopped to point at the police cars. The woman saw them and grabbed his hand.

Katherine walked toward the sidewalk without stopping to confer with the others. She wanted to have the front door in sight. It had been out of sight much too long. Grace and the sergeant joined her a minute later. Jessen stayed in the alley, and Clark walked away in the other direction.

At the entry to the apartment building Katherine pushed the button listed for the apartment manager. A woman's voice answered, and Katherine told her they were police officers and needed entry.

"I'll have to come and see," the manager said. "I can't just open the door to anybody."

"Come down, then," Katherine said urgently.

The sight of three police officers standing at the door satisfied the manager, an elderly woman who seemed to have spent the afternoon in a bar.

"I hope there's not a problem."

"We need to speak to the people in apartment 301," Katherine said.

"I didn't give permission for all those people to move in," she said. "They just did it on their own. I try to keep this place in order."

"We're not concerned about that," the sergeant said, "but we might need a key for the apartment. We want to keep this quiet, too. I imagine you can help us with that."

Katherine started up the stairs. She was not interested in listening to the intoxicated protests of the apartment manager. She wanted to find Mary. She wanted Hagan in handcuffs. She wanted to stop feeling angry and start thinking again.

Grace was close behind her, leaving the sergeant to bring up the rear. On the second-floor landing, the sergeant and the apartment manager headed off to her apartment to get a key. Katherine didn't stop until she stood before the door of apartment 301. She put her ear to the door and listened intently.

"TV," she whispered to Grace.

Katherine listened for Mary's voice. She heard a game show instead. Somebody was thrilled to win a prize.

"We hear the TV," Katherine whispered to the sergeant when he arrived with the key a short time later. "Nothing else."

"Go ahead and knock," he said.

Katherine knocked firmly on the door. "Police officers," she shouted.

She heard movement inside the apartment. Someone came to the door and peered through the peephole. Katherine leaned momentarily toward the peephole and then moved back.

A woman opened the door but didn't say anything. Katherine moved forward and stuck her foot inside the doorjamb. On the television screen she saw a face, but none anywhere else.

"We're looking for Rudy Hagan," Katherine said.

The woman took a step backward and nearly tripped.

"Is Rudy here?" Katherine asked. She entered the apartment.

"He's not here."

"Are you Mrs. Wilson?" Katherine asked. "Are you Daniel's mother?"

"Yes. What's wrong? Has he done something?"

"Where's Mary?" Katherine asked.

"She went with Rudy. Why? What's wrong?"

"Do you mind if we check your apartment?" the sergeant asked.

"Why are you looking for Rudy?" the woman asked.

"We'll explain in a minute," Katherine said. "We want to take a quick look through your apartment first."

"It's not my apartment," she said.

"Then you won't mind if we look," the sergeant said.

He and Grace walked down the hallway. Two doors opened on to it. One was closed; Grace opened the closed door first and entered the room while the sergeant remained in the hallway. Katherine was beginning to dread that they had another lost child.

"He's not here," Grace said when she returned to the living room.

"What do you want with Rudy? I told you he left."

Daniel's mother had sunken cheeks and was exceptionally thin. She was also frightened.

"When did he leave?" Katherine asked.

"I don't know. What's wrong?"

"How long, Mrs. Wilson?" Katherine asked. She was tired of people who couldn't answer even simple questions. "Five minutes, twenty minutes? It's important that we know."

The woman looked at her wrist, but she didn't have a watch. "Twenty minutes, I guess."

"Did he say where he was going?"

"Why? What do you want him for?"

"You need to help us, Mrs. Wilson," Katherine said. "Mary could be in danger."

"What do you mean by that? They just went to the store."

"Which store?" Katherine asked.

"The Safeway. That's where they always go."

The sergeant pulled his radio out of its case in his gun belt and walked over to the window that looked south to Market Street. On his radio he told Jessen and Clark that they were in the apartment talking to the mother. The suspect had left. He told them to stand by.

Katherine took Mrs. Wilson by the arm and led her over to the couch. She looked at the wall above the couch where Hagan had thrown Daniel. There were scuff marks on the wall, but there were marks everywhere.

"Sit down, Mrs. Wilson. We believe Rudy Hagan assaulted Daniel."

"Did Daniel tell you that?"

"Yes."

"Daniel makes up stories sometimes. Rudy lets his anger get out of hand now and then, but he's getting better. He's not used to having kids around like this. That's all. He's trying to change."

"Sit down," Katherine said again.

Mrs. Wilson sat down. Like Daniel, she had difficulty looking directly at Katherine. She had trouble looking directly at anyone.

"He sexually assaulted Daniel, Mrs. Wilson. We need to find him. Mary could be in danger, too."

"What are you talking about?" Mrs. Wilson asked. "He wouldn't do that. They're just kids. He's teaching them about the Bible. He reads to them every night. He's a good man. He wouldn't hurt them like that."

"He already has, Mrs. Wilson. Daniel is safe now, but we need to find Mary."

"She's just a baby. He wouldn't hurt her."

"We don't know that. We need to find her."

"I don't see how this could happen. He worries about my kids. Just today he went out looking for Daniel when he didn't come home. Daniel is supposed to come home right after school."

"Daniel was afraid to come home." Katherine said. "He went to a place down the street where he has a friend."

"To the cabinetmaker, I'll bet," Mrs. Wilson said.

"Yes," Katherine said. "That's where he went."

"I told Rudy he would be there, playing with those trains again. I knew he would be there."

Grace and the sergeant had been listening from the center of the room, and now they came closer. Mrs. Wilson looked at them with concern, but she didn't understand.

"Did Rudy go to the cabinet shop to look for him?" Katherine asked.

"I don't know where he went. When he came back, he just said he couldn't find him. Then he took Mary to get some candy." She looked at the faces intent upon her. "He wouldn't hurt her. She's just a little girl."

"Daniel is a little boy," Katherine said, "and this man raped him."

"He really did that?" Her unstable voice began to break. "He did that?"

"Yes. If Rudy is not at the Safeway store, where else would he go?"

"I don't know. He might go to the bar, but he couldn't go there with Mary. He wouldn't hurt Mary."

"Does he have friends or family where he could go?"

Mrs. Wilson didn't answer. She stared at the floor and took quick short breaths.

"Mrs. Wilson. Where is his family?"

The woman looked up with dazed eyes.

"His mother lives up in Marysville," she said with a faint voice, "but he never sees her. He never sees anybody. That's why he wanted us to be his family. He said he was going to get his job back, and we were going to get a house. That's all I wanted. Something for the kids. He was going to get his job back, and we were going to start over again. All of us."

"Where did he work?" Katherine asked.

"He used to drive a garbage truck."

"He was a garbageman?" the sergeant asked.

Mrs. Wilson nodded in the direction of the sergeant's voice.

"Until he lost his driver's license," she said. "It wasn't his fault. He got into a little trouble, and they took his license away." She spoke mechanically, without feeling. "They wanted to put him at the back of the truck, but he can't lift those cans anymore. He has a bad back, but they wouldn't listen."

"Does he have a car?" Katherine asked.

"No," she said and shook her head slowly. "He had to sell it. We were going to get a car, too, after he got his job back."

"I'll bring some more units in," the sergeant said.

"We need to move our cars," Grace said. "If he comes back and sees them in the alley, he'll know something is up."

The sergeant handed her his keys. "Move mine, will you, or have Jessen do it. Tell Clark and Jessen to search Safeway first. We'll get a complete description out as soon as we can, and I'll have Radio notify transit and the cab companies."

Grace hurried out the door. Mrs. Wilson covered her mouth as the door closed, but she could not cover the horror she was beginning to see.

"Do you have a picture of this man and the girl?" the sergeant asked. "We may need to keep it for a while."

Mrs. Wilson had trouble getting up from the couch. Katherine helped her and walked with her over to a cabinet against the south wall. Mrs. Wilson opened a drawer, which was filled with bills in unopened envelopes, and found a picture beneath them. Katherine took it from her hands.

It was a photograph of four people—two children and

two adults. For all to see, it was a family in their best clothes, smiling at the camera. She looked at the small boy's face, at his eyes. Looking at the picture, a person could deceive herself that he was a happy child.

Katherine looked out the window onto Market Street where Rudy Hagan had so often looked. The Bell Tower on Ballard Avenue reflected light off its dome into the apartment. Above her a break in the clouds allowed the sun to come through. It was the first piece of blue sky she had seen in days.

Chapter 38

Maybe he shouldn't have taken her. He hadn't had time to think it through. Unlike the boy, she had one question after another until it drove him crazy. He told her to look out the bus window so that the moving view would give her something to do. He had to think.

He hadn't meant to hurt the boy. Everything would be different if they could start over.

Maybe the boy hadn't talked. The boy's silence could drive him crazy sometimes. If the boy had obeyed, they could move away and start again. Someday the boy would understand, just as he understood. He remembered the first man his mother brought who took turns with him and his sister. There was another after him, and another. That wouldn't happen to the boy, and the boy would forget.

People were looking at him. He released his grip on the seat in front of him and wiped his forehead with the back of his hand. He looked at the girl who was on her knees with her face against the window. He looked in the direction she was looking, saw a ship, and pointed.

"Look at the ship," he told her.

She was already looking at the ship.

"What's it doing there?" she asked.

His sister had been too weak. She gave up before she learned how to twist them around, to make them crawl. He had learned to make them crawl to him, including his mother. She wanted forgiveness, and he gave it to her. He gave it to her with his fists and knocked her down with it.

"What's it doing there?" the girl asked again.

"It's unloading something."

"Can we go see it? I want to see it."

"Some other time."

The bus began to scale Queen Anne Hill, and the girl turned her head to see the ship. He had to think. Once the girl started talking, she didn't stop. The boy had learned to keep his mouth shut. Maybe he wasn't at the wood shop, but why else would the police car be there? Maybe the boy wouldn't say anything if he was in there, but why else would those two women cops be standing outside and not going anywhere?

Whoever heard of women cops anyway? For days after the girl met them, that was all she could talk about. She was going to be a cop like them, she said, and keep everybody safe. She would soon learn her place, to be quiet and obey. If the boy had done what he was told and stayed away from Ballard Avenue, none of this would have happened.

He pulled the cord above the window to signal the driver they wanted off, and the girl looked at him.

"Is this where they have the candy?" she asked. "You said we were getting candy."

"We'll walk over to the Seattle Center, and you can go on the rides."

"And get cotton candy?"

"Sure, cotton candy."

Her face was happy with the thought of cotton candy as they got off the bus. She extended her hand and waited for him to take it. Her face was quite pretty. He had known that all along. It had fine delicate features—completely unspoiled. He took her hand and led her toward the Seattle Center, where they had rides that kept kids busy. He was lucky the rain had stopped. Maybe his luck was changing.

She wanted to go on the merry-go-round. He bought four tickets and lifted her up on the first horse they came to, but she insisted he move her to the blue horse. To keep her quiet he moved her and told her to give one ticket to the man every time he came around until the tickets were gone. There was only one other kid on the ride, another girl, and she was on the opposite side of the circle. After watching the merry-go-round circle twice, he walked over to the telephone booth beside the ticket window.

In his wallet he had twenty-three dollars. It cost two dollars for four rides, and that was a weekday rate. When she came around on the horse, the girl waved to him. He didn't wave back.

He removed the envelope from his front pocket and felt how many pills were left. There weren't enough. In a few days, depending upon his need, they would be gone. The merry-go-round stopped, and he dialed his apartment as the girl gave away her second ticket. The phone rang six times, and there was a long delay from the time the phone was picked up until she said hello. He could barely hear her.

"Edith, this is Rudy. Did Daniel come home?"

There was another pause. "Yes," she said.

He didn't believe her.

"Let me talk to him."

She took too long to answer.

"He's sleeping. I put him to bed. He doesn't feel good."

"Wake him up. I want to talk to him."

"No," she said without hesitation. "Where's Mary? Let me talk to her."

"She's playing in the park. She's too far away for me to get." He lied without thinking.

"Where are you?"

"Never mind about that," he said. "Who is with you in the apartment?"

"Nobody."

"Don't lie to me, Edith. I have Mary with me. You shouldn't be lying to me."

"Bring her back, you bastard. She's just a baby."

He hung up the telephone just as the merry-go-round started again. The music was the same every time. It was like the bell in Ballard with the same sound every day. He began hating it.

He took two pills from the envelope and wrapped a piece of paper around them. With a rock he found beneath the park bench, he crushed the pills while he watched the girl. People were so stupid that they would never know what he was doing. He creased the paper and brought it up to his nose. He could laugh how easy it was. He covered the paper with his hands, but he doubted anyone would notice if he didn't. People were too stupid to notice. Through each nostril, he sniffed the crease with its delicate powder until he was sure the paper was clean.

The girl waved to him again as she went by. The merry-go-round was gaining speed. The horse moved up and down beneath her, and her dress flared into the air. He waved as she came around again, and he smiled to match hers, except that it didn't match.

If the boy had kept quiet, none of this would have happened.

He went back to the telephone again, dialed the number that he kept in his wallet, and told the man who answered where he was.

Chapter 39

With each question that Katherine asked, Mrs. Wilson withdrew further within herself so that she could barely point to the closet door where Daniel's clothes could be found. Katherine was losing patience. This was not the time for the mother to collapse.

They had not been prepared for the telephone call. She had tried to coach Mrs. Wilson in the few seconds between the startling sound of the first ring and the fifth or sixth when Katherine picked up the receiver and placed it between her ear and Mrs. Wilson's. The coaching had failed. It would have been better if she had answered the phone herself, or if they had let it ring.

Before the phone call Grace had moved their car across the street to the bank parking lot. It didn't matter now. It could just as well have been right in front of the apartment building.

Katherine guided Mrs. Wilson across 22nd with one hand and held Daniel's clothes with the other. Grace remained in the apartment, which she would secure until Homicide arrived with a search warrant. The sergeant waited with Grace, but he wasn't likely to stay long. Katherine hoped he would leave soon because Mary was nowhere to be found. Every free car in the north end, and many that were not, was looking for her. The sergeant would soon be leaving even if they didn't find the child, which was what Katherine feared more with every minute that passed.

If she and Grace had not waited for backup, Mary might be safe. She might also have been placed in greater danger. If a person would steal a child, what else would he do?

Katherine drove south on 22nd to Ballard Avenue and made a U-turn to park in front of Al's Cabinet Shop. Mrs. Wilson shrank against the door in the backseat as if she wanted to disappear through it. Katherine decided to leave her there. Perhaps if left alone, Mrs. Wilson would find some reservoir of motherly instinct, whatever that was.

Al had posted a *closed* sign on his shop door and had locked it. Katherine walked up the outside stairway. When she knocked, Al pulled the window curtain aside and opened the door.

"Is Daniel still in the kitchen?" she asked.

"Yes. I made him a sandwich. He was starved."

"Hagan took Mary," Katherine said. "We think he came here looking for Daniel and saw us."

"Oh, no."

"Don't say anything to Daniel."

"Of course not."

"I have dry clothes for him. I need to take him to Harborview. They have sex crime specialists there. Grace is still at the apartment, but I have Daniel's mother out in the car. She's a basket case."

"She must be in shock."

"I suppose, but it wouldn't hurt for her to show a little courage right now."

"You're thinking like a police officer," he said.

"Am I?" she asked.

If so, it was about time. She couldn't help Daniel or Mary if she didn't start thinking like a police officer. She had been angry at first, much too angry, but that was over now.

"I need to put Daniel's underwear into evidence," she said to Al, who had not tried to answer her question. "Do you have a plastic bag I can use?"

"Sure," Al said. "Sure I do."

She followed him into the kitchen where Daniel was sitting at the table, wearing an engineer's cap like the one he had drawn earlier. One of Al's train books lay open beside his plate. He looked at her with a ring of cocoa across his upper lip. Al opened a kitchen drawer and began pulling out one bag after another.

"I just need one," she said to him softly and picked up a plastic grocery bag from the pile heaped on the counter.

"I brought you some dry clothes, Daniel." She tried to make her voice calm and cheerful. "You can put them on, and then we'll go downstairs. Your mom is down in my car. We're all going to the hospital now."

She expected Daniel to ask about Mary, but he didn't. Instead he looked at Al for confirmation.

"Yep, we're all going," Al said. He picked up a paper towel beside Daniel's plate and handed it to the boy. "Wipe your mouth, bud." Then he pulled the engineer's cap down over Daniel's eyes.

Daniel smiled as he pulled the cap back up and wiped the cocoa from his mouth.

"Daniel, when you change, I need you to give me the underwear you have on," Katherine said. "It's just something we have to do. Don't worry about it. Al won't mind if you go in the bedroom and change. You can put your underwear in this bag."

Daniel got off the chair, and Al's denim shirt dropped past his knees. It made him look smaller than when he had been in the chair. Al shook his head as Daniel carried the plastic grocery bag and clothes into the bedroom. She didn't ask what he was thinking.

With Daniel sandwiched protectively between them, they walked down the outside stairway. As they approached the car Daniel began to slow his steps until each one was painful for her to watch. Katherine opened the back door of the car so that Daniel could get in beside his mother. His mother watched him but said nothing. Daniel stayed outside the car.

"Where's Mary?" he asked.

His mother covered her mouth and looked out the window. Katherine bent down beside Daniel.

"Mary is going to be all right," she said.

"He took her, didn't he?"

"We're going to do everything we can to find her."

Daniel looked at his mother, who continued to look out the window. Daniel looked down at his hands and began digging the fingernail of his thumb into the palm of his other hand. Katherine placed a hand over his. Someone had to touch him. He looked at her. He was afraid, but he wasn't afraid of her. His hand became still beneath hers.

"We'll find her, Daniel," she said.

A nurse led them to an examination room off a remote hallway of the hospital where sex crimes were treated. Katherine guided Daniel as gently as she could, touching his shoulder when they turned a corner, smiling whenever he looked up. From a drawer the nurse pulled out a small hospital gown, which was the right size for a child, and laid it on the examination table. She lowered a step at the back of the table. In a calm professional voice she told Daniel to take off all his clothes, put on the hospital gown, and climb up on the table. She pulled a curtain halfway around the table so that he would have a private place to change. She was well prepared to handle children.

"Mrs. Wilson, you may help Daniel," the nurse said. "The doctor will be here in a few minutes."

Katherine walked out to the hallway where Al had remained and sat down in a chair close to the door. Even though another chair was close by, Al remained standing. She began filling out the incident report just as she would with any victim. Her piece of paper would start the process of reports, investigations, and trials that might go on for months. She wondered how long it would go on for Daniel.

Before entering the examination room, the doctor stopped in front of Katherine's chair and stuck out his hand.

"Dr. Maxwell," he said. He had a large bushy mustache that exaggerated his smile.

Katherine stood up and shook his extended hand.

"Officer Murphy."

She introduced Al and saw that he still had sawdust on his clothes. She explained to Dr. Maxwell that Al was Daniel's friend, and Daniel had wanted him to come along. Dr. Maxwell shook Al's hand, too.

"I'm glad you came. Daniel needs all the friends he can find right now. So, what do we have here?" He took Katherine's clipboard and read what she had written.

"They say a lot of these guys never make it out of prison. Is that true?"

"I've heard that."

"We can hope, then. Is the mother in there with Daniel?"

"Yes."

"I understand that the assailant is still on the loose and might have taken the little sister."

"That's right."

"Jeez. The poor kid must be scared to death. Has Mindy been down here yet? She's the social worker on duty tonight."

"Not yet," Katherine said.

"She'll be down soon. You'll like her. She's real good. She'll talk to Daniel and his mother, line them up with counseling, and do what she can to get the healing started. At least we've moved out of the dark ages on that."

He pushed the door open, and she could imagine the smile he gave Daniel from the voice she heard. Then the heavy door swung closed, and she could hear nothing else. She appreciated that he used Daniel's name, that he knew a child was in the room, waiting and afraid.

Katherine walked to the end of the hallway to the drinking fountain and drank the electrically cooled water. She looked at the blank tile wall above the drinking fountain and remembered how afraid she was the time she had fallen off Silver in the north pasture of their farm. They were not going fast, just walking along a well-worn cow path that circled a ravine and led to lush grass at the bottom where water collected in the spring. She was riding bareback, singing, and imagining herself as a famous star with the audience sitting in stunned silence at the range of her voice. Wearing a beautiful dress that modestly covered her rising breasts and long beautiful legs, she was coming to the finale that would lift the audience from their seats when a jackrabbit jumped across the path. Silver shied and dumped her onto the stage. She landed awkwardly in the weeds and twisted her ankle so badly that it made her cry. Silver could have run off, but the good old horse remained, her head lowered to the ground, wondering how Katherine had ended up there.

She was a long way from home. In order to get back on Silver, she would have to get to a fence or find something that she could climb up on, but the closest fence was a half mile away and she could put no weight on her foot. It hurt worse when she tried to hop on the uninjured foot. If they had a saddle, she would be able to get back on, but her father would not let kids use a saddle. He feared that one of them would get a foot caught in a stirrup and be dragged to death.

She looked at the brown grass hills that went on and on and imagined no one would ever find her. Rattlesnakes would sneak up on her in the night and kill her without caring who she was. Coyotes would eat the flesh from her bones. It would be better to be dragged to death than die like that. They would all be sorry, even her sister, but they would never know what happened to her.

Her father came an hour or so later, before the rattlesnakes, driving his pickup truck along the path. She stood up silently from where she was resting, still holding Silver's reins, not far from the place she had fallen. She had stopped crying by then.

Her father looked worried. She knew the lecture would

go on and on like the brown hills with green grass only in the ravines. The more he worried the more he lectured.

"Are you hurt?" he asked.

"My ankle," she said. "I can't walk."

He took the reins from her and lifted her as easily as she might lift a kitten in the haymow. She put her arms around his neck, and tears began to drop from her eyes. She didn't want to cry, but tears came anyway. He carried her to the pickup and put her gently onto the seat.

"Scoot over to the middle and put your foot up on the seat," he told her.

He removed her shoe and pulled down her sock. Her ankle was swollen and turning a dark ugly blue.

"Mom will take care of this," he said.

Then he turned to the horse that had waited patiently beside the pickup with the reins dropped to the ground.

"Good old girl," he said and rubbed the horse gently on the forehead. "I spotted Silver from the windmill," he told Katherine. "Next time tell me where you're going."

He tied Silver's reins to the back of the pickup, turned around, and slowly drove home. She leaned against him with her foot up on the seat, and he put his arm around her to steady her over the ruts. Her ankle hurt fiercely, but she was not afraid anymore.

When the doctor came out of the examination room, both Katherine and Al were standing. The doctor's face no longer had the smile that greeted them when he first came down the hallway. He spoke to Al first.

"Daniel was wondering if you were still here. I told him you were right outside. I think it would be okay if you went in there and talked to him awhile. I've finished my examination."

After Al entered the room, Dr. Maxwell turned to Katherine.

"We have a few problems. Daniel has been sexually assaulted. That's certain," Dr. Maxwell said. "There are tears in the rectum and clear evidence of trauma. He has bruises on his back and quite a lot of soreness in his stomach. Here's the really swell part: I'm pretty sure Daniel has been infected with gonorrhea. I'll have to run a lab test, but I don't have much doubt."

His mustache covered his entire mouth as he clamped it tightly shut.

"Is it serious?" she asked.

"You mean the gonorrhea? Naw, probably not. We'll treat it with antibiotics. It's just the idea, that's all. I'll need to examine the mother now. The assailant probably gave the infection to her, too. Of course, she might have been the one infected first and gave it to what's-his-face who passed it on to Daniel. Wouldn't that be a swell deal? She doesn't seem very involved with the boy," Dr. Maxwell said, "but you never know how these things will work out. Did Mindy show up yet?"

"No."

"Well, I'll go find her. She can talk to the mother. Bless her heart, she's good at that."

Dr. Maxwell walked off down the hallway in search of Mindy. Katherine sat down in a chair outside the room and tilted her head back against the wall. The fluorescent light in the ceiling tiles was as harsh as the naked sun in the north pasture. She wondered if Mindy would come before the rattlesnakes.

Chapter 40

"**O**kay, Rudeass, where is she?" Gillette asked.

Rudy jumped up from the bench. The voice scared him. Everything about Gillette scared him.

"Over there," he said, pointing to the merry-go-round.

It had cost him another four dollars for tickets. He had bought her cotton candy, and they had walked around the fountain and watched it spray different designs. The girl wanted to go home. He had to buy more tickets for the merry-go-round so that she would stop complaining.

"Where?" Gillette asked.

"On the merry-go-round. She's coming around now. The one on the blue horse."

"Jesus Christ, you didn't tell me she was that young. Keller will never go along with that."

"So leave him out of it. Somebody will pay a lot for this. You and me can split fifty-fifty."

"What happens to the kid?"

"I'm taking care of her. She'll do what I say. We'll make it a game. She won't even know the difference."

"You got to be kidding."

"Look, don't worry about it. We do this, and I'm gone. Nobody hears from me again."

"How come you're so hot to leave? I thought you had a good deal set up."

"It changed. A couple cops got to know the girl and her brother, and now the cops want to be heroes."

"How old is the brother?"

"I don't know. Ten, eleven, something like that."

"Where is he?"

He knew where Gillette was leading with his questions. Gillette liked to make fun of him about the boys he brought, but they made money with them. They would make money with the girl, too. With the right contact they could make a lot of money. It might take a little time, but it would be worth it. Gillette knew that.

"What do you care where he is?"

"You getting shy all of a sudden, Rudeass? You want me to be your partner, I got to know these things, or you find somebody else."

"He's with the cops."

"Jesus. You've been messing in your own backyard, haven't you? Haven't you?"

"I didn't expect the kid to talk. Nothing would have come of it if everybody had minded their own business."

"Well, they didn't, did they? You think I'm crazy enough to get into this when you got cops after you? Get real, Rudeass. You're wasting my time."

Gillette turned and started to walk away. Rudy followed him, but he didn't know what to say. Without Gillette he would have to leave the girl and take off on his own. Twenty bucks and the cops after him.

"Wait," he said. "We can make a lot of money on this. You know that. Wait. You can't just walk away. They find me, they find you, too."

Gillette stopped so suddenly that Rudy almost bumped into him. Even though they were only a few feet from the cotton candy stand, Gillette looked at him as if it didn't matter to him whether anyone was around or not. Rudy was afraid that Gillette would tear him apart right there in front of everybody.

"You threatening me?"

"No. I didn't mean that. Look," Rudy said, turning his back on the cotton candy stand so that nobody would hear what he had to say. "I just need to get some money, and then I'm gone. If everybody minded their own business, none of this would have happened. A couple women cops. Who ever heard of that?" The smell of the cotton candy almost made him sick.

"Women cops?" Gillette asked. "What do they look like? Are they black and white? Is one of them colored?"

"Yeah, I guess so," Rudy answered. "What difference does it make?"

"It makes a difference," Gillette said. "Do you know their names?"

"No. All I know is that they talked to the kids a few times, let them blow the whistle or something, and now the girl thinks she's going to be a cop when she grows up." He nodded toward the girl on the merry-go-round. She had stopped waving when the circle reached their side.

Gillette stared coldly at the merry-go-round, but he was not looking at the girl. "We'll go sixty-forty," he said.

Rudy didn't bother to ask who got the sixty percent. He knew he wasn't in any position to bargain. Still, he couldn't give in without trying to argue. Gillette would take even more if he thought he could get away with it.

"Look, I'm bringing the girl. She does what I tell her. You get nothing without me."

"You get nothing without me. Play with the girl yourself. You like that anyway."

"All right, but let's get out of here. I need to take her someplace. You want to go to the King Arthur Motel?"

"No," Gillette said. "Not there. I've got another place in mind."

"Where?"

"You'll find out. What are you going to tell the girl?"

"Leave that to me. I'll come up with the perfect story."

Chapter 41

As a precaution Grace placed her chair, which creaked each time she shifted her weight, close to the hallway door on the hinged side even though she expected no one except her to open it. Grace lowered the volume of the police radio that the sergeant had left her so that it was barely loud enough to hear.

In block letters on an officer statement form, she described what she had seen, heard, and done so far. She used Daniel's name the first time when she described the victim, which meant listing his name, age, and race—all that was required for justice. After that she used the word *VICTIM* instead of his name. She described the rape of the small boy and the kidnapping of his sister in detached terms as though she were describing the green shag carpet that covered the apartment floor. "State facts, remove emotion," the report-writing instructor had said in the academy. "You are not a voice crying in the wilderness." Nevertheless, it was an ugly carpet, whether she cried or not.

Daniel had not wanted to talk about the rape. He wanted to draw the engineer's hat and think about trains. He didn't want to hate anybody or get revenge. He wanted Hagan to go away, to leave him alone, to leave them all alone. At least that's what she thought he wanted. Who knew? Who could possibly know?

A box of breakfast cereal stood on the table. A blanket lay on the floor beside the couch. On the stove a blackened frying pan with egg scraps was on one of the electric burners, and a pot with beans sat on the other. Neither had a lid. The sink was stacked so high with dishes that the removal of one would cause a catastrophe. She wouldn't use that many dishes in a week.

Grace flipped to the second page on the statement pad and described the phone call from Hagan. Katherine had listened with Mrs. Wilson and tried to signal what she should say. She became angry when Mrs. Wilson called him a bastard, but Grace was not sure at whom. In the report there was no anger. The report said only that the mother had demanded the return of her child.

She heard footsteps in the hallway and turned the radio volume all the way down. The walker stopped outside the door. Grace put the clipboard on the floor, quietly stood, and moved closer to the wall. When she realized the person was entering the apartment across the hall, she remained standing for a minute or two after the opposite door was closed.

At six-fifteen Grace heard Detective Markowitz ask Radio to alert her that they were outside on the sidewalk. Grace pushed the door button on the intercom that unlocked the outside door. She waited for the detectives in the hallway. Markowitz came up first, then Richards. Anne Smith trailed behind, slightly out of breath.

"Are you here by yourself?" Markowitz asked.

"Katherine took the boy to the hospital, and the mother went along. After the suspect called, we were sure he wouldn't show up here."

She gave Markowitz her statement pad so that he could read her description of events. Like Daniel she didn't want to tell it again. Markowitz read the report quickly and gave the statement to Anne.

"Officer Murphy called us from the hospital," Anne said. "The doctor confirms that the boy has been raped. When the judge heard that, he issued a warrant that lets us look for anything we want."

"I'll leave a copy of the warrant on the table so that we're official," Markowitz said. He slipped it under the box of breakfast cereal.

Richards knelt on the carpet, opened the evidence case, and pulled on a pair of latex gloves. He handed another pair to Markowitz and spread a sheet of plastic on the carpet. He lifted the blanket to make room for the plastic and uncovered an open black book lying facedown on the carpet. He reached over and picked it up with his gloved hands. He used his finger to save the open page and flipped to the inside cover.

" 'To James R. Hagan,' " he read, " 'From Mother.' " He held the book up so that they could all see the Bible. He opened the book to the saved place. "Genesis. Let's hope he got beyond the first chapter."

Richards stuck a small evidence envelope into the Bible to mark the page and laid the book on the plastic sheet.

"I don't suppose anyone saw our victim come in here or somebody like him?" Markowitz asked.

"Which victim?" Grace asked.

"I was thinking about the boy in the garbage compactor."

"The mother didn't see anyone, but she was gone a lot. She's a bartender on Ballard Avenue. Daniel didn't either. We haven't talked to anyone in the apartment building yet. Do you want me to do that?"

"No," Markowitz said. "We'll have plenty of time for that. We'll process the apartment the same way regardless. If there is evidence here, Bill is going to find it. Am I right, Bill?"

Detective Richards stood up from the open evidence case. He had a camera in his hand and was ready to begin.

"I'll start down there." He pointed to the bedroom doorway.

"Is this a picture of the suspect?" Anne asked. She stood beside the window facing Market Street.

Grace joined Anne and looked at the picture lying on the top of the cabinet even though she knew what it was. Richards and Markowitz came up behind them.

"That's him," Grace said, "and that's Daniel and his little sister, Mary."

"What do you think, Fred?" Anne asked.

Detective Markowitz moved closer and lifted his glasses. "What are you thinking?" he asked.

"The movie," Anne said. "I think it's him. The guy with the boy. He had a hood over his head, but he's the right size, skin color, build—the whole package."

Markowitz lowered his glasses and stood upright. "Might be," he said. "What do you think, Bill?"

"To tell you the truth," Richards said. "I didn't watch it too close."

"I guess I didn't either," Markowitz said, "but it could be him."

"You guys are a big help," Anne said. "The lab should be finished with the video by now. Let's see if we can get Yoshida down there. I want to see that movie again tonight."

"We'd better put a stakeout on Keller," Markowitz said. "If Hagan is the guy in the movie, he might try to contact Keller."

Anne looked back at the picture, and Grace thought she was studying the suspect again.

"Jesus," Anne said. "I think we had better find this little girl."

Chapter 42

Katherine sat with Daniel and Al in the small waiting room at the end of the hall. Mindy had given Daniel a book of Indian stories to read. She had none about trains. Al read the story aloud to Daniel, who didn't want to read the book by himself. Every time someone walked by, Daniel looked up expectantly.

Katherine had nearly finished her officer statement when Mindy returned to the waiting room. She walked as silently as the Indians in Daniel's book, and Katherine saw the long brightly colored dress before she saw the worried face. Mindy smiled at Daniel through her worry and asked him about the book. It was good, he said, but he wondered when they could leave.

"Soon, Daniel," she told him. "Keep reading. The best part is yet to come."

When Mindy turned away from Daniel, she motioned with her hand for Katherine to follow her. They walked down the hall to an examination room next to the one where Daniel had been.

"Have you seen Daniel's mother?"

"No," Katherine said. "Why are you asking?"

"I think she's gone," Mindy said. "I brought her in here so that I could talk to her privately. I explained Daniel's infection and asked if she had had sexual relations with the supposed boyfriend. She had. I told her that she was at risk, too, and would need to be examined and treated if she was infected. I'm afraid the poor woman has been hit with more than she can handle."

"You don't know where she is?" Katherine asked.

"I've checked all the bathrooms. I've checked the nurse's station. They haven't seen her. I've checked all the empty examination rooms, too. She's not here. I've never had anybody just walk out before."

"How long has she been gone?"

"Not more than ten minutes. I left her here to disrobe. When I came back she was gone. I found the hospital gown on the floor."

It was still there, next to the examination table. Nothing else in the room looked out of place.

"I'm worried about her mental state," Mindy said.

"I'm worried about Daniel's," Katherine said. "Where is Dr. Maxwell?"

"He's with another patient."

"Send a message to him anyway. Notify hospital security and give them Mrs. Wilson's description. Maybe she's still wandering around here. I'll tell police radio that we have a walk-away. She's not under arrest, so I guess she can leave if she wants. It's a lousy thing to do, though."

Katherine pulled the radio from her gun belt by its short antenna. Mindy did not leave immediately as Katherine expected, and Katherine saw for the first time how young the other woman was. It was rare for her to feel older than anyone with whom she worked.

"Maybe I didn't say the right things," Mindy said.

"What can you say?" Katherine asked. " 'Cheer up, life will be better tomorrow'? Get Dr. Maxwell and call security. After that we'll talk about what to do next."

Mindy headed out the door and left Katherine alone in the examination room. She switched to F5, the frequency for the East Central District, and listened for a minute to make sure the air was clear. She brought the radio up to her mouth and looked at the fluorescent light in the ceiling. "2-Boy-8 on F5," she said.

The East Central operator acknowledged her.

"I have a walk-away from Harborview. Her name is Edith Wilson. She's a white female, twenty-six years old, five foot four, thin build, short brown hair. She's wearing a green long-sleeve blouse and black pants. I would like the district cars to keep an eye out for her. If she's found, I would like to have her picked up and returned to Harborview for Boy-8. Her mental state is uncertain, but she is not under arrest. Repeat. She is not under arrest."

Radio repeated her message to the East Central patrol cars, and two cars came on the air and said they were in the area. Katherine wondered what she would do if they found her. What could she do? She could take Daniel and his mother back to the apartment so they could spend the night cleaning up the mess that the detectives were certain to leave. Wouldn't that be a fine way to end their day?

Katherine searched the hallways again, but she didn't find Daniel's mother. Nobody did. When she was certain that more searching was a waste of time, she went back to the waiting room and pulled a chair over to where Daniel and Al sat on the couch. They had finished the book and had moved on to magazines. Daniel did not say a word as she sat down in front of him. Mindy stood behind her. Daniel looked up at Mindy and then to Katherine.

"Dr. Maxwell wants you to take this pill," Katherine said. "You have an infection that we need to fix."

He extended his hand obediently and took the pill from her fingers.

"Put it in your mouth," she told him. "Here is some water to wash it down."

He washed the pill down.

"Drink a little more," she said.

He still had not said anything. Why should he? He had not heard anything good from her yet. He emptied the paper cup, and she took it from his hand and put it on the floor.

"Your mother went somewhere, Daniel," Katherine said. "She didn't tell us where she was going. We're looking for her, but we haven't found her yet. I'm going to take you to a nice home for a little while until we figure out where your mother is. Mrs. Linden is waiting for you there. I talked to her on the telephone. She sounds like a very nice lady."

"You can take the book with you," Mindy said. "Would you like to do that?"

Daniel looked down at the table where they had put the book. On the cover a smiling boy rode a smiling horse. They were chasing buffalo, an entire herd of buffalo running across the prairie. Daniel shook his head. He didn't want the book.

"Can Al go with me?" he asked.

"I'm afraid not," Katherine said.

Al patted Daniel's knee, smiled, and struggled to keep the smile from breaking down. Daniel did not look at anyone around him. He looked at the book he did not want to take.

"I'll have a car swing by and pick you up," Katherine told Al.

"Don't worry about that," Al said. "I'll get a taxi."

"I don't want to bring you down here and then leave you on your own."

Al shook his head and didn't want her to talk about it anymore. "Come on, bud," he said. "I'll walk you out to the car."

He stood and held his hand out for Daniel. Daniel scooted off the couch and put his hand into Al's.

"Maybe my mom went to look for Mary," he said. He looked up to Al to see what he thought.

"I'll bet she did," Al said, and then he repeated the words as if that would make them true. "I'll bet she did."

Chapter 43

It was nearly seven-thirty by the time Grace left the apartment building. Katherine was going to meet her at Rigmor's store as soon as she took Daniel to the foster home. Markowitz and Richards were still inside the apartment gathering evidence and would be for another couple hours. Anne Smith had called for a patrol unit to take her back downtown where she would coordinate the search for Mary.

Grace listened to the police radio as she crossed Market Street, hoping there would be some new information. There had been nothing new since a bus driver reported that he had picked up a man and little girl matching the police description in Ballard and had dropped them off on Queen Anne Hill. His radio hadn't been working properly, and he had missed the first broadcast about the kidnapping. Patrol cars flooded the area, but it was too late.

There was no further sighting of Mary, none of Hagan, none of the mother. All of them gone, vanished without a trace, and, so far, without a way to trace them. Three hours had passed since Mary had disappeared, and each hour that passed was more critical than the one before.

Grace heard her name being called as she walked past the Bell Tower and crossed Ballard Avenue on the brick divide.

"Officer Stevens," Jack Morton said again as he hurried to catch up with her.

There was no traffic, and she waited for him on the brick street. His heavy work boots pounded the bricks as he approached.

"I was on the roof when I saw you guys pull up in the alley. I knew something had to be going on. At first I thought it might be a robbery at the bank, but then I saw you go into the apartment. I was wondering if it had anything to do with the boy we found."

"Have you been running?" Grace asked. He seemed to be out of breath, although he was trying not to show it.

"Yes. I guess I'm out of shape. I was in my office when I saw you leaving the apartment, so I ran down the stairs to try to catch up. I ran across the red light, too."

"We'll let that go this time," she said. "I'm on my way down to Rigmor's. Why don't you come along with me? You can help me close the store, and I'll think about what I can tell you."

When she was a girl her mother would not let her go beyond the brick divide. She could play hopscotch on the sidewalk in front of Rigmor's store, or go upstairs to Rigmor's parlor, but she could not go across the bricks to the park where the bums hung out. Even after they built the tower and cleaned up the park, she could only go there when Arne rang the bell.

Her sister ignored the rule of the brick divide when her mother left the two girls with Rigmor. When Rigmor scolded her for breaking it, her sister would come up with one excuse after another: She saw a dog that was limping; her ball got away from her; she thought she saw Arne, but it turned out to be somebody else. Rigmor never reported her sister's transgressions to their mother, but Grace wouldn't go beyond the divide even when her sister encouraged her. Sometimes she would hopscotch to the end of the block and around the corner on the sidewalk, which had ideal rectangular blocks of concrete, but she didn't break the rule. Her sister was now in Los Angeles, as scornful of rules as ever, while Grace was still on the same block.

Grace propped open the front door of Rigmor's store and told Jack Morton to pick up one end of the produce table.

"No *ja,*" Rigmor said as Grace backed into the store with the first vegetable table, Jack Morton carrying the opposite end. "*Hvor er* Katrin?" Rigmor asked.

"She'll be coming soon. It's a long story," Grace said.

"And not a good one either, I'll bet."

"*Nej,*" Grace said. "Mr. Morton has volunteered to help me close."

"That's very kind of you, Mr. Morton," Rigmor said.

"My name is Jack. I wish you would call me that."

"I guess we can do that," Rigmor said, "especially since we have you working. The pay here is not so good, you know."

"That's all right," Jack said. "I'm used to working for nothing."

When they went out for the second table, Jack went to the far end, reached under the table, and waited for her to lift.

"We're looking for a man who lived in one of the apartments," Grace said. "We think he has something to do with the boy you found. He kidnapped a little girl this afternoon. The girl and her brother and their mother were living there with him. He assaulted the boy, and we went there to arrest him. He took off with the girl before we got there. His name is Rudy Hagan. Ever hear of the guy?"

"No," Jack said.

"I've only seen his picture, but he looks like a big man. Over six feet tall, more than two hundred pounds. He's got short dark hair. It looks black in the picture, but it might be dark brown. He's only been in the apartment for two months. Have you seen anybody that matches that description?"

"I don't know. There are a lot of big guys around here."

"Yes, there are. Some detectives might show you a picture of this suspect in the next day or so."

"I hope they do."

"I told them about Thomas's theory. It helped a lot," Grace said.

"I'm glad to hear that."

"These detectives might be surprised if you already know the suspect's name."

"Don't worry. I have trouble remembering names."

"I should have warned you, Jack. Once you start working at Rigmor's, it's almost impossible to stop."

Chapter 44

Katherine called Anne Smith at eight in the morning and learned that Anne had worked late into the night. There was still no trace of Mary, and nothing had turned up from the stakeout of Keller's house. Anne told her that Markowitz and Richards had been at the apartment until midnight gathering evidence and lifting fingerprints. "Can you imagine how many fingerprints there are in an apartment with two kids?" she asked. The lab had already begun looking for a match from evidence they had taken from the compactor and the garbage close to the girl they found in Fremont. Markowitz found garbage bags beneath the kitchen sink that were the same size and color of the garbage bags that surrounded the boy and the girl. The lab was working on that, too. Most important, they had made a positive comparison between the picture of Hagan and the man in one of the films.

Katherine dreaded asking, but she asked anyway. "Was Daniel in the movie?"

"No, thank God, but I'll have to ask the poor kid if this creep ever took any pictures. Hagan has been charged with a bunch of minor crimes—solicitation, trespassing, stuff like that. Nothing serious, but at least we have his prints on file.

"Fred and I have talked it over, and if we don't find Mary today, we're going to circulate her picture to the newspapers and television stations. It's a risk, but we think we have to take it. We've got to find her soon."

"What about the mother?" Katherine asked. "Any sign of her?"

"No, and she's not at the top of my list either."

"I thought I would go out to the foster home this morning and see how Daniel is doing," Katherine said. "I can't just sit around here."

"Good idea," Anne said.

"Anything else I can do?"

"Not right now, but I'll call if anything turns up."

"I'd appreciate that," Katherine said.

"What were those meatballs called that Rigmor made? I've looked in my cookbooks, and all I see is Swedish meatballs. They weren't Swedish, were they?"

"I don't remember what they're called, but they weren't Swedish."

When Katherine hung up the telephone, she smelled a different kind of food than the meatballs Anne was trying to remember. Dale was baking, and the smell was stronger than usual. She opened her door and saw that he had left his door open across the hall.

"Knock, knock," she said.

"Here," Dale said from the kitchen.

"It's not fair when you do that," she said.

"What?"

He poured coffee into a large mug and handed it to her. She leaned against the kitchen counter and took a drink.

"When you leave your door open while you're baking. What are you making?"

"Brioche," he said. "A brand-new recipe. It'll be ready in ten minutes."

He opened the refrigerator, which was stuffed as always to its extreme limit, pulled out a small jar of red jam, and put it on the table.

"I found this at the market yesterday. Berringer Farms. They make preserves from their own berries. Raspberry preserves on a warm brioche. How does that sound?"

"Delicious."

"The apartment beside Mrs. Rabin is empty," he said. He had turned away from her and was looking into the oven. "The guy moved out last week without paying the rent. I'm thinking about renting it and setting up a catering service from there. What do you think?"

He stood upright and waited for her answer. She knew it wouldn't matter what she thought, so she didn't think.

"Interesting," she said.

"The landlord always has trouble renting it. It's too close to the sidewalk. If he would upgrade the electricity, I could put in a commercial refrigerator. We already have gas in the building. Ground level. Easy access. I could have private parties as well as on-site catering. I could use the storeroom in the basement for a wine cellar. The apartment is below me so it wouldn't bother you if we went a little late. I could put an entrance door directly outside so that nobody would have to come into the hallway and jeopardize building security. What do you think?"

"The noise wouldn't bother me."

"No, I mean about the idea. Here, look at this."

He handed her a book titled *Catering in the Pacific Northwest* and pulled a chair out from the kitchen table. She sat down, opened the book to the center, and leafed back to the front.

"Lots of competition," she said.

"But not a single one around here."

He opened the oven door, flapped a towel to dispel the heat, and turned on the vent fan above the stove. Katherine turned the bottle of preserves so that she could read the label.

"Mrs. Rabin could provide the flowers," she said. She wondered why she said it.

"Terrific idea. Homegrown flowers. Why not?"

He plopped down at the table with her and fanned himself with the kitchen towel. His enthusiasm for her idea worked across his face.

"We could build her a greenhouse in the alley so that

she could have fresh flowers all year long, and we could sell the extra flowers through one of the flower stalls in the market. Have you been there lately? The tulips are in full bloom right now."

"We? Who is this we?" Katherine asked.

Dale laughed high into the ceiling and reached to his shirt pocket where there had once been the package of cigarettes. "Oh, damn," he said as he realized that his ideas would have to keep him high without the nicotine boost.

She heard the telephone ringing in her apartment and jumped up from the table.

"We've got a match," Anne Smith said as soon as Katherine picked up the receiver. "We have the dead boy's prints inside the apartment—the boy you found in the garbage compactor—but, just as important, we have Hagan's prints on that little cross Markowitz found in the garbage. He's pleased as punch about that. Homicide will have a warrant issued within a few hours."

"Any prints from the two suspects we arrested?" Katherine asked.

"Not yet, but they're still looking. Guess where they found the boy's prints in the apartment."

"I have no idea."

"They got a print on an empty bottle of vodka beneath the kitchen sink. It was behind the trash can, and they found the other print on the bottom of the toilet seat. Can you imagine looking there?"

"No."

"Me neither. I would have overlooked that one."

"What about the girl they found at the dump station?"

"No match on her yet," Anne Smith said. "I planned to talk to Daniel this morning, but I don't think he's doing very well."

"What do you mean?" Katherine asked.

"The foster lady said he wasn't talking."

"He's probably scared," Katherine said.

"I mean, he's not talking at all. He won't answer any of

her questions. He won't move away from the window. He just sits there like she doesn't exist. He won't say if he is hungry or if he hurts or anything like that. The woman doesn't know what to do with him. She's afraid to let him out of her sight. The social worker is heading out there to see him. I'm wondering if I should even try to talk to him," Anne said.

"I'm heading out there now," Katherine said. "I'll meet you there. He might talk to me. At least I'll be a familiar face."

Dale was not disappointed that she had to leave quickly and could not hear more of his plans. Anything quick pleased him, and he rose to the occasion with a large bag of provisions. She was just going across town, she told him, not on a weeklong vacation. Nevertheless, she took the bag with her and ate a brioche in the car, managing to keep the jam on the bread as she dropped down to the freeway and headed north.

Anne was waiting in her car as Katherine parked in front of the foster home. On both sides of the street, small painted houses fit together with years of accommodation, and the house hid behind tall fir trees that stood guard in the front yard.

Anne walked over to her car. "I'll make sure you get overtime for this," she said.

"Don't worry about it," Katherine said. She closed her car door and brushed off crumbs of brioche from her pants.

Anne rang the front doorbell and dug in her purse for her badge case. The foster mother pulled aside the curtains from the window at the top of the door and studied the two women on her porch. Anne raised her badge.

"Mrs. Linden, I'm Detective Smith," she said. "I called you this morning."

Mrs. Linden unlocked the dead bolt, opened the door, and invited them inside. Katherine was sure the woman did not recognize her.

"You have met Officer Murphy," Anne said.

"Of course," Mrs. Linden said. "You look different without the uniform. The social worker is with Daniel right now. He seems a little better. He's talking to her, at least."

Katherine stood in the door to the bedroom where Daniel and a new social worker sat on the small twin bed. It had been a girl's room once, probably a daughter's room. Dolls and stuffed animals filled the bookshelves.

Daniel sat as close to the end of the bed as he could. He recognized Katherine right away. His eyes opened wide, and for a moment he looked like he might smile. Then trouble clouded his eyes again. She smiled as much as she could for both of them.

"Good morning, Daniel," she said.

The social worker stood up and the adults introduced themselves. The social worker for the morning was Elaine. Mindy didn't start until three.

"I need to make a few phone calls," she said. "I'll be right back."

Katherine sat down in the impression Elaine had left on the child's quilt. She folded her hands in her lap. Daniel's small shoulders were hunched as he leaned forward, and his feet hung over the edge of the bed. He was wearing clothes that were too big for him.

"This is Detective Smith, Daniel. She's a police officer like me."

Anne barely had time to smile before Daniel looked down again. He seemed far away. Katherine wished she could put him on her lap and rock back and forth the way her father did whenever she had been sick as a little girl. She was afraid to touch him, afraid that he would pull farther away. How much farther could he go?

"Detective Smith and I came to see how you are doing," she said.

"Did you find Mary?" he asked.

"No, but we're looking very hard. A lot of people are looking for her."

"He might hurt her, too."

"I know. That's why we're looking so hard."

"Did my mother come back?"

"Not yet. Do you have any idea where she might go?"

He shook his head. "She didn't go anywhere since we started staying with Rudy."

"How about before then?"

He raised his head, and she could see that he was thinking hard. Softly, with a voice so low that she wouldn't have understood him if she had not seen his lips, he said, "I don't remember before that."

Katherine patted the bed between them and left her hand in the space. "Can you move a little closer?" she asked. "I can hardly hear you."

He shifted his position on the bed so that it looked like he was trying to move, but at most he was an inch or two closer than before. Elaine returned to the bedroom and bent down so that her head was no higher than Daniel's.

"I talked to the doctor," Elaine said, "and he thinks maybe you should come back to the hospital and talk to him. Maybe you could stay there a little while, too. Would you like to do that?"

Daniel turned away from the social worker, he turned away from Anne and Katherine, but he could not find a place to look where somebody was not looking at him. They all waited for him to agree because there was nothing else for him to do. Katherine could almost imagine herself in his place.

He didn't answer Elaine's question. Instead Katherine felt a delicate movement beneath her hand. It reminded her of a little bird seeking shelter. She was afraid to move from fear that he would fly away. Gently she squeezed his hand that he had slipped under hers. He looked directly at her and did not fly.

"Do I have to go back there?" he asked.

Katherine had become accustomed to people asking her questions. She was supposed to be an expert on everything from traffic jams to marital solutions. In distress she was supposed to find relief. In danger she was supposed to find safety. From chaos she was supposed to find a simple solution. Sometimes, not nearly as often as she wished, she did.

Chapter 45

Al came as soon as Katherine called, but it wasn't simple. First she talked to the social worker, and then the foster mother, and then Dr. Maxwell, who called the child psychiatrist who called Katherine at the foster home and then talked to the foster mother and the social worker, who called her office, and so it went. If it took as long to get anything accomplished for Mary as it did to bring a friend to Daniel, the little girl would never be found. Katherine had run out of patience long before Al's old pickup truck stopped in front of the foster home.

From the back of the truck Al picked up a box that held a small train set, blocks of wood, nails, and a child-size saw and hammer. He brought books and magazines and the engineer's hat, which Daniel was wearing when Katherine left them on the back patio of the foster home.

When she opened the car door she smelled Dale's freshly baked brioche. She wasn't hungry, and it seemed a shame to waste them. Despite her impatience, despite her sense of urgency to get to the station and start doing something, anything, she grabbed the bag and hurried around to the back of the house, where she delivered them to Al and Daniel. If Dale had seen the pleased expression on Al's kind face, he would have spent the rest of the day baking pan after pan of brioche.

As she drove to the station, she thought about Dale and Al and realized that if Dale had not moved next door to her, she might not have called the other man. She might have let the jokes that she had carried with her from high school, the farm, and right through college into the police department keep a friend away from Daniel, the only friend he had. She might have persuaded Daniel to go to the hospital, knowing that he would have no choice, feeling that she had no choice herself. If Dale had not moved in beside her, she might not have stuck her finger in front of the cop with his cruel sarcasm. There was plenty more sarcasm, she knew as she walked into the North Precinct, from where that came.

Katherine immediately recognized the woman sitting in the public waiting area. The woman was asleep, and her head drooped onto her chest while her hands grasped the metal arms of the chair as if she were afraid of being dragged away.

Katherine stopped at the counter. The First Watch clerk pushed away from his desk and came up to her. He rested his elbows on the counter and leaned toward Katherine, who remained on the outside.

"She came in asking for you," he said, nodding toward the sleeping woman. "She wouldn't tell me what she wanted. I told her you didn't come to work until noon, and she said she'd wait. I tried to call you at home, but nobody answered. You must know her."

"Yes," Katherine said. "What time did she come?"

The clerk looked back over his shoulder at the wall clock.

"Eight, eight-thirty," he said, looking back at Katherine. "Something like that."

"And she's just been sitting here?"

"That's right. I tried to talk to her, but she said she wanted to talk to you. She wasn't causing any problems. I just left her there."

"Okay, thanks," Katherine said.

"Anything you want me to do?"

"No. I'll handle it."

The patrol clerk went back to his desk, and Katherine looked at the sleeping woman. Katherine had imagined the woman drinking herself into a stupor, or finding some other worthless man to put her up for the night, or finding some way to escape her responsibility to her children. She had never once imagined that Daniel's mother would come looking for her.

"Mrs. Wilson," Katherine said as she sat in the adjoining chair. Katherine touched the woman's arm. "Mrs. Wilson."

Daniel's mother turned her head slowly and looked at Katherine with bleary unfocused eyes. Her hands began to tremble despite their firm grasp on the chair arms.

"I'm Officer Murphy," Katherine said. She wasn't sure that Mrs. Wilson recognized her.

"I know," the woman said. "Did you find Mary yet?"

"No," Katherine said. "Did you?"

Mrs. Wilson was surprised by the question.

"Daniel was hoping that you left him to find Mary."

"How's he doing? Is he okay?"

"No, he's not okay. He won't be okay for a long time, maybe never. How could you walk off and leave him?"

"I don't know. I just couldn't handle it right then. Sometimes I think my kids would be better off without me."

"Did you know what Rudy was doing to Daniel?" Katherine asked.

"No. I knew something was wrong, but I never thought Rudy would do that."

"Did you ask Daniel what was wrong?"

"We didn't have anyplace else to go. What was I supposed to do?"

"You'll have to answer that question yourself," Katherine said. "What were you doing all night?"

"I just walked. I tried to call their father, but he must have moved. Somebody else answered the phone. I walked out to Ballard. When I was on the bridge, I thought about crawling out to the edge and just letting go. I thought maybe my kids would be better off if I jumped."

Mrs. Wilson's face became contorted with pain as she

looked once more into the dark water. On the bridge Katherine might have offered false hope, and she would have extended her hand to the woman. In the safety of the police precinct Mrs. Wilson's large silent tears made little impression on her even if they were sincere. Katherine wasn't thinking about helping this woman. She was thinking instead of the two children who needed her hands more.

"The Ballard Bridge isn't high enough to kill anybody," Katherine said. "You'd have to drown if you wanted to die there. Anyway, you didn't jump. You came here. Now what are we going to do?"

Chapter 46

The girl's screams were getting on his nerves. He shook out the last three pills from the envelope but put them back. Gillette had promised more, but he hadn't brought any yet. As far as he knew, Gillette had not left the room where he kept the whore he had picked up on Highway 99 the night before.

The girl shrieked again like she was drowning. He took a drink of vodka from the hotel glass and closed his eyes. He didn't care if she was drowning. The boy might whimper now and then, but he never made noise like that.

She was getting on his nerves—begging for this, begging for that, always asking questions. He could make it stop in a hurry. He would, too, if something didn't change soon. He had done it before. He took another drink from the glass.

Her screams faded like she was being pulled down farther and farther into the water. Peace would soon come. Peace on earth. Peace on water. Farther and farther down she went.

"Hey, Rudeass, what are you doing? You're supposed to be watching the girl."

Rudy opened his eyes and saw Gillette sitting in the next chair smoking a cigarette. Gillette picked up Rudy's hotel glass and smelled it. He tossed the liquid into the swimming pool.

"You maybe want to pay attention for a few minutes so that the girl doesn't take off. What happened when you gave her the dope?"

"She fell asleep."

"What do you mean, she fell asleep? Did you talk to her? Did she do what you told her?"

"She was tired. She fell asleep. Don't worry, she'll be okay."

"Look, nobody wants to watch her sleep. How much did you give her?"

"A quarter of the pill, just like we decided. She doesn't like to sniff it. I put some in her nose with my finger. She says it hurts. But don't worry, she'll do what I tell her. I need more pills, though. I used up the last of mine today."

Gillette blew smoke into the air and dropped a sealed envelope on the table. Rudy opened it.

"There are only four here," he said.

"There'll be more. Save one for the girl."

"Maybe you want to work with her. You got such a way with women."

Gillette blew smoke into Rudy's face and stared into his eyes.

"You should be careful how many of those pills you take. They make you talk too much. You keep talking, we'll see what happens."

He chose not to keep talking. Gillette had a way of keeping things quiet. Even the girl had become quiet. She floated quietly on the rubber toy as far from them as she could get.

"Did the girl say anything else about the cops?" Gillette asked.

Gillette continued to ask questions about the cops who had arrested him. The girl wouldn't talk to Gillette about them. She wouldn't talk to Gillette about anything.

"She won't tell me any more. Do you want me to bring her over here so you can ask her?"

"Never mind," Gillette said. "I know all I need to know."

Gillette pulled another cigarette from his pack. He lit it and took a long drag. The smoke curled out of his nose in a pulsing angry stream.

Chapter 47

A soft knocking stirred Dale from the sketch he was revising at the kitchen table. He was moving the dining entrance to the back of the apartment where he imagined a trellis of clematis through which his guests would pass as they left the public sidewalk. The path would set the mood for their entry into the kitchen, which was the friendliest room in any house. He was imagining himself in the kitchen, and he tried on various jackets in his imagination before settling for traditional white. The white lingered in his mind as he opened the door.

Mrs. Rabin stood in the hallway with daffodils in one hand, using the hoe to steady herself. She leaned her shoulders back to look up.

"Come in, come in," he said. He had expected to see Katherine, but he should have known the knock was not hers.

"I can't stay," she said. "I brought you some flowers." Mrs. Rabin rarely left her apartment in the evening.

"Thank you." He took them from her and held them up. "They're beautiful."

She smiled and nodded her head. Her head nodded most of the time, and she always seemed to be in agreement with whatever she was doing.

"Have you noticed that man out there?" she asked. Her smile faded with her question.

"No," Dale said. "What man?"

"He was here yesterday, too," she said. "I knocked on Katherine's door, but she's not home."

"She left this morning after she got a phone call from work," Dale said. "She probably went swimming again after work."

"I don't like it," Mrs. Rabin said. "He was in the alley looking in the windows of that apartment across from me."

"Nobody lives there anymore," Dale said. "What's-his-name moved out last week."

"I still don't like it," she said.

"Maybe he's interested in the apartment. Oh, God, I'll bet he is, and I have an idea for that place, too. Come in for a few minutes, and I'll tell you what I'm thinking. It will stop all these people from moving in and out before we even know their names. How about some tea? I have Market Spice. I know that's your favorite."

At the prospect of Market Spice tea, Mrs. Rabin smiled and nodded her agreement. Dale took her arm, and she started forward. Her first step was wobbly, but she steadied herself with the staff of the hoe. Once she started moving her steps were more certain.

"I'll take your hoe," he said. Then he laughed with how silly it sounded. Imagine, he thought, greeting a guest in his kitchen and offering to take her hoe.

Mrs. Rabin settled into a kitchen chair, and he leaned her hoe next to the door. He turned on the gas burner and filled the teakettle with water. There was no time to lose. He would talk to the landlord tomorrow.

He looked out his kitchen window. The streetlights had come on while he had been working on his sketches, and the evening crowds were massing on Broadway. Time passed so quickly. He could plan all he wanted, but there was always somebody out there who would ruin everything. It made him sick to think that somebody else would want the apartment just when he finally had the perfect idea.

He opened the can of Market Spice tea and scooped three tablespoons into his teapot. The perfume of the spices filled the kitchen. He breathed in the aroma and imagined afternoon tea in the dining room. The ladies would come from all over the neighborhood. They might come from even farther away. Mrs. Rabin had given him a great idea. He would tell her about his plans. It might take a while, but there was no time to lose.

Katherine shut off the headlights before turning into her parking space so that the light would not shine into Mrs. Rabin's bedroom. Instead of opening her car door, she sat in the dark and closed her eyes to the darkness. She didn't think she would be able to sleep even though she had pushed herself as hard as she could in the swimming pool, adding lap after lap to burn out the frustration.

She had taken Mrs. Wilson downtown to Sex Crimes, where Grace had joined her and Anne Smith in the afternoon. They had spent the rest of the day there. Katherine had wanted to look for Mary, but she and Grace never left the fifth floor of the Public Safety Building. And Mary wasn't there.

At least the mother showed up, Katherine thought. Mindy had come for her late in the afternoon and would have another chance to counsel. It didn't look like Mrs. Wilson would be leaving the psych ward of Harborview any time soon.

Showing up was more than she could say about the father. Katherine had finally reached him on the telephone at his apartment in Mukilteo. She shouldn't have bothered. After a minute in their conversation Katherine was on her feet shaking her finger in the air as if the man on the telephone in Mukilteo could see it. He didn't want to be involved, he said. He should have thought of that eight years ago, she shouted.

"Let it go," Grace had told her after she slammed down the receiver.

Remembering Grace's words, Katherine nodded her head in agreement and reached for her gym bag on the seat beside her. As she walked around the apartment building to the front door, she saw a light in Dale's kitchen. He was probably still scheming with his latest idea. She unlocked the door to the lobby. Before she started up the stairs she got her key ready for the dead bolt on her apartment door. She tiptoed on the stair treads so that Dale would not hear her. It had been a long day, and she wanted to be alone. She wanted to crawl into bed with a book and take her mind to some other place. Maybe she would find the books she had bought about Mexico and Hawaii and compare the two places again. She would read about swimming in a warm ocean with only whales and dolphins to keep her company.

In front of her door was a paper sack with Dale's latest gifts. She didn't even want to look, but she hoisted the strap of the gym bag over her shoulder and picked up the sack. There was a jar of pickles inside and the rest of the raspberry jam. Why would he give her pickles? She unlocked the dead bolt. The sack shifted suddenly, and she lost her place on the key chain. She hugged the sack closer to her body as she manipulated the keys with her right hand. She could imagine the mess if she dropped the sack. She had too many keys—police station, locker, front door, back door. Finally she found the key for the doorknob, which was in sequence on the chain next to the dead bolt key, and slipped it into the slot just as she heard the footsteps.

She turned her head, expecting to see Dale coming up the stairs. She would tell him that she was tired. She did not want to hear one more plan that he had made in the hours she had been gone. Even if he was disappointed, his plans would have to wait until the morning.

The man came fast as soon as he saw her. She saw the gun, dropped the sack with jelly and pickles, and pushed her way through the door. She tried to open her gym bag where she had stuffed her gun, but there wasn't enough time. His body crushed her to the floor as she lunged inside. He grabbed her hair, pulled her head back, and rammed the gun barrel against her throat so hard that it made her choke.

"Quiet." His voice was as ugly as she remembered from the motel room.

She had not said a word, but she could feel the scream of terror rising inside her. He pushed her face into the floor and moved the gun barrel to the back of her head. She heard him kick the door closed. He was breathing hard, covering her with his body and breath so that she could hardly breathe herself.

He was wearing rubber gloves. She had seen them as he raised his gun in the hall.

"Do exactly what I say, and I won't kill you. Do you understand?"

She said nothing, and he pushed the gun barrel harder against the back of her neck. His lips touched her right ear.

"Do you understand?"

"What do you want from me?"

"Nothing. I'll take everything I want. Let's see how you like these."

He grabbed her left hand and twisted it behind her back. She felt hard steel against her wrist. At first she thought he had taken her handcuffs, but she never took her handcuffs out of the station. He had brought his own.

A howl poured from her as she pushed away. She would not be bound even if he killed her. She jerked her hand free and began to turn beneath him. The blow struck her temple, and she could not break free from the silence that held her as she felt herself dragged from the door.

"Did you hear that?" Dale asked.

"It sounded like something broke out in the hallway," Mrs. Rabin said.

"That's what I thought. Did you hear Katherine come home?" he asked.

"No, but she can be real quiet if she thinks I'm in bed."

"I'll check and make sure everything is all right."

He got up from the kitchen table and walked through his dining room to the hallway door. He looked through the peephole that exaggerated everything in its view, but he saw no one in the hallway. He didn't hear anyone either. Katherine's door was closed.

When he opened his door to look down the hallway, he saw the paper sack he had left for Katherine. The jars had broken inside, and pickle juice stained the paper and flowed along a crack in the wooden floor toward the stairs.

He thought he heard a sound inside Katherine's apartment. He put his ear to the door and heard it again. It sounded like she was dragging something, or maybe she was sick. He knocked on the door and put his ear back to the wood. The noise stopped.

"Katherine," he said. "Katherine, are you all right?"

He did not like this at all. He knew he had heard sounds inside the apartment. He twisted the doorknob to see if she had locked the door. The doorknob turned freely. He opened it an inch and peeked inside. Her apartment was dark. He opened it completely and heard a noise in her bedroom.

"Katherine, it's me, Dale. I heard the jars break. Are you okay?"

It was quiet for too long, but then he heard her voice.

"I'm okay," she said. "Dale, can you hear me? I'm okay."

He knew her voice. He knew her voice when she was happy and excited. He knew it when she was angry. He didn't know this voice.

Then she shrieked. "Run, Dale! Run! He has a gun. Get the police!"

Her voice scared him so much that he did exactly what she said. He slammed Katherine's door and turned to run down the stairs. But then he saw Mrs. Rabin standing a few feet inside his open door. She would not be able to run anywhere. He changed course and ran into his apartment.

"Katherine's in trouble!" he shouted.

He slammed his door and threw the dead bolt lock. His heart was beating so hard that he thought he was going to have a heart attack.

"Call the police," he told Mrs. Rabin. "Katherine's in trouble. I'll hold the door."

The door bounced in its frame, and he knew he would not be able to hold it. He started for the kitchen where he had knives, but the door burst open before he got to the kitchen doorway. He looked around for something, anything, to throw and saw Mrs. Rabin's hoe arcing toward the man's face. The man screamed, stumbled over the stuffed chair, and covered his face with his hands. Dale saw the gun in the man's hand and reached for the first thing he could find.

The last blow had glanced off her head, but her face still felt numb. She rolled off the bed where he had dragged her and tried to slip her feet past her handcuffed wrists. She had seen kids do it, but they had more limber bodies.

She heard a scream in Dale's apartment. Then she heard another. She was sure that the second had come from Dale.

Her shoulders felt like they were being pulled out of their sockets as she tried to get her hands in front of her. After rolling to her side she gave one final kick and her feet slipped past the cuffs. She crawled into the living room and saw her open door. Her gym bag was beside the door, and she lunged for it, unzipped it, and pulled out her revolver. With hands bound by the handcuffs, she grasped the gun. She tried to stand but felt too dizzy, so she crawled toward the door, her finger on the trigger and the gun pointing forward.

She crawled over the sack with broken jars and saw Gillette lying facedown on the floor inside Dale's apartment. One foot moved uselessly in slow motion. Dale stood over the man's head with a glass vase poised to strike. His arms were shaking, and he had a wild look in his eyes. Katherine saw Gillette's gun on the floor a few feet from his hands. His hands were not moving.

"Okay," she said to reassure herself and Dale as she crawled over to Gillette. She pushed his gun away from them with her foot. With her hands cuffed, she could do no more than that. "Okay," she repeated.

Dale slowly lowered the vase. Flowers and broken glass covered the floor. Dale's face dripped with water, and his shirt and pants were soaked. Mrs. Rabin was on her knees struggling to raise herself. Dale kept the vase in his hand as he helped the old lady to stand.

Katherine put her knee into Gillette's back so that she could feel his body if he started to move again. She thrust her gun barrel into his right shoulder. If he moved, the first shot would go there.

"Dale," she said. "Reach in his pockets and see if he has a key for these handcuffs."

Dale put the vase on the floor and eased forward. He did not want to get as close as she instructed.

"Hurry up."

Dale knelt down beside her and looked at the handcuffs on her wrists.

"Who is this man?"

"Never mind about that. There may be another man with him. You've got to empty his pockets."

Dale reached under Gillette into the right pocket of his pants and jerked the pocket inside out. Among the articles that flew out was a key ring with a dozen or more keys in a circle. She instructed Dale to pick up the keys and show them to her. She saw the small handcuff key with its hollow tip.

"The little gold one," she said.

His hands were shaking as he selected the smallest key on the ring. Katherine raised her hands and twisted her wrists apart. Her gun was in her right hand, and she tried to point it away from him. He focused on the gun.

"Hurry, Dale," she said. "Unlock this one first." She wiggled her left hand. "Put the key in and turn it."

She felt the steel give up its grip. It felt like it released her whole body. Dale was gathering himself, and his hands began to steady.

"Now this one," Katherine said. She switched the gun to her left hand and turned her right so that he could see the keyhole. She stuck the gun back into Gillette's shoulder.

Dale freed her right hand. Gillette moaned and tried to raise his head. Katherine reached for his left hand but didn't have the leverage to bring it behind his back. Without instruction, Dale grabbed Gillette's wrist and jerked it back for her. Katherine pinned down his arm with her knee. Gillette groaned again.

"Put the cuff on his wrist," Katherine said. She looked at the hand, which was encased with a transparent rubber glove. She did not intend to remove the gun from Gillette's shoulder blade. His muscles bunched with the movement of his arm. Using both hands, Dale encircled Gillette's wrist with the ends of the cuff and pushed the teeth into the waiting jaws. Katherine squeezed the cuff together as tightly as she could.

"Now the other hand. Pull it back here."

Gillette's right arm was under his body and did not move when Dale pulled it. Dale scrambled over to the right side of Gillette's body, reached under him for a grip closer to Gillette's wrist and pulled again. He pulled much harder. Katherine heard popping in Gillette's shoulder socket, and Gillette raised his head and growled in pain. His face was covered with blood. Katherine pushed her knee and her gun harder into his body.

She gritted her teeth. "Freeze," she said without opening her mouth. "Police officer. You're under arrest." She was not sure if he heard or understood, but she had said the words. That was enough.

Dale's eyes opened wide as she pushed the gun into Gillette's shoulder, but he did not give up the other man's arm. He pulled it back so that the wrist was close to the other. He wrapped the second cuff around it and squeezed the steel pieces together more tightly than Katherine could ever have done. No blood would be passing through Gillette's wrist into his hand.

There was plenty oozing out of his face, however, especially from his eye. The eye socket was completely smothered in blood. Gillette breathed hard and spit blood away from his mouth. His face contorted with pain as he began to regain his senses.

"He's the one I saw, all right," Mrs. Rabin said. Unaffected by the blood, she leaned toward Gillette's face to get a better look. "I didn't like the looks of him the first time I saw him."

Gillette could not see her through his bloodied eye. A red gash ran from the eye down to his cheek.

"She hit him with the hoe," Dale whispered close to Katherine's ear. "She hit him, and then," he said, looking at the broken shards of glass scattered on the floor, "oh, God, I hit him with the Chihuly."

In disbelief he picked up a piece of broken orange glass and looked over his shoulder at the specially designed stand that was now empty. Suddenly he burst into a shrill harsh laugh.

"Dale," she said. "Listen to me. We have to get help. I need your phone. Will your cord reach this far?"

He stopped laughing as abruptly as he had begun and hurried into the kitchen.

"Dial 911 and hand the phone to me," she said when he returned with the telephone. "We're going to get help here in a hurry."

As Dale pushed the buttons she reached for her badge case in her back pocket. It wasn't there. She had a faint memory of Gillette's hands on her body after he dragged her to the bedroom. He had touched her breasts, pulled off her belt.

Dale handed the receiver to her. Somewhere, far off, she heard the telephone ringing over and over into empty space. Finally an operator answered and began the standard questions. Katherine shook her head to clear herself of the foggy disconnection and cut off the woman's mechanical voice.

"I am Seattle Police Officer K. A. Murphy, serial number 5004," she said. "An officer needs help. Put me through to the chief dispatcher."

"What is your location?" the woman asked again.

"This is Murphy, put me through to the chief dispatcher now."

"Go ahead, Officer Murphy," said another voice, one that she recognized. She was now talking to a cop.

She gave the chief dispatcher her address. "I have an assault suspect under arrest," she said. "He broke into my home. He was armed with a forty-five-caliber automatic. There may be more suspects in the area. I need help now."

"Stay on the line with me, Officer Murphy," the chief dispatcher said.

Katherine heard the three beeps that made every cop in the city with a police radio stop and pay attention. Help would soon be pouring in.

"Dale," she said, "go into my bedroom and see if my police badge is on the bed or on the floor. I'm going to need it. Hurry."

"We have units responding," the chief dispatcher said. "Give us your description, Officer."

"White female wearing a beige shirt and blue pants." She looked at the rest of what she could reveal of herself. Her jeans were smeared with blood, but it was not hers. "I'm armed," she said. "I have another citizen with me in the apartment, a white female, eighty years old."

Radio repeated her description to the incoming cars.

Dale returned to the apartment out of breath. He had her badge case in one hand and a black bag in the other. "Is this yours?" he asked. He raised the bag. "I found it on your bed."

She shook her head.

"There's a camera inside," he said.

She felt a sharp pain in her stomach.

"Open up the bag," Katherine said. The chief dispatcher was answering units who were responding, and Katherine could hear sirens in the background. The sirens might have been coming to her through the radio dispatch, or they might have been coming from outside. Dale knelt beside her and opened the camera bag. He started to reach inside the case.

"Don't touch the camera," she said.

"Are you with me, Murphy?" the dispatcher asked.

Katherine could not make the transition back to the telephone as quickly as the chief dispatcher expected.

"Do you need an aid car there, Officer?" the chief dispatcher asked.

"No," Katherine said. Gillette might need one, but she wasn't going to order it. "A citizen will meet the officers at the front door of the apartment building and let them in. He's a white male, forty-five years old, wearing a white shirt and brown pants.

"Hang on a minute, Radio," she said.

"Go downstairs, Dale. Wave both hands over your head when you see the cop cars. Make sure the cops see your hands," she said. "Tell them what I look like. I'm not in uniform, and they won't know who I am. Tell them I have a gun."

As she heard Dale's heavy footsteps on the stairway, she put the receiver on the floor next to the telephone base and inched forward on Gillette's back.

"Mrs. Rabin," Katherine said. "Sit down in that chair." She pointed to the dining room chair closest to Mrs. Rabin.

Mrs. Rabin pulled the chair away from the table. She turned it to face Katherine. Katherine reached for her badge case and saw the camera again. She had been fighting to survive, fighting to save herself and Dale. Now she saw much more. What she saw was coming into hard clear focus. Gillette. Movies. Hagan.

She dropped her badge on the floor, grabbed Gillette's hair with her left hand the way he had grabbed hers and twisted his head around so that his good eye was looking at her. He winced but said nothing. She put her gun within an inch of the eye that could still see.

"You have the girl, don't you? Where is she? Where's Mary?"

"Fuck you," he said. The words seldom made her angry anymore, but this time they gave her anger that she had not known before. She pushed his head back onto the floor and tucked her gun into the waistband of her pants. She put her knee on his neck and picked up the hoe that lay on the floor beside them. His hateful eye stared at her with disdain.

"Where did you take the girl?"

Again he spit out his reply in profanity and blood.

She placed the blade of Mrs. Rabin's hoe into his crotch and pulled one corner in as far as it would go. His eye lost its disdain.

"Where is the girl?" she asked. She enunciated each word so distinctly that each was like its own sentence.

She heard a voice in the telephone lying on the floor, but that was not the voice she wanted to hear. She hung up the telephone. She wanted an answer from Gillette that wouldn't be recorded by police radio.

"Mary," Katherine said. "Where is she?"

Without waiting for a reply she leaned on the handle with all her weight leveraged into his scrotum, lifting herself from his neck as he screamed first in pain and then with a word: "Portland. They took her to Portland."

No matter what he said, she would not believe him. She wanted to crush him not for truth, because there was no truth in him. She wanted to crush him the way he meant to crush her, the way the others had been crushed. She wanted to crush him for what she feared for Mary.

The phone was ringing through his screams, and she pulled the hoe away. She felt as if she had swum miles and miles. Her whole body was tired. She dropped the hoe down beside him so that he could see the blade of the implement that had made such an impression on him. He turned his head away and panted like a dog through his open mouth. She picked up the telephone.

"Murphy," she said.

"We lost you there for a minute, Murphy," the chief dispatcher said. "Is everything still under control?"

"It's under control," Katherine said.

The chief dispatcher broadcast to all the units responding that he had reestablished telephone contact with the officer. By then she could hear a car engine whining through the sound of the siren. It was close enough that Dale would be flagging it down. She was disgusted with herself. Mrs. Rabin had seen it all, and Katherine was ashamed to look at her. It was dangerous to lose control. She wasn't sure how it happened. It was happening too often.

"I'm sorry I did that," Katherine said to Mrs. Rabin.

"My, my, dear, don't worry about that," Mrs. Rabin said. "On the farm we used to cut them off the young bulls with a knife. It was a lot faster."

Katherine heard voices down in the foyer and heavy footsteps on the stairs. She heard Dale's voice over them all. She could hear the police officers telling Dale to wait, but he would have none of that. His voice led them up the stairs.

"Katherine," he shouted. "We're coming up, Katherine."

Katherine knelt on top of Gillette again. She picked up her badge case, flipped it open to reveal the shiny silver badge, and held it toward the door. Two police officers appeared there with Dale right beside them.

"That's her," Dale said. "That's Officer Murphy. She's a police officer."

The police officers could see that. They were holstering their guns even as Dale talked.

"This man broke into her apartment, and then he chased me over here. He had a gun and was going to kill us all. If Mrs. Rabin hadn't hit him, we'd all be dead."

One of the police officers knelt beside Gillette and grasped the handcuffs. Katherine stood up and placed her hand on Dale's arm. He had begun the circle of explanation again.

"It's all right, Dale. They understand."

Dale took a deep breath and nodded his head. He wiped his mouth with the back of his hand.

"Sit down beside Mrs. Rabin," Katherine said. "Make sure she's okay."

She was not worried about Mrs. Rabin.

Dale placed his hand across his chest and breathed deeply as he walked around Gillette's head and joined the old woman at his dining room table. With her one good eye Mrs. Rabin watched everything with keen interest.

More police cars arrived outside and the second officer with the portable radio stood in the hallway door and told all other units to slow down. Then he went downstairs to open the door, which had locked again behind them.

"Is this man shot?" asked the officer who remained with Gillette. He felt Gillette's neck for a pulse. Gillette was still panting deeply, but he had stopped making any other noise.

"No," Katherine said. She remained standing, away from Gillette, away from the anger she had felt. "Mrs. Rabin hit him in the eye with a garden hoe, and Dale hit him on the head with a flower pot."

The officer, who continued to hold Gillette's bound hands, looked over at the two citizens sitting side by side on dining room chairs. He was younger than Katherine. He still had an innocent smile.

"You guys do good work," he said.

"I hit him you know where, too," Mrs. Rabin said. "My husband always told me you could make the biggest fellow listen if you just hit him in the right place."

More officers came tromping up the stairs along with a sergeant. Katherine briefly explained her previous encounter with Gillette to the sergeant. He sent two officers to check her apartment and others downstairs to check Mrs. Rabin's apartment and the vacant apartment next to hers.

"What about a car?" the sergeant asked. "He must have one somewhere around here?"

Katherine reached down to the floor where Dale had dropped the keys and saw a rolled wad of money next to his body. A few inches beyond that was a piece of paper, which had been folded into a square packet. She straightened up, handed the keys to the sergeant, and carefully unrolled the paper. There were twenty or more small pills inside. One dropped onto the pine floor, and she watched it bounce beside a book of paper matches. She squatted down and carefully laid the folded paper on the floor. She picked up the book of matches. The green cover stood out distinctly against the brown wood floor. She should have seen it before. She should have seen everything before.

The sergeant squatted beside her, and she showed him the matchbook. She opened it and saw that three matches were missing from the front row. The edges of the paper cover were sharp and shiny. Raised gold letters gave the name of the hotel and its address.

She heard more voices in the hallway and looked up to see Sergeant Parker and two Vice Squad officers pushing their way through the door with their badges raised in front of their plainclothes. Parker came straight toward her and squatted beside her.

"Jesus, Murphy," he said, "are you okay?"

"I'm okay."

"We were down on Pike Street when I heard your name come over the radio. What the hell happened?"

Katherine nodded toward the man who lay groaning on the floor.

"It's Gillette," she said. "He came after me in my apartment."

"Son of a bitch," Parker said.

Parker looked at Gillette's bloodied face with the rage she had felt before. She put her hand on his arm to steady him, then stood up and motioned for Parker to follow her. Both sergeants trailed her into Dale's kitchen.

"Do you know about the little girl who was kidnapped?" she asked Parker. Parker could not push his mind forward or backward fast enough to understand. "The little girl out in Ballard," she said.

"Right. I know about that."

"Gillette knows where she is," Katherine said. "These people are all involved. Gillette, the man who took the girl—his name is Hagan—probably Keller, too. I'll bet they're all involved. This was in Gillette's pocket." She held the matchbook in front of his eyes. "It's new. There are only three matches missing. She might be at this hotel."

"Highway 99," Parker said. "Out by the airport."

Katherine nodded as the familiar highway surfaced again.

"I'll get my squad out there right now," Parker said.

"I'll go with you," she said.

"Maybe you should stay with Gillette. You ought to have a doctor check you out. You don't look too good. You're getting a real shiner there."

"I know this little girl," she said. "I'm going with you."

"All right," Parker said.

"I'll call Grace. I want to make sure she's okay. Detective Markowitz and Detective Smith will want to know about this, too."

"Sergeant," Parker said to the patrol sergeant, who had listened intently to everything they said, "I think your troops have this place secured. Murphy and I are going to take a little trip out of the city. You'll want to get Homicide here. Ask for Detective Markowitz or Richards. They're handling a homicide and kidnapping that this is tied in to."

"It looks like we'll have to take your suspect to the hospital," the sergeant said. "I'll call for a quiet ambulance. We'll keep two officers with him all the time. That old lady really whacked him. I think he'll lose that eye."

"I haven't searched him completely," Katherine said. "He might have something else in his pockets. Maybe he's got a receipt or something. It would be nice to have more than a matchbook."

They walked back into the living room, and the patrol sergeant called Radio to order a quiet ambulance. Parker knelt down beside Gillette and removed a wallet from his back pocket. He tossed it up to her. He reached into the other back pocket. It was empty.

There were no receipts, but there was money and a Washington driver's license with matching Social Security card. They looked old and worn, except the name. The name was new.

"Look at this," she said, showing the driver's license to Parker. "He has a new name now. Warren Shackelton."

"This time we'll book him as John Doe," Parker said.

Parker turned John Doe onto his side and emptied the one pocket that was not already turned inside out. He found only a few pieces of change inside it. For good measure he frisked John Doe thoroughly, roughly searching all the vital spots. John Doe gritted his teeth and swore blindly.

Chapter 48

As he paced before the windows his shadows followed him in gross distortions on the opposite wall. The streetlights burned through his shadows like fire. His book was open at the table, in the beginning. The girl sat on the floor in front of the television set.

Everything was good, he read—light and dark, the firmament and earth, plants and living creatures, man in His own image, the likeness of God. And on the seventh day He rested. By the sixth chapter, He was sick of them all— His creation, His image, His likeness—and He destroyed everything, washed the earth clean, and began again with the chosen few.

Rudy looked out the window toward the lights and saw himself in the glass—the image of God, the chosen few. The image trembled, gripped with a desire so strong that it must be from the source.

He looked down to the street, which was an evil place in his mind, a Gomorrah waiting for destruction. Like pillars of salt, the columns of the parking garage at the airport rose from a desert of concrete. Deafening noise from the heavens rained down upon them.

The girl watched the television and ate potato chips. Earlier he had tried to read her Revelations so that she would understand mysterious ways. " 'Then I saw an angel coming

down from heaven, holding in his hand the key of the bot-
tomless pit and a great chain.' "

She didn't want to learn. She wanted to watch television.
She wanted to go home. She had yet to learn obedience,
to submit to a superior will. He had turned back the book
to the beginning.

It was ten o'clock, and Gillette had not returned. He had
lied again. There was no end to the evil in that brutal man's
heart. Gillette had promised money, but there was no
money. Gillette had promised him the pills needed to overcome his problems, but Gillette had brought only a few.
Rudy Hagan removed the folded white paper from his
pocket and felt the last round forms within its folds. They
were a message to become free of artificial awakenings and
find simple purity in the wilderness. It would not be long.

He walked behind the girl, who sat on the floor two feet
from the television screen as if the rays from the box would
shield her from the truth. "Know the truth," he mumbled
as he passed her.

In the bathroom he placed the folded paper on the plastic counter and crushed the final four pills inside with a
glass until the paper was flat. He unfolded the paper and
sniffed in the powder, half to each nostril. He looked into
the mirror and saw a white fleck above his lip. Gently he
pushed it higher with the tip of his finger and drew it in
with a single sniff.

In rain and storm he would walk the highway and train
his mind to think in simple purity. He closed his eyes and
breathed deeply.

He would make the girl sleep. Then, without money, he
would begin his journey, cast away all his worldly possessions, and walk barefoot out of Gomorrah. He would find
the true bliss of freedom. For forty days and forty nights
he would journey in the wilderness and seek truth no matter where it lay. He would find a place of refuge and call
the children to him.

Chapter 49

In the cemetery Katherine stood with the cops who gathered around the hood of Parker's car. The others looked at the crude map he had drawn on the back of a blank report, but Katherine had already seen it and watched the street instead. She knew Parker had followed the proper procedure in meeting with King County officers, but time was passing. They had waited too long last time.

They were two blocks from the hotel drawn on Parker's map. The noise of jet engines disturbed the deadly peace of the graveyard. Flashing lights and neon advertised a special price for the strip joint across the street, but the souls who lay beneath the black earth were not buying.

The police officers gathered at the top of the circular drive that led into and out of the cemetery. Anne Smith stood between Parker and Katherine. A King County sergeant rubbed his chin as he looked over Anne's shoulder at Parker's map. Four uniformed King County deputies were with him.

"I've got six officers watching the hotel now," Parker said. "All the officers have county commissions. We have two guys inside the lobby, two in the parking lot, and two around back. They'll see anybody who tries to leave. The girl is only four years old. She should be easy to spot.

"Detective Smith, Officer Murphy, and I will go in first.

We don't want to spook our suspect with marked cars and uniforms. We think that might have happened before when he snatched the girl. We've called Judge Townsend, and he's waiting for us to call back. He'll give us verbal approval for a search warrant if we find out which room the girl is in. You know Townsend, don't you?" Parker asked the King County sergeant.

The King County sergeant smiled with his knowledge.

"Old Townsend has had a few drinks," Parker said, "and he's ready to hang somebody. If the girl is in one of the rooms, we'll knock and go. We're not going to wait for them to answer the door. Sergeant, we'd like your guys to be close and come in if we need you, but stay out of sight until then. I'm thinking one car north of the hotel here on 99"—he circled an X on the map—"and another car to the south." He circled a second X. "But you know this area better than we do, so if you have other ideas, let us know."

The King County sergeant bent closer to the map. "This is fine," he said.

"We might be on a wild-goose chase anyway," Parker said. "We're not sure the girl is here, but it's our best shot."

Another car turned into the cemetery drive and highlighted them for a moment with its headlights. Katherine recognized the car and walked toward it. The headlights went off, and the car approached slowly in the dark along the ornate fence and parked behind the King County cars. Grace got out of her car.

"I was afraid you wouldn't get here in time," Katherine said. "We're about ready to go."

"Are you okay?" Grace asked.

"I'm fine," Katherine said.

Grace put her fingers on Katherine's chin and tilted her head to catch the light from the closest lamp.

"How did he find out where you lived?"

"I don't know," Katherine said.

"Bastard," Grace said. She removed her fingers from Katherine's face.

"Come on," Katherine said. "We need to get going."

Katherine led Grace into the circle of police officers. Those on the outside cleared the way for them.

"This is my partner, Grace Stevens," Katherine said. "She'll go in with us. Are we ready?"

"We are," Parker said.

The Emerald Star Hotel was four stories tall, one of the largest along the strip of hotels that served the airport. Katherine rode in the car with Parker, who found a stall close to the lobby entrance. Grace stayed away from them even though there was a stall open next to Parker. Anne rode with her.

Inside the hotel Katherine could feel Mary's presence. She could hear her voice as if the child were calling. She knew it was the right place.

Katherine immediately picked out the two Vice Squad officers. Their clothes did not fit with the large ornate chandelier in the lobby. They looked as if they belonged on Pike Street. One of the officers was reading a newspaper in an overstuffed chair beside the unlit fireplace. Katherine and Parker walked up to the stained oak reception counter. Parker put his hand on the brass corner. A young man stood behind the counter.

"May I help you?" he asked.

He wore a white shirt and black tie. He did not smile in courteous hotel fashion. Katherine looked past him to a young woman with a matching black tie and white shirt who was sitting at a desk behind the counter. The young woman could not hide her distress when she saw Katherine's face.

"Seattle Police," Parker said. He showed the hotel clerk his badge. Then he flipped open a leather pocket inside his badge case. "This is my King County commission."

The young man reached out as if he were going to take the badge case for closer inspection. Parker pulled it back.

"Just look at it," he said.

Katherine also showed her badge to the young woman

behind the desk. Anne and Grace joined them at the counter. Grace turned to watch the lobby. The young woman pushed her chair back and came up to Katherine.

"We're looking for a man and a little girl," Parker said. "We think they might have checked in here yesterday or maybe today."

Anne opened her purse and showed them a copy of the family picture she had taken from Daniel's apartment.

"Have you seen this little girl?" Anne asked. She pointed to Mary even though Mary was the only little girl in the picture.

The young man shook his head. His name tag said AN-DREW J. BARROWS, ASSISTANT MANAGER. "We have two hundred rooms," he said.

"I've seen her," the young woman said. Her name tag identified her as Sharon Brown. "She was in the swimming pool this afternoon. That man was with her." She pointed to Hagan's face in the picture. "Is there something wrong?"

"She's been kidnapped," Anne said. "Do you know which room she's in?"

"No," the young woman said. "What name would they have registered with?"

"Try Hagan," Anne said. She spelled the name.

Sharon moved around the assistant manager and picked up a computer printout. "There's no Hagan," she said. She bit her lip as she began flipping through the guest file.

"Can you tell which rooms have children?" Katherine asked. She would knock on every door if she had to.

"Usually, but I'll have to go through the file one room at a time. We don't charge for children, so we might not have any record."

"Try Warren Shackelton," Katherine said and spelled the last name.

Sharon looked at the computer printout again.

"Shackelton," she read. "Warren Shackelton. Two rooms—442 and 444." She flipped through the guest file and pulled out the registration forms. "There is no child listed, but, like I said, that may not mean anything."

"We're supposed to record everyone who stays with us," Andrew J. Barrows, Assistant Manager, said.

"Yes, but sometimes the customer doesn't tell us."

Katherine read the check-in forms. Warren Shackelton had registered for both rooms. On one form was an address in Port Orchard. The address on the other was blank. He listed no car.

"We'll need keys for both rooms," Parker said.

"I don't have the authority to give out keys," Andrew Barrows said. "I'll need to call the hotel manager at home for approval."

"You may not have the authority," Parker said, "but I do. And you won't be making any phone calls until I tell you it's okay. This little girl is in danger."

Sharon unlocked a drawer and put a gold key on the counter. "This will open every room in the hotel," she said. "Do you want me to come with you?"

"No," Parker said. "We want you to stay here, but I need to use your phone."

Sharon lifted the telephone from the low counter in front of her to the high one next to Parker. He dialed the telephone number for Judge Townsend, and Townsend instantly gave his approval.

"We're set to go," Parker said as he hung up the receiver.

"What are the rooms like?" Katherine asked Sharon. "Are they connected?"

"No," Sharon said. "They each have two double beds. There's a bathroom right inside the door."

"How about two keys, then," Katherine said.

The young woman opened the drawer again and handed Katherine another key. "Will you tell us if you find her?"

"Sure."

Parker sent the two Vice Squad officers up the stairways on both ends of the building. Then he turned to Barrows.

"Nobody makes any phone calls," he said.

Katherine and Grace got on one of the two elevators, and Parker and Anne Smith got on the other so that all the routes were covered. They arrived on the fourth floor moments apart. Katherine saw the Vice Squad officers at both ends of the hallway. She started walking, noting the room numbers she passed. When she got close to the room where she hoped to find Mary, she pulled her gun from its holster.

The two rooms registered to Shackelton were side by side. Katherine stopped at the first one, room 442, and put her ear to the door to listen for noise, to listen for a child's voice. There was neither from 442. She shook her head to tell Grace that she heard nothing. Grace had stopped at the second room, 444.

"TV," Grace mouthed with her lips. She also had her gun ready.

Parker stood in the space between them. Anne stood behind Katherine. She had her hand on top of her purse, but she was the only one who did not have her gun drawn.

Parker motioned for the officers at the end of the hall to join them. Grace and Katherine backed away from the doors, and they regrouped fifteen feet away, although Katherine continued to watch the door of 444.

"We'll go into both rooms at the same time," Parker said. He looked directly at Katherine. "Pick the one you want."

"Grace and I will take 444," Katherine said.

"I'm with you," Parker said. He gave his key to one of the Vice Squad officers. They had all been customers at the King Arthur Motel, but Katherine could not remember their names. "We'll go into both rooms at the same time," he repeated. "We'll unlock the doors first, knock, shout 'Police,' and go in. I'll follow you," he said to Katherine. "If the girl is in there, you two get her. I'll check the bathroom behind you. Anne, you cover the hall in case we miss something."

They divided into two groups at the two doors. Katherine placed her key into the key slot above the door handle and put her hand on the door lever.

"You knock," Katherine said to Grace.

Parker nodded to her and turned to give the same signal to the officers at the next door. Katherine inserted the key and turned it. She pushed the lever down and moved the door open with her shoulder. Grace banged twice on the door and shouted, "Police." Then she and Katherine went through the door side by side.

"Police," Katherine shouted. She heard the same word shouted beside her, behind her, and from the next room.

Mary was sitting on the double bed closest to them, and Hagan stood dumbly at the window. The child recoiled from their harsh voices and guns. She slid back as far as she could and pressed against the headboard. Hagan reacted slowly, as if he heard voices that were too far away to understand. His face was blank. He did not raise his hands. He did not move at all.

Katherine jumped between the two beds, between Mary and Hagan. Grace went straight after him, grabbed his right hand, and jerked him around so that he faced the window.

"Bathroom is clear," Parker said as he holstered his revolver. He pulled his handcuffs out of a belt pouch and clamped them on Hagan's wrists. Katherine holstered her gun and turned toward the little girl.

"Don't be afraid, Mary," Katherine said. "Do you remember me?"

The little girl nodded her head vigorously and stopped pushing against the headboard. She peeked around Katherine to look at the man who had brought her to the room.

"You're safe now," Katherine said and turned off the television set. She sat down on the bed with Mary, leaving a space between her and the girl. It was too big a space for such a little girl. Katherine reached out to Mary. "Come here."

Mary sprang forward and wrapped her arms around Katherine's neck. The little girl nearly knocked her off the bed, and her arms gripped so tightly that Katherine had trouble breathing. She was willing to tolerate the loss of air.

"The other room is empty," one of the Vice Squad officers said. He stood in the entry.

Parker pulled Rudy Hagan past Katherine and Mary. With her head buried in Katherine's shoulder, Mary did not see him go. Hagan did not look at the child either. He followed the pull of the next hand that grabbed him.

"Take him into the next room," Parker said. "I'll be right there."

Sergeant Parker sat down on the bed beside Katherine. Katherine held the girl gently and did not ask Mary to ease her hold. Mary would have to do that on her own.

"I'm sorry we scared you like that," Parker said. "I'm a police officer like Officer Murphy. I have a daughter the same age as you. She would be scared, too."

Mary lifted her head a few inches to look at the man who had a daughter like her. Mary still had bright eyes. Fear was leaving them, and they were without the troubled veil that covered Daniel's eyes.

Parker patted Mary on her shoulder, but the girl was not ready for that. She pressed her face back into Katherine's shoulder. Parker stood up and smiled, but Mary did not see it. His smile faded into an expression that was almost sad.

"I'll talk to Hagan and leave this brave little girl with you guys."

Mary eased down into Katherine's lap after Parker left. Anne pulled a chair over to the bed and Grace stood behind her. Anne's bright lipstick outlined her smile. There was no sadness in it, and Mary had no fear of her.

"I'm a police officer, too," Anne said.

"You're all lady policemen," Mary said. She looked up at Grace, who had let her turn on the blue lights on the police car.

"That's right," Anne said. "We came here because Rudy should not have taken you away. He's done some bad things. We were afraid that he might hurt you. Did Rudy hurt you?"

Mary shook her head. Her wispy hair brushed across her face.

"Where's Daniel? Where's my mom?" she asked.

"Your mom is okay," Katherine said, "and Daniel is safe."

"What happened to your face?" Mary asked.

"I'll tell you about that some other time."

"Does it hurt?"

Katherine smiled even though it hurt to stretch her skin. "No. It doesn't hurt. Were there other men here with you and Rudy?"

"One man. I wanted to go home, but Rudy said we couldn't. He said we were on a vacation with that other man, but I didn't like him. I didn't want to be on vacation with him."

"Did that man hurt you?" Anne asked.

"No, but I didn't like him. He made Rudy scared."

"How did he do that?" Anne asked.

"Just by talking, I guess. He scared me, too. He made me smile when I didn't feel like it. He told me to put the dragon around me and smile. He took my picture."

"What dragon?" Katherine asked.

"It's in the bathtub," Mary said.

"I'll get it," Grace said.

It was quiet as they waited for the dragon. The little girl shifted on Katherine's lap and looked up at her face. Katherine smiled, but she feared her smile would not reach the child. She feared she could not push down, push back, push away all the emotions she felt. Squeezing Mary gently she brought the child's face in contact with the unbruised side of her own face.

Grace returned with a child's swimsuit and an inflated dragon that a child would use in a swimming pool. She laid both on the opposite bed. The round green creature smiled from his painted face as if he was their best friend.

"Where did he take your picture?" Anne asked.

"In the bathtub," Mary said. "He wanted me to put on the dragon and smile like it was my favorite toy. I did it, but I didn't want to."

"Were you wearing your swimsuit when he took the picture?" Anne asked.

Mary looked at the swimsuit beside the dragon.

"No."

"Did you wear something else?"

The little girl shook her head.

"Rudy said I needed new clothes, so I just had the dragon. He said Uncle Charlie would buy me new clothes and toys."

"Who is Uncle Charlie?" Anne Smith asked.

"I don't know," Mary said, "but Rudy said that when he got here Uncle Charlie would buy me all the toys I wanted."

Chapter 50

Grace looked at her watch. Five minutes had passed since the last time she checked. She sat with Anne Smith by the window, seeking fresh air from the two-inch limit of its opening. Intermittently the roar of a jet engine announced the departure of another airplane. The departures were becoming less frequent. The colored glow of the television set and the small lamp above the closest bed produced a mixed light within the room. The jokes of *The Tonight Show* were turned low. They waited for Uncle Charlie.

"Do you think he'll come?" Grace asked.

"I don't know," Anne said. "Didn't you hear Hagan? He's never heard of Uncle Charlie. He's just rescuing the little girl from her evil mother. It's his mission to save as many children as he can from the sins of their fathers. And their mothers, I guess. We forgot to ask him to pray for us."

"The slime bag," Grace said. "Wanting to take the Bible with him. Who does he think he's kidding? We should have asked to him to take a hike out the window."

"Right now I'll bet he's praying for a lawyer, especially if Katherine interrogates him. She's tougher than she looks."

"She is," Grace said. "Once she gets her teeth into something, she won't let go."

"I don't think that little girl will either," Anne said.

Mary had wrapped her arms around Katherine's neck as Katherine carried her down the hall, escorted by the Vice Squad officers, who towered over both of them. If they hadn't found her, Mary would probably have been asleep by now—the deep sleep of a child. Would this man, this Uncle Charlie, come to wake her? Would he frighten her, would he threaten her? What kind of person could destroy a child's life, take away childhood itself?

"Oh, God, all kinds," Anne said when Grace voiced her thoughts. "Selfish people, sick people, people in the gutters, people in fine tall buildings. Priests, lawyers, judges. White, black, blue, green. I even had a cop once. He at least had the decency to kill himself."

"I couldn't do it," Grace said. "Your job, I mean. I couldn't do this every day."

"Of course you could," Anne said, "and you'd be damn good at it, too. I'm the one who couldn't do your job, or Katherine's. If somebody hit me across the head like that, I'd be in the hospital."

"So would I."

"No, you wouldn't," Anne said. "I watched you two go through that door. You wouldn't let a bump on the head stop you. I'd like to do that just once. I'd like to kick down the door and bust into a room like I knew what I was doing."

"There's not much to it," Grace said.

"There would be for me. I feel like I'm either pretending or placing everybody in mortal danger whenever I take out my gun. You guys were good. When I go into a room like this, I want you in front of me."

"You should go to the range with us and practice. We could give you some tips. Katherine finished second in marksmanship in our academy class."

"I've practiced. It doesn't do any good."

"How do you qualify?"

"Pencil jabs."

"What?"

"Pencil jabs," Anne said. "After we fire off our rounds and walk up to the targets, I stick mine a half dozen times with a sharp pencil. Then I dare anybody to say something. It works just fine."

"You have your gun with you, don't you?"

"I do," Anne said. She patted her purse on the table in front of her. "Don't worry. If anybody gets too close, I'll stick him with my pencil."

Anne began to laugh but choked it off when a soft knock filtered through the laughter from the television show. They moved toward the knock with equally soft footsteps, Grace in the lead and Anne a step behind. At the door Grace rested her right hand on top of her holstered gun. She looked through the peephole and signaled to Anne that Uncle Charlie had arrived. His balding head barely rose to the level of the peephole. Although his image was grossly distorted, he looked about fifty years old, maybe older. He looked harmless. He was carrying a doll.

As planned, Parker opened the door of the next room, where he waited alone. They didn't know which room Uncle Charlie would come to, if he would come at all, but Parker was to come to the hallway to greet him. Grace heard Parker's voice, and the man turned toward the voice and moved out of her sight. She heard Parker's door close, and then it was quiet.

"He went into Parker's room," Grace whispered.

"Now we'll see what kind of salesman Sergeant Parker is," Anne said. "Come on, Parker. Get him to tell you his most intimate desires. Get the money."

They waited by the door for something to happen. They waited as Johnny Carson finished his monologue on *The Tonight Show* and advertisements went by one after the other. Finally there were two taps at the door, and then three more. Anne Smith smiled at the signal.

Grace opened the door wide enough so that the man would be able to see her but not Anne Smith and not her gun still in her holster. She saw the small man with his doll and Parker behind him. Parker raised green bills for her to see.

"Are you Charlie?" she asked.

"Yes." He had a weak timid voice.

"Uncle Charlie?" she asked. She pronounced each word distinctly, as if it were a curse.

"Who are you?" he asked.

"Officer Stevens," she said. "Seattle Police Department."

The man stepped back and dropped the doll. Grace thought it was ridiculous that he would even think about running, but he turned and his arms flew out to propel himself away. He had not completed his first step before she grabbed the collar of his fine blue suit and pushed him into the wall.

"I know my rights," he said. "I've done nothing wrong. You have no authority to stop me."

Grace gave the man her answer. With her hand still on Uncle Charlie's neck, she reached under his suit coat, grabbed the belt of his pants, and pulled his feet back. He tried to catch himself with his hands, but he was too late. His head bounced authoritatively off the wall of the hallway where he had walked moments before with such anticipation.

Chapter 51

Katherine stared straight ahead as a parade of lights flashed across the windshield of Grace's car. Mary was asleep in her lap, oblivious to the parade and their destination.

Katherine could not accommodate, reconcile, or accept the rush of images that swept past her as she held on to the child. It had come too fast, this flood. It had been too strong. It was her, her life, but in another way it seemed apart from her. She felt as numb as the side of her face where Gillette had hit her.

Grace found a rare open spot on the street in front of the apartment building and pulled next to the curb. Katherine looked at the building but did not move. She wondered if she had the strength to climb the stairs.

"Give her to me," Grace said. She had walked around the car to Katherine's door. "I'll carry her in."

Grace reached for the little girl and slowly lifted her from Katherine's lap. Mary's head rose momentarily from sleep, and she mumbled words from a dream before settling into a new position in Grace's arms. Katherine got out of the car and walked stiffly to the front door of the apartment building. The entire second floor was lit. She was glad, at least, that the rooms were not dark. She unlocked the front door and led the way up the stairs.

Above her a machine was whining. From the stairway she saw a man in a gray suit kneeling in front of her open door, wiping the floorboards with a wet towel. She smelled vinegar, but nothing remained of the broken jar. The machine stopped, and Dale appeared in her doorway with his upright vacuum cleaner in tow. He was about to speak to the man in the gray suit when he saw Katherine.

"My God, your face," he said.

Markowitz turned toward her and rocked back on his heels as Dale squeezed past him. Katherine walked up the last few steps to meet him.

"We'll put some ice on it right away," he said.

"I've had ice on it," she said. "What are you doing?"

"Cleaning up," he said. "They're done with the powder and all that other stuff."

Markowitz folded the towel neatly and placed it beside her door. He stood and brushed off the knees of his pants.

"It seems like we just follow you around these days," Markowitz said. "Are you okay?"

"I'm fine. I didn't think you would still be here," Katherine said.

"We're done. Just cleaning up a little. It's a special service for one of ours. I think Dale is almost satisfied. Dale?"

Dale did not hear him. He was looking down the steps at Grace, who had stopped behind Katherine.

"Is this the little girl?" Dale's voice dropped to a whisper, which still could be heard throughout the hallway.

"Yes," Katherine said, "and my partner, Grace Stevens."

Grace had both arms wrapped around Mary, and she shifted the child higher in her grasp. Dale headed for his apartment, beckoning them to follow. He grabbed his vacuum cleaner on the way and dragged it behind him. Katherine knew it was useless to resist.

In the living room Dale arranged pillows on one of his two burgundy couches that formed a wide V below the west windows. He lifted a knitted afghan that was draped over the back and shook it gently.

"Put her here," he said.

Grace laid Mary on the cushions of the couch. Mary remained sleeping and curled into a ball. Dale spread the afghan over her. Then he hurried into the kitchen past a cardboard box, which held the broken pieces of his Chihuly vase. Katherine heard ice trays banging in the sink.

"Why don't you sit down," Markowitz said. He had followed them into Dale's apartment. "You don't look so great."

"I'm all right," she said.

"Sit down, Katherine," Grace said.

Katherine sat on the couch beyond Mary's feet, rested her hand on top of the afghan, and patted the little girl through the yarn.

"Did you find anything here?" Katherine asked.

"Richards got some good plaster footprints outside the window on the apartment below this one. That's where Gillette got in. He pried open a window and made himself at home there. We took prints inside the apartment, and we've got fiber samples at the window. He had a pry bar in his camera bag, and it matches the pry marks on the windowsill."

"Why did you dust my apartment?" she asked. "He was wearing rubber gloves."

"I know. We wanted to make sure he wasn't there before."

"Did you find any?"

"Some that were big enough, but Dale thought they might be his. Anybody else we need to screen out?"

"Probably not," she said.

"It doesn't matter," Markowitz said. "We'll compare them to our suspects and see if anybody matches. We've got all we need on Gillette to keep him gone for a long time. Same with Hagan. He might even get the big one. We'd like to wrap up Keller a bit tighter, though. So far we've just got him dancing along the edge."

"What kind of dance?" Katherine asked.

"Not sure yet," Markowitz said. "How did you get the little girl released to you?"

"It wasn't hard," Katherine said. "It will just be for a day or two until we can figure out where she and Daniel can go. Their mother is in Harborview, and she can't take care of them yet. We might have to move Daniel to a new place so that they can be together, and I wasn't going to start that process tonight. Mary has had enough for one night."

"She sure is a cute kid."

"Yes," Katherine said, reaching over to Mary's face and brushing her hair back. "She's a cute kid."

"I'm going downstairs to get Richards, and then we'll get out of here. You get some sleep. We'll talk to you tomorrow."

Markowitz stopped at the kitchen door to tell Dale that he was leaving. Dale's shrill voice rose to say good-bye and dropped mid-sentence to a penetrating whisper. A moment later Dale hurried into the living room with a plastic bag filled with ice. He wrapped a tea towel around the ice bag. Katherine recognized it as one that his mother had left him. It had delicate time-consuming stitches that formed a border of roses.

"Put this on your face," he said.

She placed the rose-covered ice bag next to her eye and tilted her head back. As she felt the cold of the ice reach through the towel, she closed her eyes—only for a moment.

"I'll get you a pillow," he said.

She heard his footsteps disappear into the guest bedroom. Grace remained standing beside her.

"Do you want me to stay tonight?" Grace asked.

"Of course not. Go home. We'll be fine."

"Hell of a day," Grace said.

"We got Mary back."

"You got her back."

"I'm not sure I like what it took to do that," Katherine said. She pursed her lips together so that they would not tremble, and she forced her eyes tightly shut. "I'm not sure I like the person who did it either."

She felt Grace's hand on top of hers over the ice pack. It felt strong and warm. Katherine opened her eyes.

"I like her," Grace whispered.

Tears soaked into the towel cooled by ice but roamed freely down the other cheek until Grace placed a hand there, too.

"Get some sleep. I'll call you tomorrow. I think Dale is going to take good care of you and Mary."

Katherine smiled between Grace's hands, and then Grace released her and walked toward the door. Grace waved good-bye to Dale as he emerged from the bedroom with two pillows and a large wool blanket. He waved back with his arms full of bedding. He arranged the pillows on the second couch and fluffed out the blanket.

"You'll stay here tonight," he said.

Katherine moved to the adjoining couch and laid her head on the pillows. She could hear Mary breathing next to her. She thought about checking her apartment but decided to wait. She didn't want to go in there yet. She didn't want to do anything yet. Dale pulled a stuffed chair over to them so that it was within the V of his matching couches.

"Thank you, Dale," she said, closing her eyes as tightly as she could.

"The detectives took Mrs. Rabin's hoe," he said. "We'll have to get her another one tomorrow."

Chapter 52

Katherine woke so often during the night that when she woke again she didn't realize it was morning until she heard Dale in the kitchen. Mary was curled on the couch beneath her arm, where she had come during the night, shrinking the narrow space even more. Despite waking often Katherine had slept with such heaviness that the girl's crowding and Dale's snoring in the upholstered chair next to her had been temporary interruptions until she heard his banging pans.

She stood in the kitchen doorway and watched him open cupboard doors and arrange a row of ingredients on the counter. He looked like he was sleepwalking.

"What are you doing?" she asked.

He snapped his head toward her, suddenly awakened.

"Making pancakes," he said. "Every kid likes pancakes."

"You look exhausted," she said.

"You don't look so good yourself. How's your face? You got a black eye, you know."

"I know," she said, although she didn't know. She had not looked at herself in the mirror. "Thanks for letting us sleep here last night."

He flicked his hand as if there were nothing more to talk about on that subject.

"I wasn't quite ready to go back to my apartment."

"Of course not. Stay here until you're ready."

"I'm ready," she said. "I have to go to the bathroom. Would you keep an eye on Mary in case she wakes up?"

"Use my bathroom," he said.

"No. I need a shower. Would you watch Mary, though?"

"I'll watch," he said. "Leave your apartment door open."

Dale watched her stop at the couch where she arranged the blanket over Mary, and he watched her open his door and enter the hallway, which still smelled faintly of pickles. She imagined he was still watching as she stepped inside her apartment, leaving the door open as he instructed.

She expected to see or feel or smell some trace of the other man, but it was as if he had never been there. Dale had placed his mark on everything the man may have touched before him. There was more order in her apartment than when she left. In the doorway of her bedroom she stood looking at her bedspread, which Dale had pulled taut and smooth, and could see no imprint of herself or the man who had dragged her there.

It had happened so fast, in another time. She remembered her fear and desperation, and then a vague helplessness as he dragged her into the room. She didn't remember how she got onto the bed. He dragged her there, certainly, but she could not remember. If she chose, she could imagine well enough how it happened, but she would not imagine anything. She would not. She entered the room, reached under the bedspread for the mattress cover beneath the sheets, and pulled each corner free. After bundling all the bedding into a ball, she carried it into the kitchen and stuffed it into a garbage bag. She tied off the bag and dropped it beside her open door.

Mary liked the pancakes. She knelt on a chair and leaned forward into the kitchen table as she ate them, smothered in maple syrup, strawberries, and sugar. Although she wasn't hungry, Katherine ate one pancake with maple syrup. Dale finished half of his. There was a large platter in the middle of the table with more pancakes than anyone would eat.

All through breakfast Katherine prepared herself for the child's questions. Where was her mother? Why had she left? Where would she stay until her mother came home? Katherine had questions, but not the little girl. Mary ate the pancakes as if she ate pancakes in Dale's kitchen every morning. She was careful not to spill on the table, not to make a mess, even with syrup dripping from every bite. She told Dale that his pancakes tasted good, especially the strawberries. He piled more strawberries on top of them.

After Mary could eat no more, Katherine took Mary's hand and led her into her apartment.

"Is this where you live?" Mary asked.

"Yes."

"I thought you lived with Dale," Mary said.

"Just last night. I was so tired that I fell asleep on his couch."

Mary looked at the still-open apartment door. It was only a few feet from Katherine's door to Dale's. A child could see that no one could be that tired. But again, Mary did not ask the question Katherine anticipated.

She asked plenty of other questions, however, as she followed Katherine from room to room. Who were the people in the pictures? Did she have a dog? How about a cat? Where did she keep the police car? Where was her gun? Did everybody have to do just what she said or go to jail?

Mary stood at the bathtub with her questions while Katherine filled the tub with water. Katherine lifted a fresh towel from the open stack above the vanity and put it on the floor beside the bathtub.

"You can take off your clothes, and I'll wash them," Katherine said. "I have a nightgown you can wear until they dry."

"Where are you going now?" Mary asked.

Katherine▪was standing in the doorway.

"I'm just going into my bedroom for the nightgown," Katherine said.

"Will you come right back?"

"I'll come right back," she said.

Mary was pleased with the nightgown that she wore after her bath. She lifted it from her feet as she walked. Through the open doors the smell of homemade bread filled the apartment. Katherine would have to close her door again, but she knew it would be hopeless today. Dale had already called the hospital, taken the day off, and begun making enough chicken soup to feed the neighborhood. Every fifteen minutes or so he came into the apartment with something new—a bright quilt for Mary, a small figurine of a girl, a flower vase that reminded him too much of his Chihuly. And he had ideas. The child's face became excited each time he came into their apartment.

While they waited for the clothes dryer to finish, Katherine called Daniel at the foster home. Then she handed the telephone to Mary. Katherine listened to the girl explain to Daniel what had happened since she had seen him. She did not mention Gillette, but she described in elaborate detail how Katherine had come into the hotel room with her gun, and how they had taken Rudy away. Mary told Daniel about Dale's pancakes and the strawberries she put on top. Katherine waited for her to explain who Dale was, but the girl went on as though Daniel already knew. The telephone drifted away from her mouth and then back again. Sometimes neither child said anything, but Mary still didn't want to break off the connection.

After the telephone call Mary was restless. She had questions she forgot to ask Daniel. Katherine sat down on the couch and picked up a book of children's poems Dale had found. The girl settled into her lap. Katherine held the book in front of them.

The telephone rang, and Mary jumped from her lap. She thought it might be Daniel calling back. She lifted the bottom of the nightgown above her knees and hurried to the stand where the telephone waited. Katherine thought it was more likely Anne Smith or Markowitz. She hoped Mary was right.

"Got your dancing shoes on?"

Both had guessed wrong, and she smiled above the girl who looked up to the telephone covering Katherine's smile. Katherine covered the receiver with her hand.

"It's not Daniel. It's somebody I know. Why don't you read the book by yourself for a little bit," she said.

"I can't read."

"You can look at the pictures."

Mary retreated to the couch, to the book she could not read. She opened it and meandered through the pages. The pictures did not interest her.

"I'm back," Katherine said into the telephone.

"Is this a bad time to call?"

"It's fine. I have a little girl with me. Her name is Mary, and she is four years old and reading poetry." Katherine smiled at Mary over the telephone.

"I don't know about Mary," Joe said.

"I know. It's a long story."

"I called several times yesterday," he said, "before your shift and after. Ring, ring, ring. Nobody home. I thought maybe you moved to Ireland."

Dale was in the doorway holding a wide-brimmed straw hat. Mary got off the couch and ran over to him. Katherine asked Joe to wait again, and her hand covered the receiver once more.

"Important call?" Dale asked.

"Yes," Katherine said.

"I'll take Mary with me," he said. "It was for the trip you keep talking about but never make." He held up the hat and put it on Mary's head. "You'll have to get another."

He took Mary's hand and guided her into the hallway. The hat covered her eyes as she lifted the nightgown to walk. Katherine laughed softly into the telephone.

"Dale just came and got Mary. He's spoiling her rotten."

"Dale?" Joe asked.

"My neighbor across the hall. Another long story. Where are you?"

"Working. I was hoping we could get together soon. Anything planned for tonight?"

"I have to take care of this little girl for a day or so. Her brother, Daniel, is in a foster home, and her mother is in the psych ward at Harborview. They've had a tough time."

"Who are they?" he asked.

"That's a good question," she said. "I'm not sure I know. They're two kids who live in my district. I kind of got wrapped up with them before I knew what was happening. The mother left them. The father left them. And they're such sweet kids."

"Kids you met at work? The police department lets you do that?"

"Yes. This time anyway."

"But, Katherine, you can't bring home every kid who's having a tough time."

"I know. I didn't. This is just one little girl. There was nobody else. If you had been in my place, you would have done the same thing. I know you would."

There was noise behind his telephone that took him away from her. She wanted him to come back so that she could explain how Daniel had put his hand beneath hers and how Mary had hugged her. She wanted to tell him how well he danced.

As she listened for him to come back, she saw Mary standing in the hallway just outside her door. Dale had tied a string around her waist so that she wouldn't trip in the nightgown. He had put a feather in her straw hat and had tied a cape around her shoulders.

"I'm Wondergirl," she said and skipped back to Dale's apartment.

"Ah, geez," Joe said. "Somebody just cut off his thumb. How the hell do you do that? Look," he said, and she looked but didn't see him, "I've got to run. I'll have to call you back. Will you be there for a while?"

"I think so," she said.

"Bye, then," he said.

"Bye," she said, but by then he had already run.

Chapter 53

The day had come to leave the recycling shed, and Thomas had choices to make. The day before Jack had reminded him again about the basement apartment down the street, and for some reason there had been no new cardboard for the last three days. Jack had also brought him a letter from his brother in Chicago. They missed him, his brother said. Who was they? Thomas wondered.

He spread the contents of his plastic sacks onto the stack of cardboard inside the shed. Even with no new cardboard and carefully arranged layers compressed with his weight and all the gravity Einstein could theorize, the stack now rose more than three feet. He didn't have to bend to inspect his possessions.

He could stay longer, he supposed. It was pleasant not to hide and to have people wave at him as they drove in or out of the garage. The pretty lady—he wished he could remember her name—had given him a red flannel shirt, and George had given him a pocket chess set that was missing only two white pawns and one black knight. It was interesting to play with missing pieces, to see which side had the advantage. Thomas discovered that he could play against himself without cheating.

Thomas picked up the chess set and put it into a sack. On top of the chess set he carefully set Whitman's poems, which had traveled with him from Chicago. The book had been in his hand the day he left. He chose his extra pair of socks and underwear, a sweatshirt, and khaki pants.

Jack had run a hose out of the garage with a spigot on the end that allowed Thomas to turn the water on and off when he chose. Jack gave him a bucket and soap, too.

Thomas knew that if he stayed, he would have to make choices he couldn't make—friendship with Jack or the basement apartment, wearing the flannel shirt or the old sweatshirt he liked, playing chess on the field of squares or letting his mind roam unbounded. It would be like choosing between Einstein's relativity and quantum mechanics. Both theories are correct but incompatible when pushed together.

He selected a toothbrush, a bar of soap, and a half roll of toilet paper and saw that he still had room in the sack for the last can of beef stew. Finally he lifted the Swiss army knife that Jack had given him, turned it in the sunlight, and stuck it into his pocket.

Thomas feared that Jack would lose patience with him sooner or later if he didn't use the bucket and hose, if he didn't move to the basement apartment. No one had been kinder to him than the people in Jack's building, but too often kindness expects a return. He feared he couldn't give the expected return. He didn't want to see Jack's face again as it had been that morning when Jack first opened the door to the recycling shed. Instead, he wanted to always remember the moment Jack lifted the cardboard up to his eyes and understood the photon clock.

Thomas gathered everything else—books, newspapers, a half-eaten bag of potato chips, paper cups from the coffeeshop, rags, a thermometer, pliers, a broken hammer—and stuffed them into the remaining two sacks. He picked up every scrap of paper, every crumb, every foreign object, so that he left no sign of himself. Finally he closed the door of the shed and wedged a stick into the hasp. He picked up his three sacks and walked down the alley. An old blue pickup truck drove slowly by on the street, and a man waved to Thomas. The truck was gone before Thomas had time to wave back. Thomas stopped at the garbage compactor and placed two of his three sacks neatly beneath the locked jaws of the machine.

Daniel paced back and forth on the sidewalk waiting for Al. The day had come to return home. He knew it was going to be the best day he had ever had since Mary came back. Mary was inside with Ruth, who was their new foster mother. She was helping Mary put on the dress Katherine had brought yesterday. Katherine had brought him new clothes, too, but he could put on his shirt and pants by himself. He didn't want any help.

His mother had been in the hospital, but she was better now. When Al came they would get in his pickup truck and drive to their new duplex where his mother was waiting for them. Ruth, just like Mrs. Linden, had been nice to him and Mary, but she wasn't their real mother. He couldn't wait to see his real mother again, and he wanted to go home, even if he didn't know exactly where it was.

Daniel hoped they could get a cat and call him Hercules like the cat they used to have. He hoped everything would be like it was before they moved in with Rudy. Maybe he could get Al to marry his mother. Then everything would be the same except better.

Al said that the duplex was close enough to his shop that Daniel could walk down and visit him anytime he wanted. Daniel didn't know what duplex meant except what Al told him. Somebody else lived right next door, but there was still a yard with grass and trees. Hercules would like the trees.

Ruth read stories to them at night before they went to bed, and Mary would always ask her to read one more. Before falling asleep Daniel would think about the stories, and sometimes he wouldn't wake up until morning. Then he would see the room and know that he was safe. Katherine told him that Rudy would never hurt him again. He believed her, but sometimes at night he hurt all over again in his dreams. The stories helped him forget. Maybe he and Mary could get their mother to read stories. He wanted to hear her voice again.

Daniel looked up through the tall evergreen trees beside the sidewalk and wondered if any of the trees at the duplex were as tall. He hoped there would be at least one tree with branches that he could reach, at least one that got rid of its leaves in the winter and started all over again in the spring. That was the kind of tree he could climb. The evergreen trees were pretty, but he couldn't see what good they were. Even Hercules wouldn't climb one of them.

He saw Al's blue pickup truck coming toward him, and he ran inside to tell Mary. He had packed his cardboard box the night before, and it was at the door waiting for Al and the truck. They didn't need a truck for their two boxes, but Al didn't have anything else.

Daniel carried his box out to Al's truck and then went back for Mary's. Ruth kissed Mary good-bye and started to come toward him. Daniel got into the middle of the truck even though he liked to sit on the outside. He looked for the seat belt as Ruth helped Mary into the pickup. He couldn't look at Ruth, even when she said good-bye to him and closed the door. He didn't know why.

He didn't know why he got mad at Mary either. Mary was sitting where he wanted to sit, but he had moved to the middle of the seat himself. It wasn't her fault, and he didn't want to be angry. This time he would forget about it. He wouldn't say anything to Mary or push her like he did sometimes. The other lady who came to see him told him to remember that Mary was not the one who had hurt him. Daniel knew that, but he didn't want to think about Rudy anymore. It seemed that Rudy was all that anybody wanted to talk about. Except Al.

Al sat down behind the steering wheel and started his pickup truck.

"Are you ready, bud?" he asked Daniel.

"Ready," Daniel said.

It didn't take long to drive to their duplex. Daniel thought they would have to drive all the way across the city, but before he had time to get ready, Al was parking the pickup truck.

When Mary saw their mother in the door of the duplex, she jumped out of the pickup and ran up to her. Their mother lifted Mary in the air like on television. That was what he wanted, too. He imagined that his mother would lift him so high that he would finally forget about Rudy. She would lift him high enough that he wouldn't miss his father anymore. If he had been on the outside instead of Mary, he would have been the one to run up to his mother and hug her. He walked slowly ahead because his mother already had Mary in her arms. His mother was crying. He was sorry that she was crying. He hadn't had time to think what he would do if his mother was crying.

He turned around and saw that Al had stayed beside the truck. Al looked sad, too, but he wasn't crying. Daniel walked back to the truck.

"Aren't you going to give your mom a hug?" Al asked.

"I'll carry in the boxes first," Daniel said.

Chapter 54

Katherine stood alone on the forward deck of the ferry and looked for landmarks on the Olympic Peninsula. Two hours earlier from the west window of her apartment, she had seen heavy clouds cresting the two southern mountains in the Olympic range. The clouds had tumbled down the eastern slopes and now hung so low over the Sound that they hid the two mountains and the rest of the range to the north. The clouds hid nearly everything.

The wind was cold as it swept over the water on its way toward Seattle and the Cascade Range. The Cascades would subdue the wind temporarily until it gathered strength again on the high plateau farther east. Anne Smith had arranged free days for her and Grace, and Katherine had considered following the wind east where she could settle into the comfortable routine of the farm and her familiar place at the dinner table. She decided to go west instead.

She didn't check the map to see how far it was, or the ferry schedule for the best time to leave, or the laundry basket in the closet that would remind her how many chores had been neglected. From her meager clean supply she gathered clothes, stuffed them into a bag, and put on her coat. She considered calling Joe to tell him where she was going, but he would be at work. He was always at work. She pushed a note under Dale's door and left.

She was surprised how good the cold air felt.

She was going to a place Dale had told her about one day months earlier when he had seen her reading a travel book about someplace she never went. Dale said there were cabins on a cliff above the ocean and fresh cinnamon rolls every morning at a bakery next door that smelled so good you wanted to wake up early just for them. How far can you see, she wanted to know. As far as you want, he told her.

Years earlier she had camped with somebody in the rainforest on the western side of the Olympic Peninsula. It was after she had taken him home for a weekend on the wheat farm. He couldn't imagine how she had tolerated living there with no water, no trees, and no people. There were trees, she told him, wherever there was enough water. There was water, but you had to look for it and wait for it. And there were people, and she was one of them. In the rainforest where he took her, the trees were so tall that she couldn't see the sky and so close together that she couldn't find her way. No matter how hard she tried—and she had tried—she could not acclimate herself to them. For two days she felt like running away like the horses on the farm when confronted with danger—real or imagined. She had not wanted to make conversation or anything to him there. He told her that her response to the majestic trees was irrational. She supposed it was, but she hadn't gone back.

She wouldn't see anything from the cliff either if the clouds were as low there as they were on the Sound. It didn't matter. Where she was looking, she could look in clear weather or clouds.

The bruise on her face and the black around her eye had faded enough so that she could conceal the lingering discoloration with makeup, but she had bad dreams that wouldn't go away. In her dreams her wrists were bound again, and she struggled to break free until she woke sweating from exertion. In her dreams it wasn't always Gillette who bound her. Gillette's appearance had grown vaguer so that now she usually sensed more than saw a looming evil that held her and wouldn't let her go.

The dreams did not frighten her as much as her reaction to them. She lay awake and fought in her imagination, and her dreams began to adapt. When it came in her sleep, when she sensed the presence of its evil form, she would fire her gun into it. If her gun didn't work, she would scratch at his eyes. If it had no eyes, she would grab it and bite like an animal, and her fear became rage and her rage became a person she didn't know.

She wanted order and a system like the one she had studied in the police academy that contained and controlled the evil. She wanted to sit in the courtroom, present the case, and have the judge order everything properly. But what happens when you're alone, she asked, and evil comes to you? What happened to Daniel, to Mary, to herself? How do you fight without becoming the evil yourself?

The ferry horn blared, and she looked up from the fathomless water and saw that they were coming into the dock at the ferry landing. As she walked down the metal stairs to the car deck, she felt the reverse of the propellers slowing the boat and bringing it to a gentle stop against the pilings.

Katherine drove south around the mountains and west toward the ocean. The ocean was like a magnet pulling her through the rain that beat ferociously on her windshield once she passed the protection of the two mountains that stood invisibly off to her side. There was little traffic. She avoided the primary roads until she came to the ocean where there was only one road. On it she turned north and looked for the cabins on the cliff.

They were humble impermanent structures among weather-beaten trees bent permanently from the wind. It was not tourist season, and she had her choice of cabins. She selected the one farthest from the road.

Rain streamed down the west-facing windows of her cabin until gusts of wind blew the streams of water diagonally across the glass. Sometimes the wind shook the cabin so hard that she wondered if it would hold. She wondered, also, if she should go back home. She wasn't going back.

Later in the afternoon, despite the weather, Katherine walked down the wooden stairway on the face of the cliff. The wind was so strong that it took her breath away. She was willing to let it go. At the bottom of the cliff she found a river that emptied into the ocean. It was a small river—no match for the storm waves that crashed high onto the shoreline and pushed the river far back into itself. She walked inland along the edge of the river until they were both out of the reach of the waves. There the river flowed evenly as if it didn't know what lay ahead. It was shallow enough and gentle enough that a child could wade across. The river came from the direction of the two mountains, brother and sister without names, and Katherine believed it originated on their weeping slopes. She followed the river until she was in tall trees that sheltered her from the wind. The river was like a friend, and she wasn't afraid.

She missed Grace. If Grace was with her, they could follow the river until they found its source. They could talk about the two children they had found. She could ask Grace if she had bad dreams, too.

That night Katherine dragged the mattress into the living room beside the fireplace. She built a fire, fed it wood late into the night, and listened to the wind. She felt inadequate against the ocean storm, but she wasn't alone. Everything was inadequate. Eventually the trees would bend too far, the buildings would rot, and the cliff would crumble.

Sometime during the night the rain stopped and the wind quieted, and she heard only the roar of surf. The waves surged and receded, gathered strength and surged again. She listened even in her sleep and did not dream of being bound.

When she woke in the morning she thought of the cinnamon rolls Dale loved. She had never felt so hungry before. She dressed, intending to walk down the road to the bakery, but stopped first at the edge of the cliff. The tide had gone out during the night, drawing with it the ocean surf. Below her in the sand the river had quietly and resolutely reestablished herself.

Acknowledgments

I thank my daughter, Sonya, for her keen understanding of where a story should go and my wife, Patricia, for encouraging me to follow that story.

I thank my great advance readers, who did all they could to offer various views, expertise, and encouragement: Amy Jorgensen, Robert Vanderway, Neil Low, Carol Brown, my astute aunt Mary Youngdahl, Marlene Blessing, Tammy Domike, A'Jamal Byndon, and Polly Partsch.

I thank my editor, Genny Ostertag, for her professional and artistic assistance, and Jimmy Vines, my ever-optimistic agent.

I am particularly grateful to Brian Greene for his book, *The Elegant Universe*, which gave this writer a euphoric moment in understanding the photon clock.

Finally, I thank Steven Brumbaugh for his insight and his gift of friendship, which I will always cherish.

LC